A LITTLE TEMPTING

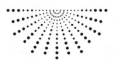

KELSIE RAE

Family Connections

Colt & Ashlyn
(Don't Let Me Fall)
Jaxon
Griffin
Dylan

Biological Siblings
Colt & Blakely
Theo & Macklin

Theo & Blakely
(Don't Let Me Go)
Ophelia
Tatum

Macklin & Kate
(Don't Let Me Break)
Everett
Finley

Henry & Mia
(Don't Let Me Down)
Archer & Maverick (twins)
Rory

PROLOGUE

REEVES

Funerals are a bitch. I've been to more than I can
count. Okay, I could technically count if I wanted to
pull up a spreadsheet, but who has time for that shit?
It's surprising how many single women will pay for someone
to be their plus-one instead of showing up to a funeral alone.
With fake tears and a fake boyfriend half their age on their
arm, the combination has only amplified my apathy for the
whole thing. When I die, they can donate my body to science
and throw a kick-ass party with alcohol, ladies, and food.

Good food.

And no one's allowed to wear black, either. I hate black.
Black is like a virus. It spreads. It devours. It swallows every
other color and transforms it into more of the same. Black.
Black. Black. I hate black.

The service was nice, I guess. Maverick, my best friend,
and his family spoke. They shared some pretty funny stories
and had the guests laughing, which is no easy feat considering the circumstances. At least they weren't fake. To be fair,
I've known the Buchanans for a while now. None of them
are fake. Ever. I appreciate it about them. The food's decent,

too. Not my style. I'd take a big juicy burger or a slice of chocolate cake over a chicken salad sandwich and fruit any day of the week, but I'm not complaining.

We just gotta make it through today.

Don't get me wrong. My best friend lost his twin. His parents lost a son. I lost a roommate, teammate, and friend. So did the rest of the guys. Yeah, accepting Archer's absence will be a bitch for all of us, but we're gonna be okay. Gonna get through this. I should know. I'm a pro. Been getting over family deaths since I could walk. Fuck, I had family dying before my first breath. My mom passed while giving birth to me, and my dad? Well, let's say he won't let me forget it.

Yeah. Everyone moves on. Everyone has to. Disney had it right. It's the circle of life, even when we don't want to accept it.

I snatch a grape from the banquet table and pop it into my mouth, scanning the large room for entertainment. I like watching people. Seeing how they interact. How they handle their grief when no one's looking. And even if they catch me watching them, it's not like they care. I'm Reeves. The shallow asshole with his head up his ass. It's not like I'm paying attention anyway, right?

I watch Mav and Ophelia, his girlfriend, talk to their parents with their hands interlocked. He's right out of the hospital after a two-week stay. Apparently, recovering from a heart transplant isn't for the faint of heart.

Ha! No pun intended.

Maverick's staying with his parents for the next little while, and I doubt I'll see much of Ophelia until he's back in our house. It's a shame. I kind of like her. I wonder if her roommates will be just as scarce, but I doubt it. Finley's a social butterfly and isn't afraid to force Dylan to be her wingwoman.

Good.

Dylan needs someone to push her.

I tear my attention from Mav and Ophelia, browsing the room like I would Netflix.

Griffin, Everett, and Jaxon are throwing back a few beers with some of Archer's internship buddies. I bet a hundred bucks they're replaying some of Archer's finest moments on the ice since they all huddle around Everett's phone. I might be wrong, but I doubt it. And Rory's in the corner, her eyes swollen and puffy as she stares at Jaxon from across the room. Fuck, the longing in those baby blues is gonna land her in trouble one day.

It's a good thing Jax is oblivious, or I'd break his hand for touching someone underage. To be fair, he wouldn't cross the line even if he did know the girl's in love with him. Jax doesn't have a dishonorable bone in his body. It's one of the main reasons I respect the bastard. But as soon as Rory turns eighteen, I have a hunch all bets will be off, and she'll get sick of waiting for him to see her as anyone other than a little kid.

And when the day comes, I'll pop some popcorn because that shit will be entertaining as fuck.

With a smirk, I steal another grape and continue perusing today's crowd.

Aaaand there it is.

Finley, Finley, Finley, I tsk.

She curses at someone on her phone. I bet it's her boyfriend. I heard they're having problems despite Finley's insistence it's all rainbows and butterflies between her and Drew. Two hundred bucks says he's already sleeping with some sorority girl in one of his classes. Finley's smart, though. She'll figure it out. She might have to take off her rose-colored glasses and overcompensating optimism to get there, but I have faith in her.

And then there's Dylan.

My gaze falls on the little wallflower despite myself. Black glasses are perched on her button nose, and I tilt my head in surprise. I've never seen her wear glasses.

We've hung out a couple of times. Not one-on-one. The girl would probably have a heart attack if we did, but since one of her brothers is my roommate, and my best friend is dating her cousin, we've crossed paths a time or two. She reminds me of Daenerys Targaryen. Not the seventh-season badass, but the baby deer from season one with wide eyes and a hint of naivety that's hot as fuck.

Pretty sure her brothers would kill me if I started messing with her. Pretty sure Everett would, too. Everett's another of my roommates. I can't figure out if his fascination with her is due to her being a family friend or if his feelings run any deeper.

I'm not sure I want to find out.

Or maybe I do.

I've always been a sucker for poking the bear, especially when the stick up his ass is practically welded there.

Snatching another grape from the banquet table, I toss it into my mouth, stride toward Dylan, and tuck my hands into the front pockets of my slacks.

When she catches me approaching, she shrinks in on herself and folds her arms.

"You know," I start. "I heard a rumor that if a dude takes Viagra and dies, his dick stays hard indefinitely."

She covers her snort with her hand and shakes her head. "Tell me you're joking."

"Definitely joking. You think I'd Google that shit?" I shiver. "I might look like an idiot and have even convinced Maverick to Google a thing or two, but I learned my lesson in sixth grade when I had to write a book report on Harry Potter." I drop my voice a little lower. "Fell down the rabbit hole of Dramione, and let me tell you, there is some fanfic art you cannot unsee, my dear Dylan."

"What's Dramione?"

Brows raised, I explain, "Draco and Hermione? Dramione?"

She frowns. "Doesn't she end up with Ron?"

With a scoff, I throw my arm over her shoulders. "Aw, my sweet, innocent little Dylan. She might end up with Ron in the real books, but everyone's a sucker for a good opposites-attract, enemies-to-lovers story, don't you think?"

"I, uh," she hesitates. "I never really thought about it, so... I'm not sure?"

"Is that a question?" The edge of my mouth curves up.

She lifts a shoulder, and her blue-green eyes fall to the ground. Even with her glasses shielding her, I notice how puffy they are. And damp and free of makeup. Like she didn't give a shit about getting ready for the outside world today. No. This is Dylan Thorne. The original girl next door.

She's a pretty little wallflower. I'll give her that much.

"Since when do you wear glasses?" I prod.

She touches the edge of her black frames. "Oh. I, uh... always, I guess?"

"I've never seen you in them."

"I usually wear contacts, but sometimes they give me a headache, especially when I've been crying a lot and—"

"Dylan!" Everett snaps from across the room. "Come over here."

Peeking up at me, Dylan slips from beneath my arm and scoots her glasses along the bridge of her nose. "Nice chatting with you, Reeves. I'll, uh, see you around."

She darts across the funeral home into Everett's waiting arms like the baby deer I pegged her for.

Yeah, I fucking called it.

Everett wants in Dylan's pants.

The question is, does she want him there?

Only one way to find out...

5

1
DYLAN

It's official. I hate the first day of school. To be fair, I've always hated the first day of school, and this isn't my first rodeo, but for real. I hate it. New classes. New teachers. New schedules. And this year, I get to add a new home, new people, and a new reality, thanks to one of my close friends dying a few weeks ago.

Yeah.

Talk about turning a girl's world upside down.

This year's going to be a real treat, I can tell.

Tucking my thumbs beneath my backpack straps on my shoulders, I take a deep breath and head inside the massive brick building in front of me. The long hallway is jammed with students, each rushing toward their class like the rest of us. Keeping my eyes glued to the ground in front of me, I dodge a couple arguing on my left and run smack-dab into a very hard chest.

A pair of hands fly to my elbows to keep me from falling flat on my butt, though I'm too surprised to be grateful.

"Whoa, you okay?" a familiar masculine voice asks.

7

I lift my chin and draw in a breath. It's laced with relief when I meet a pair of familiar blue eyes. "Oh. Hey, Everett."

My best friend's older brother ushers me to the side of the long hallway and lets me go. "You shouldn't be looking at your feet when you walk, Dylan."

"Yeah, but if I look up, I have to make eye contact with people, and if I make eye contact with people, they might try to talk to me, and talking to people gives me hives, so…"

"You're talking to me," he points out dryly.

"You don't count. You're family," I remind him.

Okay, technically, we aren't related. Still, all of our parents went to college together and raised their kids to be one big, happy family of cousins. So, blood or not, he means way more to me than anyone else in this building. He's actually seen me in my not-so-awkward glory, which is kind of a miracle since awkward is my go-to whether I like it or not.

With a wrinkled brow, Everett pulls the backpack strap a little higher onto my shoulder, his cool blue eyes rolling over every inch of me as if he's searching for said hives and whether or not he has time to grab some cream from the nearest pharmacy when a girl calls his name behind me.

"Hey, Everett!"

His gaze flicks away from me toward the culprit while he pastes on a smirk most girls would swoon over. "Hey, Morgan."

"You gonna walk me to class?" She bats her long, dark lashes at him, and I bite back my snort.

Subtle, girlfriend. Really subtle.

"Give me a sec," Everett replies. He turns to me again, his brows bunching. "Where's your class?"

I lift a shoulder, take my phone from my back pocket, and pull up my already-memorized schedule. "Photography. Room 301."

"I'll walk you."

"Dude, I'm fine."

"Do you know where you're going?" he challenges.

No.

"Yes."

He doesn't believe me, so he motions to the stairs on my right anyway. "Two floors up. First room on the left. You got it?"

"Yup."

"You sure?" he pushes.

"One hundred percent." With a mock salute, I repeat, "Two floors up. First room on the right."

"Left," he corrects me.

"Right. *Left*." I pat his chest and step away, wiggling my fingers in a half-assed wave. "See you around, Everett."

"Not if you're staring at your feet," he counters.

I roll my eyes but don't reply as I make my way toward the stairs. Everett's always been this way. Overprotective. Bossy. And with a side of holier-than-thou. It makes me want to smack him more often than not. Then again, he's also thoughtful, sharp as a tack, and drop-dead gorgeous thanks to his dark, straight hair, almond-shaped eyes, and a wide smile with straight white teeth he uses to lure in the ladies. The combination allows him to get away with almost anything, including the less-than-adorable traits I already mentioned.

Yeah. Good ol' Everett. Can't live with him. Can't live without him. But at least I know where I'm going now. Thanks to my less-than-stellar sense of direction, it's a freaking miracle. I tug my backpack straps a little tighter and take a deep breath.

Photography, here I come.

～

THE CLASSROOM IS EXACTLY LIKE I EXPECTED. SMALLER, maybe, but otherwise? Yup. It's exactly like high school. Tan walls. A whiteboard at the front of the room. Rows of black, rectangular desks set up with two chairs tucked beneath them. And scratchy, dark carpet to camouflage any spills.

Yummy.

I make my way to the back of the room, slip off my backpack, tuck it beneath the vacant, two-person desk, and sit down on the far end. Maybe if I'm lucky, the chair beside mine will stay empty. A girl can dream, can't she? When the cool plastic seeps into my bare thighs, I shiver, making a mental note to wear jeans for the rest of my classes since, apparently, the school enjoys blasting the air conditioning way too much for me to be comfortable in shorts and a tank top.

After pulling out a notepad and pen, I check the clock on the wall. There are still a few more minutes until class starts. The room slowly fills with people, but the chair to my right remains empty. I thank my lucky stars, playing with my cell and counting down the seconds. Maybe this class won't be so bad after all.

"Ladies and gentlemen," the teacher announces. Dr. Broderick. Or at least it's the name on my schedule. His navy button-up shirt stretches across his broad shoulders, almost camouflaging the beer belly hidden underneath. There's a slight stain on his khakis, and his hair is a disheveled mess of brown and silver. He's probably in his...forties? Honestly, I'm not sure. He isn't smiling, though, and I can't decide whether or not we'll vibe well or if my clumsiness will get on his nerves.

I've tried to curb it. The way my balance catapults me into awkward scenarios. But thanks to my head injury, my equilibrium isn't always one hundred percent. While some find it endearing, others find it annoying. And annoying your teacher isn't exactly a goal one should have if they want to pass the class. Trust me, I know from personal experience.

Leaning his butt against the desk at the front of the room, he continues. "Welcome to Photography 101. My name is—"

The door slaps against the tan-painted cinder block wall, and my head snaps toward the room's entrance. The girls in front of me giggle quietly when they recognize the culprit. Reeves lifts his head when he hears it, catching them as they blatantly check out one of LAU's favorite hockey players. With a shameless smirk, he lifts his chin at them in a silent hello. It's casual and innocent and so freaking smooth I'm full-blown jealous. Not of the girls in front of me, but at how the bastard's so damn comfortable in his own skin, it's borderline annoying.

Then again, I guess he's earned his right to be confident and comfortable.

Our school is known for quite a few sports, but hockey? Around here, it's king, and the fans are all loyal subjects. Everyone knows the players, including my older brother, Griffin. Griff is the new captain this year after replacing my *other* older brother who graduated at the end of last season. Everett is Griffin's right-hand man on and off the ice, and... then there's Reeves. The man smirking at the girls in front of me, knowing with a single look he could have any of them at his beck and call. Hell, he probably already does.

Yeah, I'm well aware of who the infamous Reeves is. He's so high and mighty the guy doesn't even need a full name. He's like Cher or Madonna or...I dunno? Who else is famous and only uses one name? Pop culture is the last thing on my radar, but it's not the point. The point is, it's hard *not* to notice a guy like him. One who's cocky and sarcastic and has every right to wear his confidence the way he does. He's attractive. Talented. And even nice in an *I'm an asshole, but don't let it get to you* kind of way. I blame the warm chocolate eyes, perfectly messy chestnut hair, olive skin, and devilish smirk I'm pretty sure is tattooed onto his face. The sharp jaw, tall stature, and broad shoulders don't hurt either. He isn't known for being tied down, but from what I heard, he's more than willing to show a girl a good time. And if my best friend, Finley, is correct, he's shown a lot of girls a good time during his three years at LAU.

We've only spoken a few times, and each interaction has left me feeling more awkward and tongue-tied than the last. I'm less than graceful around almost anyone. Add a devilish smirk, a sharp tongue, and dark eyes, and I'm a fumbling mess.

Seriously. It's a problem.

It's also the last thing I need if I want to get through today unscathed.

Nibbling on the edge of my pen, I stare at the blank notepad in front of me as the teacher says, "Nice of you to join us, Mr. Reeves."

"Sorry for interrupting," Reeves replies.

"Take a seat."

I keep my attention glued to my desk while Reeve's firm footsteps echo off the walls as he searches for an empty spot in the room.

Please don't notice me, please don't notice me, I silently chant.

"This seat taken?" the familiar voice interrupts.

Perfect.

My shoulders fall, but I shake my head, answering his question while refusing to face the culprit head-on. With a low chuckle, he slides into the chair beside me, not bothering to wait for an invitation while the teacher continues summarizing the syllabus.

I should be used to talking to attractive guys or at least being around them without falling over my own feet. I have two older brothers who are athletic and pretty good-looking dudes. Why do I mention Jax and Griffin? Because attractive guys hang out with other attractive guys. I'm not sure why it's a thing, but it is what it is. Growing up with handsome brothers with whom I'm actually really close means I'm around their friends, too. It's simple hot guy math. The problem is my brother's friends are way more interesting than boring numbers on a piece of paper. I learned pretty quickly to keep a wide berth or put them in the friend zone if I wanted to survive hanging out with them without sticking my foot in my mouth every two minutes.

Overall, it's been a pretty nifty solution, and even though it's a hit to my confidence, the guy friends haven't complained about being friend-zoned. But Reeves? Well, he's a different story. For one, he's new. Okay, technically, *I'm* new if we're talking about LAU's campus, but he's new in a more intimate sense. Like I said, my family is pretty tight-knit. I had no choice but to get used to hanging out with Everett, Maverick, and Archer. We grew up together. Anytime one of the guys brought home a new friend, I simply made myself scarce until they left. Afterward, I'd come down from my room and hang out with everyone else. Cowardly? Sure. Convenient? I dunno, sometimes? It beat being all tongue-tied and klutzy, then mercilessly teased for said awkwardness, that's for sure.

Unfortunately, I can't hide in my room and wait for Reeves to disappear. He's Griffin's roommate, friend, hockey teammate, *and* my next-door neighbor. Apparently, I can also add classmate to the list.

Perfect.

It doesn't help how the girls in front of me won't be quiet so I can actually focus on the teacher I blocked out for the last five minutes. The girls whisper to each other while casting glances over their shoulders at the guy beside me. Giggling, they each scribble something onto a piece of paper, and, with a quiet rip, the blonde removes the message from her notebook, folds it in half, and slips it onto my desk right in front of Reeves.

Seriously?

From the corner of my eye, I catch his mouth lifting as he unfolds the paper and chuckles under his breath.

I have no idea what he read. Was it their numbers? An offer to meet them in the bathroom for a quickie? A compliment on how good the guy looks in his dark jeans and olive green henley? Honestly, I should envy the girls for their boldness, but I'm kind of swimming in secondhand embarrassment. Because if it was me? I would probably fall off my seat while passing said paper and split my head open or something instead of coming off as smooth and confident.

I wish I was kidding, but I'm not.

Seriously, though. Who just hands their number to a guy? Who does that? Man, even the idea of attempting something so daring makes me want to melt into the walls and disappear entirely.

Nope. No, thank you.

Reeves leans toward me, resting his forearm on the space separating us as he drops his voice low. "There a problem, Thorne?"

Thorne?

Seriously? Did he forget my name?

I mean, it's not like we're close, but he's my brother's roommate, teammate, *and* friend. He seriously doesn't even remember my first name?

I shake my head but don't look at him, keeping my attention glued to the teacher in front of me as he writes his name on the whiteboard. Mr. Broderick. Yup. The trusty schedule was right.

Noted.

Reeves leans even closer, and the same low breath of

amusement causes goosebumps to race along my skin. "You look like you're sunburned," he murmurs. "Spend too much time outdoors this weekend?"

Is this guy baiting me?

I'm blushing because he's talking to me. It's a sick, twisted bodily response I suffer from when anyone even remotely attractive looks at me, let alone talks to me. Add it to the fact I was already drowning in secondhand embarrassment while imagining passing my number to a random dude, and I have no doubt I look like a ripe tomato thanks to my pale complexion. Why, oh, why didn't I inherit my dad's olive skin like my brothers? Oh, wait. Because I'm unlucky, that's why. I blame my mom. Blonde hair. Pale skin. But, where she's absolutely gorgeous, I'm...well, what am I? Cute. Yup. I'm cute. And let's be honest. There isn't anything wrong with cute. Puppies are cute. Kittens are cute. And me? I'm cute. Forgettable, yes, but cute all the same. Then again, when you're a girl like me, there isn't anything wrong with being forgettable. It helps you stay out of the spotlight, which is precisely what I need if I want to get through this semester.

Please stop looking at me, I silently beg as my thumb finds the end of my pen, and I click it over and over again.

"You're cute when you blush," Reeves notes. Giving me some space, he stretches his long, muscular legs out beneath the table.

I force my lungs to expand, grateful for the reprieve.

"Look around," the teacher announces. Mr. Broderick. *Right.* "The person next to you will be your partner for your first project this semester."

I squeeze my eyes shut as the words wash over me.

I hate projects. And I hate partners. And I *really* hate projects with partners, especially when said partner is my brother's friend who, apparently, doesn't even remember my name.

Untucking my hair from behind my ear, I use it as a shield while attempting to focus on the project's guidelines and how I can get out of it without pissing off my new teacher.

"Emotion," Dr. Broderick announces. "It's what I want you to capture in your portfolio for this project. Happiness. Sadness. Desire. Discomfort. Peace. Surprise. The options are endless." He rubs his hands together. "I want you and your partner to each choose two emotions. They can be the same. They can be different. I don't care. What I do care about is how you capture those emotions and ensure the viewer of your work feels the same depth of said emotion as your model in the photograph. You and your partner will have the opportunity to take photos and star in them. I expect examples of each to be turned in. The first piece is due in one month. Any questions?"

The girl in front of me raises her hand. "What if our partner sucks at modeling? It isn't our fault—"

"You'll be graded together on this project. Both in front of and behind the lens. As you're all aware, you presented a portfolio to be accepted into this class, so I know you all understand how to use a camera. Today, we're looking at examples of how to show those emotions through photographs." He walks toward the edge of the room and flicks off the light. Images flash on the massive whiteboard at the front of the room from the projector at the back.

It's hard to focus on Dr. Broderick's examples. I'm too busy attempting to steady my breathing so I don't hyperventilate. There's a reason I like holding a camera, and it isn't because I want to be in front of it, that's for sure. I'm not particularly in love with photography, but it's fun, and the class is way better than some other electives. Or at least, it was until Reeves sat next to me.

"Thorne?" Reeves prods. His voice is still low as he leans closer to me. "You okay? You look like you're about to puke."

"Why do you call me Thorne?" I ask, surprising us both with my boldness. I'm not bold. Hell, I'm the furthest thing from it. But he's right about the puking part, and I'm desperate for a distraction, even if it means fraternizing with the Greek god beside me.

Reeves pulls back, clarifying, "It's your last name."

"So?"

"So?" he repeats, looking as lost as I feel.

"So, do you seriously not remember my actual name?"

"I remember, *Dylan*." My name sounds like a caress as it slips past his lips, making my stomach clench even more.

He does know it.

Noted.

If only it explained why he doesn't use it.

"Oh," I murmur. "Okay, then." I turn back to my paper, unsure what to do or say after opening my stupid mouth.

"Why did you think I forgot your name?" he questions.

My pen hovers an inch above the paper as I debate whether or not I should even reply. If I do, I'll probably blush again, and if I don't, he'll think I'm a bitch, which is the last thing I need, considering the fact we're partners in this class. Finally, I give in and look up at him again. "You called me Thorne."

"Your last name *is* Thorne."

"Well, yeah, but why call me Thorne if you know my first name?"

"Maybe I need the reminder that I know your brothers." His mouth lifts, but it only fans my confusion.

Tucking my hair back behind my ear, I ask, "Why?"

"Because I'm pretty sure they'll kill me if I forget." His

attention drops to my mouth, and his amusement grows. "And if your brothers don't, Everett will."

My forehead wrinkles. "What about Everett?"

"I'm sure he'll explain one day," he offers cryptically.

"Should I call you by your last name, too?"

"You already do."

My brows cave. "Reeves is your last name?"

"Surprised?"

Uh, yeah. Kind of. I literally never hear anyone call him anything else. I guess I assumed...

As I fiddle with my pen, my curiosity gets the best of me, and I blurt out, "What's your first name?"

"No one calls me by my first name."

"Obviously, or else I would've heard it by now."

"Excuse me," Mr. Broderick snaps from the front of the room.

My eyes bulge when I find his gaze pinned on me, his bushy brows pulled low in disappointment.

Way to go, Dylan. Pissing off your teacher on the first day.

Now, everyone's looking at me.

Ground, please open up and swallow me whole.

"Sorry," I squeak.

"As I was saying..." Mr. Broderick turns back to the whiteboard, continuing his spiel as Reeves leans even closer to me.

"Can I have your number, Thorne?"

He's close. Too close. I can almost feel his breath against my cheek. Or maybe I'm imagining it. Maybe I imagined this entire interaction. It wouldn't be the first time I daydreamed about having a simple conversation with the opposite sex without making a fool of myself. Oh, wait. I kind of already did make a fool out of myself, thanks to Dr. Broderick calling us out, so apparently, we're still very stuck in reality, and I need to focus.

"Thorne," Reeves repeats, "What's your number?"

Refusing to look his way, I seethe, "Will you please be quiet?"

"Let me guess. This is the first time you've ever been in trouble for talking in class. Am I right?" Amusement taints his voice, but I can't decide if it's mocking or innocent, and I'm not about to look at him to find out.

Then again, I'm not sure it matters, anyway. He's still causing a scene, and if Dr. Broderick calls me out again, I'll lose it. Scooting my chair a little further away from my new partner, I let out a quiet huff and throttle the pen in my hand as if it were Reeves' neck.

The same familiar rip sounds from his side of the desk, but I don't acknowledge it when a piece of lined paper is placed in front of me.

Ignoring it, I try paying attention to Mr. Broderick's lecture. But it's hard. Like, really hard. Especially when the stupid piece of paper is in my periphery. Taunting me. Making me curious and anxious and—

"Class is dismissed," Dr. Broderick announces. "I'll see you next week."

I grab my things and shove them into my bag, leaving the paper on the desk as I stand, or at least attempt to. My foot catches on the chair leg, and I practically face plant into Reeves' lap.

His. Freaking. Lap.

In an attempt to catch myself, I brace my arms in front of me, grazing his crotch with my palm as I stand there shell-shocked. The only thing between me and his semi-hard dick is the denim of his jeans.

Holy shit, I'm touching a dick.

I've never touched a dick before. I've never even seen a dick up close and personal. Well, at least not one outside of a textbook picture. And here it is. In my freaking hand.

My head snaps up, and my eyes widen in shock when they connect with a very amused Reeves as the snake in his pants twitches beneath my palm.

"You know, if you wanted to cop a feel, all you had to do was ask."

I jerk away from him and stand up, fumbling with my backpack at our feet as my brain races to catch up with what the hell just happened. Yup. I most definitely felt up whatever-his-first-name-is Reeves in front of my entire class. Kill me now. Our classmates laugh around us while my cheeks burn with an embarrassment so deep I feel it in my soul. Keeping my eyes glued to the ground, I slip past the back of his chair and race into the hall.

It's official.

I need to drop photography. Stat.

2

REEVES

S natching my number from the desk, I follow Dylan into the hallway, waving to a few familiar faces as I catch up to her.

"Slow down," I order.

"Nope. No, thank you." Dylan dodges between a group of people exiting one of the rooms, and I follow suit until we make it outside. Reaching for her arm, I yank her to a halt and say, "Breathe."

Her nostrils flare, and her hands tighten around her backpack straps. The girl looks like she's about to puke as her eyes dart around the rolling green hills and tall brick buildings surrounding us, desperate to look at anything but me.

"Where's the main office?" she asks.

I frown. "Huh?"

"You know, the main office. For adding and dropping classes and stuff."

"You want to drop a class?"

Finally gracing me with a glimpse of those aquamarine irises that are somehow bluer than Griffin's and greener than

Jaxon's, she gives me an are-you-stupid look. "Uh, yeah. Duh."

Shaking off the reminder of whose little sister I'm dealing with, I press, "You want to drop photography?"

"Ding, ding, ding, we have a winner."

The girl's sassier than I expected. I guess all it takes is getting her fired up long enough to get out of her own head. I make a mental note, tucking it away for later. "You can't drop photography."

"Why not?" she demands.

"Because you're my partner. And call it a hunch, but I don't think you're in photography for an easy credit like I am."

"It doesn't matter why I signed up, I just…felt up your lap in front of everyone, including your little fan club, which is absolutely the highlight of my day, so if you'll excuse—"

"Fan club?"

She rolls her eyes. "You know what I mean. The idea of going back there once, let alone the rest of the semester, sounds like hell on earth, so yeah. I'm dropping the class."

She dodges around me again, but I follow suit, blocking her escape. "Look, you're cute when you're all riled up, Thorne, but—"

"Stop calling me that."

"What? Thorne?" I ask.

"Yes. It makes me think you're talking to my brothers, and I'm not my brothers, so stop calling me by my last name," she snaps.

"Okay, Dylan." I lift my hands in defense. "Let's start over. Hi. I'm Reeves." Offering my hand, I wait for her to take it, but she stares at it like it's a prickly cactus. "I heard we're partners this semester," I continue, "and I'm really looking forward to it. Can I give you my number so we can set up a time to talk about our project?"

"Dylan!" a voice booms.

I glance over my shoulder in time to find Everett striding toward us. Seriously, the guy might as well pull out his dick and piss on her. Don't get me wrong, Everett and I are fine. I'd even argue to say we're friends, but teammates and roommates are probably more fitting. After I fucked the guys over last season, I've been on his shit list, and he's yet to let it go.

"There a problem?" I ask him, but he ignores me.

"What happened, Dylan?" Everett demands. "I saw you running down the hallway like a bat out of hell. You okay?"

Her eyes slice from Everett's to mine, and she nods. "Yeah, I'm fine."

"What happened?" he repeats.

Crossing her arms, she stares at the ground and clears her throat. "I pulled a Dylan and did something embarrassing."

"That's all?" He sighs in relief and presses his hand along her lower back. "Shit, you scared me, Dyl. Come on. I'll walk you to your next class—"

"I still need to give her my number," I interrupt.

His muscles coil as he turns to me, his gaze narrowing. "Why?"

I stare at Dylan. Giving her a choice. Just a hunch, but I doubt she's used to having those. Not when her older brothers or Everett's involved anyway.

She peeks up at me, wariness tainting her blue-green eyes yet somehow making them more vibrant. More alluring. And she honestly thought I didn't remember her name? The girl has no fucking clue.

Pretty little wallflower, I see you. Don't worry.

"Dylan?" Everett prods.

"He's my..." Her attention flicks from me to Everett. "He's my partner for a project."

"You two are in the same class?"

"Uh, yeah." She gulps. "I guess we are."

"Great," he mutters under his breath. With a wave of his hand, Everett motions for me to get on with it. Does he think he's subtle?

Dylan pulls out her phone, her fingers hovering over the numbers while refusing to look at me again. I could push it, but I won't. The girl seems like someone who prefers careful coaxing more than being bombarded with testosterone. That is if I wanted to push her in the first place. Fucking up my relationship with my roommates over a girl isn't exactly on my itinerary. Not when they already view me as a selfish prick.

Giving in, I rattle off my phone number, and she types it into her phone, saving my contact information.

"I'll, uh, I'll call you later," she murmurs.

"Can't wait." I back away from her and head inside the building for my next bullshit class. I wasn't kidding when I told her I signed up for photography for an easy credit. Well, I also lost a bet during registration, but my diploma's nothing more than a technicality I'm stubborn enough to achieve so I can shove it in my dad's face. Therefore, I don't give a shit about what's on the transcripts as long as I have the credits to graduate. Hockey's my future, thanks to being drafted my sophomore year, and despite my fuck ups, I've put a lot of blood, sweat and tears into the sport. I refuse to give it up for anything.

Lions, here I come.

PRACTICE IS A BITCH, BUT WE GET THROUGH IT. *BARELY.* WE fucking suck this year. We didn't, but we lost two of our best players, and now, it's like we can't catch a break.

It's weird not having either Buchanan playing. My best friend, Maverick, had heart surgery, and his twin, Archer, passed away in a car accident. In some fucked-up twist of fate, Mav received Archer's heart. Now, he's living with his parents while he recovers, and the rest of the team is trying to figure out how to play without two of their best defensemen. If they moved away or some shit, it would be one thing, but having a teammate fucking die? It's messing with all our heads, making it impossible to concentrate on anything, let alone winning.

Our first game is in a couple of weeks. Bluntly put? We're not ready. I'm not usually the sentimental type, but my entire body is sore from how hard I've pushed it on the ice to honor the twins' absences. I'm not the only one. The whole team eats, sleeps, and breathes hockey, but you wouldn't know it. Nah, after today's practice, I'm convinced you could strap a pair of skates on a flock of geese, and they'd still look better on the ice than we do.

Rumor has it the Lady Hawks, LAU's women's team, are showing up, which is saying something, considering Ophelia's involvement with the twins and her position as a goalie. She's gotta be as fucked in the head as the rest of us, though it isn't showing in her playing time. So, what the hell is wrong with us?

Toweling off my wet hair, I head to my locker, hating how quiet it is. But the worst part is how I can't escape it. The quiet. Not at home. Not at practice. Fucking nowhere, and it's slowly driving me insane.

I hate the quiet. I've hated it since I was a little kid when my dad would be at work or disappear on a bender until his next shift, and I would spend my days all alone in my trailer. Yeah, those were the good ol' days.

Cue the sarcasm.

After I was accepted to LAU, I vowed to never go back to the quiet. The loneliness. The fucking itch crawling along my skin anytime I'm by myself. And so far, it's worked. I had

Maverick and my teammates and hockey and parties and girls. I had the fucking world. Now, Archer's dead, Maverick's living with his parents while he heals from surgery, and the rest of the team prefers drowning their sorrows in silence. It doesn't matter how much I fight it. The darkness is starting to creep in, and I'm not sure how long I can take it.

The rest of the team has gone home except me, Griffin, and Everett. We showered in silence—my favorite—each of us well aware of the uphill battle we'll face in our first game if we can't get our heads out of our asses.

Griffin straddles the bench between the lockers with the Hawk's playbook spread open in front of him. Since his older brother, Jaxon, graduated last year, the team voted for Griffin to take his place as captain, and he's been doing his best to stay focused. Considering Archer's funeral was last week, I'd say it's easier said than done.

"Aren't they the same plays as last year?" I joke, opening my locker and grabbing my boxers.

He doesn't bother looking at me as he flips the laminated sheet to the next page. "Smartass."

"You avoiding home, too?" I prod. I've never been a fan of walking on eggshells, and after the last few weeks of doing exactly that, I'm throwing in the towel.

Griffin looks up at me. "Who says I'm avoiding home?"

"Come on, man. We've all been avoiding home. No use being dipshits and lying about it."

He looks back at the plays but doesn't deny it.

"We should have another Game Night," I decide. The idea sounds better and better as it hangs in the air. Since our freshman year at LAU, we've thrown Game Nights ranging from Truth or Dare to Musical Chairs to The Floor is Lava. It sounds childish, but when mixed with some alcohol, cute girls, and my teammates, they're some of the best nights I'll ever have.

"A Game Night?" Griffin questions.

"Yeah. We could play Spin the Bottle or Hide and Seek or...I dunno?" I lean the back of my head against the cool metal locker and stare up at the ceiling. "Fuck, anything is better than the silence in our place."

Stepping out of the shower area, Everett wraps a towel around his waist and interjects, "You really think a Game Night is a good idea?"

"I think anything to lift the curse is a good idea," I argue.

Griff cocks his head. "Curse?"

"You know what I mean," I push. "The silence is starting to go to my head, Griff. I swear, I'm going crazy, and after the shitshow Coach called a practice earlier? I know I'm not the only one feeling it."

"It was rough," he mutters, turning back to the weathered pages in front of him. Coach Sanderson is old school and refuses to upload the plays onto an iPad, terrified it'll jinx us on the ice. If only he knew what losing a teammate would do.

"If we can't get our heads on straight by the first game of the season, we're fucked," I tell them, driving my point home.

Everett scoffs. "Just because you don't know how to respect the dead—"

"Reeves is right," Griffin interrupts. "We're all playing like shit, and we're all avoiding home because none of us want to walk past Archer's room when we all know it's empty."

"Aunt Mia and Uncle Henry cleaned it out two weeks ago," Everett points out.

"Because that makes it better," I mutter under my breath.

Sometimes, I hate being the black sheep. I should be used to it by now, but the reminder of how close everyone else is compared to me can be a bitch. Everett and Griffin aren't related to the Buchanans, but they grew up together. Their parents went to school at LAU together. Their dads played hockey together for Henry Buchanan's NHL team,

KELSIE RAE

and since I was signed as well, it made sense for me to live there.

Even now, they spend most Sundays together for brunch. Everyone does. Everyone but me. Hearing Everett call Maverick's parents aunt and uncle reminds me exactly where I fall on the totem pole. The very. Fucking. Bottom. Honestly, I'm surprised I got a room at the house with the guys in the first place. If I hadn't become friends with Maverick during summer training, I probably wouldn't have. The guys? They're knitted tighter than a scarf. And me? Well, I'm the loose strand they could cut at any second.

"Aunt Mia and Uncle Henry cleaning out Archer's room doesn't mean everything's back to normal." Griff scrubs his hand over his face. "Fuck, I feel guilty for even saying I want it to be back to normal."

He's right. There is no normal after losing a friend or a brother or a cousin. But living the way we have? It's fucked.

"Yeah, well, being in limbo isn't doing us any favors," I point out. "You think Arch would want us to sabotage our season all because we're distracted he's gone?"

"So what? We pretend he never existed?" Everett argues.

"I'm not saying we pretend he doesn't exist," I grit out. "I'm saying we honor him the way he deserves. By not being whiny little bitches." Dropping my towel, I slide my boxers on, adding, "Let's have a Game Night. Everyone can write down memories of Archer on the way in, and we'll give them to Mav and his parents during our first game. And then, we'll get shitfaced, maybe hook up with a couple of girls, and celebrate the start of the semester."

With a quiet slap, Griffin closes the playbook and stands up. "Make it a costume party, and I'm in."

"You wanna do a costume party?" I ask, my brows raising as his suggestion sinks in. Any Game Night is crazy, but a costume party? Those are legendary. We usually only throw one or two a year.

"If we do this, we might as well do it right," Griffin says. "Get it done."

I slip my shirt over my head and reach for my cell, preparing to send an invitation to the masses while ignoring an annoyed Everett at the edge of the room. "I'll make it happen."

3
DYLAN

Ophelia went home for the weekend. Actually, that's a lie. She went to Maverick's parents' house for the weekend. And by weekend, I mean, she stopped by to grab a fresh change of clothes, since she basically moved into the spare bedroom across from Maverick's ever since his surgery. They've been hooking up for a while now, and after a messy turn of events, they made things official a few weeks ago. Don't get me wrong. I'm happy for Lia and all. But being left alone with a social butterfly like Finley as my sole roommate for the foreseeable future when a party is happening in the duplex connected to ours is more than I can handle.

"Are you ready yet?" Finley asks from the hallway bathroom.

When I don't answer with an enthusiastic hell yes, her head pops through the doorway, and she narrows her eyes. "Why aren't you dressed?"

I glance down at my sweats as I sit cross-legged on the family room couch. Fiddling with my glasses, I tell her, "I figured I'd stay in and watch a movie instead."

"Nope. No deal." She slips the mascara wand back into its pink tube and marches toward me. "Come on. We're doing college the right way, with or without our third musketeer."

"But I hate parties," I whine.

"You hate parties because you're still sober. Once we get you a shot or two of tequila, you'll sing a different tune. Trust me."

"Says the girl who doesn't drink," I point out.

"Hey, it's not my fault I have epilepsy, and alcohol triggers seizures. At least let me live vicariously through you, you know? Now, up you go." She grabs my wrists and tries to yank me to my feet, but I keep my butt planted on the cushion. With a huff, she pushes, "I already laid an outfit on your bed, and you need to put in your contacts."

"But my head hurts," I pout.

I probably shouldn't pull the migraine card so early, but I can't help it. Sometimes there are perks to being smacked in the head with a puck when you're thirteen years old, causing you to have vision problems, equilibrium issues, and nasty headaches you wouldn't wish on your worst enemy, and dammit. If I wanna use said perk tonight to get out of a party, I will.

Finley's eyes thin as she studies me carefully. "Are you lying?"

"Would I use my health issues as a way to get out of something?"

"Uh, yes. I do it all the time," she counters with a laugh. "The question is, are you or are you not lying to me?"

Dammit. The girl is way too good at sleuthing, and I crack almost instantly.

"Fiiiine, I'll go."

Grudgingly, I raise my hands into the air, and Finley grabs hold, letting me use her as leverage. Once I'm on my feet, she lets me go, then pats my butt. "There's my girl. Now, go change. It's a costume party."

I freeze in the hallway and look over my shoulder at her. "You're joking, right?"

"Come on, I hear they're super fun."

"I don't have a costume."

"You *didn't* have a costume," she clarifies. "But don't worry. As your self-appointed fairy godmother for the evening, I took care of it. And before you ask, no, it's not pink, and there isn't any glitter on it, so, you're fine. Now, shoo."

She waves me off with a flutter of her fingers, and my nose wrinkles in defeat.

"Fiiiine," I repeat, knowing if I don't give in, she'll keep bugging me until I do.

I DREW THE LINE AT LIPSTICK BECAUSE IT'S NOT ME. FINLEY still managed to pin me down and wipe shimmery stuff on my cheeks and eyelids, though, as well as some thick eyeliner our Aunt Mia would be proud of. She also curled my hair and gave me messy pigtail buns on top of my head, adding a black nose and more faux freckles. I'm a deer. A helpless baby deer. The instructions for the girls tonight were to dress up as weak prey. Rude? Kind of. I'm already insecure enough as it is, thank you very much. Still, even I can admit I look pretty cute in my camel-colored shorts romper and white sneakers. Finley chose the skunk route and pulled her hair into a faux mohawk, spray painting the center white while keeping her natural dark hair on the sides and sporting a skin-tight black tank top and jean shorts. Not gonna lie. The girl looks hot, and if her boyfriend saw her like this, walking straight into a den of wolves, he'd probably be questioning his choice of attending a college across the country from us.

But that's on him, so…suck it up, buttercup.

I've been to two Game Nights besides this. The first one, we played Never Have I Ever, and it ended with my best friend, Ophelia, running away in tears. The second time, we played an altered version of Cards Against Humanity. The outcome had me seriously questioning my brothers' sanity and who they're friends with. Reeves being the main culprit.

I haven't seen him since photography class, and I haven't reached out, either. If I want a good grade, I should, but who needs good grades? Well, technically, I do, but I might rescind my conclusion if I make a fool of myself tonight.

The guys' duplex is a mirrored replica of ours, with a large family room, a set of stairs hugging the left, and a kitchen at the back of the house. A table sits in the entryway covered with envelopes, cardstock, and Sharpie markers. There's a piece of paper taped to the wall next to it. It says, "Share a favorite memory of Archer Buchanan. Cards will be given to the Buchanan family during the Hawks' first game of the season. RIP #22."

I stare at the scribbled handwriting on the paper for a solid ten seconds until someone bumps me from behind.

"Hey, watch where you're going!" Finley scolds, offering me one of the Sharpies. "Here."

"Thanks."

Uncapping the marker, I bend down, staring at the blank piece of cardstock as tears gather in my eyes.

I have so many memories with Archer. It's hard to choose ONLY one, but the first one to come to mind is actually kind of recent.

At prom earlier this year, I made a

complete fool of myself with my date, like multiple times. I felt stupid and exhausted, and after I went home, I took a shower, vowing to NEVER acknowledge my date from hell ever again. Lo and behold, as I was climbing into bed, I received a text from Archer.

He asked how I was doing, then joked about how my date was a tool and I could do so much better, even though we both knew my date was the one who made it clear he wasn't interested in going out with me a second time and not the other way around. Honestly, part of me thinks the only reason he asked me in the first place was so he could possibly have an "in" with my brothers or something.

Regardless, Archer spent the next few minutes making me feel like I dodged a bullet. I don't know...it meant a lot to me, and it's one of my favorite memories. Archer was so amazing at making people feel seen. Feel comfortable. Feel like they belonged. Even when they didn't believe it themselves.

Love you, Arch. Miss you so much.

I scribble my name at the bottom, slip the cardstock into one of the envelopes, and drop it into the large glass bowl in the center of the table.

Finley does the same, mirroring my movements and dabbing at her glassy eyes with her fingertips.

"Well, that sucked," she says.

"Yeah." I sniff. It really did.

"Come on," she adds. "Let's get you a drink. At least one of us can drown our sorrows, right?" She guides me down the hall leading to the kitchen. The granite countertops are littered with glass bottles, red Solo cups, and different kinds of soda and juices. Finley pours herself a cranberry and Sprite, then sets it aside and makes another replica, adding a hefty splash of vodka. My nose wrinkles as I imagine how strong that bad boy must be.

With a knowing smirk, Fin hands it to me. "Drink up, Dyl."

"I'm under twenty-one, remember?"

"And you're at a college party."

"Because you made me come."

"Stop being a sourpuss and drink," she pushes. "It'll settle your nerves."

The girl knows me too well. Keeping my sour expression, I swallow half the cup's contents and hand the drink back to her for a refill. She doesn't even bat an eye as she adds more liquid to the cup and picks up her own alcohol-free beverage.

Sometimes it's nice. Having a consistent designated driver as a best friend. Other times, I'd kill for Finley to be able to drink so she could let go of the reins every once in a while and keep her nose out of my business. Unfortunately for both of us, Finley's epilepsy isn't a fan of alcohol. Her mom, Kate, has been great at showing Fin the ropes of what not to do with her condition.

"Hey," someone says.

I glance to my left, finding a pair of large hands cradling a cup. Slowly, my eyes trail up the very tall frame, and my neck cranes until they land on a pair of baby blues. They're bright and expectant and—I can't do this.

Tongue-tied, I turn around and face Finley completely, praying she notices my bulging eyes as I mouth, "Help me!"

She chuckles under her breath, well aware I'm seconds from having a full-blown meltdown, then takes the lead, slipping closer to me and the stranger behind me and cutting through the awkward silence I created by my lack of response.

Greeting the guy behind me, Finley says, "Hi."

"Hey," he repeats. "I'm Todd."

"Hello, Todd." She offers her hand. "I'm Finley, and this is Dylan."

I glare at my best friend but don't bother turning around to face Todd, choosing to hook my arm through Finley's and tug us both to safety and as far away from Todd as possible.

Practically jogging backward to keep up with my escape, she waves her hand, calling out, "Bye, Todd!"

We're swallowed whole by the crowd almost instantly, and I breathe deep in an attempt to keep my anxiety at bay once we find an empty corner of the room.

"Dude," she says through another laugh. "You're the worst wingwoman ever."

"Never claimed to be anything different, Fin," I mutter. "Is he gone?"

She rises onto her tiptoes, glancing over the crowd. "Pretty sure."

The fight drains from my muscles, and I sag against the wall behind me. "Good."

"What's good?" Everett asks. He approaches us while pinching the neck of a beer bottle with his fingers.

"Dylan dodged a cute guy who tried talking to her," Finley quips.

Everett nods. "Still afraid of the opposite sex, Dyl?"

I roll my eyes but don't bother responding.

Turning to his sister, Everett points out, "Your shorts are too short."

"That's why they're called *shorts*," Finley replies.

Gritting his teeth, he motions to her cup. "Any alcohol in there?"

"No, *Dad*, but thanks for your concern. Is the game starting soon?"

Everett shrugs as he looks around the crowded room. "Depends on Reeves. This was his idea."

With a grin, Finley replies, "I knew I liked him. Now, run along. I'd really like to not be known as Everett's little sister for the next four years."

He tosses his arm over her shoulder and lifts his chin at one of his friends across the room like he hopes to do exactly that.

She elbows him in the ribs. "Ev!"

"Be good," he warns, then his eyes find mine. "Both of you."

"Yeah, yeah. Now, shoo."

Grumbling, he drops his arm from around her, then disappears through the crowd as Finley fusses with the bottom of her faux hawk. "I'm going to use the bathroom real quick."

"You can't ditch me," I seethe. "What if Todd comes back?"

"You'll be fine." Wiggling her fingers back and forth, she calls, "I'll be right back. Tootaloo!"

As she weaves through the crowd, I scowl at her retreating form, tossing back more of my drink.

"Someone's thirsty," a low voice notes.

I jump at the sound, and the last of my drink splashes onto a pair of very flashy sneakers.

The guy bounds back, hands raised. "What the fuck?"

"Sorry!" I rush out. "Shit, your shoes."

"It's fine." His face is more of a snarl than anything else as he looks down at me. Something flashes in his eyes, though I can't quite place what it is. He's cute in a snooty, I'm hot, and I know it kind of way. Which is bad. Really bad. Because if he knows he's cute, my body does, too. And if my body knows he's cute? Well, this could turn really bad very quickly. His shoes will be the least of my worries if I don't get out of here as soon as possible. I might try to run my fingers through his hair or spill what's left of my drink all over him, or hell, maybe I'll trip over my own feet and wind up with his dick in my face. Oh, wait. I already did that once this week.

My spine is a steel rod as I clear my throat and take a step back. "Okay, then. Bye."

"Wait," he orders. "You're new."

Get. Out. Of. Here.

I paste on a fake smile and turn to dart away, but he moves around me, blocking my escape.

"And pretty," he adds.

"Pretty something," I mutter under my breath as I stare at his stained shoes. Sucker shouldn't have bought canvas. Poor guy. They're most definitely ruined.

"Something?" the guy prods.

"I don't..." My nose scrunches, and I look up at him. "I don't know? What are we talking about?"

"What's your name, new girl?"

"My friends call me Dylan, and my family calls me Dylan. Or Dyl sometimes. It depends on the situation, but, uh... yeah."

"So your friends and family call you Dylan, but it isn't your name?"

"No, it is," I tell him. "My name's Dylan." Glancing around him, I search for Finley reappearing, but the brat is yet to be seen. "Did I not make it clear? Sorry, I'll explain. My name's Dylan Becca Thorne. Although I'm pretty traditional, so when I get married, I'll probably take the guy's last name, which feels weird, ya know? Because then I'm dropping my own last name. My parents told me they debated on not giving me a middle name so my last name could fill the spot once I get married, but I really like my middle name, so I'm not disappointed they wound up giving me one, you know?"

He blinks. Slowly. His jaw falls an inch, leaving his mouth gaping as he digests my word vomit.

I did it again. I made it awkward.

"Welp..." I grimace. "See ya later."

Without another word, I dodge past the poor guy, and this time, he lets me. I'm not surprised. He probably wanted to end the conversation as quickly as possible, too, now that he knows I'm a crazy person.

"Dylan!" Finley calls from the hall.

I rush toward her and loop my arm through hers so she can't ditch me again. Peeking over my shoulder, I see the stranger's gone.

Shit. I didn't even ask for his name.

Good one, Dylan.

Even landing in Reeves' lap during photography felt less embarrassing than my interaction with...whoever he was. Maybe it's because Reeves doesn't look at me like I'm growing a second head despite my...moments. Or maybe he's simply better at hiding it.

"You okay?" Fin asks.

"Fantastic," I grumble. "So, how long do I have to stay here until I can go home without you giving me shit?"

With a laugh, she shakes her head and turns me around, leading us back to the large kitchen and family room. "At least an hour. Oo, it looks like the festivities are about to begin."

Reeves jumps onto the coffee table in the middle of the family room. His entire body is draped in black, and a mask hangs from his fingertips as he scans the space. When his gaze lands on me, a smirk tugs at the corner of his mouth, and I look down at my empty cup, my cheeks heating.

"Listen up!" he calls.

The buzzing around the room quiets, and so does the music, blanketing the space in silence.

I peek up at him again. He isn't looking at me anymore. Nope. Now, he's addressing the entire room, making each and every one of the people sandwiched together feel like he's talking to them.

"Welcome to Game Night!" he continues. "Because we have a few new players this evening, here are the rules. One. What happens at Game Night stays at Game Night. If we hear you sharing anything or taking photos of anything, you're banned for the rest of your life. Second. Leave your jealousy at the door. This is a game. Emphasis on the word *game*. As in fake. As in, not real. As in, keep your head out of your ass, all right?" Lifting the gaudy gold medallion from around his neck, he raises it into the air. "Usually, the winner of Game Night is awarded this medallion and is required to keep it safe until the next Game Night, which allows them bragging rights and the opportunity to choose and judge the next game. As you can all see, I was the previous winner and would like to announce tonight's game."

An even heavier hush falls over the crowd, each of us hanging on every single syllable said by the stupid Adonis in front of me. "But tonight, I decided to make us all winners." Low laughter rings throughout the room, and I glance at Finley beside me, feeling like I'm missing something, but she lifts a shoulder. She's as confused as I am.

"Rules are simple," he explains. "Hide and seek. Girls against guys. The entire neighborhood is free reign. Girls hide first. You have three minutes until we come searching. If someone finds you, they get to kiss you on a location of your choosing. As always, we're big fans of consent around here, and if anyone pushes the boundaries to where you aren't comfortable, let me, Everett, or Griffin know, and we'll take care of it." His gaze darkens. "And if anyone's stupid enough to push the boundaries, let me make this clear. You won't walk away from this party. You'll leave in a body bag." I give Finley another curious look but keep my lips pressed together as Reeves adds, "Guys who came here with their girl, I suggest you hunt quickly so someone else doesn't find her first. Girls who came here with their guy? Well, I suggest you choose an innocent place for your wolf to collect his payment if you're caught by a wolf you don't belong to." Another round of amusement rolls through the room, and Reeves basks in it before asking, "Any questions?" His look skims the crowd, falling on me again. Smirking, he slides the mask he's holding into place. It's a wolf. With gray fur. And glow-in-the-dark eyes. I look around the room as every other guy in the house slips on a matching mask, making it impossible to tell whose face hides under it.

My heart rate ratchets up a notch as I take in the crowd surrounding me. There are so many of them. A pack of wolves ready for the hunt. Reaching up, I touch one of the messy buns on my head. A deer. Prey. Well, if they wanted to make the game interesting, they succeeded. If I can keep my adrenaline in check so I don't faceplant once the game starts, that'd be great.

I glance at the masked Reeves again, curious about what he's waiting for. His head cocks a few degrees when I catch him staring at me. It makes me feel like he can see right through me. Like he can sense exactly what I feel. Like he truly is a wolf. And even though his entire face is covered, I swear I can feel him grinning beneath the mask before he yells, "Run!"

Like the prey we are, all the girls race toward the entrance, spilling out the door, one after another, and spreading across the front yard and further onto the driveway. It's dark out. Like, extremely dark. Most of the street lights are covered in garbage bags, shielding the glow from lighting up the sidewalk. It's borderline freaky but clever as hell. I'll give them that much.

It seems the boys have thought of everything.

Squeals and giggles mingle as one of the girls in front of me stumbles in her heels, practically faceplanting on the sidewalk. Her friend helps her up, and they rush behind a neighbor's house, each of them dressed like Playboy bunnies, complete with fishnet tights and fluffy white tails pinned to their butts.

Seriously. I give it ten minutes until someone calls the cops for trespassing.

"How is this allowed?" I ask.

"I heard they give everyone on the street season passes to LAU games to make up for their shenanigans," Finley explains. "Now, hurry up! We need to find a good spot to hide!"

"Who's they?" I ask as we dart around the corner of a house and book it toward someone's deck, crouching low when whooping echoes from the main house.

Finley doesn't bother answering me, choosing to cover my mouth with her hand while giving me a death glare warning me to be quiet or I'll feel her wrath, as loud howls echo from the guys' house, followed by sneakers scuffing against the pavement.

I guess our three minutes are up.

"Ready or not, here we come!" masculine voices announce.

My heartbeat throbs in my ears, making it hard to hear anything else as I look around the edge of the house with wide eyes. Okay, this is terrifying. What if someone catches me? I didn't sign up for this. I mean, I didn't *not* sign up for this, but my heart is pounding, my palms are sweaty, my skin feels hot and tight, and I seriously might pass out at any second. Ripping Finley's hand from my mouth, I force my breathing to calm as I listen for...something, but it's eerily quiet. Seconds later, a few girlish squeals cut through the sound of feet pounding the ground. It's followed by low laughter, and before I realize what's happening, a loud "Boo!" from behind me makes us both jump out of our skin. Then, we're running as fast as we can. Whoever it was is still far away, at least fifty yards, but the glowing eyes and wide stance are enough to light a fire under my ass, and I pump my arms back and forth, searching for an escape.

Rounding the edge of the street, I spot a tall fence ahead of me. Finley dashes to my right, but I stay straight and use an empty flower pot as leverage, grasping the edge of the fence, pulling myself up, and sliding down the slick surface on the other side.

The cold from the metal seeps into my romper as I try to catch my breath, waiting for the stranger to hurdle over it like I did, but I'm gifted with silence. He must be following Finley instead. The footsteps recede, and within seconds, I'm left with nothing but my own unsteady breathing for company.

Holy shit, it worked.

I'm...well, I don't know what I am. Terrified? Yes. Shocked? Definitely.

Did I really do that?

I feel...exhilarated. Invincible, almost, which is ridiculous, but still. I cover my mouth to hide my laughter when another set of squeals grabs my attention from the main street, twenty feet in front of me.

Do I stay? Do I leave? Dammit, I have no idea.

Where's Finley?!

Okay, Dylan. You can do this. You can...I don't know?

Maybe make it back to the house? Sneak in through your back door? Hunker down until...what exactly?

Slowly, I tiptoe along the fence and dash across the grass. With my back pressed to the side of a house, I peek around the corner. Finley's nowhere in sight, but there are two men in masks. I don't recognize either of them.

Shocker.

With legs spread wide, they stand in the middle of the empty road, scanning the surrounding houses for girls.

"Truck," one of them grunts. He lifts his chin toward a white F-150 parked in a driveway. In a flash, they run toward it, closing the distance within seconds. When they reach the truck, they pull themselves up until they each stand on the tailgate, towering over whoever chose the bed as their hiding spot. More squeals of surprise cut through the night air, and the wolves laugh, each spotting their own prey. The one on the left leaps into the truck bed with the girls. My eyes widen when the other joins in, pouncing on them.

I catch myself smiling as I wait for them to reappear, but all I hear is, "Time to pay up, Lace," as another group of wolves round the edge of a yard on the opposite side of the street. They spread out like a legion, their heads swiveling from left to right until I'm pretty sure I'm seconds from being caught if I don't start moving. Keeping them in my sight, I start to back away when a hand slides over my mouth. I gasp, clutching at the wrist as the masked stranger spins me around and pushes my back against the house, pressing his forefinger to his lips.

With my pulse thrumming in my ears, I hold my breath but stay quiet, waiting for...honestly, I don't even know. The man in front of me leans closer, whispering, "Caught you."

My brows tug, and I swear I recognize the voice, but I'm too amped up to place it, let alone reply. My mouth feels like it's filled with cotton as I watch him, the glowing eyes staring down at me, his body pressing into mine while his friends check the front of the house we hide behind. The wolf mask hides his expression and true identity from me, but he's tall. With broad shoulders and the same dark clothes as every other guy on the street. He peers around the edge of the house and watches the rest of his pack leave as I continue staring up at him, taking in every minute detail, no matter how few there are, in an attempt to place the culprit, but I'm as lost as ever.

Once we're gifted with retreating footsteps, I wait for him to back up and give me some breathing room, but he doesn't. He continues pinning me to the house, his hard muscles pressing against the front of my body in a way I've literally never experienced in my entire life. He's warm. Hard. Every inch. The rough stucco scratches me through the thin cotton of my outfit, and I wet my lips, unsure what to say or do since he caught me and has me right where he wants.

"What happens now?" I whisper.

He lifts the edge of his mask, revealing his strong jaw and mouth as it curves up on one side, keeping most of his face hidden from view. "Now, you pay up." I gulp, and his smile widens. "Where do you want your kiss, baby deer?"

"Who are you?" I ask.

"Does it matter?" There's a growl in his tone. Like he's altering it on purpose. Like he doesn't want me recognizing it or *him*. It makes my heart pound faster.

Who are you?

He leans closer, his breath kissing my lips. It's too dark. If I had more light, I might be able to tell who's jaw this is, but right now? I'm clueless. My pulse flutters faster and faster with every passing second. "You won't tell me who you are?"

"What's the point of the game if you know who I am?" he counters. "Now, choose your location, Dylan Thorne." He touches the side of my face, letting his gloved hand trail

45

down my cheek and along the curve of my neck. It's slow and sensual and turns my insides into mush.

"I, uh, I'm not sure," I whisper.

His mouth lifts. "Would you like me to choose for you?"

When I nod, my forehead slams against his mouth, and I gasp in horror. "Shit, sorry!"

His deep chuckle swallows my curse and pulls low in my belly as he rubs the edge of his full mouth with his gloved hands. "Giving me a fat lip in exchange for your payment?"

"Apparently," I mutter. My face feels like it's on fire, and I look down at my feet. I'm standing in a flower bed, the green plants smashed beneath my shoes.

Oops.

My nose scrunches, and I add, "I should go."

"You haven't paid up yet," he reminds me. "And since I'm not sure I'll ever get another opportunity…" He shifts even closer, somehow planting his left foot between mine. Since we're already close, the heat of his leg warms my inner thighs, leaving me even more curious than ever.

Lifting my eyes to the glowing wolf's, I ask, "You still want to kiss me after I headbutted you?"

"You gonna do it again?"

My eyes narrow. "Maybe."

His smile spreads. "Worth it."

He angles my head toward him and bends down, waiting for the briefest of seconds for me to push him away. I like it. The unspoken request for permission despite him technically having earned the right already. When I don't ask him to stop, choosing to stare at his barely parted lips mere centimeters from mine instead of the wolf mask that's both terrifying and weirdly a turn-on, he kisses me.

Holy shit, he's actually kissing me.

It isn't soft, but it isn't hard, either. It's calculated. Perfected. As if he's had plenty of time refining the art of kissing until he's nothing short of a master. My eyes flutter closed as I lose myself in the feel of his lips against mine. Then, he slides his tongue along the seam of my mouth and goes deeper, dipping it into me. Tasting me. Teasing me.

I've never been kissed before.

Okay, that's a lie. I've been kissed twice. But neither experience was like this. Neither kiss was nothing short of exquisite. Perfect pressure. Perfect taste. Like sweet bread. Orange, maybe? It's the yeast from his beer. It should be gross, but it isn't. Actually, I kind of want to taste him more. I open my mouth wider and reach up, grasping his wrist as he continues holding me in place. He's strong. I can feel it beneath my fingers. Like he's holding back. Like he could do whatever he wanted to me in this moment. And honestly, I'd probably let him. Which is stupid on so many levels. I don't know who this is. It's dark. He's barely said a word, and even then, he's only whispered. He's wearing a mask. He's wearing black. He's a stranger, and I likely couldn't pick him out of a lineup even if I tried. He could be anyone.

Anyone.

And here he is, kissing me. Making my knees weak and my core tighten in a way I've literally never experienced in my entire life.

But he knows my name.

It has to count for something, doesn't it?

I whimper, clenching my thighs, belatedly realizing his knee is still between them.

Shit. Did he feel it?

With a low groan, he pulls away and rests his forehead against mine.

I'll take that as a yes.

"Fuck," he breathes out. "You taste even sweeter than I expected."

"Is that a bad thing?" I whisper.

His quiet laugh fans across my cheeks, and he leans away, pulling his mask back into place. "Guess it depends on whether or not I want your brother to beat the shit out of me." He tilts his head as if he's debating the pros and cons, then clears his throat and steps away. "You should head back to the house."

"H-house?"

"The party," he clarifies, his voice as quiet as ever. "You should get back."

"Oh." I wipe at the corner of my mouth with my thumb, then move around him. "Right. I should probably find Fin, too."

"Good idea."

On shaky legs, I walk away, forcing them to work, when he calls out, "See you around, Dylan."

I glance over my shoulder to find him disappearing into the darkness like a ghost. A figment of my imagination. Hell, he might as well be. I don't know who he is. I don't know anything about him. But for the first time in…I don't know how long, I'm curious.

Dammit, I'm curious, which is both exhilarating and frustrating. The question is, does he hope to find another girl to prey on, or is he heading back to the house, too?

And why do I care?

4
DYLAN

I head back to the house like a good girl, my mind spinning like a top. I'm not sure if you can get drunk on lust, but if I ever needed convincing it's a possibility; tonight's the night. I'm lightheaded. I can't stop smiling or laughing to myself. My stomach keeps flip-flopping. And the hangxiety is already setting in.

Was I a good kisser?

Did he like it?

Did I seriously kind of rub myself against his thigh like a pervert?

Yup.

Hello, anxiety. Nice to see you again.

Man, I need another drink.

Twisting the top off of the vodka bottle, I pour a generous splash into a cup and add Dr. Pepper. When some of it spills over the rim, I set everything down on the counter and force my shaking hands to relax as I take a slow breath. *In through the nose, out through the mouth,* I remind myself. It's weird. Sharing the best kiss of your life with a faceless stranger. To be fair, he didn't have a lot of competition, but still. I'm surrounded by the

49

same people from earlier, but I can't stop looking at them now. Studying the lower half of their faces. Attempting to piece them together with the stranger from ten minutes ago. Eavesdropping on every black-shirted wolf, dissecting every single gruff voice in the room, and comparing it with the one who rumbled my name before kissing me. It's useless. I take a sip of my drink and head to the nearest corner, blending in with the gray walls as I continue my pitiful inspection. If the guy wanted to keep his identity hidden, it's official. He nailed it.

I have no idea who kissed me, and I'm not sure I ever will. But the idea of never figuring it out feels like an unscratchable itch in the back of my brain, and it's driving me crazy.

"Dylan!" Finley squeals when she finds me. Her grip is like an anaconda as she squeezes my bicep. "How'd it go?"

"It, uh..." I clear my throat. "It was fine?"

"Fine?" She pulls back, assessing me carefully. A Cheshire grin spreads across her face. "Well, if my little doe didn't find a big, strong predator to eat her alive."

My face flames, and I groan, "Fin."

"Seriously, you're a terrible liar," she notes. "Okay, tell me everything."

"There's nothing to tell."

"Yeah, and I'm the queen of England." She snorts. "Come on. You're blushing like a virgin." My eyes widen, and my expression turns into a warning glare. She raises her hands in defense. "Kidding," she sing-songs. "For real, though. What happened?"

I stare down at the caramel-colored liquid in my cup. "I played the game and was found."

"And where'd you let him kiss you?" Her brows bounce up and down. "Actually, let's cut to the chase. Did you or did you not at least have a better experience than your first two kisses? And when I say better than your first two kisses, I'm aware of how low the bar is, thanks to one of the guys almost barfing in your mouth, and—"

"Technically, I was the one who almost barfed," I mutter.

Another amused chuckle slips out of her. "Oh, yeah. I forgot. So? Was it at least better than those?"

"I mean, it was a..." My mouth goes dry as I replay the kiss.

"Ah!" She claps her hands. "It was good, wasn't it? I knew it was gonna be good."

"Dude, breathe," I tell her as a few people around us start staring. Grabbing her shoulder, I drag us down the hall, searching for privacy. "It wasn't anything crazy, okay? It was..."

"The best kiss of your life?" she finishes for me.

"Well, when the bar is already on the ground...then, yeah. Sure. It was the best kiss of my life."

With another excited squeal, she tugs my arm back and forth like her cute little quarter-Asian body can't even handle her enthusiasm. "I am so freaking excited for you! So who is he?"

I glance around her tiny frame, confirming we're still alone, and admit the very pathetic truth. "I have no idea."

Her face falls. "You don't know?"

"How would I know? He was wearing a mask."

"You didn't rip the damn thing off him so you could see who he really is?" she scolds.

"Was I supposed to?"

With a shrug, she reaches for my cup and brings it to her lips. "I would've—"

I snatch it back from her before she has a chance to drink any. "Yo, epilepsy, remember? And I thought taking off their mask was against the rules."

"You're kidding me, right?"

51

Her pointed look makes me squirm, and I lift a shoulder while stealing a sip of my drink. "I don't know?"

"So you have no idea who kissed you?"

I wish.

"Nope," I answer.

"Hmm…" She taps her manicured finger against her chin. "Okay, as your self-appointed private investigator—"

"Oh, so now you're a PI *and* my fairy godmother?" I rest my hand on my hip and quirk my brow.

"Uh, heck yes, and I nailed the fairy godmother position, so shush. Let me continue my sleuthing, shall we?"

Glowering at her, I wave my hand around. "Be my guest."

"Why, thank you." She clicks her tongue against the roof of her mouth and drags me back to the edge of the main area so she can peruse her options. "How tall is he?"

"I dunno? Tall?"

"Wow, you're super helpful," she notes. "Was he taller than you?"

"Yes, definitely."

"Taller than Everett or Griffin?" She gasps. "Ohmygod, what if you kissed my brother?"

My heart leaps into my throat. "I didn't."

"You don't know for sure," she argues. "You could've most definitely kissed my brother."

"He would have had to be hunting specifically for me, and Everett wouldn't track me down when there are a shit-ton of other girls at tonight's party."

"Hey, you don't know that," she starts, but I lift my hand and cut her off.

"Seriously, Finley? It's *Everett*. The guy might be overprotective, but I'm pretty sure he draws the line there, right? I mean…" I go silent, replaying the moment, a frown tugging at my lips.

"You're not so sure, are you?" Finley assumes.

I hesitate while honestly considering the possibility, no matter how far-fetched it feels. "It was dark, he talked quietly, and I'm pretty sure I could hear my own heartbeat in my ears, so..."

My back hits the wall, and I slump against it as the idea of kissing Everett Taylor filters through me. It makes me feel... confused? Curious? Anxious? I don't even know. Would he have kissed me? Would he have wanted to? I don't...I don't know.

"So, you're not sure," she repeats.

My attention clicks to her. "I guess not."

"But you liked it?" she pushes. "The kiss?"

The knowing gleam in her eyes makes me purse my lips. "I already told you I did."

"Then I say we try to figure out who it was, even if we have to ask every guy on campus point-blank."

My body fights to curl in on itself, but I stand strong. Pushing away from the wall with a deep breath, I attempt to remember how ridiculous this entire conversation really is. "Finley, it was just a kiss."

"For ninety-nine percent of the people at the party, sure. But for my cute little doe?" She steps closer. "I think not."

She's right. I might not want to admit it out loud, but it's true. I'm not...I'm not a casual kisser. I've tried to be, and it didn't take. So much so we have a rule with Truth or Dare or any other game involving a bet. For me? Kissing is off the table, simple as that.

"We should drop it now instead of making this into something it isn't," I decide.

"Admit it, you're basically living out Cinderella."

"Yeah, if I was the prince," I mock, rolling my eyes as the realization hits full force. Seriously. This is ridiculous.

"Oh, come on," she argues. "They've made loads of different versions."

"So, what? He's my Cinderell-o?"

"Noooo," she drags out. "Obviously, he's your Cinder*fella*."

I snort. "Pretty sure that's even worse."

"Look, the name isn't the point, even though I think Cinderfella is pretty adorable." Her chest puffs out with pride as if she's the most clever person alive. "The point is, you're officially in a fairytale, and I'm the one who got you there, so you're welcome."

"I wouldn't celebrate quite yet," I mutter. "Besides, the guy called me by my first name, so it's not like he doesn't know who I am, and since he clearly wanted to hide his identity from me, I'm pretty sure tracking him down is a bad idea."

"Aw, come on," she begs. "It'll be fun."

"Potentially being turned down by a cute guy all because I'm stalking him? Yeah, sounds like a real hoot."

"Wait, how do you know he's cute if you didn't see his face?"

Looking down at my feet, I shift from one foot to the other as my cheeks flood from the memory of the kiss. "Trust me, I could just...tell."

"How?"

"You know how it is," I hedge.

"Spell it out for me, babe."

With a sigh, I look up at her again. "With the kind of confidence this guy was sporting, he's...definitely comfortable in his own skin. We'll have to leave it at that."

"Mm-hmm. Okay. Totally get it." She nods as if collecting data and storing it for later. "If we're gonna track this guy down, I need every detail you can remember."

"Or, we can drop this whole thing, go home, and watch a movie," I suggest.

"Or you can give me all the details, and I'll make a mental note of every person at this party who fits the description, and—"

"Finley," I beg.

"And *then*," she emphasizes, "we go home, watch a movie, and I give my detective skills a rest until tomorrow." She nudges her shoulder with mine. "Deal?"

"On one condition," I decide. "You can't flat out ask any guys if they kissed me tonight. It would be...weird."

"Not even Everett?"

"*Especially* not Everett."

"All right, fine. Deal. Now, let's see. What's first? Beard? No beard? Low voice? High voice? Would you say he's white or black? Blonde hair or dark hair? Give me something to work with."

Fighting through the onslaught of questions and how much they overwhelm me, I answer, "Uh...he had scruff, olive skin, probably dark hair if I had to guess, but I might be wrong on that one?" I bite my bottom lip, searching my memory for clues but shake my head in frustration. "Like I said, he whispered, so I have no idea what his voice actually sounds like. He knew my name, though."

"He knew your name?"

"I already told you—"

"Okay." She lifts her hands in defense. "So, he knows you."

"We don't know if he really knows me."

"Why else would he use your name, Dyl?" she counters.

My lips gnash together, but I don't argue with her.

Satisfied she's won, she adds, "Honestly, it makes this scenario so much juicier. What about his eyes?"

"He had a mask on, remember?"

She frowns. "Good point. Hmm. Okay, how 'bout teeth? Straight? Crooked? Yellow? White?"

"White teeth. Straight."

"How 'bout his lips? Thick? Thin?"

"Uh...full, I think? I don't know? They were kissable. He had kissable lips."

"Kissable, huh?" She smirks. "All right, I'll be sure to keep an eye out for *kissable* lips."

Shoving at her shoulder, I grumble, "You're making fun of me."

"I'm not making fun of you. I simply think it's refreshing how we found you an actual guy you're interested in *and* connected with. Damn, I'm a good fairy godmother."

"You're something, all right," I mutter. "Any more questions?"

"Um..." Her attention catches on someone in the family room, and her breathing stalls.

"You okay?" I ask.

"Yup, let's get out of here, shall we?"

I try following her gaze but wind up empty as she hooks her arm through mine and guides us out the back.

"So, speaking of the chase and all, how'd it go for you?" I prod.

"Meh." She shrugs. "Griffin caught me, so I let him kiss me on the cheek."

My eyes widen. "Griff, as in my brother?"

"The one and only."

"How do you know it was Griff?"

"Because he pointed out how Drew would probably be pissed if he knew I was playing this game."

"Yikes." I grimace. "Is that why you wanted to get out of there?"

"Didn't feel like having another lecture," she grumbles. "Usually, it's Ev with his panties in a twist, you know what I mean? But apparently, Griffin felt like taking the stick from my brother's ass and stuck it up his own this time, so..." She opens the back door to our place and lets me step inside before joining me. "It's not like I was going to let anyone kiss me in the first place. Well, other than on the hand or cheek or something. I might talk a big game, Dylan, but I'm not

56

stupid. I refuse to jeopardize my relationship with Drew over a silly game."

"Good," I say, not because I particularly like Drew or anything. But I have a feeling if Finley did something stupid like cheating, she'd never forgive herself. Collapsing onto the couch, I start unlacing my shoes, adding, "Can I ask you something?"

She plops down next to me and reaches for the remote on the coffee table. "Sure, what is it?"

"Do you love Drew?"

She freezes, and her hesitation leaves the air around us with an uncomfortable weight I'm not sure how to carry. Drew and Finley have been together for almost a year, but as far as I know, they spend more time fighting with each other than being a happy, healthy couple. Don't get me wrong. I've met Drew once or twice, and he's fine, I guess, but I don't know. She clings to him in a way I don't understand. Maybe it's because Finley's family moved away when we reached middle school after her mom got a job promotion. After leaving, she always felt kind of...alone. Like, without me or Ophelia in high school, she didn't really have anyone. Not because she couldn't make friends —the girl's the most social person on the planet—but friends like me and Ophelia? Friends who are more like sisters? Those are hard to come by. Fin's the one who drew the short stick and had to find her own solution for being across the country from her other musketeers. Then, Drew came along and...I don't know. It's like it fixed the hole for a little while. But now, she's here, and she doesn't have quite the same void, so I guess I'm a little lost as to why she's still with him. It doesn't mean I have a right to pry, though.

"You don't have to tell me," I rush out.

Rubbing her fingers along the edge of the remote, she

murmurs, "He was my first. I think you always love your first."

"And you're not scared about the long distance?"

"I'm terrified of the long distance," she admits. "But I wasn't going to sacrifice my friendships with you and Ophelia and my relationship with my brother over my high school boyfriend, no matter how much I love him. And I'm not stupid enough to forget how young I am, and rear-ranging my entire life for a boy is...not necessarily the mature way to handle the situation, you know what I mean? But I'm also not ready to give up on me and Drew and every-thing we've been through and experienced together. So... here we are. Taking it one day at a time and...yeah. I guess we'll have to wait and see."

"I think you're brave," tell her.

"Or stupid." She smiles, but it doesn't reach her eyes. "Now. I think it's time for our movie, don't you?"

"Yup."

"Perfect. Let's pick something gory."

I snort. "Whatever you say, Fin."

5
DYLAN

Seriously, I can't turn it off. The need to scan each and every masculine face scattered in the quad as I walk with Finley toward one of the very few classes we have together this year: Math 1050.

"If you keep staring at people like this, you'll end up with a reputation," Finley points out.

"What do you mean I'll end up with a reputation?"

"For being a creepy stalker," she clarifies without bothering to look up from her phone while she continues typing away.

Honestly, I'm impressed she caught me perusing the opposite sex in the first place.

"I'm not stalking—"

"You're trying to figure out who kissed you at the party."

"I'm not—"

"You are, but it's fine." She pushes send on whatever message she was texting, then gives me her full attention. "I'm trying to figure it out, too, and I'd be a lot more help if I had anything to actually go off. But olive skin, possibly dark hair, and scruff, which may or may not have been shaved off this morning, is like looking for a needle in a haystack. Not to mention straight white teeth being my only other clue, and thanks to braces being a thing in the US, it narrows things down by like ten percent, maybe. Don't worry, though. I put out some feelers with a few other girls I met who were at the party." Her phone buzzes in her hand. Her eyes light up, and she turns back to her cell.

"Finley," I groan. "Can we not drag every stranger at the party into your sleuthing, please?"

"Don't worry. I didn't mention your name, but I feel we might get somewhere if we simply give it some time."

She goes back to tapping away on her cell as we head toward class when someone yells, "Watch out!"

I turn around and barely dodge a football coming straight for my head. Finley doesn't even flinch. It bounces off the black pavement and rolls onto the grass a few feet behind me. I look around the grassy space and find a grimacing Everett a few feet away, aka the culprit who yelled at us.

"Nice throw," I note, my voice practically dripping with sarcasm as I fold my arms.

"Sorry." Jogging toward me, he asks, "You okay?"

"We're fine," I answer, trying to calm my racing heart.

Yup. I'm pretty sure I saw my life flash before my eyes and may or may not have peed myself. Okay, no, I didn't pee myself. But I could have, for sure.

Everett bends at my feet and picks up the ball, tossing it to a shirtless Reeves twenty feet away. Across the space, Reeves' muscles bunch and flex as he catches the torpedo with an annoyingly attractive ease, and it somehow suits him perfectly.

The ease. The confidence. The laid-back persona.

Seriously? The guy's...well. Perfect. He's perfect.

Which means there's no way he would've kissed me last weekend...right?

"Hey, Drew's calling," Finley announces beside me. "I'll meet you in class."

"Sure thing," I murmur, not bothering to look at her as I continue studying half the hockey team throwing a ball across the grass, hoping to place my Cinderfella.

"Dylan," Everett barks.

My neck snaps toward him. "Mm-hmm? Yeah?"

"Maybe be a little more subtle when you check out my teammates, yeah?"

His jaw tics, and my cheeks flame as I look at the ground.

Good one, Dylan.

"I'm not checking them out," I mutter.

"Yeah, and I'm the king of France."

I peer up at him again. "Does France have a king?"

"Honestly, I have no idea." He rolls his shoulders, which is when I notice he isn't wearing a shirt, either. As if my eyes have a mind of their own, I scan his taut chest. I can't help but wonder if his body was pressed to mine this weekend. If those are the abs. The biceps. The hips. Everett's stronger than the last time I saw him shirtless. His muscles look like Michelangelo himself carved them, and the joggers hanging low on his hips? It's, uh, it's quite the combination.

"You doing okay?" he asks.

My attention flicks to his, and I clear my throat. "Yeah, why wouldn't I be?"

"You left the costume party early the other night. I haven't seen you since."

Probably because I've avoided anyone and everyone in hopes of either forgetting my encounter with my wolf altogether or finding the culprit like it's my last dying wish.

"I guess I'm hunkering down, trying to figure out college life," I tell him.

He nods. "You still planning to work at Rowdy's?"

"Uh, yeah. I started last week. It's been nice, you know? To, uh, to have a distraction."

"I get it. We're all looking for distractions lately." He tucks his hands into his pockets and kicks a stray pebble.

It skitters across the pavement as I twist my hands in front of me. "Tell your dad thanks again for hooking me up with the job."

"Yeah, no worries." He shrugs and peers down at me. "They're always looking for cute waitresses."

Rowdy's is a western steakhouse right outside of town. Macklin, Everett's dad, invested in the company after winning the lottery a couple decades ago. It's also where Uncle Mack and Aunt Kate went on their first real date. There's line dancing, a mechanical bull, and the nicest manager-slash-owner you've ever met. My interview with Rowdy lasted about five minutes, but I'll never forget his thick southern drawl as the old man fixed the cowboy hat on his head and offered me the job. Boy, did I need it. Not for the money. But for the distraction, like I mentioned. It's weird. Losing a friend. Feeling guilty for having fun. Having memories of him pop up at the most random times. And the quiet? The quiet is when it hurts the most. So, yeah. I think all of us have been grateful for whatever distractions we can muster. Hockey. Homework. A new job. We'll take what we can get.

"Well…" I continue fiddling with my short, trimmed nails. "Still, tell your dad thanks for hooking me up."

"I will."

"Yo, Ev!" one of his teammates calls. "You comin'?"

"In a minute!" Everett replies. He squeezes the back of his neck, and his biceps bulge as he turns to me again. "So, uh, you doing okay?"

I blink and force myself to look at his face instead of his toned arms. "You already asked me that."

"Guess I'm not convinced with your previous answer." He steps closer. "How was the party for you, anyway?"

My lips part, but I hesitate as a wave of suspicion washes over me. "What do you mean?"

"Finley said you kissed someone."

"I mean, it was kind of part of the game, right?"

"I guess so," he murmurs. "Any idea who kissed you?"

Why do you want to know? I want to ask, but I stay quiet. He's always been protective. It would make sense for him to be curious even if he isn't the one who kissed me so he could warn the culprit to keep his distance or so he could warn me about the guy and his *likely* sordid past if the wolf's excellent kissing skills are anything to go by.

But what if Everett's bringing it up because it was him? If he's the wolf? He isn't. Is he? I analyze his jaw, then glance at Reeves and the rest of the team again while they toss the football back and forth with each other. It's strange to think, but it could be any of them. Literally. Even knowing my name isn't a stretch, considering they all play hockey with Griffin. It would make sense for them to know his little sister's name and keep a wide berth from me.

Finley was right. It really is like looking for a needle in a haystack.

Clearing his throat, Everett prods, "Finley said you were —and I quote—smitten."

"Finley would use that term," I mutter, as fascinated as I was earlier watching Reeves jog to the opposite end of the field. The way Reeves' muscles tighten and pull. The way his tan skin glistens in the sun. The sheen of sweat. The way he moves so effortlessly. "And, no. Not smitten. Curious."

Everett tracks my line of sight to exactly where my focus strayed. A low breath of annoyance slips out of him. "Be careful with Reeves."

Jerked back to the present, my eyes snap to Everett. "What?"

"He's bad news for a girl like you. You'd be smart to stay away from him."

I frown. "I thought we were talking about the party?"

"We were until you were distracted by Reeves," he counters.

Apparently, I'm not very subtle.

I rub my lips together. "Aren't you two friends?"

"We are," he clarifies, though I'm not exactly convinced. Sensing my hesitation, he squeezes the back of his neck, adding, "We're teammates and roommates, and he's Maverick's best friend. We don't always see eye to eye on shit, but I don't mind hanging out with him, and yeah, I consider him a friend overall."

"Quite the explanation," I note.

"Yeah, well, once you get to know Reeves a little better, you'll understand the clarification."

"Who says I'll get to know Reeves better?"

"Trust me. If I had any say, you wouldn't, but we're neighbors. There isn't exactly a way to keep you two apart."

My eyes thin. "Did you give Finley this same lecture?"

"I should," he grumbles. "But it seems like Reeves isn't interested in anyone but you."

With a light scoff, I shake my head. "He's not interested."

"I think you might be surprised."

"And I think you're smokin' somethin'."

"I'm serious," Ev pushes. "I know girls love a good bad boy and shit, but with his rap sheet—"

"Rap sheet?" I jerk back. "As in...literal rap sheet?"

Scrubbing his hand over his face, he lets his hand fall to his side and drops his voice low. "Let's just say he's been in and out of cuffs since he was a freshman in high school."

"Seriously?"

"Yeah. And even if he had a good reason for some of those, you need to remember he'll always look out for himself. Growing up in the kind of home he did, he had no choice, so I get it. But I don't want you hurt."

"You say it like you know from personal experience. How he always looks out for himself," I clarify.

Darkness swallows his blue irises, and I almost take a step back. Not out of fear but surprise. Everett might be bossy, controlling, and stubborn, but this? This is new. There's history here. I don't know how I know, but I do.

"What happened, Ev?" I ask.

"Not the point, Dylan. Reeves is..." He pauses, his molars grinding. "He's bad news. Especially for someone as trusting as you."

"I'm sorry. Should I be offended?"

"All I'm saying is, he loves the chase, casual hookups, and being paid to take women on dates, all right? A girl like you... he'll only hurt you, Dyl."

My brows raise toward my hairline. "Did you say Reeves gets paid to take women out?"

Seriously, did I enter an alternate dimension? Because I'm pretty sure Everett is speaking gibberish.

Everett's lips push to one side, and I know he's said more than he wanted to.

"Are you saying Reeves is an escort or something?" I push.

"Just..." He runs his hand over his face again. "Stay away from him, all right? You deserve better."

It's weird. Seeing Everett so worked up over something so inconsequential. It's Reeves we're talking about. The guy could have any girl he wants, and even though he's been nothing but friendly with me, all I've seen so far is him being nothing but friendly with *everyone*. I have absolutely zero reasons to believe he's interested, let alone the guy who kissed me, so, I'm not sure why Everett's freaking out over nothing.

Bumping my shoulder against his in an attempt to lighten the darkness in his eyes, I say, "Don't worry, Ev. Even if you're right, and by some miracle, a guy like *him*"—I tilt my head toward his teammate—"is interested in a girl like me, which I don't think he is, we both know I have zero interest in the opposite sex, either, so..."

"Not even after the steamy kiss with your masked man?" he challenges.

My muscles lock. "Who said it was steamy?"

"You said you were smitten."

"Technically, Finley said it, and even if it was true, me being smitten doesn't mean it was steamy."

"So you *are* smitten."

"I didn't say I am."

"Sure you didn't." He lifts a shoulder and starts walking backward toward the rest of his friends. "Get to class. You're gonna be late."

He turns and walks away, his swagger both attractive and confusing on so many levels. When he reaches his teammates, Griffin says something to him, then waves at me from across the grass. I return it with one of my own. Reeves notices and makes a comment to Everett, though I don't hear what's said. It must piss Ev off, though, because the guy looks furious. And like an out-of-body experience, I watch Reeves grab his T-shirt from the waistband of his sweats and start jogging toward me. *Me.*

Why me?

My heart rate kicks up a notch as I take in his steady strides before turning on my heel and rushing into the nearest building like a monster's on my tail while refusing to acknowledge the slight twinge of disappointment when I realize he didn't follow me inside.

6

DYLAN

Class is fine, and so is the work the next day. But this morning? This morning, I'm dragging. Probably because I saw a handful of girls walk out of the guys' side of the house as I was leaving, and I couldn't help but wonder if one of them slept with my wolf.

My wolf.

He isn't mine.

I don't even know who *he* is.

Besides, the wolf probably doesn't even live next door to me. Statistically speaking, there's a huge possibility my masked kisser isn't Reeves or Everett. He could be anyone. Sure, whoever he was, he knew my name. But it isn't hard to learn a person's name, especially when my entire family is LAU alumni, and my brothers were hockey royalty long before I ever came here. It could even be the stranger I word vomited on. I blanch at the possibility, then shake it off. No. After our awkward encounter, he would've run in the opposite direction if he had seen me during the game.

Wouldn't he?

"Miss?" the barista in front of me says.

"Oh. Right. Uh…" I look up at the Bean Scene's menu, shaking my head. "Pumpkin spice latte, please." As soon as the words slip out of my mouth, a deep warmth unfurls in my stomach. It hits out of nowhere, and I glance over my shoulder, nearly swallowing my tongue as I face straight ahead again like I'm a freaking mannequin at the mall.

It's stupid to assume Reeves hasn't noticed me. He's literally right behind me. And the smirk on his annoyingly attractive face when we made eye contact? Yup. He definitely noticed me *and* my response to the bastard's presence. I tuck my sweaty palms into the crooks of my elbows and stare straight ahead.

"Miss?" the barista repeats.

Shit.

Again?

How long has she been talking to me? And how long have I been completely spacing out in front of her?

I clear my throat and paste on an awkward smile. "I'm sorry, did you say something?"

Heat spreads along my neck and shoulder when a forearm comes into view in front of me. Tucked between two fingers, Reeves offers the barista his credit card. "I'll have what she's having. Thanks."

The barista smiles up at Reeves and takes his card, swiping it in her little machine while my brain attempts to catch up with what happened.

Reeves bought my drink.

Reeves. Bought. My. Drink.

It's not a big deal. Or at least it shouldn't be, but a stupid voice in my head points out how the only people who buy me drinks are my family and two dates, both of whom wound up burnt by said coffee. Not on purpose, mind you, but the aftermath was the same.

Yeah, it was a real hoot, and I prefer to *not* make it a hat trick this morning.

The barista hands Reeves his card back and sets a steaming cup of coffee on the counter. I grab it, veering left to keep a wide berth from the man behind me so I don't spill my fresh java all over him. Because with my luck? It's almost a sure thing.

"Dylan," Reeves calls, but I don't answer him. I continue on my merry way like I've officially gone deaf.

Yeah, this isn't awkward at all.

"Dylan, wait up!"

I duck my head and push the exit door open, anxious to get the hell out of Dodge as quickly as possible.

"Why are you avoiding me?" Reeves calls out.

His tone reeks of exasperation, so I spin around and fold my arms, careful not to jostle my cup as I face him fully. "I'm not avoiding you."

"It seems like you're avoiding me."

"Maybe I'm protecting you."

"From what?"

"From winding up with second-degree burns." I lift my cup as if to prove my point.

His smirk makes my heart thump a little faster as he moseys toward me. "I think I'll take my chances."

"And I think I should get going."

"And *I* think your avoidance tactics are not very subtle."

Molars grinding, I repeat, "I'm not avoiding you."

"Could've fooled me," he notes while his long legs eat up the last bit of distance between us.

Do I recognize his gait? Is it the same one from the costume party? And if it is…would I still be interested? He's an escort, for Pete's sake. An. Escort. There's no way I could ever be interested in someone like that, and even if I was, he'd have to be interested back, and…there's so much red tape surrounding all things Reeves, it's…it's annoying and unnecessary, and I don't need to forget it.

"Thanks for the coffee." I lift my cup into the air again. "I'll see you in class."

I start to sidestep him, but he moves in front of me. "Why are you avoiding me, Dylan?"

Frustrated, I mutter, "You should know you're annoyingly stubborn."

"It's one of my best traits." He grins. "So tell me the truth. Why are you avoiding me?"

"I already told you I'm not—"

"You don't avoid Everett."

"What does this have to do with Everett?"

The same knowing smirk toys at the edge of his lips as he takes a sip of his coffee, blowing out the heat in the cool autumn breeze. "Everett lives next door. I live next door. Everett says hello. I say hello. Everett's at a party. I'm at a party. And yet, Everett gets, at the very least, a smile, and I get the cold shoulder. *Why?*"

"What? You want a smile?" I challenge.

His dry laugh kisses my cheeks. "I mean, yeah, I'd kill for a smile, but you're missing my point." The same smile is etched across his face, but it's different now. More forced, maybe. It doesn't reach his eyes and is almost strained as he adds, "Do you have a thing for Everett?"

"What?" Now it's my turn to laugh. "No."

"Then, what is it?"

"What is what?"

"Why don't you avoid Everett, but you avoid me?" he pushes.

"I don't avoid Everett because Everett is…Everett."

"So, you admit you're avoiding me."

"I'm not—" I growl and drop my chin to my chest.

Looking back up at him, I try explaining a little better. "Everett is…he's family and a…*friend*."

"A friend?"

"Yeah. A friend."

"And what am I?"

"You're…" My voice trails off, and I bite my bottom lip, unsure what to say.

He steps closer, crowding me and stealing my space as well as my oxygen as I stand helplessly in front of him. "I'm what, Dylan?"

"I dunno?" I lift a shoulder. "You're Reeves, I guess."

He chuckles softly. "Is that a bad or good thing?"

Staring at how his shirt stretches across his chest, I concede, "I'm not sure."

"Do you not like me?"

"I hardly know you."

"Yet you treat me like I'm infected with cordyceps."

"Cordyceps?" The foreign word is lost on my tongue, and I glance up at him, confused.

His eyes widen. "You've never seen *Last of Us*?"

"Am I supposed to know what it is?"

"Seriously?" He looks at me like I've grown a second head, then pinches the bridge of his nose in defeat. "I want you to know your brothers failed you."

"Yeah, well, I guess you'll have to take it up with them." I turn on my heel and keep making my way across campus, but those same long strides catch up to me in an instant. "Why aren't you leaving me alone?" I demand.

"Because you're avoiding me, and I hate to break it to you, Dylan, but I'm kind of a catch."

"Then maybe you should spend your time stalking one of your other girls."

His heels dig into the ground, and he cocks his head. "Who says I have other girls?"

"Call it a hunch," I answer vaguely, but the guy's eyes spark with understanding.

"Everett said something to you, didn't he?"

The knowing look in his warm brown gaze makes me want to cower, but I manage to stand my ground, refusing to throw Everett under the bus for being a good friend to me.

"Don't flatter yourself," I reply.

"Did he tell you to stay away from me?"

"I stay away from everyone."

"Everyone except Everett."

"And Griffin," I offer.

"Griffin's your brother. It's different."

"I'm not sure how," I argue. "Everett's been part of my life as long as Griffin has. And even if he hadn't, I keep everyone at arm's length, Reeves. *Everyone.* So don't take it so personally." The words leave a bitter taste in my mouth, the memory from the costume party fluttering through my mind like a dying butterfly, but I push the thought away. Maybe the wolf is right not to approach me in the light of day. To keep his distance. Knowing it's the way I prefer things.

"Why do you keep everyone at arm's length?" Reeves prods. Carefully. Like he's treading on thin ice. Then again, maybe he is.

"Because if I don't keep my distance, then I catch feelings," I admit, "and then I turn into a bull in a china shop, or...whatever, and it isn't good for anyone.."

"Ah, so that's what it is." His smile is warmer this time as he drinks from his cup while studying me over the rim of his black lid. "You don't push Everett away because he's a friend. And since he's officially earned the label, you don't feel the need to impress him or be on your best behavior or pretend you're someone you're not, which makes you feel comfortable, and you rarely feel comfortable. Am I getting closer?"

It's disarming. How observant he is. How spot-on he is. With reading me. My thoughts. My feelings.

"Am I getting closer?" he repeats.

"Maybe." I peek up at him again. "Is this the part where you ask if you can be my friend?"

"Depends," he murmurs. "Are you gonna friendzone me if I do?"

"Are you asking if I friend zoned Everett?"

"I don't know, did you friend zone Everett?" he challenges.

Part of me wants to say yes. The other part? Well, I can't help but question if Everett is my masked Cinderfella.

Dammit.

Did I really use the term Cinderfella?

I'm seriously going to kill Finley when I see her again.

Regardless, if Everett is my masked Cinderfella, is it a bad or good thing? I'm not sure, but I *am* sure if he is, it would turn my entire world upside down. Is it wrong of me to have never thought of him that way? Even when we were younger and played Truth or Dare…I don't know. I never felt the romantic vibe from him. Then again, my romantic radar's always been broken, so…maybe I'm wrong? Maybe I've *always* been wrong. Or maybe his feelings are new? Maybe he never looked at me in a romantic way until recently? Or maybe he still doesn't, and I'm overanalyzing everything. It wouldn't be the first time, especially with a little bird named Finley whispering in my ear and blowing everything out of proportion. And maybe I shouldn't be spiraling in front of one of his teammates who's still staring at me.

I gulp but stay quiet, pulling another confident grin from the bastard. "Yeah, I think I'll take my chances with awkward Dylan," he decides. "Besides, you'll have to get over it one way or another because we'll be spending a lot of time together."

"Uh, no, we won't."

"Uh, yes, we will," he mimics.

"Says who?"

"For starters, our photography professor."

Shit, I forgot.

"Why are you in photography, anyway?" I snap.

With a shrug, he answers, "Lost a bet."

"A bet?"

"Yeah." He steps even closer, practically wedging his foot between mine. "Game Nights aren't for the faint of heart, Thorne."

Thorne.

He isn't joking about the last part. Game Nights definitely aren't for the faint of heart.

When I realize he's waiting for me to reply, I mutter, "How...inconvenient."

He chuckles quietly. "For one of us, sure."

My gaze flicks to his again.

"I don't mind the long game, Dylan."

"There is no long game."

He tilts his head. "You sure?"

"Positive."

"Agree to disagree, then." His grin widens. "Just remember, I'm not afraid of the chase."

His words wash over me like sunshine, spreading ooey-gooey warmth over every inch of my skin until I'm hot and bothered and well aware I'll be burned if I stand here much longer.

Maybe he was the one in the mask.

My teeth dig into the inside of my cheek as he takes another sip, shamelessly checking me out. Maybe his choice of words is a coincidence. Maybe he has no idea about the kiss. Maybe it was someone else who gave me the best damn toe-curling kiss in existence, and I'm grasping at straws.

"You're still cute when you blush," he notes. "Not sure I'll ever get used to it."

Curling in on myself, I cradle the coffee to my chest and take a small step back. "I'm not blushing."

"Sure you aren't."

"Fine," I snap, desperate to end this conversation as quickly as possible. "I guess we can be...friends if it'll get you off my back."

"Friends?"

I nod. "Yeah. You asked why I treat Everett differently, and I think it's because Everett is my friend, so...I guess you can be, too."

I offer my hand for him to shake as if we're ironing out a deal like a pair of stiff businessmen. It hangs between us for a solid two seconds before he takes it, surprising me, though I'll never admit it out loud. When his warmth seeps into my palm, the callouses scratching against my soft skin, I almost melt into a puddle right at his feet.

He shakes it once but doesn't let me go. The scent of pumpkin spice clings to his breath and tickles my senses as he tugs me closer to him. "Not gonna happen, Dylan."

With wide eyes, I peek up at him. "What?"

"Not gonna happen. It's cute how you think I'd say yes to your arrangement, though."

"So, now you don't want to be friends?" The back and forth from this conversation is giving me full-on whiplash. "Seriously?"

"I don't picture my friends naked, Dylan." His eyes roll over me. "And I don't want the same arrangement you have with Everett, either. You free Friday?"

I blink slowly, way too caught up on the whole picturing friends naked bit. "F-Friday?"

"For our project."

"Oh. Right." I shake my head. "Uh, I don't know? I'll have to check my schedule."

"Playing hard to get." He grins. "I like it."

I'm not playing hard to get. I can't think straight when an attractive guy looks at me like this, let alone holds my hand and strokes the back of it with his thumb. The possibility of being able to recall my schedule for the week is laughable at best. Throwing in the possibility of him being my masked Cinderfella? Yeah...it's messing with my head.

"I see how it is," he jokes. "All right. Well, use my number this time, will you? So we can set everything up."

I gulp. "I'll see what I can do."

"Good. 'Cause if you don't, I'll have to track you down again." With a wink, he lets my hand go and steps back, giving me more space. "And would you look at that? You didn't even spill your coffee."

I look down at my cup still clutched to my chest.

"See you soon, Dylan," he adds.

7

DYLAN

It's been days, and I still haven't texted him. I should. I know I should. But I haven't. Honestly, I'm not sure why. Probably because he said he doesn't want to be friends, which is pretty much the quickest way to trigger a girl like me. Because if he doesn't want to be friends, then... what else is there? Okay, I'm not stupid. I know what the other options are, but still.

What if I make a fool out of myself? What if I open up to him, and he takes one look and decides he doesn't like me anymore? He hasn't officially said he *does* like me, but...I don't know? I still can't figure out how I managed to not spill my coffee all over him. It's a modern-day miracle. Knowing he's interested in more is like hooking up my entire body to a battery and turning it on, leaving me a frazzled mess. Add in the fact he may or may not be Cinderfella, and I'm an awkward wreck.

Sitting in the same seat as last week, I try to look busy while waiting for class to start and cursing myself for not bringing a jacket. It's legit freezing in this room, and my skin prickles as I shift on the cold plastic seat.

A group of guys are hanging out near the back wall, and one of them laughs. The sound teases my curiosity. It's almost familiar. Or maybe it isn't, but my ears perk up nonetheless. Subtly, I steal a glance over my shoulder, taking in the tall one with long, wavy hair and veined forearms. He's good-looking. A little younger. Maybe he's a freshman, too? Tilting my head, I attempt to picture half his face covered and focus on his jawline.

Are you my Cinderfella?

I suck my bottom lip into my mouth, my face growing hot as I replay the moment for the hundredth time, slipping the guy across the room into the memory to see if he fits.

"Don't get me wrong," a familiar voice interrupts. I nearly jump out of my skin as I turn to find Reeves staring down at me. "You're cute when you're hot and bothered, but should I be jealous?"

Without a word, I turn in my seat, untuck my hair from behind my ear so I can use it as a shield, and start doodling on the edge of my notebook, attempting to appear unaffected by my classmate's presence while my stomach flip-flops over and over again.

"Aw, so I take it I *should* be jealous," Reeves notes as the familiar scrape of his chair vibrates down my spine, and he sits beside me. "I'll keep it in mind." A quiet tap follows. I look to my left, finding a Bean Scene cup scooting toward me. "Pumpkin spice, right?" He offers me the cup, then brings a matching one to his lips and takes a swig.

"You bought me coffee?" I ask.

He nods.

"Why?"

"Guess I was craving something sweet and figured you might be, too."

My lips gnash together, and I stare at the cup like it's

laced with poison, but I remember my manners and how freaking cold it is in this classroom.

"Don't worry," he adds, "You won't spill it on me."

Praying he didn't jinx me, I lift the cup and taste. "Thanks." Sweet warmth coats my throat and heats my belly as I bring it closer, practically hugging the cup to my chest.

With a quiet rumble of amusement, he asks, "You cold?"

"I'm fine," I lie.

His eyes thin, and he slips off his maroon LAU hoodie, offering it to me. "Here."

"I'm okay," I start, but the bastard ignores me, scrunches up the fabric, finds the neck hole, and slips it over my head without waiting for my approval. It's soft and worn like it's been washed a thousand times, making the thick material more pliable and cozy, proving it's one of his favorites.

"Reeves," I mumble into the toasty fabric, but the words die on my tongue as his woodsy cologne and comfortable warmth wash over me in unison. Seriously. Why does he have to smell so good?

Fingers brush against mine as he steals my cup, helping me thread my arms through.

With a quick tug, he pulls the hood from the top of my head and leans back in his chair, grabbing his coffee and drinking some more. "Better?"

I feel like I'm wrapped in a warm hug. A super good-smelling, warm hug.

I nod softly, whispering, "Thank you."

"No problem. So." He scoots a little closer and leans his forearms on the desk. "Why were you blatantly checking out the guys in the back?"

My face flames, and I clear my throat. "No reason."

"Liar."

"I thought I maybe recognized one of them."

He checks out the group behind us, then turns to me again. "From where?"

Shit.

Opening up the can of worms with the bold label "Costume party featuring Cinderfella" is the last thing I want to do.

"Uh, nowhere?" I lie.

"Liar," he repeats wryly. "Tell me."

"Seriously, it isn't a big deal."

"If it wasn't, you'd tell me."

I glower at him but give in anyway. "I just, uh, I thought I might recognize them from the costume party or something."

"Ah, so that's why you were blushing like a little virgin." He tugs on the ends of my hair playfully. "Trying to figure out who kissed you, am I right?"

I press my lips together and ignore him.

"It must've been good," he continues, "for you to be out here, days later, trying to figure out who he is. But here's the real question. If it was such a good kiss, why hasn't he tracked you down?" Grabbing the base of my seat, he drags me closer to him. "Maybe he's waiting for the right moment. Or maybe he's grotesque." He shivers and rests his elbow on the table, cradling his chin with his massive hand while I drown in his full attention. "Or maybe he's Everett and wanted to steal a taste without stepping out of the friend zone." His eyes dance with mirth. "The possibilities are endless, right? Fuck, maybe you're talking to him right now."

My eyes snap to his. "What did you say?"

"Did I say something?"

"Are you?" I push.

"Am I what?"

"Are you Cinderfell—" My jaw locks tight, and my eyes pop as the stupid nickname makes its debut.

Reeves' deep chuckle spreads goosebumps along my skin,

and he bends even closer. "Were you about to say Cinderfella?"

I turn back to my mess of a paper and mutter, "No comment."

"You were, weren't you?" Another laugh rumbles past his lips. "That's a Finley nickname, right?"

My eyes pop—again—and I turn back to him. "How did you—"

"You're not exactly one for classic movie references. Which reminds me, I gotta catch you up on some solid Dramione fan fiction still," he adds, mentioning the comment he made at Archer's funeral. Honestly, it didn't even make sense. Hermione ends up with Ron, not Draco. So, why would people be 'shipping them together?

"That, uh, won't be necessary," I tell him.

"Aw, but it's so fun, Dylan. And if you're all worked up from a simple kiss with your Cinderfella, imagine what some good ol' smut could do for a girl like you."

"Reeves," I warn.

"Back to the question at hand." He brushes his knuckle against the back of my hand still clutching my paper cup. It causes a zing to shoot up my arm, and it's both exhilarating and foreign in a way I can't even wrap my head around. Slowly, I inch away and take a nervous sip of my drink. Waiting. For what, I'm not sure.

"Are you asking if I'm the guy who kissed you, Dylan Thorne?" he prods. The words are warm and sweet, like my coffee. But laced with depth, too. A richness, maybe. I don't know what to think or how to handle how close he is. So close I can taste his sugary coffee breath. Feel the weight in his gaze. The confidence radiating off him. It's familiar, almost.

"Are you?" I whisper. "Are you him?"

His attention drops to my mouth.

"All right, class," Dr. Broderick interrupts. I jerk in my seat and scoot away from Reeves, hoping the distance will help clear the fog in my head.

"Today, we're focusing on planning your project," the teacher explains. "Take the entire time to talk with your partner and plan your first shoot. Make sure to focus on colors, props, etcetera. If you have any questions, let me know."

Great. I don't even have a lecture to fall back on.

Stealing another taste of my coffee, I clear my throat and glance at an unflustered Reeves, who's currently staring at me like I'm the most amusing thing in the world.

"So…emotions," he prods.

"Yes. So. All right. Emotions," I ramble.

"Which one do you want to focus on first?"

"I don't know? Uh, let's see. There's sad? Angry? Happy? Horny?" My eyes bulge. "Happy. Let's focus on happy."

He leans closer, clutching his coffee as he crowds my space. "Did you say horny?"

"I didn't—"

"You did. You definitely did."

"And then I said happy," I rush out. "So…let's focus on that, shall we?"

"Aw, but horny would be so much more fun, don't you think?"

The same swell of embarrassment spreads through my chest, leaving my cheeks burning as I stare at my paper.

"Hey," he croons, keeping his voice quiet so no one but me can hear him. "I know I said you're cute when you're awkward and all, but I don't want you to be uncomfortable. Not around me."

"I'm fine," I mumble.

I can feel his gaze on the side of my face. The way he studies me leaves me even more vulnerable, but I don't look up at him. I don't acknowledge him and keep staring at my paper while attempting to control my breathing.

Did you really say horny, Dylan? I silently scold. *You don't even know what horny is. I mean, you do, but every time you even tried to explore it, you always tense up, and—*

"What makes you happy, Dylan?" he prods.

I stay quiet, surprised at how easily he pivoted our conversation when he could literally tease me for a solid ten minutes with the ammunition I accidentally laid in his lap. I'm grateful for it, though. Surprised but grateful. He might be all about teasing, but only if it doesn't make others uncomfortable.

Licking my lips, I answer, "Ice cream. Family. Puppies. Fall." His smile widens, and I frown. "What?"

"You gave me an idea."

"What kind of idea?"

"For the shoot."

"Ooookay? So I can stop telling you about what makes me happy?"

"I mean, I can listen to you all day," he counters, "but I have a feeling you aren't one for the spotlight, so if you'd like me to take a turn, I can."

"Actually, yes," I decide. "What makes you happy?"

"Uh...let's see." He clicks his tongue against the roof of his mouth and stares at the cup in his hands for a moment, then finally offers, "For one, hockey."

"Hockey?"

"And friends. And ice cream. And fall. And puppies," he adds, mimicking me.

My gaze narrows. "You stole all my ideas."

"I didn't mention family," he points out dryly, swallowing the last of his drink and tossing it in the bin across the room.

As it hits the edge of the garbage can and tumbles in, I ask, "Does your family not make you happy?"

The same lifeless grin nearly splits his face in two, and I'm surprised by how quickly I've learned to tell the two apart.

"My family makes me wanna hit something."

"So, *anger*." I nod. "Got it."

He chuckles sardonically. "Guess you could say that."

It goes quiet. Not the room. No, everyone around us is still chatting away, but the sound grates on me. The silence. His silence. He isn't quiet. He's chatty and confident and fascinating. But quiet Reeves makes me feel even more on edge than confident Reeves, and I don't think I like it. As his silence seeps between us, weaving its way into the crevices and making me squirm, I click my pen a few times with my thumb while my anxiety eats a hole in my gut.

"Wanna...talk about it?" I ask. The words come out breathy and forced. I can't help it, though. I'm curious. Especially after everything Everett hinted at a little while ago. Reeves' rap sheet. His home life. His history.

"Not much to talk about," he replies. "It's me and my dad, and he's an asshole."

"Got it," I repeat. I look down at my paper again and scribble dad and asshole on the top line.

"Yeah." He sighs. "But uh, *happy*. Hockey makes me happy, and I didn't steal that one."

"Hockey. Yup." I write the word down on my notepad and underline it. "Anything else?"

"Seeing a cute girl in my hoodie."

Avoiding his gaze and the fact I am most definitely wearing his hoodie, I add the words hoodie and girl next to hockey, then clear my throat. "Anything else?"

"I could think of a few more things, but I think I'll save those for our next session when we focus on horny, right?"

"Reeves!" I smack his shoulder.

"Hey, you brought it up."

"It slipped out, okay? I told you I'm awkward."

84

"Cute, not awkward," he clarifies. "There's a difference. Well, with most girls. You?" His mouth quirks. "Let's just say you're good at riding the line, and it's addictive as fuck."

I pull my lips into my mouth and stare at the label on my cup, unsure what to say or how to handle this kind of attention from anyone, let alone a guy like him. A guy who's paid to be an escort. A guy who's charismatic and cocky.

"You still busy on Friday?" he asks.

"I, uh, I'm not sure."

"We have to start this project at some point, Dylan."

"Mm-hmm. Yup. We sure do."

"So...Friday?"

"What about Thursday?" I counter, peeking up at him.

"Can't. I have practice."

"Tonight?"

"Practice again."

"Sunday?"

"What's wrong with Friday?" he asks.

Because Friday kind of, sort of makes it feel like it's a date, and I do not need the added pressure of spending one-on-one time with Reeves to feel like a date. Not if I want either of us to survive the interaction. I mean, we haven't struggled so far, but doesn't it mean the breaking point will be even more catastrophic?

"Are you busy Friday?" he questions.

"No?"

"So we can do the first photo shoot on Friday, then?"

Puffing out my cheeks, I give in and nod. "Okay. I can do the afternoon but not the evening."

"You're busy Friday evening?"

I'm not, but it isn't the point.

As if he can read my thoughts, he smiles and settles back in his chair, giving me space to breathe.

"Okay, Dyl. Friday afternoon, it is."

8

REEVES

I 'm either an idiot or a fucking genius. Probably both. Checking the time on my phone, I wait for Dylan to arrive at the arena. She hasn't texted me, which means I still don't have her number, and I doubt it's a careless mistake on her part. She doesn't seem like a late person, though. I scan the parking lot again, searching for her, when I find Everett's SUV slowing at the curb.

Of course, he brought her.

I would've offered to ride together since she doesn't have a car, but I had to pick up one of my props for today's shoot and figured she'd catch a ride with Griffin or something. Everett, though? I should've known he'd take one for the team and bring her. As she slips out of the passenger seat, she turns back, says something to Everett, shakes her head, and waves, closing the door behind her.

I climb out of my car at the same time and call out, "Hey, Dylan!"

When she sees me, she smiles, offering the same small wave she gave Everett.

"I'll be right there," I add, opening the back door. I bought my camera from a thrift shop a few months ago. It's about ten years old, but after a quick Google session where I learned the gist of using a DSLR, I took some sample photos, and Dr. Broderick assured me it would do the job.

I still can't believe a drunken game of Truth or Dare the night before fall semester enrollment, combined with a few botched credits during my freshman year, brought me to this moment. Sharing a class with the one and only Dylan Thorne.

What are the fucking odds?

People say you're supposed to spend your freshman year figuring out what you want to do for your degree. Yet, here I am, a fucking senior, and the only thing I want in life is to play hockey. It makes bullshit things like a degree and what classes I should take feel so damn inconsequential at this point. I'm doing nothing more than passing the time until graduation. Or at least, it was my plan until Mav wound up with a heart condition, shattering his future in the NHL. Maybe my degree means something, after all.

I squeeze the camera bag in my grasp, letting the nylon strap dig into my palm before tossing it over my shoulder as I shove aside the reminder of exactly how screwed I'll be if hockey doesn't pan out. With one final glance at the hail-mary prop in my back seat, I close the door behind me, choosing to keep it hidden until we're situated.

Everett hasn't pulled away from the curb. Not surprising. His eyes follow me from the side mirror as I approach a waiting Dylan.

Yeah, yeah. I see you, Ev. Afraid I'm encroaching on your territory?

Giving him a smirk, I walk up to Dylan and smile down at her. "You look pretty."

She tucks her white-blonde hair behind her ear and looks at the ground. "Uh, thank you. Shall we…get started?"

"Sure thing. Mind if I go first?" I lift my camera bag, and she nods.

"Yeah, sure. Might as well get it over with, right?"

"Don't sound so excited, Thorne."

"There's the nickname again."

"You know, I've been debating what else to call you."

"Huh?"

"Since you don't like Thorne and all," I explain.

"Who says I need a nickname?"

Ignoring her question, I study her profile, loving the light shade of pink as it spreads across her cheeks from being smothered in my full attention. "I'm thinking...Pickles."

Her head snaps to me. "Pickles? For a nickname?"

"Yeah, you know, Dyl? As in dill pickles?"

"You're ridiculous."

"What? You don't like dill pickles?"

"I like my name. *Dylan*," she emphasizes.

"And don't get me wrong, it's an adorable name. But can you blame a guy for wanting to stand out?" I toss my opposite arm around her shoulders and guide her toward the side of the building. The landscape is covered in grass and has tall trees scattered throughout. Reds and yellows have started swallowing the usual shades of green, turning the space into a fall lover's dream.

It's perfect for what I need.

"Let's stop here," I decide.

She looks around the open space. Curious. Hesitant. On edge. A little indent forms between her brows, but she turns back to me and smiles. "Let me guess. Fall?"

"Yup."

"You're lucky I'm easy."

I bite back my amusement at her slip of the tongue but don't call her out on it as she tucks her thumbs into the back pockets of her jeans and lifts her shoulders.

"So, where do you want me?" she asks.

I motion to one of the nearby trees. "Why don't you sit beneath this one."

"Okay?"

She walks over and carefully sits down, looking about as natural as a kitten in heels on a runway.

Sensing my mirth, she looks at her lap and wipes her hands along her jeans. "What? Is something wrong?"

"Not at all. Although, I'd hardly call you easy," I add, unable to help myself. "You don't look very happy to be here."

Her expression pinches. "Let's just say I didn't sign up for photography to be in *front* of the camera. Now, if Finley was here…"

"She'd eat this shit up," I agree. "Let's pretend you're not here. Well, with me." My brows crease, and I set my things down, pulling out the camera I purchased. "Actually, let's pretend you're still with me, but I don't have a camera in my hands."

"Ooookay?"

"Close your eyes," I prod.

She closes them, but the same wrinkle between her brows stays firmly in place.

"And stop trying to look constipated," I joke.

Those aquamarines open and pin me with a scowl. "Maybe it comes naturally to me."

"Looking constipated?" I laugh. "I hope not, but if you'd like, I'll be happy to bring you coffee every morning. It works like a charm."

"Anyway," she drags out, hiding the blush of her cheeks with her long blonde hair.

Fuck, this girl's gorgeous.

My fingers itch to push the strands over her shoulder. To see if they're as soft as they look. To see if I can feel her pulse race against my thumb if I drag my hand along her throat. To

89

see if she'd let me push her against the tree and kiss her like I did at the costume party. I can still taste her. Sweet. Soft. Fucking perfect.

I clear my throat and attempt to focus. "Close your eyes and take a deep breath. Try to relax. I'll make this as painless as possible, then we can get to my turn, and you can be behind the camera instead of in front of it, all right?"

Grumbling under her breath, she leans her back against the tree and lets out a slow breath. "I really don't think this is going to work."

She's cute when she's feisty.

"Stop fidgeting," I order. "I have to grab something from my car. Promise me you won't open your eyes."

Her eyes pop back open. "What do you need to grab?"

"It's a surprise. Trust me?"

"Yeah, sounds like an excellent idea," she snarks.

I chuckle softly. "Are you gonna close them or not?"

Her lids flutter, and she takes a deep breath, settling back against the tree. "Fiiiine."

"Good girl."

"I'm not a dog."

"Nah, you're my good girl," I remind her.

Her lips purse. "I'm not yours, either."

"Yet."

I jog back to my car, noticing Everett's SUV still parked where it was. Ignoring him, I open the back door and pull out the kennel I'd tucked inside. There are perks to knowing certain people, and even though I rarely call in favors from my connections, I couldn't help it with this one.

Careful not to jostle the puppy, I head back to where Dylan hangs out. The wrinkles between her brows have softened, and she looks almost peaceful as she tilts her head up at the sky, soaking in the rays of sunshine peeking through the branches while keeping her eyes firmly closed like a good girl.

Lifting my camera with one hand, I snap another photo, and she flinches, the quiet sound pulling her back to the photo shoot instead of the calm reality she slipped into while I was away.

"Don't open your eyes until I tell you," I remind her.

I set the kennel down and mess with the camera settings until I'm confident they're where I want them. Once I'm satisfied, I unlock the kennel and tuck the wiggly puppy under my arm.

"You ready?" I ask.

"Ready for what?"

"Don't open," I repeat while the puppy fidgets in my hold, desperate to run its little heart out. It's small and white, with big brown eyes, floppy ears, and a long, curly tail whipping faster and faster with every passing second.

"Seriously, what's that sound?" she asks.

I let the puppy go a few feet from Dylan's lap, and it climbs up her thighs. With a gasp, Dylan's eyes pop open, and she picks the puppy up, a light squeal slipping past her parted lips.

"Shut up." She brings the puppy an inch from her nose, and it licks the tip with its little pink tongue. With a laugh, Dylan's entire expression lights up like a little kid on Christmas morning. Well, a kid who wasn't with a shitty dad on Christmas.

Wielding my camera, I take photo after photo. Some are close-ups, while others are more landscape and show the entire ambiance Dylan's basking in. I love how her nose scrunches and her eyes brighten whenever the puppy steals a kiss. She snuggles closer, her entire body radiating with pure, uninhibited joy in the setting sun.

I knew she needed a distraction from me and the camera

if I had any hope of pulling this off. But seeing her like this? It's even better than I expected. I catch myself smiling behind the camera as I snap another dozen pictures.

"Where'd you get a dog?" she asks. "Is she yours?"

I shake my head. "Nah. A friend's."

"And your friend let you borrow their puppy for the afternoon?"

"I can be convincing."

Her eyes narrow as if she doesn't believe me. She gives in almost instantly, muttering, "That, I believe," against the fluffball's white fur. "So I guess this means I can't keep her, right?"

"Afraid not."

"Bummer." She kisses the top of the puppy's head. "Well, I hope you got what you came for because if I have to hold her for another second, I might steal her from your friend."

With a low laugh, I take the squirming puppy from her hands and put her back in the kennel.

"Speaking of stealing, did you ever figure out who your Cinderfella is?"

"Not yet," she mutters. "And how does my Cinderfella relate to stealing?"

"I had to bring him up somehow."

Lips bunched, she studies me for a second, then says, "You're not one for subtlety, are you."

It isn't a question.

Grinning back at her, I counter, "What do you think?"

Her eyes hold mine. Those long lashes bat slowly, and she looks down at her feet instead. "I think we both know what I think."

She's right. I know exactly what she thinks. That I'm bad news, and I'll only break her heart. She's probably right, but it won't stop me.

I like her. More than I expected. I like how genuine she is.

How I don't have to question her smiles or whether or not she's hiding something or faking shit—in general, or when it comes to me. Growing up, I honed my bullshit meter long before most of my friends, and, for some reason I still don't fully grasp, it doesn't alarm when I'm around her. It's like she has nothing to prove. Nothing to hide. And for a guy who's told more lies than he can count—both good and bad—it's puzzling. Addictive, even. As if her simplicity is leading me to so much…more. And even though I have no doubt it will bite me in the ass with my roommates, I can't help but want to peel a few more layers from her to see how deep her genuineness goes.

"Tell me, what made it so special?" I ask, unable to hide my curiosity.

"What?"

"The kiss," I clarify.

A light blush spreads across her cheeks, and I know she's replaying the moment as she tucks her hair behind her ear and stares at the grass surrounding her. "I, uh, I don't know?"

"Aw, come on," I push. "You have to have kissed more than a few guys in your life. What made this one so special?"

"I think you overestimate my experience with kissing."

"No shit?"

"Don't make it weird," she begs as her cheeks heat even more. It's innocent and fucking adorable.

"I'm not. I'm…surprised, is all."

"Why is it so surprising?"

"Because you're gorgeous, and I'm not the only one who's noticed you around campus. Or at parties," I add knowingly. "And, yeah, sex is one thing. I get it. But a kiss is just a kiss."

"For you, maybe."

"And it isn't *just* a kiss for you?" I challenge.

Toying with her fingers in her lap, she murmurs, "I mean, it can be. But those are all forgettable, right? No chemistry.

93

No meaning. It's two mouths smashing together and swapping spit."

My nose wrinkles. "Nice picture."

Her gaze connects with mine. "Hey, you brought it up."

I laugh. "Good point."

"Those are the kisses I could do without for my entire life. But the kiss I shared with...the masked dude..."

"Cinderfella," I finish for her.

"Yeah, *him*. Well. I dunno. The chemistry was definitely there, and when I don't usually feel chemistry with many people, feeling it with him was...refreshing. I guess it made an impression on me."

"A good impression," I assume.

"Mm-hmm."

"Even though he hasn't contacted you or revealed his identity to you since."

"Maybe there's a good reason," she offers.

"Like knowing your brother."

She lifts a shoulder. "Maybe."

"Or knowing the weight you're holding to it," I add. "A single kiss."

Cringing, she picks at the grass. "You make me sound like a creepy stalker."

"Nah, an invested one," I tease.

With a huff, she tosses the pieces of grass onto the ground and scowls up at me, pushing to her feet. "Look, is it so wrong to want to get to know a guy after kissing him? It's not like I expect us to get married and have babies or whatever. Wanting to see where things go doesn't feel like I'm asking for anything crazy."

She's offended. Flustered. Like she thinks I'm making fun of her. Growing up, I was always kind of a dick, learning early on if you don't have thick skin, you won't survive in this world. But Dylan? She's managed to keep a softness to her I can't help but envy. Not for myself. But for the life she was raised in to be able to keep it.

"You're not crazy," I murmur.

"You don't think?" Those big, doe eyes nearly knock me on my ass, so I do the only thing I can. I break it. The chemistry pulling us together.

"Well, not for wanting to get to know a guy you have chemistry with," I reply. "You *are* crazy for fawning over a guy who's too much of a coward to claim you, though."

"So, he *isn't* you," she decides. "Interesting."

Almost offended by her assumption, I cock my head. "Who said he isn't me?"

"You don't seem like the cowardly type."

"And you know me so well?"

"I know you show people what you want them to see."

Well, fuck. No one has ever pegged me so easily.

Brushing off the realization, I question, "And what do I want you to see?"

"For today?" She hesitates, lifting her camera bag into the air. "Happy. Am I right?"

"Maybe," I say, stealing her response from earlier.

"Well, no time like the present. Why don't you put the puppy back in your car since it isn't too hot, and I'll meet you inside."

"Inside?"

"I may have asked Everett to do me a favor and figure out how to get us in the building."

Everett.

Of course, he did her a favor.

"Not Griff?" I ask.

"He's seemed a little...stressed lately when it comes to hockey, so..."

I nod. "Yeah, I get it. I'll see you inside."

"Can I ask you something?" she calls before I even take three steps.

Facing her again, I say, "Sure."

"Why'd you choose a puppy?"

"Hmm?"

"I mean…you actually found a puppy for the photo shoot when we both know I mentioned other things that make me happy. Ice cream. Family. I feel like the puppy was the most work, you know?"

She isn't wrong. I borrowed Winnie from one of my clients in exchange for me attending her ex's wedding in a couple months free of charge. After seeing Dylan light up, it confirmed my decision, no matter how stupid it was at the time. Honestly, I could buy a puppy for less, but I didn't have the heart to return it once I was done using it for the photo shoot. My real problem is I have a feeling I'm willing to sacrifice a lot more than one weekend for a girl like Dylan. No. For *her*. Dylan and *only* Dylan.

Lifting my shoulder, I admit, "I'm not afraid to put in a little work, Dyl. I'll see you in a minute."

"Okay."

9

REEVES

Everett's in the bleachers beside Dylan. I shouldn't find it annoying, but I do. She's showing him something on her phone, and his arm is wrapped around the back of her seat, making the two look like a happy little couple.

Yeah, he definitely wants in her pants. The question is, what will he do about it now that she has someone else interested in her? Can he feel the clock ticking? The way she's slowly slipping through his fingers? Is he worried?

It's a stupid question. He's here, isn't he?

Yeah. The bastard's worried. Good. He should be.

"Hey, Ev," I say as I make my way down the cement steps and pause by the red plastic seat he's lounging in.

"Hey," he replies.

"What are you doin' here?"

He keeps his arm planted around the back of Dylan's seat, answering, "I'm giving Dylan a ride home after you guys finish."

My eyes slice to Dylan's. "I can give you a ride."

"Nah, it's all good," Everett answers for her. "Your skates are on the bench."

Annoyance simmers beneath my skin, but I don't acknowledge it. "Great. Thanks."

I take the stairs two at a time, finding my skates where Everett said they'd be, although there's a second pair beside them. Seeing them there makes me pause.

"These yours?" I ask as Dylan follows behind me on the concrete steps.

"Yup."

"You skate?"

"I have two older brothers who play hockey and a professional hockey player for a dad," she replies. "What do you think?"

"Well, all right, then." I scoot over on the bench and start lacing up while Dylan does the same. It's one of the first times I've seen her confident in something. She slides the white laces into place along her hockey skates and loops them into a knot like a seasoned pro. Part of me wonders if she plays. The other part knows how clumsy she can be. The likelihood of adding slippery ice to the equation is probably a bad idea. Still, I am curious. Once we're both ready to head onto the rink, I start skating backward, watching as Dylan joins me, balancing her camera on her shoulder.

"So if you have two older brothers who play hockey and a professional hockey player for a dad, why don't you play?" I ask.

"I did." She lifts the camera and snaps a quick picture.

"But not anymore?"

"There was an accident," she answers vaguely, making my spidey senses tingle almost instantly.

"What kind of accident?" I push.

"Uh," her eyes slash to Everett in the stands, then return to me. "A freak accident. Come on, show me a smile."

Part of me wants to push. To demand answers. But it's only taken me a few times being around her to know pushing is the exact opposite of what I should do. So, I tuck aside the sliver of information she gave me and spread my arms wide.

With a cheesy grin, I allow her to snap photos as she skates around me. Once she makes a complete turn, she looks at the pictures and frowns. "These all look fake as crap." She peers at me again. "How'd you make it look so easy?"

"What do you mean?"

"I mean, you spent fifteen minutes snapping photos, and yours looked awesome. Mine look..." Her face scrunches. "Like dog poop."

"Careful," I joke, "You're taking pictures of *me*, remember?"

"Well, could you try to look like you're happy, at least?" she quips.

"Not sure what you want from me. I'm smiling, aren't I?"

"Well, yeah, but..." Her brows cave as she sorts through the images a few more times, probably looking for anything to even remotely work with. When her eyes snap to mine, she raises her forefinger. "I'll be right back."

"Where are you going?"

"Just...give me a minute." Skating to the edge of the ice, she yells, "Ev! Get my bag from the back of your car, will you?"

"Sure thing." He disappears through the exit, and she pulls out her phone, letting her camera hang from the strap around her neck as she types furiously.

"What are you doing?" I ask.

"Did you know your eyes are like IKEA?"

I frown. "What?"

She clears her throat and looks up at me. "Did you know

99

your eyes are like IKEA?"

"No?"

"Well, they are, 'cause I can get lost in them all day."

I snort. "Did you just try to use a pickup line on me?"

With a light laugh, she looks down at her phone again. "Give it a minute. I'm only getting started."

"You're Googling pickup lines?" I question.

"I think we both know I'm not clever enough to come up with these on my own, but I got you to smile, so we're going with it."

She's cute when she's focused. The way her eyes move from left to right and her lips silently form the words she reads.

A second later, she looks up at me and grins. "Okay, I've got one."

"All right, let's hear it, Thorne."

She lifts the camera, pointing it directly at me. "Boy, you're the only proof I need to know aliens are real."

"How so?" I ask.

"Because I think you *abducted* my heart."

My mouth twitches. "You're right. That one was worse."

Undeterred, she skates toward me, her camera poised and ready. "Hey, Reeves, hey, Reeves."

"Yes?"

"If you were a fruit, you'd be a *fine*apple." She laughs. "Get it? A *fine*apple?"

I hold back my grin, and my head swivels as I watch her skate around me in slow circles. "Wow."

Letting her camera hang limply around her neck, she scans a few more pickup lines, her eyes shining with excitement.

"Oh! Oh! I've got it!" she announces.

"Yes?"

She lifts her camera again but doesn't look through the

lens, choosing to skate closer until we're almost chest to chest. The proximity isn't necessarily new, but Dylan enforcing it is. Fuck, this girl's gorgeous. It's the hundredth time I'm hit with the realization, but every time is like its own gut punch. Fucking beautiful. Her smile. The color in her cheeks. And those eyes? Fuck, those big aquamarines are the clincher. They make her look straight out of a Disney movie where she's the starring princess, and I'm—

"Hey, Reeves," she whispers.

I squeeze my hands at my sides to keep from reaching for her and tugging her against me. "Yeah, Dyl?"

"Did you know…" She bites her bottom lip, shooting for coy, and fuck me, it's ridiculous enough to work.

"Yea, Dyl?"

"Did you know not even Snape could *Severus* apart?"

A bark of laughter escapes me, and it's followed by a *snap, snap, snap* from her camera as she tries to capture the moment. "That was lame."

"Hey, you're the one with a thing for Harry Potter."

"No, I have a thing for Dramione," I counter.

"I still don't know what it is."

"It's Draco and Hermoine. Dramione."

"And it isn't real because Hermoine ends up with Ron," she reminds me.

"Yeah, but only because—"

"Dylan!" Everett interrupts.

Realizing how close we're standing, Dylan clears her throat and glides away from me, meeting Everett at the edge of the ice.

"Is this what you needed?" He raises a red and black duffle bag into the air.

With a nod, Dylan skates closer to him, examining whatever he's holding. "Yeah, this is perfect. Thanks."

"Sure thing."

"By the way, Reeves was right earlier," she adds. "You don't have to stay. He can give me a ride."

"I don't mind."

"I know, but I feel bad making you wait."

"I'm going home right after this," I interrupt. "You know, since we're neighbors and all, it's no trouble."

"No trouble, my ass," Everett mutters under his breath. If he's trying to be subtle, he's doing a shit job.

"Unless you *want* to stay," I challenge dryly.

Everett's attention shifts to me. Annoyance. Restraint. Jealousy? They all shine in his blue eyes.

You ready to show your hand yet, Ev? I don't say it out loud. I don't need to. The guy knows me all too well.

"Fine," he concedes, though I don't miss the twitch of his nostril. "I'll go. *If* you promise to keep it in your pants, Reeves."

Clutching at my chest, I counter, "Would you expect anything less?"

His jaw squeezes, but he steps back, giving Dylan some distance. I doubt she noticed how close they were standing. It's like the girl has blinders on or some shit. Fascinating but confusing as fuck.

Does she really not know he's into her?

"I'll see you at home," he tells her.

"Yup. Thanks again for the ride. You're the best, Ev." She gives him a hug. His hands find her waist, his attention shifting to me again as he squeezes her tight and lets her go but stays close, keeping his voice low. "Be careful, yeah?"

"Yup," she repeats. "I will. See ya."

With one final look at me, he turns around and leaves me alone with our girl.

My lips lift.

Perfect.

When she faces me again, her doe eyes are in full-blown

wet dream mode. Clutching the duffle bag in her arms, she clears her throat.

"Whatcha got there?" I ask.

"Something that may or may not make you smile."

My brow lifts.

"Close your eyes," she orders.

"You serious?"

"Hey, you made me close mine earlier."

Dropping my chin to my chest, I let my eyelids fall shut. The sound of rustling fabric hits my ears, along with a quiet, muffled curse.

"You okay over there?" I ask.

"Just a second," she grumbles before the familiar crunch of ice echoes in the arena. She's skating toward me. It takes everything inside of me to keep my eyes sealed, but with folded arms, I do.

"Can I open yet?" I question.

She's circling me, the familiar click-click of her camera building my curiosity as my head swivels with her movements, though I don't open my eyes like she asked.

My mouth lifts. "What are you doing?"

"You know, I'm impressed," she notes.

"Why?"

"Who knew you could follow directions?"

My eyes open to find her a few inches in front of me, her camera haphazardly pointed in my direction and her finger resting on the trigger. But her hoodie does me in. Well, my hoodie. It's the same one I let her borrow during class. My lips pull tighter in amusement. "You look good in my hoodie."

"And you look like you like seeing me in it."

Click. Click.

Slowly, I push off the ice, gliding forward a bit. She doesn't back away but does keep snapping photos with a

103

smile stretched across her pretty face. I like her like this. With her guard down. I'm not sure how I made it happen— fuck, it probably has nothing to do with me—but I like it nonetheless. With her distracted by a mission to make me smile, she isn't so lost in her thoughts. In the anxiety hidden there. In the fear constantly holding her back. From communicating. From making jokes. From letting her true self shine through.

Hello, Wallflower.

Nice to finally meet you.

"That's the one," she murmurs, looking at the photos she took with the same soft smile I can't help but admire. Giving in to my lack of restraint, I grab the edge of her camera and lower it to her side.

"You're cute when you're proud of yourself," I point out.

Peeking up at me, she says, "Careful. It's my Aunt Mia's camera." Those blue-green jewels shift from my left to right eye and settle on my mouth. I doubt she even notices she's staring at my lips, but she is. My pulse thumps faster. Harder.

So sweet. So innocent.

Like a ripe peach hanging on a low branch. Easy for the picking, especially when you're as seasoned as I am. And boy, do I want another taste.

With my opposite hand, I grab onto her waist and tug her closer, feeling her curves beneath the thick fabric of my hoodie. "Is this a habit of yours? Stealing things not belonging to you?" I tug at the fabric again, and her front presses against mine.

"Aunt Mia said I could use it."

"And this?" Twisting my hand in the fabric, I let it pull against her curves.

Her lips part on a gasp, and her palms land on my chest as she keeps a breath of distance between us. "Pretty sure you said I could use it, too."

"Use it, sure. Use it against me?" I tsk. "Hardly."

"Who says I'm using it against you?"

Damn, those doe eyes.

The girl has no fucking clue what she does to me. And the crazy part? It isn't an act with her. It's full-blown, genuine innocence, and for a kid who hasn't known or even experienced genuine innocence since—shit, I don't even know when—I can't help but want to touch it. To grasp it and hold on for dear life, even if it means ruining her in the process. I don't want to ruin her. To ruin her innocence. Her outlook. But I'm selfish enough to not give a shit about the fallout if it means I can push this a little further. Experience her a little more deeply. I bend closer. The drive to kiss those pouty lips is almost more than I can bear, and with the signals she's giving me? Fuck, I'm ready for another taste.

"Dylan!" a voice booms.

Dylan flinches, jerking away from me like I'm a fucking pariah. Her legs kick up as she flails, fighting for balance, and I almost lose my left nut when the blade of her skate cuts toward my crotch. I block her at the last second. As my forearm connects with her shin, I balance her aunt's camera with one hand, and my opposite stays twisted in the fabric of my hoodie in hopes of slowing her fall. With a soft thump, she lands on her ass and groans.

"Shit," Everett mutters from the top of the steps after scaring the hell out of her. He takes the stairs two at a time, rushing toward the shitshow he caused by spying on us.

Crouching beside her, I grasp her forearm and help her sit up. "You okay?"

"Uh, yeah." She stares at her lap, wiping the slush from her jeans and refusing to look at me. "Just a bruised tailbone and ego, but hey? What else is new?"

"You okay?" Everett shuffles toward us on the ice, and she waves him off.

"Seriously, I'm fine."

"You sure? You fell flat on your ass."

"I'm aware," she grouses between clenched teeth. Pushing to her feet, she dusts off a bit more ice from her backside, looking at me through her thick upper lashes. There's fear there. Resignation. Embarrassment. Like she shouldn't have expected anything less than making a fool out of herself. It pisses me off. Seeing the way she wants to go right back to being unseen. To blend in. Like a turtle who finally managed to pop their head out of their shell, only to slip back into the comfort of their home as soon as the outside world got the best of them.

But what's worse? I want to know if she cares. Why she cares how Everett caught us together with my hands on her waist and how I was this close to tasting her again.

"You sure you're okay?" I keep my voice low so only she can hear me.

She nods but doesn't bother looking at me as she reaches for her aunt's camera still balanced in my hand.

"Did the camera break?" she asks.

"Camera's fine."

"Phew." Her relief is palpable as she finally gives me a small smile. "Thanks."

"Don't mention it."

"You get everything you need?" Everett interrupts.

Her gaze darts across the ice as if she almost forgot he was here.

"Dylan?" he prods.

"Uh, let me look." Lifting the camera, Dylan flips through the photos one more time. The same soft smile plays at the edge of her mouth as she loses herself in the images, the last of her embarrassment finally dissipating. "Yeah. Yeah, these will definitely work."

"All right, let's go." Everett orders.

"I thought I told you I'd catch a ride with Reeves," she counters.

"Yeah, I know, but I noticed you left your backpack in my car. I came back to give it to you, and since you're already done, I figured you might as well ride with me, right?" He offers his arm and waits.

A beat passes, and I swear she's gonna send him packing again, but she turns off her camera and loops her wrist through the crook of his elbow. I stay on the ice, watching them shuffle toward the bench with an ease I envy. Watching her with him. How comfortable she is. The way his hand touches her lower back once they reach the bench. The way she gives him a smile while sitting down and reaching for her laces. The way he stands over her, folding his arms like a bodyguard or some shit, refusing to look at me. To acknowledge I'm here.

Asshole.

Oblivious to the tension swirling in the air, Dylan unlaces her skates and slides on her shoes. Once she finishes, she tucks her camera back in her bag, tugs it and the duffle bag over her shoulder, and turns to Ev. "You ready?"

Everett stares at my hoodie engulfing her body. His jaw tics, but he doesn't call her out for keeping it on. He also doesn't answer her.

"Ev?" she repeats.

With a jerky nod, he turns away from her and starts heading up the stairs. "Let's go."

She stays at the base of the steps, watching as he walks toward the exit. Once she's sure he's not watching, she peeks at me on the ice. What I wouldn't give to know what's going through her mind. To know if she feels the same tension I do.

"I'll, uh, I'll see you in class, Reeves."

"See you then."

10

DYLAN

"**Y**ou're home!" Finley gushes from the family room.

Too distracted by my weird afternoon, I barely glance her way as I drop my keys on the kitchen counter and lean against the edge, my exhaustion finally taking over. "Yup, I'm home."

"Someone looks tired," another voice adds.

My attention catches on Ophelia beside Fin, and my enthusiasm sparks, bringing with it another wave of energy while replacing the lingering embarrassment from my strange afternoon with Reeves and even stranger drive home with Everett.

"Hey!" Rushing toward my best friend, I pull her into a hug. "*You're* home!"

"I'm home," she repeats with a light laugh. "I had to grab a few things, but I'm heading back to Mav's in a few."

"Totally get it." I let her go, shoving aside my disappointment. I love Mav, and I love how much he loves Ophelia. But we spent years dreaming about college and what it would be like. Moving in, having late nights, gossiping about boys, eating too much junk food, and sharing clothes... Then Archer passed.

It's weird. How much his absence affects everyone. Don't get me wrong. I know it's a selfish perspective, but no one can deny how everything changed. Even minute details I never thought would be affected. Like this. My relationship with Ophelia and how she's distanced herself from everyone but Mav. I would never hold it against her, but finding a new normal and a new reality than the one we always talked about takes some getting used to.

"Well, tell Mav hi for me," I add.

"I definitely will, but first." She collapses onto the couch and pats the cushion beside her.

Giving her the side-eye, I sit on the edge.

"So..." Ophelia starts, and I brace myself. "Finley told me about your Cinderfella."

With a groan, my face scrunches. "Please don't call him that."

"Why not?" she asks. "I kind of love the name."

"And I kind of love being known as your fairy godmother," Finley teases from the opposite end of the couch.

I hang my head in my hands, unable to form a response or argue with the delusion Finley wears like a second skin, so I stay quiet.

Ophelia nudges me. "Any progress finding the guy?"

"Not really," I mutter into my palms and sit up again. "But I'm not holding my breath."

"Why not?" she asks. "You finally felt chemistry with a guy. If finally feeling something for a guy isn't worth digging into, I don't know what is."

"That's what I've been saying!" Finley interjects. "You should've seen Dylan afterward. She was all flushed and couldn't stop checking out all the guys at the party. It was adorable."

Leaning around Ophelia, I glare at Fin. "You know I want to smack you, right?"

"Come on, you know you love me."

"Mm-hmm," I hum, clearly unconvinced.

"Speaking of Cinderfella, were you able to cross Reeves off the list?" Finley adds.

She suggested I do my own sleuthing during the photo shoot, and even though I want to say yes I most assuredly crossed him off the list, the fact I almost kissed the dude and probably would've if Everett didn't interrupt means...

"No freaking way." Finley gasps. "Dude, you're totally blushing."

"I am not!"

"Oh, you most definitely are," Ophelia agrees, scanning my face with a massive, knowing grin. "Then again, I'm pretty sure Reeves has this effect on everyone."

"Yeah, he's hot," Finley chirps. "Does this mean Reeves is your Cinderfella?"

I hesitate but shake my head. "He said I'm crazy for fawning over a guy who's too much of a coward to claim me without a mask to hide behind, so I'm gonna go with no."

The girls grimace as Finley mutters, "Yikes."

"Yeah, I don't see Reeves calling himself a coward," Ophelia admits. "Actually, I don't see him being a coward in general. Hell, he was the only one who had the balls to stir the pot and convince Mav to give our relationship another try."

"No, he's not a coward," Finley concludes. "But he did get under your skin during the photo shoot, am I right?"

My cheeks flame, and I cover my face with my hands again. "No comment."

"Nuh-uh." Ophelia reaches for my hands. "You can't say no comment!"

"Lia's right. Sorry, Dyl," Finley adds. "The best friend rules state—"

"Okay, fine." I drop my hands to my lap. "We had fun. Like…a lot of fun, actually." My mouth tilts up as I replay the sound of his husky laughter during the Severus pickup line.

"Okay, I need details because"—Finley waves her finger in front of my face—"with a look like this? I'm getting second-hand butterflies for you."

"It's not a big deal," I tell them. "It's just…I was able to make him laugh, and he made me feel comfortable enough not to make a fool out of myself, which we all know is basically a miracle. And when I was pretty sure he was thinking about kissing me, Everett showed up, and—"

"Noooo," Finley drags out the word and clutches at her chest as if he's dealing the final blow to her personally when it was my moment with Reeves he managed to obliterate. "Tell me you're joking."

"Definitely not joking. Then again, it's probably for the best since Everett is also the one who told me to stay away from Reeves in the first place and—"

"He's totally your Cinderfella," Finley interrupts.

Confused, Ophelia shakes her head. "Who? Reeves?"

"No, Everett."

"No way." Ophelia's jaw drops. "*Everett?*"

Finley nods. "Yup."

"No," Lia repeats with another shake of her head. "No way."

"Uh, one hundred percent, yes."

"How do you know?" I ask.

"Okay, I don't technically *know*," Fin admits. "But I've been suspicious of Everett for a couple days now. From the info I gathered from a bunch of the other girls at the costume party, Everett is definitely still on the list of possibilities. And it makes sense why he isn't owning up to it, too, because he's scared to ruin the friendship or whatever. And let's not forget how he warned you to stay away from Reeves and, come on. You gotta see where I'm going with this." She turns to Lia, probably looking for backup. "Why else do you think he's so protective of her?"

Ophelia shoots me a look and frowns. "Well…"

Silence follows, and I touch the scar along my hairline as the memory resurfaces, and I let my hand fall. "Aaaand, I'm done with this conversation."

"Why? I think it's awesome," Fin argues. "You basically have two hot guys fawning over you. I say go for it."

"Everett's your brother," I remind her.

"So? He's a cutie."

"Not the point," I start.

Ophelia cuts me off. "She's right. The point is, you're a catch, and either guy would be lucky to have you. The question is…who do you want to pursue?"

I scoff. "We're talking about me, remember?"

"Okay, who do you want to be pursued by?" Ophelia amends.

I open my mouth to answer but close it quickly. It's weird. Thinking about one guy pursuing me, let alone two. I'm not the pursued-by kind of girl. I'm the friend. The buddy. The *hey, your friend's cute, mind if you introduce us?* girl. Honestly, I'm still the same girl, so this entire conversation is a moot point. Either A, Cinderfella reveals himself, and we ride off into the sunset or B, Reeves winds up actually liking me and…

Okay, apparently, Finley's delusion rubbed off on me.

"Technically, we don't know if Everett is Cinderfella, and *technically*," I repeat, "we don't know if Reeves is even interested in pursuing me."

"You said he tried to kiss you," Finley reminds me.

"I said I *thought* he was going to try and kiss me," I clarify.

"But this wouldn't be the first time I completely misread a situation."

"So we all need to take a deep breath," Ophelia orders, giving Finley a sharp look. "And we all need to be patient and see if Everett reveals himself as the real Cinderfella or if Reeves contacts you and asks you out. Until then, we wait. What do you guys think?"

I think I'm about to have a panic attack. Puffing out my cheeks, I wipe my sweaty palms along my still-damp jeans as the possibilities circle through my brain like a carousel. What if Cinderfella is Everett? Would I be okay with it? Disappointed? Elated? I don't know? And what if Reeves does ask me out? Would I be okay with that? I have no idea. Not when he's supposedly an escort.

He's. An. Escort.

What the hell is wrong with me? Of course, I can't date him.

"Don't get me wrong, great idea, Lia," Finley says, interrupting my spiraling thoughts. "But while you guys are waiting, I think I'll do a little more digging on who Everett may or may not have kissed during the costume party, and I'll also see if I can give Reeves an itsy, bitsy, teeny, tiny push—"

"Don't you dare," I snap.

She lifts her hands in defense. "Okay, okay. I'll wait…for a little while."

"You're relentless," I point out.

"I like to call it dedicated, but thank you."

Rubbing at my temples, the day finally catching up with me, along with the knowledge Finley isn't going to drop this anytime soon, I stand from the couch. "I think it's time for me to call it a night. Ophelia, it's good to see you again. I've missed you like crazy. And Finley, you're a pain in the ass, but I love you anyway. Goodnight."

"'Night," they say in unison.

I head down the hall and close the bathroom door behind me.

Maybe Everett was lying. Maybe he is ballooning Reeves'...job. Maybe Reeves really is interested in me.

And maybe pigs can fly.

One thing's for sure. If Finley opens her big, fat mouth to either of them, I'll seriously slip a frog into her bed.

The thought makes me smile.

I push myself away from the door and turn on the shower.

11

DYLAN

Tonight's my first shift at Rowdy's without a trainer. It shouldn't be nerve-wracking, but it kind of is. Finley's here, though I haven't seen her much. The place is too busy. Peanut shells crunch beneath my cowgirl boots as I wipe my hands against the black apron wrapped around my waist while a guy is thrown from the mechanical bull in the corner. His name is Bruce. Not the guy, the bull. Apparently, he's been here since the place opened and is even more of a celebrity than the restaurant owner, Rowdy, who's almost always somewhere. Greeting the regulars. Introducing himself to the new faces.

Yeah, this place is something else.

I make my way toward my fourth table for the evening and glance at the band on stage playing a Luke Bryan song. It's an oldie but a goodie.

As I stare at the cover band, I start my nightly spiel. "Hey. My name's Dylan. I'll be your server tonight. What can I get started—" My words dry up as I turn to the customers and realize who's sitting in the booth. It's Reeves in all his bad-boy glory. Fitted T-shirt. Five o'clock shadow. Messy yet perfectly quaffed hair. And dark, penetrating gaze as soon as it locks with mine. If I didn't know better, I'd say he's as surprised to see me here as I am with him. "Oh. Uh, hi," I offer.

"Hi," the woman sitting across from Reeves replies.

My attention snaps from Reeves to her as the pieces fall into place. He's on a date. Reeves is on a date. A stone drops in my stomach, and I swallow the bile coating my throat as my eyes bounce back and forth between them. Seriously. I think I might puke.

"Hi," I repeat. It's breathy and forced and—

What the hell?

I haven't seen Reeves since the rink. Actually, that's a lie. I've stared at his face on my camera off and on for days, even spotting him with his shirt off on the side of the road while he was on an evening jog when Griffin drove me home from work last night. But talking to him? Having an actual conversation when we almost kissed the other day? Yeah, no. It hasn't happened, and now, I definitely don't want it to. Not when he's clearly here on a date while I was delusional enough to think he felt a spark for me.

I should probably blame Finley since she's been unable to drop it, either. Well, anything related to Reeves or Everett has been a hot topic on our side of the house lately, and I seriously regret telling her anything at this point. Then again, now isn't the time to silently curse my best friend for helping me get my hopes up. Nope. Right now, I need to serve Reeves and his…*date.*

Shaking off my jealousy, I click the back of the pen and stare down at my notepad. "Can I, uh, can I get you anything to drink?"

"I'll take a whiskey," she replies. "Jameson."

"Yeah, because *I'm* the girl who'd order a fruity little drink 'cause she can't shoot whiskey," I mutter.

"Excuse me?" the woman interrupts.

"It's a line from an old Carrie Underwood song," I mumble, stealing the courage to look back at her instead of the jumbled words on my notepad. She's gorgeous. Older. Like, my mom's age or something, but gorgeous, nonetheless. "Nevermind. I'll have the bartender deliver a...whiskey? Wait. Do you want a glass or a shot or...?"

"Two shots, please. Jameson." The woman looks at Reeves. "And what would you like?"

He's staring at me. I can feel him. His gaze. The way it brands the side of my face makes my cheeks heat with frustration and embarrassment and jealousy. I can't actually look at him again. Not when my stupidity threatens to burn me up from the inside out.

Did I seriously misread everything that happened at the rink?

"Reeves?" the woman prods.

"Water's fine," Reeves says.

I don't bother looking at him as I scribble *water* on the notepad, heading to the bar to place the woman's order. I'm still under twenty-one, so I can't technically serve alcohol. I can, however, pass along the order so someone legal can deliver it to the table. It feels a bit like a loophole, but if it keeps me away from their table for a little while, I won't complain. I need a minute. To collect myself. To remind myself exactly who I am and what type of relationship I have with the man at table four. A non-existent relationship, or at best, a friendly one. Which is fine and completely normal, so I need to stop making it weird and awkward.

Stop. Making. It. Awkward.

My hands shake. It's stupid, but it's true. I throttle the pad and pen when a firm grasp encompasses my arm and yanks me down the hall.

"Shit," I screech.

"Hey, Dylan."

Recognizing the culprit, I yank out of Reeves' grasp. "What are you doing here?"

"I could ask you the same question."

"I work here. What's your excuse?"

"Also working."

My brows shoot up. "Working? Is that what the guys call it these days?"

The bastard simply smirks and steps closer, crowding me. "You're cute when you're jealous."

Not realizing how close I am to the wall, I step back and run into it with a soft thump. The air whooshes from my lungs, but Reeves doesn't stop his pursuit as he corners me against it.

Staring at his chest, I murmur, "I'm not jealous."

"And I'm not on a date."

"It looks like you're on a date."

"And it looks like you're jealous," he volleys back. I can hear the amusement in his voice. It pisses me off. How nonchalant he is. Like I have no right to feel affected. Then again, I guess I don't. He owes me nothing. Absolutely nothing.

"Whatever you say, Reeves." I force a smile, trying to slip past him. "Now, if you'll excuse me, I need to get back—"

He mirrors my steps, keeping me exactly where he wants me. "She hired me, Dylan."

My breath stalls. "H-hired you for what?"

"To take her out."

I blink. Twice. Hating the fact Everett was right all along. I pretended he wasn't, but he did warn me about Reeves being an escort. After the costume party. Before *and* after my photo shoot with Reeves. I pushed aside all of the warnings simply because of how nice it felt to be...silly and fun with someone. To see the curiosity in Reeves' eyes. The attraction.

And I swear it was there, even if it only lasted a few minutes. I don't know. I liked it, though. How thoughtful he was to bring a puppy simply to see me smile. How genuine he seemed. How interested—even if I didn't admit it aloud to Finley or Ophelia. And now...now, I have front-row seats to the guy who made me feel capable of attraction and flirting, along with confirmation he's literally paid to give exactly that to anyone willing to cough up a chunk of change to be in his presence.

Of course, he's an escort. And a good one, too. I can attest to it firsthand.

So why am I blindsided?

I feel his stare again. The way it scalds me. Holds me captive. The problem is, I have no idea what I'm supposed to say.

"Okay, then," I mutter.

"I'm a...platonic, non-physical escort," he clarifies.

"Platonic," I mimic.

"Yeah, platonic."

"And non-physical."

"Exactly."

"Escort." The word makes my nose scrunch as it rolls off my tongue.

"I'm more like Hitch," Reeves offers with the same heavy dose of nonchalance from earlier.

My gaze flicks to his, veering from the safety of his very broad chest. "Hitch?"

"You know, the old movie with Will Smith?" he explains.

"I have no idea what you're talking about."

"It's a movie."

"Ooookay?" I take a step to my right, desperate to get out of here so I can lick my proverbial wounds in private. "Have a good night."

He blocks my way again. "Humor me, Dylan."

Annoyed with myself, I bite the inside of my cheek, then grit out, "And why should I?"

"Because we both know if you walk away, you'll over-think what you saw for days, so let me explain it to you and save you the sleepless nights, yeah?"

I keep my feet planted and cross my arms, hating how right he is. How I will overthink this and for a hell of a lot longer than a few days. I thought he…liked me. Was I that far off?

Taking my lack of leaving as a sign to continue, Reeves explains, "People pay me for one of three reasons. One, so I can teach them how to date and be desirable. Two, so I can be their fake boyfriend when their exes won't leave them alone. Or three, when they have a wedding or a funeral to attend or—"

"So you *are* an escort."

"Yeah, but not like…sex and shit."

"Not sex and shit," I repeat. "Got it." I start to step around him again but stop and shake my head, finally stealing the courage to look at him. "Why are you telling me this?"

"Because I'm not a fan of the miscommunication trope."

I shake my head once more, convinced I slipped and fell in the bathroom or something because this? This is *not* reality. "What do you mean?"

"You know…when a simple conversation will pretty easily clear up any drama. Like right now." He steps even closer, the heat from his front burning through my clothes, leaving me aching. Reaching up, he tucks my hair behind my ear, causing every inch of my skin to prickle with awareness. "She's a job. Fuck, she's not even that. She's a potential job."

"A potential job?"

"I don't take on every client who approaches me like I used to. Not anymore. Between hockey and school, finding time for a regular job was hard, so I had to be creative."

Why is it so hard to breathe right now? Oh. I know. Because I can smell him. His cologne. Or maybe it's simply Reeves I smell. His natural scent. He smells good. Almost like Christmas. Pine. It's pine and warmth and—forcing air into my lungs through my mouth, I slowly give him a shrug, unsure what he wants me to say or how he wants me to handle this situation or the way he's practically pinning me to a wall.

"What's your point, Reeves?" I gulp. "You don't owe me anything. Hell, I don't even know your first name."

"It's Oliver." He tilts my chin up. "But no one else who matters knows it. And my point is...I need you to stop looking like I kicked your puppy."

The callus on his thumb tickles the underside of my chin, but I don't pull away as my tongue darts out, moistening my lips. "I'm not looking at you like you kicked my puppy."

His mouth quirks. "You kind of are."

"Well...what do you even mean, anyway?" I lean away from his touch and rest my head against the wall behind me, desperate for space. "I don't have a puppy, so—"

"It means you seeing me with another woman hurt your feelings, and trust me, Dylan. Hurting you is the last thing I want." He lets me go and takes a small step back. "I didn't even know you work here."

"And if you did know I work here?"

"I would've found a different place to take her."

"So, hiding it is better?" I challenge.

He shrugs. "I like to keep my business separate from personal relationships."

"We don't have a relationship," I remind him.

"Yet."

Or ever.

I puff out a deep breath and square my shoulders. "Look, if you wanted to hide this, there's no need. Everett already told me what you…do." I wave my hand around, surprised by how much the extra space between us bothers me, making my head foggier instead of clearer like it should be. "I mean, technically, he called you an escort when, apparently, you're more of a G-rated gigolo, but—"

A quiet snort escapes him, and he shakes his head. "I'll be sure to add the title to my business card."

"You do that," I mutter. "Besides, it's none of my business anyway, and neither is how you, apparently, also have a habit of being selfish and only thinking of yourself, so…" I grit my teeth to keep from spewing out any more bullshit, hurtful things. I'm not a mean person. And I'm not one to try and hit below the belt. So what the hell was that?

Unflustered, Reeves asks, "Is that what Everett said to you?"

My lips press into a thin line, but I stay quiet.

"Did he give you specifics?" he prods.

I shake my head as shame threatens to suffocate me.

"Of course, he didn't," he mutters. And I can't decide if he's pissed or amused at how he can read me and Everett so easily. "Do you wanna know? What happened?"

I shrug but don't say anything else.

"Yeah, I'll tell you," he decides. "Because, like I said, I'm not a fan of miscommunication."

"I'm not trying to pry."

"Yeah, you are,"—his mouth ticks up—"but it's all right. I'll forgive you this time." Again, he steps closer, but I have a feeling it isn't an excuse to touch me this time. No, he's crowding me because he doesn't like this information being spread as much as he'd like me to believe. Like this is private. Personal. Delicate. It makes me more curious.

"Bluntly put, I fucked up." He says it like we're discussing the weather. Like he isn't connected to the conversation at all. Like black is black and white is white, and there is no in-between. "I got a DUI the night before LAU's playoff game last season," he continues. "The team counted on me, and I was too busy hanging out in jail, waiting to make bail instead of being on the ice where I should've been. We lost the game. Because of me. It's why your buddy, and probably your brothers, thinks I'm a selfish, unreliable, arrogant prick who's only loyal to himself."

He steps back, giving me space as his confession hangs in the air while a few of the other waitresses skirt around us. I should get back to work, but honestly? I'm so taken aback I'm frozen. By his brutal honesty. His emotionless assessment. The way it's unbiased and so...blatant. It leaves me speechless, but clearly, he's waiting for my response because he won't stop staring down at me. Does he actually care what I think, or am I delusional?

Licking my bottom lip, I murmur, "Yikes."

With a smirk, he tucks his hands in his pockets and lifts his shoulders. "Yeah."

"Why did you drink before a game?"

"I was on a job, had a drink, then ran into my dad, and, uh, let's just say things spiraled from there. Even then, it was a shitty thing to do, and I fucked up, but there it is. The real reason why your friend hates me. The question is...do you?"

My eyes drop to his mouth. The slight curve. The full lips. It's almost believable, his carefree persona, but I don't buy it for a second. That this doesn't affect him. The way his friends don't trust him. How they haven't forgiven him for making a mistake, even if it was a big one. He's been carrying it. Hiding it behind sarcasm and a give-no-shit attitude when, clearly, he does. Give a shit.

"I think we're all allowed to make mistakes," I murmur.

"Me too." His eyes soften, but whether it's from relief or attraction, I'm not sure. Regardless, it's dangerous. He's dangerous. How easily I could fall for him. How easily I could open up to him. How much I want to open up to him.

This. Is. His. Job.

"So…are we good?" he prods.

I look down at my hands and play with the edge of my apron. "Why wouldn't we be?"

"You're a shitty liar, Dylan."

"I'm not lying," I argue, "and honestly? If I ever need your services, I'll be sure to let you know."

"My services?" he growls.

I pull back, surprised by the animosity in his voice. Apparently, he *doesn't* hide all of his feelings, and I obviously pissed him off.

"You know. Like…" I gulp. "If I ever need to hire you for a date or something. You probably pieced together how I'm not great with the opposite sex, and since you're evidently very good at what you do, maybe you could help me out or something, or I don't know—"

He scoffs like I personally offended him. "Not gonna offer you my services, Dylan."

My brows tug in the center as I hold his steely gaze. "Why not?"

"Because I don't date my clients."

"Isn't it exactly what you're doing?" My focus shifts to the main area of the restaurant where I know his client is waiting.

Rolling his eyes, he mutters, "Okay, I date them, but I don't *date* them."

"Well, that's about as clear as mud," I note.

"Would you like me to make it more clear?" He steps closer again, and my back hits the wall behind us like we're in a twisted version of deja vu.

"I don't touch my clients, Dylan. I don't wonder what they

taste like. I don't picture them naked, and I sure as shit don't imagine them in my bed."

The imagery makes my knees tremble as I stare at his lips. They're so close I can almost taste them, and if I were a different girl, I would. I'd lift my chin and take what I want. I'd quench my curiosity. I'd—

My phone rings, and I jerk at the foreign sound. Pulling it out of my apron, I check the name on the screen, then peek at Reeves.

Something flashes in his warm brown eyes when he sees my mom's name. "Answer it," he orders.

"I'm at work."

"It's your mom."

"I'll call her back."

"Answer it, Dylan."

"Seriously? You never ignored one of your mom's calls?"

"My mom's dead. Now, answer it."

Like a punch to the gut, I exhale, too surprised by his revelation to do anything but follow his orders. As my thumb slides across the screen, I bring the phone to my ear. "Hello?"

My mom rushes out, "Tell me you're okay!"

"What?"

"Are you and Finley okay? Lia's with Mav, but—"

I plug my opposite ear. "Mom, I'm at Rowdy's. What's going on?"

"Oh, thank goodness."

"Mom, what's wrong?" I try again as Reeves stares at me, not even bothering to hide the fact he's most definitely eavesdropping on my conversation, or at the least, my end of it.

"The house, it's… Oh, Colt." Rustling sounds through the speaker, and my dad's voice replaces my mom's.

"Hey, Dyl. You there?"

125

"Hey, what's going on?" I ask for what feels like the hundredth time.

"The fire department called. Your house is on fire."

My heart leaps into my throat, and I blurt, "What?"

"Is Fin with you?"

"Uh…" My head bobs up and down with a nod as I search the restaurant, finding Finley with her cell pressed to her ear. She's probably hearing a rundown of the situation from her parents like I am with mine. "Yeah. Yeah, she's here."

"Good." My dad sighs. "The fire department is putting it out right now, but we don't know how much damage there is. From what I understand, it only affected your side of the duplex, but it may have spread. I'm not sure. We're on our way to check everything out right now."

Still reeling, I close my eyes. "What can I do?"

"I don't know," he mutters. "I'll call you as soon as possible with an update. I love you, Dylan."

"Love you, too." I hang up the phone with my mind spinning.

"What happened?" Reeves asks. His brows are pulled low, and his muscles are tight. Like he already knows something's wrong, and he's determined to protect me from the fallout. It's…unexpected and confuses me even more.

I pinch the bridge of my nose and fight off my impending headache, or at least attempt to. Then again, impending is a bit of a stretch. The thing pulses behind my eyelids. The sooner I take my contacts out, the better.

"Dylan," Reeves prods.

Dropping my hand to my side, I look up at him and tell him the truth. "My house is on fire."

"Yeah, I caught that part." His mouth lifts, but he backs away, giving me some room to breathe and think straight.

But the smile does me in. "I'm sorry, why is this funny?" I ask.

"It isn't. But I always knew I had hot neighbors. Didn't think they'd catch their house on fire, though."

My nose scrunches. "Was that a pickup line?"

"It was a compliment."

"A terrible one."

"Ah, come on." He bumps my shoulder with his. "Look at it like this. I just got out of my date."

"Yeah, because that makes this situation so much better," I argue dryly. "I need to find my manager."

"You mean the guy Finley's with?"

Sure enough, Finley's already talking to Rowdy. As if they can feel my stare, Rowdy glances in my direction and mouths, "*Go home. I got this.*"

"*Thank you,*" I mouth back to him and slowly walk toward the main area of the restaurant.

"See? And you get tonight off," Reeves adds as he follows me. "Sounds like a win to me."

I roll my eyes. "Not sure it's an even trade-off."

"Maybe not, but you gotta look at the bright side, Dylan."

"Not sure there's a bright side in this," I argue.

"There's always a bright side."

I stop walking and face him fully. "How do you do it? How do you always...turn shit around? You did it at the funeral. You're doing it now. I don't get it. My whole life might be up in flames, and..."

"And here you are. *Okay*," he emphasizes. "Pretty sure you guys being okay is all that matters."

"Yeah, but my things—"

"Can all be replaced. There's only one you." He boops my nose then turns on his heel. "I'll talk to my client. Why don't you grab your things, make sure you're good to go with your boss, and I'll meet you outside in five."

"Reeves, you don't have to—"

"Too late." He walks backward toward table four while

holding my stare. "Tell Fin I'll give her a ride, too. We need to check out the damage."

He's right. We do. And if I have to wait for Griffin, Jaxon, or Everett to give me a ride, it might be a while.

Forcing my legs to move, I murmur, "Thanks," while untying my apron.

12

DYLAN

There's a lot of it. Damage. But it's not as bad as I expected after my phone call with my dad. Half of the kitchen is burned to a crisp, and most of our bedding and clothes will have to be replaced thanks to the smoke damage, but otherwise? The firefighters said we were pretty lucky. I was even able to save the froggy shower curtain in the bathroom, which is pretty much the bane of Finley's existence. When I found out, I even managed to laugh.

My parents are here to assess the loss as well, but there isn't anything they can do. Their hands are as tied as ours.

We walk along the charred flooring, inspecting the damage while Griffin, Everett, and Reeves hang out at the entrance. When Everett saw Finley and me climb out of Reeves' car, he didn't look too happy about it, but I didn't care. I was too busy freaking out over the fire truck parked in front of our house. Now, here we are, our minds reeling as we inspect our torched kitchen.

"What are we going to do?" Finley asks.

"Henry already has enough on his plate," my dad mutters,

mentioning Maverick's dad, "so I called the insurance company for him. They'll send someone out tomorrow to get the ball rolling with everything. We need to find you girls a place to stay."

"Why don't they stay with us?" Griffin offers. "Everett and I can share his room, and the girls can share mine on the second floor."

"You don't mind?" my mom asks. "We could always look into a short-term lease or—"

"As long as the guys don't mind, I'm fine sharing with Finley," I interrupt. "You already have enough on your plate, too, trying to figure out this mess. I don't want to make your lives any harder."

"Yeah, and I definitely don't want to stay in a hotel long-term," Finley adds. "Besides, I bet my left boob all of the available housing near campus is already booked solid for the school year. At least if we stay with the guys, we'll have a kitchen."

"And we'll have another badass cook under our roof," Griffin chimes in. He's talking about Finley and Everett. Their dad's an amazing cook and passed on his skills to both his kids. Seriously. Finley's Belgian waffles are legendary, and Everett's soups, pasta, and, well, basically everything the guy cooks are pretty freaking incredible, too.

With a sigh, my mom pulls me into another hug and sags into me. "Are you sure you guys don't mind?"

I hug her back. Griffin takes my place when I let her go. "Sure thing, Mom," he tells her. "Not a big deal."

"And you?" My mom gives Everett a pointed look.

"Happy to help, Aunt Ash."

"What about you?" She turns to Reeves.

He hasn't said much since we pulled up. Part of me wonders if he feels uncomfortable. Being here. Like this is a family matter or something, and in a way, I guess he isn't wrong, but I've never seen Reeves out of his element. Right now? With the way he's leaning against the entrance doorjamb, his hands tucked into his jean pockets, the majority of his body staying out of the house, and the lack of smart-ass comments coming from him. I don't know. He seems...off.

Or at least he did, until my mom addressed him, and now he's in the spotlight. As if he's a well-seasoned actor, he gives my mom his signature smirk and announces, "I've always been a sucker for a sleepover."

My mom's eyes widen, and I interject, "Mom, he's kidding. Er, half-kidding, but...do they know what caused the fire?"

"They think it was some of the wiring," my dad answers as he shifts his phone from one ear to the other, "but they're still investigating."

"At least I have my medication." Finley pulls her orange prescription bottle from her purse, lifts it into the air, and shakes it back and forth.

"Yeah, we're all very impressed," Griffin jokes, but my mom elbows him in the ribs.

"Be nice. It's one less thing we have to replace. But for now..." She sighs again. "I guess we need to shop for a few essentials." Pulling out her phone, she checks the time on the screen and frowns. "It's getting late, though. Hmm."

"Don't worry, Mrs. Thorne," Reeves adds. "Dylan loves borrowing my clothes, so I'm sure we can pull together a few things for her and Finley until tomorrow." My dad pins him with a warning stare, his phone call forgotten, and Reeves lifts his hands. "Platonically, of course."

"Platonically, huh?" My mom quirks her brow.

With a nod, he replies, "I've been nothing but a gentleman, I swear. Why don't you guys go to the hotel and get some rest? I'm happy to take the girls shopping tomorrow if you and Mr. Thorne need to be here to meet with anyone."

KELSIE RAE

She smiles back at him and opens her mouth to say something, but I cut her off.

"Pretty sure it won't be necessary. Not the whole getting rest part, but the whole taking me shopping thing."

"Aw, come on, Dylan," Reeves quips. "I can even wait outside the dressing room, and you can model all your choices like a solid 90s movie."

My eyes glaze, and I shake my throbbing head. "I don't even know what that means."

"Well, apparently, I've failed you as a mother," my mom interjects. "Because I know exactly what he's talking about."

"I bet you know what Dramione means, too, am I right?" Reeves asks, his eyes practically gleaming.

With a light laugh, she turns to me, giving me a startled look and making me feel like I've been living under a rock. "You don't know what Dramione means? Sweetie...I know screens haven't always been your friend, but Harry Potter? Should I be ashamed or impressed?" She pulls me into another hug and rubs her hand up and down my arm. "Okay, we should have a Harry Potter marathon. What do you guys say? Not today or anything, but—"

"Mom, my house just burned down," I remind her.

"Which is even more of a reason why you need a distraction," she argues. "Honestly, we all do. Besides, it's almost Halloween, and Harry Potter involves witches, so, obviously, the timing couldn't be more perfect." Her eyes glow with enthusiasm as she bounces her brows up and down. And it's nice. Seeing her smile when we all had a shitty day.

Defeated, I mutter, "I'm not sure Harry Potter should get the Halloween movie label, but fine. Can we nail down logistics later, though? After everything that happened tonight, my brain feels like mush."

"Yeah, of course." She waves me off. "I'll send out invitations later."

132

"I don't think we need invitations for a Harry Potter marathon," I point out.

"Mrs. Thorne is right," Reeves interrupts. "You definitely need invitations."

My mom grins back at him. "See? I knew I liked you, Reeves. Keep an eye out for your invitation in the mail, all right?"

"Okay, *Grandma*," Griffin teases.

"Oh, shush," she calls back to him. "I want to make this feel authentic."

Chuckling, Reeves squeezes the back of his neck and nods. "Sure thing, Mrs. Thorne. I'll watch for it."

"Thank you, *Reeves*." She tosses a mock glare at her son. Everyone says their goodbyes, and within another ten minutes or so, my parents climb back in their car, pull onto the street, and wave goodbye through the passenger window.

"Well..." Finley rubs her hands together. "Who's ready for a sleepover?"

"Dude, I want to climb in bed and sleep for eternity," I tell her.

"Where's the fun in that?" Finley argues. "We should play a game."

My mouth bunches on one side as I shake my head. "Seriously, I'm exhausted, and my head is killing me. Why don't you guys play without me or something?"

"I'm game," Griffin offers.

"Me, too," Everett adds.

They both turn to Reeves, waiting for his two cents. But Reeves? He simply stares at me. "I think I'm gonna call it a night, too. Come on, Dylan. I'll get you situated."

"I think I can handle it," Everett mutters.

"I thought you were gonna play a game?" Reeves counters.

"Yeah, come on, Ev," Finley pleads. "I'm pretty sure Reeves can take care of my good friend here, right, Reeves?"

The bastard doesn't even bother hiding his smirk as he nods and rubs at the corner of his mouth, looking sexier than sin. Satisfied, Finley gives me a grin, slipping her arm through her brother's. "I think the board games in my room are still safe. Let's go pick one. Griffin, you, too. Chop-chop!"

With his hands tucked in his pockets, Griffin turns to Reeves. "You good showing her where the spare sheets are and shit?"

"I think I can handle it," Reeves replies, mimicking Everett from moments ago.

Griff hesitates, and I swear there's a weird, manly undercurrent passing between them. Finally, my brother gives Reeves a single nod, then heads back to my side of the duplex. It's weird. From the outside, you'd never know the kitchen was burned to a crisp.

Finley glances over her shoulder at me and Reeves. "Goodnight, you two. Sleep tight." *And you're welcome*, she mouths, tacking on a wink as she guides Everett into the house.

Reeves' chuckle is low as he watches them disappear. "That girl is something else."

"You have no idea," I mutter. Then, it hits me...it's only me and Reeves now.

Holy shit, it's just me and Reeves.

A guy I most definitely shouldn't be crushing on.

My head hurts too much for this.

As if reading my thoughts, he gives me a boyish smile. "Looks like it's just you and me now."

I gulp. "Yup."

With a wave of his hand, he motions toward the front of his house. "Ladies first."

13

DYLAN

N erves buzzing, I walk up the steps and push open the front door to the guys' side of the duplex. It's dark, and I pause at the threshold, unsure what to do. Heat skates across my shoulder as Reeves reaches around me and flicks on the light.

"Home sweet home. But you already knew that." I can hear the smile in his voice, but I don't bother looking at him to confirm it as he adds, "Do you know whose room is whose?"

"I did until Jax graduated, and everyone switched rooms," I admit. "Griff is on the top floor, right?"

"Yeah. Follow me." He closes the front door with a quiet click, then heads up the stairs. They creak softly under our weight as I follow him, feeling like it's the first time I've ever taken this path, even though it couldn't be further from the truth. Once we reach the second floor, he taps his knuckles against one of the closed doors as we walk past it. "This one's mine. And this one"—he pauses at the last door on the right —"is now yours."

Cool. We're neighbors. Well, more so than before. It's

totally normal, right? Being neighbors with a guy you should have nothing to do with?

Cool. Cool. Cool.

With a twist of his wrist, Reeves pushes the door open. He doesn't have a chance to step back when I jump the gun and start to walk inside, belatedly realizing there's only so much room in a doorway, and we've now used all the space. And I mean *all* the space.

Nice one, Dylan.

When my chest brushes against his, I freeze. The same pulsing heat passes between us, along with his scent. Is it him? Is this just the way he smells? Or is it cologne? Something used to lure in innocent little virgins like me? Regardless, it's working. It shouldn't be, but it is. I stare at his chest as a quiet rumble of amusement escapes him.

"Want me to walk you through it?" he murmurs. My gaze snaps to his, and he clarifies, "The *room*."

Oh. Right. Because being walked through my tangled emotions and libido is probably a bad idea.

Clearing my throat, I slip past him the rest of the way into the room, refusing to give him the satisfaction of seeing my red-stained cheeks when the bastard already has a knack for reading me way too easily.

The blinds are shut on the large window, making the room as dark as the main floor when we entered. Reeves flicks on the light like he did downstairs. The place still looks pretty bare. A large bed with rumpled sheets takes up the center of the room, along with a black dresser, a matching nightstand, and a walk-in closet. It's like Griffin has yet to make the full move from his shared room with Everett on the main floor. Considering the circumstances and the fact he's letting us kick him out for the foreseeable future, I guess his procrastination paid off.

Despite my headache, I feel Reeves' stare from behind me,

so I head toward the bed and start stripping the sheets. The sooner I'm situated, the sooner he can go away, and I can go to bed.

"I'll grab some clean ones from the closet," Reeves offers. "And if those are crusty, blame Griff."

My nose scrunches, and I drop the edge of the top sheet. "Ew. I did not need to hear that."

"Just calling it like it is," he yells from the hallway, returning with a set of crisply folded sheets in his arms.

Forcing the thought of Griffin hooking up with anyone in the queen-sized bed in front of me, I start stripping the sheets again while Reeves moves to the opposite side and helps me.

"I should be grateful he's letting me kick him out of his room in the first place," I point out.

"Griff shared a room with Everett for years until Jax moved out," he reminds me. "He'll be fine. And if he decides to bitch about it, he can always sleep in Archer's."

My body tightens, and my shoulders fall as I peek at Reeves across the bed.

"Aw, not you, too," he adds.

It's like he's almost disappointed or something, but it only leaves me more confused. "What do you mean?"

"Everyone's walking on eggshells since Archer's death. Don't get me wrong, I get it, but...not you, too."

"Maybe not all of us are as casual about death as you are."

"Who says I'm casual about death?" he asks.

"I don't know? You say his name like..."

"Like he's still here?" Reeves finishes for me. He wads the used sheets into a ball and tosses it across the room. With a quiet *phft*, it lands next to the door, and Reeves reaches for the fresh sheets on the dresser, unfolding them and spreading them across the mattress. "Let me ask you this. If you died right now, would you want the rest of us to act like you never existed? To be scared to say your name or talk about you all because it would make us miss you? In my opinion, that's the real death. The real tragedy. Archer? I fuckin' love the guy. He didn't care if I was acting like a dick. Didn't care if I fucked up like I always do. He still talked to me. Would still hang out with me. Would still treat me like I'm a teammate. A roommate. A *friend*. Why wouldn't I want to talk about him or say I miss him?"

The words burn more than I expect. I let go of one of the sheets to wipe beneath my nose as I reply, "Because it hurts?"

"Well, yeah, but life fuckin' hurts, Thorne. Isn't that the beauty of it, though? When life beats the shit out of you, you still have something to look back on and appreciate. To remember. To...I dunno,"—he shrugs—"cherish."

Pulling my lips between my teeth, I stand dumbfounded as he finishes making the bed. The weird part is he's right. I can see where he's coming from. The fresh perspective I hadn't considered. Like maybe...maybe the pain isn't a bad thing. Maybe it's a reminder of all I have. No one wants to be numb, right? But readily embracing the pain? Acknowledging it's there without pushing it away? I don't know. It doesn't sound like something we come by naturally. Not me, anyway. Then I remember his comment about his mom earlier tonight, and it all makes sense.

Once the last corner is tucked, he turns to me, and my breath hitches.

"Did I render you speechless, Pickles?" he asks.

"No, it's..." I nibble the edge of my lip, unsure whether or not talking about a dead mom is a subject I should broach.

"Tell me," he pushes.

"You sound like you know this from personal experience."

"Ah, yeah." His hands find the back of his neck, and he threads his fingers together, resting them there as he stares at me. "Forgot I dropped the *dead mom bomb* on you at the restaurant. I'd apologize, but, uh, it is what it is."

"So?" I prod.

"So, what?"

My brows crease, and I reach for one of the pillows, changing its cover. "Never mind."

"Nah." Rounding the edge of the bed, he takes the pillow from my grasp, tosses it onto the bed, and sits in front of me. "Tell me."

"It's... You're so casual about bringing up Archer and how everything went down, but as soon as your mom is brought up, you refuse to tell me anything about her."

"You didn't ask."

"You were so upfront at the restaurant I didn't think I had to."

"Good point," he concedes. "Well, I hate to break it to you, but there isn't much for me to tell. She died in childbirth, and my dad got pissed any time I asked questions, so I never had much to go off of. I know her birthday and her name, and she attended LAU. That's it."

Pity flares in my stomach, but I keep my expression blank, praying he can't feel it. Call it a hunch, but I feel like if he did, it would make him push me away, and for some reason I literally can't understand I don't *want* him to. Even if it's stupid. Even if it'll bite me in the ass one day. I want to get to know him. To see this side of him.

"Well?" The mattress dips as I sit beside him, shrinking the distance I hoped to keep between us, but I'm too invested to move away. "What was her name?"

"Heather. Heather Reeves. And her birthday is...tomorrow, actually." His eyes widen with surprise. "Fuck."

"What do you normally do on her birthday?"

With a shrug, he leans back on the bed, resting on his bent elbows. "Nothing."

"You don't go to her grave or anything?"

"She was cremated, and I'd rather put a bullet in my skull than visit my dad's kitchen."

"Kitchen?"

"Her urn is tucked between the empty sugar jar and an overflowing ashtray." He scoffs. "Quite the resting place, right? Why do you do that?"

"Do what?"

He touches my hand beside my face, and I realize I'm putting pressure on a particularly sharp point of my headache. I hadn't even noticed.

Dropping my hand to my lap, I shy away from him. "It's nothing. Just a headache."

"You still have your contacts in?"

I nod.

"Where's your case and glasses?"

"Probably in my room," I admit. "I should probably—"

"Stay here." The bed creaks as he stands up and heads into the hall. The familiar *thump thump thump* of feet on stairs echoes, only to be replaced with silence as I close my eyes, counting the seconds. When I reach eighty-seven, a squeak from the front door sounds, followed by the same beat of footsteps.

"Here." Reeves hands me my backpack, glasses, and contacts case. As I take them, he adds, "I'll be right back," then disappears like he did a minute ago, returning with his arms full of clothing. "Take this."

"What is it?" I ask while multitasking like a champ and removing my contacts.

"Something for you and Finley to sleep in."

"I can borrow something of Griffin's—"

"And let me miss out on Everett's face when he sees you and his baby sister wearing my shirts?" A low laugh escapes him. "Come on. Consider it an early birthday present for my mom."

Mirth coats the inside of my chest as I slip on my glasses, then lift a pair of gray sweats into the air and inspect them. "You have a twisted sense of humor."

With a wink, he drops the rest of the clothes onto the foot of the bed. "You have no idea. How's the headache?"

It's still there, but it's duller. More manageable.

"I'll be fine," I answer.

I can tell he wants to push me on it. To ask me questions and demand answers. Instead, he sighs. "Okay, then. I left a toothbrush on the bathroom counter since we're sharing now, and, uh…" He rocks back on his heels. "I think that's it?"

"I guess so."

"Well…" The same familiar scent washes over me as he steps closer, reaches up, and tucks my hair behind my ear. "'Night, Dylan."

"Goodnight, Reeves."

He walks back to the door but stops and faces me again. "Oh, and, uh, if you have any bad dreams or find out Finley's a shitty roommate, my bed's always open."

I smile. "How thoughtful of you."

"Now, *that's* a term I rarely hear when being described, but I'll take it." With a final tap of his knuckles against the doorjamb, he disappears down the hall. I stare at the empty doorway for a solid thirty seconds. Finally, I stand from the bed and shut the door, still reeling from the turn of events as I close my eyes and replay our conversation.

Who are you, Oliver Reeves?

And why do I care?

141

Maverick's living with his parents while recovering from heart surgery, and even though the bastard has a good excuse for not being around lately, I miss him. We all do. It's why the guys and I drove out here after a particularly brutal practice. It's my mom's birthday, which doesn't help, either.

I wasn't lying when I told Dylan I don't celebrate or anything. Fuck, I didn't even find out the specific date until I was eighteen and found my birth certificate. But it still messes with my head. Her absence. The only family who ever wanted me, and I never even got to meet her. I shouldn't have driven past my dad's trailer before practice, but after my conversation with Dylan, I couldn't help it. The strange twinge of desire to pay my respects to a woman I never met on her birthday while apologizing for killing her.

Unfortunately, the quick detour only fucked with my head more.

Shaking off my annoyance, I lift my hand and tap my knuckles against Maverick's parents' door, with Everett and Griffin flanking my sides. This afternoon, I want to hug the one person I consider family. It's strange admitting it to myself. He's surrounded by dozens of people who care about and love him. Then, there's me. With only one person who actually fits the bill, and even then, he doesn't recognize how much his friendship means to me or how our roommates are a distant second to him. One of which refuses to pass to me on the ice, all because he's pissed over the fact I gave Dylan some sweats and a T-shirt to sleep in last night.

Yeah, nice one, Ev.

The hinges are smooth as butter as Maverick's silhouette greets me through the glass, and he pulls the door open.

He's starting to look better. There's more color in his cheeks, and the scar peeking out from the collar of his white LAU T-shirt isn't as raw and fresh as the last time I saw him. His movements are still a little slow and forced, but if I didn't know any better, I'd assume he's sore from a brutal workout or something, not healing from a heart transplant. Part of me wonders if he ever tries to convince himself of the same thing. That with enough time, he'll be like he was, when we both know it's a lie. Nah, even with his transplant, the doctor told him to kiss his NHL career goodbye, and if that isn't a hard pill to swallow, I don't know what is.

"Hey, guys." Mav leans against the doorjamb and grins. "What are you doing here?"

"We missed you, brother," Griffin answers for all of us. He pulls Mav into a hug, careful not to jostle him too much. Then, he walks into the house like he owns it. Everett follows suit, hugging Maverick and joining Griffin in the family room, leaving me on the porch with my best friend.

"Hey, man. Looking good," I tell him.

"Liar." Mav opens his arms, patting my back in a brotherly hug, and I return it, slapping my hand against him with a little more force than the other guys, just to be a dick. To stand out.

143

He chuckles and shoves me back. "Ass."

"Come on, you know you miss me."

With a roll of his eyes, he shakes his head. "Yeah, whatever."

Maverick's always been my best friend. He's the guy who saw through my bullshit persona and welcomed me with open arms. Literally. He's also the one who convinced his friends to take me in during our freshman year when I'm pretty sure they would've rather stabbed me with their skates. Shit, they probably still prefer to do so. Everett would, for sure.

I let Maverick go. "For real, though. You don't look like you had the shit kicked out of you anymore."

"I guess," he concedes, rubbing his chest, though I doubt he realizes it. "Still feels like it."

"You'll be all right."

"Glad one of us is sure." Another dry laugh rumbles from him, and he tilts his head toward the inside of his house. "Come on in."

I've visited Maverick's childhood home a few times, but the place never ceases to amaze me. Dark wood. Light walls. Photographs hung, each one sporting a happy little family. It's clean and homey and smells like money. Okay, not literally. It smells like...I lift my nose and sniff. No alcohol. No piss. No smoke. No artificial bullshit to cover the underlying stench that doesn't wash out no matter how much you scrub. Just...clean.

Sometimes, I forget Mav and his family are loaded. They don't flaunt it. Don't wave it around or use it to leverage what they want. But even though their house is tasteful and shit, you can still feel it. The wealth. The class. It lingers in the air, reminding me how much I don't belong.

Noticing his family's German Shepherd is missing, I ask, "Where's Kovu?"

"Rory took her to my grandparents'," he answers, mentioning his little sister.

"The dog?"

"Yeah." Maverick forces a smile and squeezes the back of his neck. "She doesn't go anywhere without him lately."

Lately.

As in, since Archer's death.

With a slow nod of understanding, I close the front door behind me and tuck my hands into my pockets near the entrance. Forcing my feet to move, I follow Maverick further into the house. There's a sitting area to the right of the entryway. Maverick steps down the single stair, his bare feet hitting the fluffy carpet, and he makes his way to one of the leather couches. Slipping off my shoes, I follow him to where Griffin and Everett have already made themselves at home.

"So, you guys think you're ready for the first game?" Maverick asks.

Griffin props his feet on the coffee table in front of him and threads his fingers behind his head. "Dude, we fucking suck. Seriously. We miss you on the ice." He hesitates. "Both of you."

Maverick's head falls forward as if the words and the mention of his brother are a physical blow. He clears his throat when he looks up again. "Yeah, I get it. I miss it, too, and, uh, if Archer was here, I know he'd feel the same."

I glance around the room, curious to see how Ev and Griffin feel about Maverick saying Archer's name aloud. At our house, it's basically the equivalent of He Who Must Not Be Named.

They're tense. Like they're sitting on the edge of a cliff, so I decide to push them over.

A little exposure therapy never hurt anyone, right?

"You know what I love about Archer?" I ask.

"What do you love?" Mav murmurs. The same undertone

145

of melancholy taints his words, but he's trying. I can see it, and so do the guys.

"I love how, no matter how shitty we play, he always finds a way to put a positive spin on it," I tell him.

"Yeah, we could use his positivity right about now." Griffin laughs. It's forced, but it's progress, and I wanna fucking applaud the guy for giving it a shot. "Remember when I split my chin open on the ice?"

Everett chuckles beside him, his muscles softening as he shifts on the couch. "He told you chicks dig scars."

"Or the time I failed one of my tests freshman year, and I knew I'd be on the bench?" I add.

"At least you won't have to hear Jaxon bitching about everything you did wrong while he's on his man period," Griffin finishes for me, mimicking Archer's voice. He snorts. "Yeah, and take it from me, since I'm Jaxon's little brother, Archer wasn't wrong. The guy can *bitch*."

We all laugh a little harder.

"Remember the one time when I bailed on Opie on prom night, and Archer stepped in?" Maverick's eyes mist, and fuck me, it's like a dagger to my own empty chest. "Yeah. I should've thanked the fucker for making her night when I wound up ruining it."

"Always taking one for the team." I grab Maverick's shoulder and shake him jokingly.

With a sad smile, he turns to me and nods. "Yeah, man. Definitely Archer's MO."

"And he wouldn't have it any other way," I agree. "Fucking martyr."

The rest of the guys laugh again, and Maverick leans forward, resting his elbows on his knees. "I've been thinking about it, though. I, uh, I think I want to take Ophelia to Homecoming."

Griffin's brows lift. "Homecoming?"

"Yeah." Mav nods. "I know we've never gone to any of the others at LAU, and they're kind of a pain in the ass, but...I dunno. I want to take her to a dance since I messed up the last one."

"I fucking love dances," I tell him. "What do you need from us?"

With a sigh, Mav rubs his hands along his thighs. "I, uh, I want you guys to come with. Get dates, split a limo, the whole thing."

"You know Finley and Dylan will wanna come," Griffin adds, already brainstorming and fine-tuning all the details like the captain he is, both on and off the ice.

Maverick nods. "Yeah, I figured."

"Finley will probably twist her boyfriend's arm to fly in and take her," Everett adds, though he doesn't look too happy about it.

"Which leaves Dylan," I point out. A sly grin pulls at my face. "I'll take her."

"The fuck you will," Everett argues. "You're not going within ten feet of her."

"Wait, what'd I miss?" Mav looks back and forth at the both of us, but I ignore him, focusing on the prickly asshole across from me. And here I thought we were making progress.

"Ah, come on, brother. You're allowed to protect your own baby sister, but Dylan?" My tongue clicks against the roof of my mouth. "I think it's Griffin's job, don't you?" I turn to the wild card who has way more power than I usually give anyone, especially when it comes to women I'm interested in. "So, what do you say, Griff? Can I take your baby sister to Homecoming?"

As the words leave my mouth, Everett's gaze darkens, fucking blazing in my periphery, and I'm not the only one who notices. Griffin shifts uncomfortably in his seat, and like

Mav, his attention flicks from one friend to the next. I'm not an idiot. I know Griff and Everett are two peas in a fucking pod, but Griff isn't the one cockblocking me left and right since the beginning of the semester, and he's trying to figure out why his friend looks like he's two seconds from having an aneurysm.

You gonna tell him, Ev? How you want in his sister's pants?

"Hey, guys!" a girlish voice interrupts.

The sound cuts through the tension like a hot knife through butter. I turn around on the couch and lean over the back, finding the culprits looking over the second-floor wrought iron railing. Finley and Dylan flank Ophelia's sides as they take the stairs toward us.

Well, if it isn't the little wallflower herself.

Dylan's olive green pants and black crop top show a sliver of silky skin, and her hair is pulled into a high ponytail I'd love to wrap around my hand. She went shopping with her friends and their moms today, and her outfit looks new. Then again, so does her hair. It's lighter. And those glasses? Fuck me, I've always been a sucker for a girl who's unapologetically herself. Well, that and the whole sexy librarian bit. My mouth lifts as I picture Dylan in a tiny skirt.

"I thought I heard a few more manly voices down here," Ophelia adds, pulling me from my daydream. "What's up?" She passes hugs around to all of us guys like they're confetti and plops between me and Maverick on the couch.

Leaning her head against Mav's shoulder, she watches as her friends follow suit. Griffin and Everett push to their feet, pulling the girls into hugs, so I stand up as well, way more curious than I'd like to admit to see how Dylan will respond or if she'll avoid me completely with her friends around.

Without batting an eye, Finley gives me a quick squeeze, and I watch from over her head as Everett hugs Dylan. I wonder if anyone else notices the way he lingers. The way he kisses her temple, his focus locked on me. My eyes thin at the innocent contact as I let Finley go, waiting for Dylan to approach me.

She never does. Instead, she moves to the edge of the room, looking awkward as fuck with her glasses propped on the end of her button nose and her arms folded, her gaze roaming every inch of the room except where I stand.

And because I'm a glutton for punishment, and I love watching her squirm, I approach her, keeping my voice low as I watch the way her pretty little throat tightens with a gulp. "You're cute when you're shy," I murmur.

She rolls her eyes, finally acknowledging me, and offers me her hand. To shake. Like I'm a stranger.

"Oh my gosh! Dylan, you're making it weird," Finley protests.

"Am I?" Dylan's wide eyes remind me of a deer in headlights. "I don't know—"

With a laugh, I take Dylan's hand before she has a chance to rescind her offer. My own practically swallows her dainty little palm as I lift it to my lips and kiss the back. "There. I made it weirder."

Her lips bunch on one side like she's fighting her amusement and relief.

Well aware she isn't one for the spotlight, I let go of her hand and ask, "Another headache?"

"He knows about the headaches?" Everett interjects.

Dylan glances at Everett, who's back at his spot on the loveseat and shakes her head. "It's not a big deal, and no. No headache today." Giving me her full attention again, she touches the edge of her glasses. "Sometimes I'm too lazy to put in contacts."

"I like the glasses," I tell her, stepping back to give her some breathing room. Pretty sure she'd pass out if the interrogation continued for another second. But later? Yeah, I'll be investigating the *why* behind her headaches as soon as I can get her alone again. Hell, maybe I'll even sneak into her room while Finley's downstairs arguing with Drew over the phone when she thinks we're all asleep.

"So, what were you guys talking about?" Ophelia prods. "I feel like we interrupted something."

Threading his fingers with hers, Maverick says, "We're catching up on a few things. Will you give me a minute?"

"A minute?" Her eyes narrow. "Yeah, that's not subtle at all."

"Please?"

"Are Dylan and Finley allowed to stay, or are we all banned from the family room?"

He grins. "Only you."

"Should I be offended?"

"Flattered," he clarifies as Finley plops down beside Griffin, and Dylan takes a seat next to Everett while I stay standing at the edge of the room, ever the outcast.

"Hmm." Ophelia shifts toward Mav on the couch and kisses his cheek. "Fine. But only because you asked me nicely."

"Five minutes, I promise," Maverick adds.

"Mm-hmm. You're lucky I have a paper to write." With one more pointed look at her boyfriend, she adds, "You owe me." When she starts to shift away, he grabs the side of her face and kisses her, pulling a soft smile from her.

"I think we both know I have no problem paying you back," he murmurs against her lips. You'd think they were in a world of their own, and if there's any positives to Archer's death, it's this. The strength these two have found in each other. Maybe it's a little morbid, but hey. I'm not afraid to call it like it is. Honestly, I envy it. Having someone to rely on.

My eyes find Dylan like they have a mind of their own.

When I catch her staring at Mav's exchange with Ophelia, Dylan drops her focus to her lap and plays with her fingers. Nervous. Uncomfortable. Shy. The combination is like gasoline on an already stoked fire.

"I'll be upstairs," Lia tells him as her eyelids flutter, and she finally comes out of the lust-filled coma Maverick induced. Turning to her best friends, she adds, "Will you guys grab me when Mav is finished…doing whatever he's doing?"

"Yup." Finley snuggles into the cushions a little more and makes herself comfortable. "We'll be up in a few."

"Good." Pushing off the leather couch, Ophelia leaves, and Maverick leans forward, watching as she takes the stairs, his eyes zeroed in on her ass.

"Perv," I cough into my hand, not even bothering to hide my lack of subtlety. The guys laugh.

Once we have an ounce of privacy, Finley prods, "So? What is it?"

Maverick looks at the empty foyer one more time. Satisfied, he announces, "I want to take Ophelia to Homecoming."

With a squeak, Finley claps her hands quietly to keep the sound from echoing up to Ophelia's room. "Seriously? Aw, this'll be perfect!"

"I hope so."

"Do you need our help?" Dylan asks.

Mav shakes his head. "I'll take care of it, but I wanted to give you a heads-up. I'd like it if we could all go together and have a fun night."

"I'm in." Pulling out her phone, Finley starts typing a message, her fingers flying over the screen. "Let me see if Drew can come."

Everett rubs at the corners of his eyes. "Called it."

His comment is followed by an awkward as fuck silence. It hangs over the room, and Dylan curls in on herself beside him, well aware she's the elephant. "Aaaand, I'm going to the bathroom."

"Dylan," I call as she starts to stand up. "Will you—"

"I'll take you," Everett interrupts.

Her blue-green eyes bounce from Everett to me and back again. "W-what?"

Reining in my annoyance, I try again. "Dylan, will you—"

"I'm taking you to Homecoming," Everett repeats. It's a command. An order. Like she doesn't have any say in the matter, and it pisses me off.

Mother. Fucker.

My hands clench at my sides, turning my knuckles white. But instead of beating the shit out of Ev, my attention shifts back to Dylan.

Arms folded, she opens her mouth to say something but closes it quickly. She looks uncomfortable. Like ants are crawling beneath her skin. Like she has her feet in the stirrups in a doctor's office, and she's waiting to be humiliated in front of everyone. I hate it. A lot.

"Uh…thank you for volunteering to be my pity date, but it's totally fine. I'm not a big dance person anyway, so—"

"You're not a pity date," I argue.

"It won't be the same if you're not there," Everett adds. His tone is softer yet persistent. "Let me take you. Please?"

"Stop being a dick," I snap. "I'm the one—"

"I have an idea," Finley announces. She sits up a little straighter in her seat as a sheen of triumph makes her gray eyes practically glow. "As the newly self-appointed Homecoming matchmaker for this event, it's clear there are two prospects for our dearest Dylan. Well, three if we include the infamous Cinderfella, but since he's yet to make an appearance…" Her expression sours with annoyance, but she smooths her features again. "Anyway, Dylan. I think we're at a crossroads here, and I have two suggestions. One, you choose who you'd like to go with, which is the much more boring route, but hey. You do you. Or option number two, we turn this into a one-time-only, game-slash-competition, and you're the prize."

Dylan scoffs in her seat and leans back into the cushions. "I'm no prize."

"You have no fucking clue," I argue as I take a step toward her.

Her cheeks flood with heat, but she doesn't look at me. She looks back at her lap, appearing even more uncomfortable as the silence stretches around us.

I want to tell her all the reasons she should let me take her. All the reasons I'd be the luckiest bastard alive to be her date for the evening. All the reasons she should pick me. But if I've learned anything about her relationship with Everett, it's how he isn't above pushing, which makes me want to do the opposite, so I keep my feet planted on the plush carpet and fight for restraint.

"Like I said," she mumbles. "I don't want a pity date."

"It isn't a pity date," I start.

"Don't you have someone to *escort?*" Everett asks me. Like I'm the problem. Like I'm the one being an ass. Like I'm the one to blame for making Dylan uncomfortable.

It pisses me off.

Molars cracking from the pressure, I turn to him with a glare. "Is there something you wanna say, Ev?"

Everett pushes to his feet, and Griffin moves between us, his hands raised in the air. "Look, I don't know what the fuck your guys' problem is, but if both of you want to take my little sister, and Dylan doesn't have a preference, *and* it'll turn your pissing contest into something productive, then I say we do Finley's suggestion."

"Really?" Finley claps her hands again like she's her own

personal cheerleader. "Yay! So, Dylan? You don't have a preference? Officially?"

"I don't...uh." She squeezes her eyes shut. "I think this is super awkward. So." She shrugs. "Whatever ends this conversation as quickly as possible would be great."

"Perfect," Finley gushes. "A competition, it is. All in favor, say, aye!"

The room stays quiet as Griffin turns to his little sister. "Dylan?"

Like a balloon, she deflates even more, but I don't miss the way she refuses to look at me as her tongue darts out between her lips. "Aye, I guess."

"Aye," Finley chirps.

The rest of us join in, and I lift my forefinger in agreement, no matter how juvenile it makes me feel.

"Well, looks like it's unanimous," Finley announces. "So the question is...what kind of competition are we thinking?"

"First game of the season is next week," Griffin offers. "How about whoever scores the most goals during the game gets to take Dylan to Homecoming?"

My brow lifts. "Seriously?"

"Yeah, why not?" Griffin argues. "Might as well give you something to work for, right?"

"Apparently, I'm a piece of meat." Dylan slides further into the couch, taking up the extra space Everett vacated while probably wishing she could be swallowed whole.

Sorry, Dyl. You're not so lucky.

"Nah." Griffin sits beside her. "You're an indecisive little sister I'm using to kill two birds with one stone."

"Gee, thanks," she mutters.

"You sure you're okay with this, Dylan?" I ask. I hate it. Seeing her like this. Uncomfortable. Anxious. Embarrassed being in the spotlight. But it's not like I can throw her over my shoulder and make her go with me. It's not like I can make her stand up for herself. And if this is what she wants? Well, my hands are tied.

Her hesitation grates on me as she lifts a shoulder and nods. "Yeah. Sure. Why not? It'll be…memorable, at least. Right?"

With a laugh, Griff wraps his arm around her shoulders and pulls her into a side hug. "Love you, too, sister."

Well, shit just got interesting, but I'm sure about one thing. I'm not going down without a fight.

15

DYLAN

I've successfully avoided Reeves since last night. To be fair, I've avoided him for a lot longer, but especially since last night. The look in his eyes when I told him I didn't want to pick between him and Everett? I don't know? Maybe I imagined it, but I swear I could feel an iciness in him. And the iciness? It was new, and I didn't like it, which makes zero sense in the big scheme of things.

He's a freaking escort and Everett? He could be...he could be Cinderfella, and maybe Homecoming is his chance to prove it.

"Yo," Finley snaps from the fridge. "Go check on the bacon."

Puffing out my cheeks, I head to the oven and open it, eyeing the sizzling bacon laid out on the cookie sheet. I'm pretty sure I was right when I guessed one of the main reasons the guys invited us to stay here while our house is repaired is so Finley could make her famous Belgian waffles. I, the girl who can't cook for the life of her, am basically a consolation prize.

Exactly like the one my brother turned me into all

156

because I couldn't decide between the guy I kind of like even though it's stupid and the guy who might like me and is a much better fit if he does.

Speaking of… Everett, Griffin, and Reeves amble in from the front door with zero shirts and zero fucks about the lack of said shirts. Not that they should. This is their house. They're allowed to not wear clothing if they feel like it. But damn. It's quite the sight. Well, other than my brother, because, *ew*.

Like a homing beacon, my eyes fall on Reeves as he comes through the doorway. Tan skin. Black basketball shorts. Despite the cold, a sheen of sweat clings to his skin from his morning run with the team.

"Aw, come on," Griffin argues as if he's deep in conversation with the rest of his friends. "She's cute—"

"Nah, she's a walking red flag." Reeves grabs the phone from Griffin's hand and collapses into one of the chairs at the kitchen table. "Let's see what she's working with, shall we?"

I peek at the crowded dining area as the guys hover around Reeves, trying to steal a closer look at whatever's on the phone.

"Wait, wait, wait," Reeves decides. He sets Griffin's phone face down on the dark wood table and grins at his friends. "I'm gonna call it right now. Are you ready? I say, in the ten most recent photos, there will be at least one with food, one with a boat, one where she's traveling, and one at a club— potentially even SeaBird near campus—in a tight-ass dress. You ready?"

"Um, excuse me," Finley chirps. She waves around the waffle batter ladle, causing a string of batter to splat on the granite countertop, but she ignores it. "I think I can speak for me and Dylan when I say this. We're offended."

With a low chuckle, Reeves turns around and faces us,

resting his forearm along the back of his chair, showcasing the veins beneath his olive skin. "For what? For calling out a completely uninteresting girl?"

"How rude," I blurt out.

He tilts his head, surprised by my outburst. "It's *true*," he counters. "There's a difference."

"You don't know she posted all those things," Finley chimes in.

"Ah, but I do."

"No, you don't," I argue.

Pushing to his feet, he scoots out the recently vacated chair and waves his hand toward it. "Take a seat, Pickles. I want to make sure I have your full attention while I prove how well I know the opposite sex."

Part of me wants to tuck my tail between my legs and run out the back door with everyone looking at me. The other part? Well, I don't want to give him the satisfaction of backing down. Not when I already did last night.

With a huff, I steel my courage and march toward him, collapsing into the vacant seat and folding my arms. The scent of sweat and cologne envelops me as Griffin and Everett scoot closer, clearly invested in Reeves' demonstration or...whatever this is.

Leaning over the back of my chair, Reeves cages me in with his long arms as he displays the phone in front of me. He's so close I can feel him. His breath. His warmth. His smooth skin. The stubble on his freaking jaw as it brushes against my temple. I tried convincing myself I'm over-hyping my physical response to the guy. But when I find myself in positions like this, I remember how screwed I really am.

Maybe if I could find my Cinderfella—the *only* other guy who's made me feel this way—I wouldn't be so intrigued by Reeves. Especially when, if I want a healthy relationship with someone, he's literally the exact opposite of who I should be interested in.

And this conversation will prove it, I remind myself. *So, focus.*

"All right, let's do a quick recap, shall we?" Reeves announces. "I'm guessing, out of the next ten photos, there's food, a boat, travel, and a club. Oh, and probably a selfie in the car, too." He bends lower, his warm breath kissing the shell of my ear. "There's always a selfie in the car." I peek up at him from the corner of my eye, finding a devilish smirk I swear is directly connected to my core.

"You ready?" he challenges.

"Just pull up the photos," Everett grits out.

"Exhibit A," Reeves states. He slides his thumb across the screen. "A picture of her at a restaurant. Food." He slides to the next photo, showcasing gorgeous blue water and her arms spread wide as she stands on the bow of a white boat in an orange string bikini. "Boat," he murmurs. Sliding to the next photo, I find Griffin's love interest standing in a vine-yard. "Travel?" Reeves questions.

"We don't know," I argue.

He snorts. "Yeah, okay. Did you see the caption? #ItalyBa-by," he practically moans, doing a valley girl impression to make any California girl proud. When I don't disagree, he adds, "Let's see what's next." Another image shines back at me. "Would you look at that? Another restaurant picture." He slides his thumb across the screen again. The girl has a martini glass in her hand, and she's wrapped in a skimpy red dress with the caption reading, "Drink up, bitches!"

"Hmm," Reeves hums into my ear, causing goosebumps to climb up my neck. "I believe there's our bar or club photo. Am I right, Dyl?"

My teeth dig into the inside of my cheek, but I don't bother confirming what he already knows. *Duh.* Instead, I snap, "Next picture."

His thumb glides across the screen. It's a close-up of her in front of another fancy dish. Food.

"And, uh, what are we still waiting for?" Reeves questions.

Griffin slaps his hands against the wooden table, creating a drum roll as Reeves changes it to the next photo where the girl is sitting in the front seat of a car, her lips squished together as she makes a peace sign with her fingers.

"Aaaand, there it is," Reeves announces. "A selfie in the car." He sets the phone in front of me and leans closer, his lips skating across the edge of my ear. "I rest my case." Then, with his hands raised in the air, he steps away, his chest puffed with pride. "So, as you can see, Griff, she isn't anything special. And she definitely isn't worth asking to Homecoming. She's exactly like the rest of the puck bunnies who want to get in your pants as soon as they find out you play for the LAU Hawks and is, therefore, a walking. Red. Flag."

Puck bunnies. I hate puck bunnies. Not because they're all walking red flags, but because I was raised with flawless Barbies hitting on my brothers and their friends before and after games as soon as they hit puberty. Oh, and let's not forget the ones who chased after my dad and uncle when they played professionally. Yeah, a real joy. Honestly, I'm still not sure how my mom and aunts waved it off so easily.

And here's another one...staring at me from my brother's phone. Predictably gorgeous and annoyingly confident in a way I'll never be able to emulate, let alone pull off. Instead, I'm sweet, innocent Dylan. The little sister who likes to tag along. Always watching and never experiencing. Never being taken seriously. Not after the accident, anyway. And if a girl like her is getting a bad rap, then what does Oliver Reeves think of me?

Leaning back in my chair, I keep my arms folded and

glare at him, way more annoyed than I have any right to be, as he gloats shamelessly.

"I think you're being a superficial asshole," I decide.

His brows jump, but he doesn't look offended. He looks impressed. "Did you just say asshole?"

I rest my elbows on the table, attempting to hide the heat in my cheeks as everyone stares at me.

"Glad to see someone's calling it like it is," Everett interjects dryly.

Reeves' attention shifts to him for a split second but slides back to me. "What about my prediction makes me superficial?"

I should backpedal. I should stop talking altogether. I should—

"Tell me," he pushes.

"You act like you know everything about this girl based on a few photos."

"Do you wanna know what her social media tells me?" he challenges.

I nod.

"It tells me she's so afraid of being herself and standing out that she isn't worth your brother's time or anyone else's for that matter."

"Harsh," Finley calls from behind us.

He smirks back at her. "True."

"Those are a lot of assumptions coming from you," I murmur, again surprising us both. I shouldn't care. I shouldn't push. But I can't help it.

"I'm paid for those assumptions, Dylan."

"Like Hitch."

"Exactly." His smile spreads, and he pulls out the seat across from mine, flipping it around and resting his forearms on the backrest while giving me his full attention.

"Are you always this cocky?" I ask.

"Yes. Are you always this argumentative?"

"Not usually," my brother interrupts, but the bastard looks more amused than confused, and it makes me prickle more.

I open my mouth to defend myself, but Reeves cuts me off. "Let's check out your social media, shall we? See how you compare to the walking red flag."

"Oo, then do me!" Finley calls.

"We already know you'll pass with flying colors," Reeves answers her, playing the girl like a fiddle, and even though I know Finley can see right through it, the girl freaking preens.

"You're not wrong," she sings.

His grin widens. "I'm never wrong." The charisma exuding from across the table makes me want to claw my eyes out as he pulls his phone from his shorts and unlocks it. "What's your handle?"

I give it to him, and he nods, finding my profile in two seconds flat. I can't see what he's looking at, but I don't need to. I know what's there. The pictures and videos and quotes I've posted over the years. Instead, I'm given a front-row seat to Reeves' reaction to them. The tiny divot between his brows. The softening smirk. The subtle movement of his thumb as he scrolls through my profile. Pausing on some posts. Flicking through others.

My chest is tight as I wait for his reaction. His assumption. His declaration the guys will likely grasp as if it's scripture. Well, if they didn't know me, they would, anyway.

"It isn't so easy creating assumptions when you don't have much to go on," I mutter.

The gentle shake of his head fans my nerves as he continues his perusal. "Nah, this tells me plenty."

"And what does it tell you?"

A beat of charged silence passes as his eyes lift from the

screen to pin me in place. "The quote tells me you're thoughtful. The selfie with your best friends tells me you care about your loved ones and aren't afraid to share the spotlight. The no makeup, silly face tells me you're genuine. And the lack of daily posts tells me you care more about experiencing the world around you than proving to others you're experiencing it. This girl?" He leans forward and stretches out his long arms, setting his phone in front of me and showcasing a corny selfie of me from last Halloween when I dressed as a *very* unsexy scarecrow. "This girl's worth dating." He leaves it there, backs away, and stands, heading to the kitchen with a sexier-than-sin swagger. Like he didn't rock my world. Like he didn't make me question whether or not I even care if Everett's my Cinderfella anymore when I have a guy like him asking to take me to Homecoming. Part of me wishes he hadn't. That I wouldn't have to question if I'm crazy for being interested in a guy who's paid to take girls out but is willing to go out with me for free. The other part? Well, I'm seriously regretting agreeing to the whole Dylan's-the-prize bit, and there's nothing I can do about it.

16

DYLAN

This girl's worth dating.

The words circle through my brain. Over and over again as Dr. Broderick stands in front of the classroom, droning on about...well, I have no idea because I haven't heard a word. As soon as Reeves showed up with two coffees, both loaded with sugar and caffeine, I was done for.

"And that will be all for today," Dr. Broderick comments. Chairs scrape against the floor as people stand up, each heading for the exit. I wait for Reeves to do the same, but instead, he waits, kicking his legs out and staring at the side of my face like I'm the most fascinating thing in the world.

Unable to actually acknowledge his attention, I gather my things and stand up, preparing to head to my next class.

When he joins me, I give in and turn to him. "Thanks again for the coffee."

"You're welcome. How'd you like the peanut butter?"

"It was good. Different," I clarify. "But I liked it."

"Sometimes different is good."

"Mm-hmm." I walk out the door and down the stairs to the first floor. He follows me, walking by my side like we're friends. It's…off-putting but kind of nice. Still leaves me on pins and needles, though.

"So, do you buy all of your class partners coffee?" I ask when the silence grows too thick.

"Only the ones I dream about at night."

His smirk tugs at my chest, and I turn away, unsure what to do about it. About him. The guy's so…unperturbed. About anything and everything. And honestly? I guess I'm jealous. That he can be so carefree. So open, yet still respectful. About my boundaries. My surliness. Because let's be honest. I've been far from accommodating, yet here he is. Bringing me coffee.

"How'd you know I'm not allergic to peanut butter?" I ask.

"I texted Finley."

My brows hitch. "You texted Finley?"

"Yeah, of course."

"W-why?"

"Are you kidding me? I need an ally. I would text Ophelia, but she's so distracted with everything, I figured having one closer to home was probably smart."

"You need an ally?"

The same smirk toys with his lips. "When I have a stranger in a mask and a childhood friend you've known your entire life as my competition, then, yeah. Collecting as many allies as I can is a good idea."

Nearly stumbling on the stairs at the mention of, well, everything he said, I grab the railing to keep my balance as he wraps his arm around my waist. "Whoa. You okay?"

I nod. "Uh, yeah." I clear my throat and slip out of his hold. "You don't think Everett's Cinderfella?"

With a scoff, he shakes his head. "Nah."

"Why not?"

"You said your Cinderfella was a good kisser, remember?"

165

He winks. "But, hey. Think what you want. At least I'm willing to show my face. I have that much going for me, right?"

He's right. His pretty face has a lot going for him. I stop myself from checking him out, dropping my empty coffee cup into the trash can as we exit the building. "Is there a reason you wouldn't want to show your face?"

"Other than the unrealistic expectations you set for the poor bastard?" He tosses his arm around my shoulder. "With me, you know exactly what you're getting. Flaws and all."

Peeking up at him, I ask, "And what would I be getting with you?"

"You know, I asked myself the same question," he admits. "At the very least, an experience. And you, my dear Dylan, don't seem like someone who's had many of those."

He's right. I haven't. The question is, are we talking about experiences in general or dating or...the more intimate side of things? My heart picks up its pace, and my palms go sweaty at the idea alone, so I grip the strap of my backpack on my shoulder.

"Have you been to SeaBird yet?" he asks.

I shake my head, grateful for the subject change. "Uh, you're talking about the bar by campus, right?"

He nods.

"Nope, I haven't."

"Well, do you want to?" he prods.

"I can't."

"Why not?"

"I'm under twenty-one, remember?"

His husky laugh rumbles through his chest as he shakes his head. "Shit, I forgot. Do you have a fake ID?"

"Am I supposed to?"

"Aw, come on, Dyl. You gotta have a fake ID. They're a right of passage."

"Sure they are," I mutter.

"Speaking of rights of passage, tell your mom thanks for the Harry Potter marathon invitation."

I freeze. "What?"

With a smirk, he pulls a brown envelope from his back pocket and hands it to me. A black-inked owl is in the corner, and a bold red seal is on the back. Curious, I open the flap and find a slip of paper with the date and time with the location listed is my childhood home. I make a mental note, then hand it back to him.

"Well, apparently, she likes you more than me because I haven't received my invitation yet."

"Yeah, you did." He grins and hands me a matching envelope with my name scrawled across the front.

"You know, you could've given me this one instead of letting me look at yours."

"And see the surprise on your face with how I was personally invited?" He laughs. "I think not."

"Hey, Reeves!" a feminine voice interrupts.

Our heads snap in its direction. A girl with long dark hair and sunglasses sways toward us, and Reeves' head falls forward.

It's strange. Seeing—feeling—the shift in his demeanor. The tightness in his jaw. The exhaustion. The weight.

"Something wrong?" I ask.

"Wait here." Leaving me, he meets the stranger halfway across the grassy hill, and I watch, dumbfounded. I feel like I've seen her before, but I don't know where. Maybe one of my classes or one of Reeves' Game Nights? I'm not sure. My insides twist with jealousy as I watch them. They're too far away for me to hear what's said, but I don't miss the rigidity in Reeves' muscles or the way he squeezes the back of his neck. Like he's uncomfortable. But I can't tell if he's uncomfortable because he thinks I might be watching or if he's uncomfortable because of what she's saying. If only I could read lips. Her hands practically throttle the strap of her dark leather bag as she drops her chin to her chest. Reeves reaches for her, making her lift her head to look at him again.

It feels intimate, and even though I most definitely shouldn't care, I kind of do. He starts slipping off her sunglasses, but she tugs away and shakes her head, so he drops his hands back to his sides. Then he looks at me. And it isn't a glance. It's a full-blown gander. It's weighted and heavy and unsure.

Feeling like I just got caught doing something I most definitely shouldn't—you know, like trying to eavesdrop-slash-stalk a clearly intimate interaction—I tear my attention from his, turn around, and beeline it to my next class. I shouldn't care. I *know* I shouldn't. It's Reeves. He owes me nothing. Like, seriously, nothing. Especially after I brushed off his invitation for Homecoming. And he most definitely should be allowed to talk to a girl without feeling uncomfortable, which I clearly made him feel since he caught me staring at him like a creeper. And honestly? I'm glad I saw him. Glad something could smack some sense into me and confirm one of the main reasons why I didn't say yes to him at Maverick's house. Why it would be really freaking stupid to let my guard down with him.

Heavy footsteps follow as soon as I reach the dark pavement, and the sound mingles with Reeves' low voice. "Thorne! Wait!"

I quicken my pace.

"Seriously, Dylan!" he calls. "Wait for me!"

I don't, but it doesn't matter. Reeves' long strides close the distance in a few short seconds until he jogs beside me. Distracted, I trip over my own shoelace like I'm a freaking third grader and tumble to the ground. My knees hit the pavement with a heavy crash, and a hiss escapes me as my palms scrape against the blacktop.

"Shit." Rolling onto my butt, I assess the damage with a pathetic frown. My palms are angry and red, dotted with black dirt and pebbles, along with little specks of blood as it seeps out of the scraped skin.

Yup. It burns.

Grimacing, Reeves crouches beside me. His touch is gentle as he envelops my wrist and steals a look at my palms. "Damn, Pickles."

"I'm fine."

I try to tug away from him, but he holds firm and leans closer, blowing softly on my superficial wounds. "Gonna have to buy some Band-Aids for my backpack."

"That won't be necessary." I slowly slip out of his hold, and this time, he lets me. Pushing to my feet, I wipe off my jeans with my fingertips in hopes of protecting my scraped palms from any further damage while shoving down my shame for what feels like the billionth time since first meeting Reeves. Without bothering to look at him, I announce, "I should get going. I don't want to be late."

"Uh-huh, I'm sure your sudden rush has nothing to do with me chatting with a cute girl, am I right?"

I hesitate and look down at him still crouching at my feet. "So you do think she's cute."

The same deep, throaty chuckle makes my stomach coil as he stands up, but he doesn't deny it. "Look, I know neither of us owes each other anything. But, on the off chance an itty, bitty, *tiny* piece of you cares that I was talking to a girl, I want to make it clear…it was *only* for work."

"Work," I repeat. "As in, your escort service."

"Not exactly my favorite term, but if you want to call it that, then sure. She has an asshole ex, and—"

"It's none of my business."

"Maybe I want to make it your business."

Tension lines my stomach, and I shake my head. "Reeves…"

"Why don't you call me Oliver?" he asks.

I pull back, surprised. "What?"

"You're one of the only people on campus who knows my first name, but you never call me by it. Why?"

"Why did you tell me your real name in the first place if it's some big secret?" I counter.

"Maybe I want you to feel special."

"And maybe that's the problem."

He frowns. "What do you mean?"

"I mean…if you go out of your way to make every single girl you come in contact with feel special, do any of them?"

With wide eyes, he squeezes the back of his neck, look-ing…impressed? "Well, fuck, Thorne." He smiles. "Way to say it like it is."

"Don't call me Thorne," I remind him.

"Then don't call me Reeves."

"Everyone calls you Reeves."

"You're not everyone."

I lift a shoulder and take a step back. "Could've fooled me."

Turning on my heel, I prepare to make a run for it, but his hand finds my wrist, stopping my retreat.

"What do you need, Reeves?" I ask as I stare over my shoulder, holding his gaze.

"Already told you I'm not a fan of the miscommunication trope."

I look down at his hand keeping me in place. "And?"

"And I want to make something clear to you. It will look like we're hooking up this weekend, but we're not. All right?"

We.

As in Reeves and his…whatever. Client? The word feels

dirty, especially when she clearly needs help, but I can't think of another term to fit. She hired him, and who am I to care? The realization makes my stomach churn more.

But what's worse? The sincerity in his eyes. The gentleness. The concern. Not for him, or even for the girl, but for me. For how it might make me feel to see him with someone. Someone else. Someone who isn't me.

Am I really so transparent?

"Why?" I whisper, hating how I already know the answer but asking it anyway. "Why will it look like you're hooking up with her this weekend when you aren't?"

"Not all damsels need Band-Aids." He brings my hand to his lips and kisses the back softly. "Some require other solutions. We'll talk more later, yeah?"

With a gentle tug, I pull away from him and tuck my hair behind my ear. "I'll see you around, Reeves."

I head into the closest building despite knowing I won't absorb a single freaking word. But even the mindless drivel from my professor is better than wallowing in my own pathetic thoughts.

17
REEVES

Not gonna lie. I kind of want to hit Griffin for setting up this little wager, especially after the way Dylan and I left things earlier this week. I can still see the hurt in her eyes when she saw me talking to Lilah. I fucking hated it. And here I am, expected to win a bet with the odds stacked against me. Everyone knows I'm better at assists than Everett, but when it comes to brute scoring? Yeah, the bastard usually has me beat.

I don't say a word to Everett in the locker room. Sure, I might act like a dick on occasion, but it's not like I hate the guy. And sure, Everett has his head up his ass, pretending like he's some saint for being willing to take Dylan to a dance when we both know I'd willingly take her without the guise of some chivalrous pursuit. But still. The idiot's my teammate. And we're competing against each other for a girl? A girl who's known Everett a hell of a lot longer than she's known me? A girl who's pissed at me for taking a job right in front of her?

Fuck.

This entire competition's bullshit. Everyone knows it, but

I refuse to back down. I stare at Ev across the room as he grabs his stick and slaps his locker closed. He's been especially quiet, and I can't help but wonder if he's thinking about Dylan like I am. If he's ready to cross the line he's drawn in the sand with her. If he thinks it's a good idea.

Griffin steps into my line of sight, blocking Everett with his padded shoulders and a stern look eerily similar to his brother, Jax.

"It's a friendly bet," he reminds me.

"Yeah. One I'm set up to fail," I argue. "You know assists are my strength."

"Yeah, I know." He nods, then drops his voice low. "Just, uh, don't let this get between LAU and winning, all right?"

I scoff, not bothering to hide my frustration. "Wouldn't dream of it."

"Good." He slaps my shoulder pad with his gloved hand. "Because I'm trying to throw you a bone here. If you choose yourself over the team again, I'm not sure I can overlook it. I sure as shit know Everett won't."

Fucking hell.

You'd think they'd have let it go by now. My fuck up. Instead, I wear it like the girl in *The Scarlet Letter* wore her A. What was her name again? I can't remember. All I know is Emma Stone played the part in the remake, *Easy A*, and it was hilarious. But that isn't the point. The point is, I'm being lectured about something I haven't done yet, and it pisses me off. Especially when Griffin arranged this competition for his sister in the first place. But ruffling the asshole's feathers when he holds the key to Dylan is a mistake, and even though I'm as impulsive as fuck, I need to restrain myself.

Jaw tightening, I hold his gaze. "It won't happen."

"Good." He pauses. "For what it's worth, I won't be disappointed if you win the bet."

"And if Everett does?" I quip.

Griffin grins. "Won't be disappointed then, either."

"You know he likes her, right?"

"He's protective of her," Griffin clarifies, though I don't miss the way his amusement dissipates from his blue eyes. "There's a difference."

"Why does he feel the need to protect her from me, but you don't?"

"Guess I have more faith in you than Ev does." He hesitates again and cocks his head. "The question is, do you deserve it?"

I lift one shoulder. "Only time will tell."

He scoffs. "Yeah. Time and today's game. If you haven't figured it out yet, I'm giving you a chance to prove you're not a selfish prick. To me *and* the team."

"And what does it prove to your sister?" I challenge. "That she's expendable?"

With a sigh, he leans even closer, searching for an ounce of privacy in the crowded locker room. "Look, I don't know what's gonna happen on the ice, but I do know Dylan's family's opinion matters to her. It matters a lot. And if I've learned anything about you over the years, it's how you're a resourceful motherfucker. You'll figure out how to make it up to my sister whether or not you win the bet." He hesitates, eyeing me warily. "You're not planning to fuck her over, right?"

The question sizzles beneath my skin, leaving me more exposed and raw than I'd like to admit. The fact he even has to ask it and how I've asked myself the same thing more times than I can count.

But what's worse is knowing I don't have the answer. I don't know. I've screwed up so many things in my life. Is it so unrealistic to think I might add ruining Dylan to the list?

Scratching the side of my jaw, I shove the carousel of

questions a little deeper inside of me and cock my head. "I don't know. Would I fuck her over?"

His eyes narrow as he studies me for a second, then shakes his head. "Nah. I think Mav's right on this front."

"And what's Maverick's stance?"

"You might act like a dick, but you have a nice gooey center somewhere in there if we can get to it. I think he's right."

Coach Sanderson clears his throat from the front of the room, ending our conversation as we give him our full attention. Honestly, I'm grateful for the distraction. For a moment to focus on the game instead of the girl I can't stop thinking about or how I know I hurt her earlier this week.

Coach has been with LAU for decades, and it's starting to show. Leather, olive skin. Bald head. White brows. Broad shoulders and the start of a beer belly despite his years in peak physical condition. I still remember how pissed my dad was when Coach approached me about playing for LAU. How my dad told him to fuck off until Sanderson stood toe-to-toe with the bastard on my doorstep. It was nice. Seeing someone stand up to my dad. Coach is a good guy, and thanks to my history with bad ones, I learned pretty quickly how to tell the two apart. Then again, it's simply who Coach is. Sanderson isn't afraid to face off with *anyone*. The refs. The fans. The opposing team. And if this is his last year—he insists at the start of every season it is—he deserves his players to do the same and blow our opponents out of the water.

After a short pep talk I barely register, Coach tugs on the whistle hanging from his neck, lets it rest on his red polo, and leads us from the locker room and down the tunnel to the rink.

Each player takes the ice when the announcer calls our

jersey number. My attention falls to the stands. I'll never get over this. This feeling. The energy. The adrenaline. It's one of the reasons I started playing in the first place. A way to escape my shitty life and find something...better. Something to distract me. To keep me focused. To give me hope and a way out. It wasn't easy. The equipment alone was expensive as fuck. Well, if you paid for it. I found alternative solutions. Using spare equipment at the rink. Stealing shit. Receiving hand-me-downs from the peewee coaches after they witnessed my raw talent. I was like a stray dog, and for some reason I still don't understand, they let me hang around. Let me practice. Let me catch rides with them to away games. Maybe they knew what was going on in my trailer. Maybe they didn't. But I'll never forget their kindness. Their patience. Their generosity.

When my dad found out about all the things I was doing behind his back while he was either passed out on the couch or at work, he started locking me in my room. When I climbed out the window, he shoved me into the closet instead and barricaded the exit with a dresser for days.

Too bad I got my stubbornness from him, though. By the time I hit fifteen, he had given up, letting me run the streets on my own, only bothering to beat the shit out of me when it was convenient or we crossed paths, which I rarely let happen.

Shaking off the memories, I look around the arena as blown away as the first time I stepped onto the ice. The place is packed with fans, most of whom are already on their feet cheering for the home team. The Hawks. *Me.* Red, black, and white cover the area, along with a dappling of brown and gold for our opposing team, the Bulls. There are so few of them they're barely a blip on my radar. Then again, every-one's a blip on my radar as I search the rows and rows of people for one familiar face.

Where are you, pretty girl?

Then, I find her. Sandwiched between Finley and Ophelia, Dylan's sitting in the red plastic seats with her arms folded and her cheeks painted with LAU's school colors. She looks nervous. Cute, but nervous. Nah, cute isn't the right word. Fucking gorgeous. The only thing missing is her glasses. It's a shame. I hope she doesn't get a headache from being here with her contacts.

When she catches me staring, Dylan sucks her bottom lip between her teeth. I wave, causing the fans close to her to look around to find the girl who's stolen my attention since the moment we met.

She sinks further into her seat and shakes her head in silent warning. It makes me grin harder.

Not one for the spotlight, huh, pretty girl?

Her attention snags on someone behind me, and she smiles. I don't bother turning around to see who the culprit is as Everett lines up beside me.

"You ready for this?" he murmurs.

"Let the best man win," I taunt.

He joins me. "I plan to."

The announcer's voice echoing through the speakers cuts off my response, and I cross my gloves in front of me. "We want to take a few moments to show our appreciation of two key members on LAU's senior roster. Maverick Buchanan, can you please come down here?"

Maverick steps onto the ice, his LAU jersey covering a long-sleeve black shirt and jeans. The crowd stands up, cheering wildly as he smiles at the audience. "Maverick Buchanan is number twenty-three on the Lockwood Ames University hockey team, and we want to thank him for his dedication to his teammates, his fans, and the game we all know and love," the announcer continues. More cheering erupts as the coach strides toward him with a folded lump of fabric in his grasp. "We also want to take a moment to remember Archer Buchanan," the announcer adds over the speakers, and whatever anticipation thrummed through the arena quiets instantly. "This would have been his fourth year with the LAU Hawks, and he's sorely missed by his teammates, his coaches, his family, his friends, and so many more." Coach Sanderson hands Archer's folded jersey and the stack of letters we gathered from the costume party to Maverick, who takes it with reverence. Holding one of my wrists, I let the silence wash over me as I remember my brother. "Your teammates have gathered a few letters for the Buchanan family, and I'm told you'll pass them along to your parents so you can enjoy them in private. But first, we'd like to have a moment of silence." I bow my head, and so does the rest of the team. After a solid thirty seconds, the announcer continues, "May he rest in peace. And now, for the national anthem."

The rest of the pregame business passes in a blur, and I find myself on the ice, ready to start the game.

Squeezing my stick in my gloved palms, I wait for the whistle to blow, then push off. My skates cut through the ice like a hot knife through butter as Hemmings steals the puck from the opposing team's left wing. It darts across the slick surface, barely missing the edge of Cameron's stick before intersecting my path. Dribbling the puck left, right, left, right, I dash around one of the defensemen when another slams me against the glass. With an oomph, the oxygen is forced from my lungs, and I shove the player off me as Griffin steals the puck from between his skates. He races toward the goal and slaps it at the left corner of the net, but it hits the goalie's glove at the last second. The crowd boos, their frustration palpable, as the Bull's goalie passes it to someone on his team. The guy doesn't make it past the red line, and I smash into him, leaving the puck where it is.

"Hey, motherfucker." I grin at the defenseman when the alarm blares throughout the arena.

Everett's stick is raised in the air as he skates around the oval, proving he's the reason for the goal. When his eyes land on me, he grins and raises a finger. "That's one!"

Griffin hits him from behind, celebrating our first point with his best friend as I make my way to the center line. It's for the best. If he kept bragging, I would flip him off and wind up in the penalty box.

Aaaand, here we go.

The rest of the period flies by in a blur, and the Bulls score once, bringing us to a tie at our first break. During the second period, I manage to score a goal, but I'm thrown into the penalty box a few minutes later for high sticking an asshole who checked me into the glass earlier in the game. Cameron joins me within seconds for roughing a player. It's a bullshit call, and the Bulls take full advantage of our time off the ice, scoring thirty-two seconds later.

Fuckers.

Two to two.

Most of the third period stays at a standstill, and now, the clock's winding down. If we don't score soon, we'll head into overtime, and I'm not in the mood. Not when I'm tied with Everett. Not when the Hawks are tied with the Bulls. Not when my date with Dylan's on the line, along with the entire game.

As the timer taunts us from the wall, Everett heads to the middle of the rink, going head-to-head with the Bull's center but flinches at the last second, causing a face-off violation. The ref has us switch places.

With sweat dripping along my temple, I take Ev's spot at the blue line and wait for the referee to drop the puck. My opponent waits for the same thing across from me while the crowd's cheers buzz in my ears, acting like gasoline on my already heightened adrenaline spike. Instead of distracting me, I bask in it. The energy. The applause. The tension.

In a flash, the black biscuit slips from the referee's fingers, and I reel my stick back in preparation. As soon as it hits the ice, I slap the puck off the boards, passing it to Griffin on my right, and he makes a run toward the goal while two defenders race toward him. By some miracle, he's able to get the pass off in time before he's checked against the glass. As he's sandwiched between the two assholes, I take advantage, cycling the puck down the left side of the ice as the clock continues counting down in my periphery, which is when I notice Everett in the perfect position.

If I take the shot toward the Bull's goalie, whose sole focus is on me, I might miss. He could block it. We'll go into sudden death and potentially lose the game. If I pass the puck to Everett, he could make a goal, give the Hawks a win, and take the lead on our bet when we both know there isn't enough time in the third period for me to have another opportunity to match him again. Another heavy dose of adrenaline shoots through my veins, along with the knowledge it's do or die. Now or never. Be a team player or a selfish dick, losing the respect of my teammates or the girl I'm interested in.

I don't have to look at the crowd to know Dylan's watching. To know she's standing, her hands covering her mouth as the seconds wind down on the shot clock.

Seven. Six. Five.

Sometimes it sucks not being a selfish asshole.

Knowing I'll regret it, I wind up, faking out the opposing team, and snap the puck toward a waiting Everett. He scoops it right past an unsuspecting goalie into the bottom corner of the net.

The alarm blares, and I look up at the scoreboard. LAU Hawks 3. BTO Bulls 2. One second on the clock.

I put the team first, and we won.
So why do I feel like I lost?

18

DYLAN

The place is packed. I'm not sure if everyone was invited or if people assumed the guys would want to celebrate LAU's first win of the season, but the entire street is lined bumper to bumper with parked cars. Normally, I wouldn't care—you do you, boo, and all—but since the guys' house is kind of *my* house until my kitchen is fixed, I can't help but feel dejected as I take in the over-crowded street. I've slept like crap lately, thanks to the early morning banging from the construction work next door. Add in the late-night parties, and I feel like I'll never have a full night's rest again.

"Do you think they'll play any games tonight?" Finley wonders aloud as we walk up the street. We borrowed Griffin's car for the game but had to park down the block since we couldn't even pull into our own garage.

"No idea," I answer.

Ophelia went with Maverick to his parents' house after the game. I guess I don't blame her. After the really sweet but also incredibly emotional dedication to Archer, I can only imagine how they feel. I don't doubt they want a quiet night to unwind.

I wish I could have the same thing.

"So, how do you feel about Everett being the winner?" Finley prods.

"I feel like an object."

"Oh, come on. You're not an object. You're a prize."

I give her the side-eye. "Which is basically an object."

"A *shiny* object," she argues. "Besides, as we already discussed, there's a definite possibility Everett's Cinderfella, so it'll be good to test the waters and find out for sure, one way or another."

"And if he isn't the one who kissed me?"

"It's a school dance, Dylan. It's not like you have to marry my brother or anything. Ohmygosh"—she grabs my arm and shakes me—"we could be sisters!"

With a light laugh, I shove her off me and head up the driveway. "You're insane."

"Optimistic," she counters. "There's a difference. Besides, I would be the best freaking sister-in-law in the entire world. Can you imagine how awesome I would treat your kids? I'm basically a ten out of ten."

"Which is why Drew is so lucky to have you."

"And you," she points out. "You are also very lucky to have me."

"Mm-hmm." I bump her shoulder with mine. "You know I love you."

"I love you, too."

"You know, if it doesn't work out with you and Drew or me and Ev, you could always marry Griff," I suggest. "Keep the whole sister vibe going."

"Careful, or I might take you up on it." She grins. "So do we track down Everett and deliver you now, or...?"

"There's the object talk again," I quip. "And no. I don't

know how you sleep in every morning with all the construction going on, but I'm exhausted. All I want to do is take out my contacts and go to sleep."

"But there's a party."

"A party you're welcome to attend all by yourself."

"But what about my wingwoman?" she whines.

"I'm pretty sure you can handle a party without your wingwoman for one evening."

Glowering at me, she argues, "I think you're forgetting one vital piece of the puzzle."

"What piece?"

"You have to make it through the party to get to your sanctuary, remember? It's not like you can sneak through the second-floor window."

From the sidewalk, I stare up at the jam-packed house. The blinds are open, showcasing exactly how much chaos waits for me while the music reverberates from the open front door and across the yard, rattling me to my core.

Steeling my shoulders, I take a deep breath. "It'll be fine."

"Oh, it will?"

"Yes," I decide. "I'm gonna be a big girl, go through the front door, and beeline it to the second floor like a woman on a mission." I yank her closer and press a lip-smacking kiss on her cheek. "Wish me luck."

"Good luck, party pooper."

With a wiggle of my fingers, I trek across the front lawn and walk inside, dodging a couple playing tongue hockey in the entryway. Someone shoves me from behind as I reach the base of the stairs, and I toss a cursory scowl over my shoulder at the asshole who pushed me when my attention catches on someone else across the room.

Reeves.

He's standing beside a girl. The same girl from campus. Her hair is curled, and she's wearing smokey, dark eye makeup, making her look like a freaking goddess. Seriously. She's gorgeous. Reeves spreads his hand along her back and pulls her closer. He whispers something in her ear as her palm slides along his pec. She turns her head and smiles. Not at me. She doesn't even know I exist. No, the smile is for him, but it twists the knife in my back all the same.

I shouldn't care. I know I shouldn't. Especially after tonight's game.

But seeing him with her despite his warning earlier this week? Well, it's the cherry on top of a craptastic day.

Grabbing the railing, I head to my room without a backward glance. Well, technically, it's Griffin's room, but I'm too exhausted to care about the distinction. I push the door open and stop short when the familiar creak of the headboard thumping against the wall mingles with moans. I spot a very naked girl straddling some dude I've never seen before. My heels dig into the ground.

Yup. There are definitely people having sex in the bed.

I take it back. *This* is the cherry on top of my craptastic day.

Perfect.

My backpack is right inside the door, so I grab it, leaving them to their own shenanigans, grateful I was at least able to snag my personal belongings instead of being locked out for the rest of the night without them. The question is, where do I go? If I go downstairs, I'll have to brave the party—and Reeves—and I wasn't kidding when I said I'm exhausted.

Scanning the second floor for a good hiding spot, my eyes wander to Reeves' door. Before I can talk myself out of it, I hold my breath and press my ear to the solid piece of wood, waiting for the moans and groans of someone hooking up inside.

Silence.

Sweet, sweet silence.

With a twist of my wrist, I open the door and close it behind me, refusing to acknowledge how stupid this idea is. At this moment? I don't care. Besides, he's downstairs with his job. I'll be fine. Right?

Sure. Sure, I will.

Unless he decides to hook up with her or something, but hey? Why not add fuel to the fire. After finding my contacts container in my backpack, I take them out and breathe a sigh of relief as I close my eyes. I learned to keep my contacts container and an extra pair of glasses in my backpack after a particularly brutal day in middle school left me curled up in a dark room for days afterward. On nights like tonight, I'm even more grateful for the habit.

Stupid bad eyesight.

And stupid headaches.

At least I don't have one today. That's something, at least.

Once my glasses are in place, I slip off my shoes and shove off the rest of my clothes, adding them to a small pile at the base of the bed. Whoever invented sweats and leggings is officially my hero. I'm pretty sure I have a pair somewhere in my bag from the last time I went to hang out with Ophelia. If I could only find them. Standing in my bra and underwear, I search my bag for some comfy clothes when the door opens behind me.

With a pathetic screech, I cover my body with my hands and turn around, finding a shocked Reeves.

He slips inside and closes the door, resting his back against it. "If I knew you were in here, I would've come up sooner."

"Uh, excuse me. Go away."

"My room, my rules, and I think I'll stay." His eyes roll over my body, leaving my skin heated and my breathing shallow.

"Can you not look?" I snap. Remembering my manners, I add, *"Please?"*

He closes his eyes but doesn't bother hiding his smirk as he waits for me to get dressed with his back against the door, his feet spread wide, and his thumbs tucked in the front pockets of his fitted jeans. I still don't get it. How he can look so freaking attractive yet casual and confident and annoyingly perfect all at the same time. The jeans? The henley? The slight lift of his lips and tilt of his head. Like...who looks like this?

Annoyance simmers in my veins, and I grind out, "It isn't funny," as I search my bag—again—for my sweats. Unfortunately, all I find is the hoodie Reeves gave me in class a couple weeks ago.

Fan-freaking-tastic.

I wear it anytime he isn't around. It's so soft and comfortable and warm. I know it's stupid, but I can't help it.

Okay, maybe I can. But admitting my weird obsession with a hand-me-down hoodie to myself is one thing. Giving Reeves a front-row seat to said obsession is entirely different, especially when he willingly passed the puck to Everett during tonight's game instead of taking the shot himself. It shouldn't have stung, and it didn't, but it definitely proved where his priorities lie, and they aren't with me. I wouldn't want him to throw away the game to prove his interest or whatever, but—gah!

Stop. Being. Irrational.

Besides, I'm nothing more than his friend's little sister and fellow classmate. Hockey is his future. His everything, if he's anything like my brothers and Ev.

So, why do I care?

"You know, usually when I'm around a half-naked girl, I like to keep my eyes open, but this is fun. Kinky." Reeves' smile grows, and I fumble with his maroon sweatshirt.

Finally sliding it over my body, I cover my ass with a quick tug on the hem, then fold my arms. "You, uh, you can open your eyes."

When he does, they find me instantly. A heady dose of amusement and interest swirls in their depths, but concern replaces it right away. "You okay?"

"Uh, yeah." I try to lean against the bed, but the back of my thighs misses the edge entirely. I lose my balance, almost landing flat on my ass, when a pair of strong hands latch onto my biceps, keeping me in place.

"Whoa, there." Reeves' brows crease. "You sure you're all right?"

"Yup, just peachy."

"Liar."

Hating how easily he reads me, I clear my throat and shrug out of his hold. "I'm tired, is all."

He nods slowly, but the divot between his brows deepens as he takes me in.

"Seriously, I'm fine," I defend. "It's just, with the construction workers coming so early, Finley being a sleep talker, and the late-night parties, it's been hard to get any real sleep."

"Sleep," he repeats.

"Yup. Sleep."

His eyes trail down my body. "Those your pajamas?"

I look down at his worn hoodie swallowing me whole. "It was all I had in my bag, so…"

"I like it."

"I'll give it back tomorrow."

"Keep it."

"It's yours."

"I already told you how much I like seeing you in my clothes."

My mouth goes dry as he stares down at me. A spark of

amusement and curiosity ripples in his warm brown eyes and makes me squirm.

"What?" I ask.

"I'm wondering if there's a reason you're standing in my room half-naked."

"Someone was using mine, er, Griffin's," I correct, "as their own personal thumping ground, so..."

"Thumping ground?"

"You know, thump, thump." I thrust my hips forward, belatedly realizing I most definitely demonstrated the movement as if he needed a visual in the first place. My eyes squeeze shut, and I pray for the ground to put me out of my misery and swallow me. "Please scrub the image from your brain."

"Nah, I liked it." A deep chuckle makes its way up his chest. "I'm glad you're here."

"Well, since I didn't feel like battling the party downstairs, and your room was the only one available up here, I figured..."

"You'd crash on my bed?"

"Well, it was the plan until you walked in on me," I mutter. "Never said it was a smart one, but since you're here, you probably need the bed or the room for privacy or whatever."

"You saw us," he assumes.

My head bobs up and down as jealousy licks at my insides, leaving me raw and even more exhausted than when I walked into the house.

His touch is gentle as he lifts my chin, demanding my full attention. "She's a job, remember?"

The words slip past his lips, adding weight to the stone in my gut. "You mentioned that."

"Her ex was supposed to show, and she hired me to prove she'd moved on. When one of my sources said he was at

SeaBird instead, I called it an early night and was about to come looking for you."

"Got it." I nod again, feeling like a bobblehead. His grasp on my chin disappears, but the heat from his touch lingers, making me miss it even though I have no right to. Shaking off the feeling, I bend down and pick up my backpack from the ground, avoiding him at all costs. "Obviously, there's no need to come looking for me anymore. But, uh, thanks for letting me use your room and—"

He shifts in front of me. "Where are you going?"

"Uh…"

Anywhere but here?

I bite the inside of my cheek. "I can stay in Everett's—"

"Gonna stop you right there." His hand envelops mine before he steals my backpack from my fingers. "You should stay."

"Reeves, I'm fine."

"Nah. I think I owe you at least that much, don't you?"

"You don't owe me anything."

He sets the backpack on the ground, grabs one of the hoodie strings, and softly tugs on it. "I think I do."

"Seriously, Reeves—"

"I want to apologize."

I'd laugh if his words weren't so ludicrous.

Exasperated, I ask, "For what?"

"For not taking the shot."

My brows bunch, and my pulse throbs. "What?"

"For passing to Everett instead of taking the shot," he clarifies.

Fisting the sleeves of the stolen hoodie into my palms, I fold my arms. "It's, uh, it's not a big deal."

"For me, it is."

"If it was a big deal, why did you pass?" I shake my head. "Actually, don't answer. It doesn't matter anyway."

"Can I ask you something?"

It's a weighted question, and even though I know I should say no so I can end this conversation as quickly as possible and get the hell out of here, I find myself nodding.

Slowly, he leans closer, crowding me against the edge of the bed until I'll either tumble onto it or push him away, and for some reason I can't explain, I don't want to do either. "Why'd you say no when I asked you to Homecoming?"

"I didn't—"

"You kind of did," he counters. "The real question is, did you reject me because you didn't want to hurt Everett's feelings or because you actually like the bastard? Or is it because you want to hold out for your Cinderfella?"

My hand finds his chest, and I rest it over his heart, hoping to push him away, but I hesitate as his questions filter through me. The heat from his flesh seeps out from the thin fabric of his shirt, making me want to curl into him to steal his warmth. I won't. I'm not an idiot. But a girl can dream, can't she? Besides, talking about one or multiple other men while standing in nothing but a hoodie in a guy's room has to be dangerous, doesn't it?

I run my tongue along the edge of my bottom lip and whisper, "Who says Everett isn't Cinderfella?"

His chuckle is almost dark and twisted as he lifts my chin again, but instead of finding warmth in his gaze, there's a glint of iciness. It makes me want to retreat. To take back whatever I said because it's clearly cut him in a way I never intended.

"Okay, I'll bite," he mutters. "Let's say it's Everett, and he actually has a chance of living up to your unrealistic expectations based on a single interaction. You aren't pissed he's kept it from you?"

I nibble my bottom lip, unsure what to say or even if I have a strong opinion on the matter. I mean, yeah. It's kind of a dick thing to do. We grew up together, and he kisses me out of the blue and doesn't say anything when there were more than a handful of girls he could've pursued that night instead? But it's Everett. Kind Everett. Bossy Everett. Respectful Everett. It makes sense why he wouldn't want to rock the boat unless his feelings meant something...more. And the fact he asked me to Homecoming? It has to mean something. Doesn't it?

"No answer, Pickles?" Reeves prods.

"Maybe he's waiting..."

"For what?"

"I don't know?" I lift my shoulder, causing the neck hole of Reeves' hoodie to slip and expose it, but I don't move it back into place. I should, but I like the way his eyes shoot to the bare skin, practically caressing me. "Maybe he wants to make a grand gesture or something."

The same dark chuckle vibrates up his corded throat. "A grand gesture?"

"It's Finley's theory, not mine."

"Finley's watched one too many fairytales."

"Is there something wrong with fairytales?" I whisper.

"Not at all. And chemistry's chemistry, right?"

I hesitate, digging my teeth into the edge of my bottom lip. "Yes?"

"And you felt it with your Cinderfella."

"Yes," I repeat, more resolute.

"Who you think is Everett," he adds.

Again, I lift my shoulder in a shrug. "It's only a theory."

He nods. "Let me ask you this... Do you think it's possible to feel chemistry with more than one person?"

"Well, since I'm pretty freaking inexperienced, I don't think I have enough data to prove otherwise."

His mouth lifts. "Shall we do an experiment?"

"What kind of experiment?" As soon as words leave my

mouth, I know it's a mistake. I know exactly what kind of experiment he plans to implement. A shot of adrenaline races down my spine as he reaches for my hips and tugs me closer, bunching the thick fabric in his hands until cool air hits my ass cheeks and the back of my thighs. It reminds me of the rink when he grabbed me the same way.

"Do you feel it yet?" he whispers.

My stomach flip-flops, and my cheeks warm as I feel the steady beat of his heart against my palm. "Feel what?"

His mouth ticks up, and his gaze drops to my mouth. "Chemistry."

My breathing is shallow as I wait. For what, I'm not sure. Actually, that's a lie. I know exactly what I'm waiting for. I'm waiting for him to kiss me. To put his money where his mouth is and prove his point. To prove I'm capable of feeling something for more than one person. Someone without a mask. Someone I know. Someone like him. An enigma who gets under my skin. And is kind to me. And is blatantly interested in me. And is unlike anyone I've ever met in my entire life.

It's as if I'm in a black hole. As if, with every tiny millimeter of space closing between us, time moves differently. Slowing down, yet speeding up as he moves closer and closer. His eyes are locked on mine, a silent question shining back at me, daring me to tell him to stop, begging me to let him continue.

"For science," I breathe out.

The corners of his eyes crinkle. "Science. Sure."

And when his lips brush against mine softly, carefully, it's as explosive as the kiss I shared with Cinderfella. I surrender to the surrealness of this moment. My eyelids feel heavy, and I close them, savoring the kiss while analyzing every tingle. Every taste. It's confusing and confirming and mind-muddling and more addictive than any kiss has a right to be.

Spreading my fingers along his chest, I soak in his warmth as he tilts his head and opens his mouth. Not a lot. Hell, if I hadn't been so focused, I wouldn't have even noticed. The slight spread of his lips. The invitation. The dare.

I could push this further. I could kiss him deeper. I could take control when I've *never* taken control. But if I do...what then?

He dates girls for a freaking job.

Is he Hitching me right now?

Is he proving a point, or does he *want* to be kissing me?

It's confusing and conflicting and...

I pull away slightly, letting out a slow, barely controlled breath. "I think you proved your point."

"Nah, not yet." He grabs the side of my face and pulls me into him again, nipping at my bottom lip. When he deepens the kiss, my toes curl as his tongue slides along the seam of my mouth, eliciting a moan from me while I bask in the not-so-innocent contact.

Fucking hell.

Slowly, his hands trail down my body. He grips the backs of my thighs and tugs me against him, letting me feel the ridge of his cock through his jeans and against my bare abdomen. I'm not sure when the thick fabric of his hoodie rode up, but it has, and it's adding gasoline to the fire in my already throbbing core.

A kiss. One freaking kiss. And what do I do? I melt like a stick of butter in a hot pan.

Ripping his lips from mine, he presses his forehead against my bare shoulder and breathes me in deep.

"*Now*, I've proved my point." The words are muffled against the thick material hanging off my shoulder. "If that isn't chemistry, I don't know what is, Thorne."

"Yeah." His hair tickles the underside of my jaw as my

head bobs up and down, the world still spinning around me. "Yeah, it was…"

"Have you picked your dress yet?" he rasps.

I blink, attempting to convince my brain to work properly. "My dress?"

"For Homecoming."

"Oh." I shake my head. "No. I haven't."

"Wear something black, will you?"

"What?"

Lifting his head from my shoulder, he stares down at me. "Wear something black."

"Why?"

"Because I hate black."

My mind still reeling from our kiss, I ask, "You want me to wear your least favorite color?"

With a slow nod, he squeezes the backs of my thighs right beneath my ass one more time like he's memorizing the feel of my curves. I hate what it does to both of us. The way it makes his dick twitch against my stomach. The way it makes my knees weak and my body flush.

"I-I don't understand," I admit, caught between reeling from possibly the best kiss of my life with his hands still on me and a conversation about dresses when in this moment? I seriously don't give a shit.

"I'm not sure I'll be able to keep my hands to myself if you're in anything different," he explains. Letting me go, his fingers find the edge of my glasses. He drags them slowly from the glass along the frames to tuck my hair behind my ear. "Especially this color."

"What color?"

"Aquamarine," he murmurs. "Fucking hell, Dylan. It might be my new favorite." He drops his hand to his side. "But a bet's a bet. And since you're still hung up on your Cinderfella…" He grows quiet, and I swear he's about to kiss me again.

Shit, I can feel it from the top of my head to the tips of my freaking bare toes. I lift my chin, waiting for him to put me out of my misery, and I think he might.

Cinderfella, who?

"Hey, Reeves! You in here?" a girl calls through the door.

I jerk at the sound, the foreign voice acting like a gavel, solidifying every single reason why kissing Reeves again is not only a bad idea but a freaking terrible one.

"Thanks for the, uh, the demonstration." I pat his chest, then slip out from where he'd pinned me to the edge of the bed. "And for letting me hide out in your room. I'll be sure I'm out of here by the time you come to bed."

"Well, if that wasn't the most polite way of saying fuck off, I don't know what is." He smiles, but it doesn't reach his eyes. Still facing me, he steps back toward the door and dips his chin. "And don't worry about me coming to bed. I'll find somewhere else to sleep tonight."

I want to tell him he shouldn't bother, but my mouth stays closed as he turns to leave, then spins right back around, snapping his fingers.

"Do you sleep better in the dark?"

My lips turn down, and I tilt my head. "Don't most people sleep better in the dark?"

"Depends on their childhood trauma," he quips. "Do you want me to unplug the night-light?"

"You have a night-light?"

"Told you I hate black," he reminds me without an ounce of shame. Like it's normal for an adult male to sleep with a night-light and hate the color black so much even a dark room is a no-go.

Right. Trauma.

With a gentle shake of my head, I murmur, "I'll be fine. The, uh, the night-light can…stay."

"All right." He sighs. "See you around, Dylan."

He turns on his heel again, and this time, he leaves, but for some reason I genuinely don't understand, all I'm left with is a lump of...regret? Resignation? Confusion? Dammit, I'm a muddled mess, and I really don't want to know why.

I stare at the door separating me from the outside world and bunch the sleeves of his hoodie in my palms. "See you around, Reeves."

19

DYLAN

It's weird. Shopping for dresses. And even though I found at least six Finley and Ophelia swear look incredible on me, I couldn't help but settle on a silky, muted aquamarine dress with spaghetti straps and a high slit reaching mid-thigh. It's sexy and bold and makes me feel like an imposter in my own skin.

A stupid imposter.

Because who in their right mind would choose the color suggested by a guy who isn't their date for the evening?

Me. I would.

Idiot.

Because despite Reeves' job, despite the possibility of Everett being Cinderfella, despite the bet and how I agreed to be a pawn, I cannot stop thinking about the kiss.

That *freaking* kiss with Oliver Reeves.

So, here I am, kind of, sort of getting ready for a guy who isn't even my date.

It's official. I've reached a new level of low even for me, and that's saying something.

Finley recruited her older half-sister, Hazel, to do our

hair and makeup since she's a professional makeup artist. I'm not gonna lie. I almost look hot, which is strange because, until tonight, I didn't even think it was possible to transform my girl-next-door looks into a vixen. Hazel officially blew my expectations out of the water.

Ophelia looks gorgeous in a sleek red dress, and Finley looks like a full-blown supermodel in her shimmery gold ensemble, her dark, straight hair cascading down her back in a sheet of black silk.

It'd be more romantic for everyone if we weren't all staying under the same roof, but thanks to the burned kitchen next door, here we are, squished into the bathroom as the guys hang out on the main floor.

Drew flew in for Homecoming and is hanging out in the family room while the rest of us finish getting ready. When we enter the main area, I wait for his jaw to hit the floor from how hot his girlfriend is, but he's too busy staring at whatever's on his screen to notice.

Griffin, however, can't take his blue eyes off her as she walks down the stairs. My brows cave when I notice. Is there longing in those swirly depths? Or is it nothing more than casual interest? Like a person noting the weather? It's not like my brother's blind. Finley's gorgeous. She's always been gorgeous in a confident, unapologetic way I've always envied. He'd be a fool *not* to notice her, right? But this look? I don't know, it feels...different. Then again, I know my brother pretty freaking well, and I also know he cares about his friendship with Everett more than almost anything. And Everett? Well, I think we all agree he's a bit on the overprotective side. Seeing his little sister with his best friend? The guy's head would explode, and there's no way Griff would jeopardize anything with Ev over a girl who's head over heels in love with her boyfriend.

No way.

Feeling a little more confident, I continue my path toward the kitchen while an oblivious Finley ignores Griffin and heads straight toward her boyfriend. "I believe now is the time you tell me how amazing I look," she teases.

Drew's head snaps up, and his eyes widen. "Damn, Fin. You look…"

"I know, right?" She gives him a coy smile and slides onto his lap, kissing him without giving a shit who sees as the rest of us enter the room.

Finley let me borrow one of her clutches, so I grab it from the kitchen counter, stuffing my phone into it while Ophelia ignores the makeout session on the couch, heading straight for Maverick. He stands from the kitchen table and tugs her to him, whispering something against the shell of her ear. A sad smile spreads across her face.

Giving them privacy, I clear my throat and turn to Griffin and Everett, surprised to find Reeves missing. I mean, I guess I knew there was a possibility he wouldn't be here, but a tiny piece of me hoped I'd see him.

Not. Your. Date.

Shoving aside the thoughts about how good Reeves would probably look in a suit, I take in my brother and his best friend.

Damn. Even I can agree they look like a couple of models in their fitted suits. Well, if Everett didn't have the face of a father changing a dirty diaper. His nose is scrunched, and he looks like he took a shot of lemon juice as he stares at Finley and Drew on the couch.

Hoping to distract him, I stride his way and grab his wrist, shaking him playfully. "Hey, Ev."

He tears his attention from the couch and looks at me, his eyes softening. "Hey, Dylan." Hesitation clogs his throat, and he steps back, his attention flicking over me quickly. "You look…"

"Don't finish your sentence," I beg. Memories of my millionth conversation with Finley about Cinderfella's true identity swirl in my brain like a bad song, especially after my kiss with Reeves a few nights ago. And it's weird. Not knowing what I want anymore. Who I want. If I even have a say in the matter. I tuck my wavy hair behind my ear, drag it over my bare shoulder, and turn to Griffin. "Hey, big brother."

"Hey, baby sister," he returns. "I like your dress."

"Thanks." I smooth out the silky fabric, then reach for the lapel of his suit and tug softly. "You don't look so bad your-self. Where's your date?"

"We're picking her up on the way."

"Did you convince Reeves to stalk her social media before asking her?" I quip.

"Yeah, until it bit me in the ass." He grins shamelessly. "Big surprise. She failed."

"Of course she did."

"Yet, you passed with flying colors," Griff reminds me.

"It's a modern-day miracle." I glance around both of them, unable to help myself or my stupid curiosity, as I search for the devil himself.

"Reeves is meeting us at the dance," Griffin adds, reading my mind.

"Oh." I nod. "Great. Did he find a date?"

"He's probably going with a client," Everett interjects.

Casting his friend a warning, Griffin clears his throat and tugs at his pressed white button-up sleeve from beneath his black suit. "I don't think he asked anyone else. But my date's waiting, so we should get going."

"Totally agree." Finley jumps to her feet and tugs Drew with her. "Besides, we need to make time for pictures with everyone, so hustle up, guys. Let's go get Griffin's date."

A limo is waiting for us outside. And after we all climb in, we're off.

~

WE'RE LATE. OR AT LEAST LATER THAN EVERYONE EXPECTED. Finley had us stop at a pretty photo spot—her words, not mine—and made us pose for a solid twenty minutes until Everett pitched a fit, saying he was done taking pictures. Now, here we are.

I've never been to a college dance. Actually, I've only been to one dance. Period. And it was pretty freaking miserable. I practically face-planted at the entrance, spilled punch all over my date, and ended the night with an awkward handshake without any intention of ever facing the guy again. Yeah, it was a real treat.

At least I'm here with Everett. He might be bossy and controlling, but he's known me for so long I don't feel *un*comfortable around him. Hell, I'm almost excited. None of the guys have ever been to a college dance. And even now, when I know they're all inwardly moaning and groaning about attending tonight's shindig when they'd rather be hosting a Game Night at their place, it's kind of cute seeing them put on a brave face all so Maverick can make Ophelia's dreams come true and right the wrongs from his past.

Actually, it's really cute.

And their dates? Well, who wouldn't want to get all dressed up and be on the arm of one of LAU's finest bachelors? It didn't hurt ticket sales for the dance when word started getting around that most of LAU's hockey team would be attending, and damn. I don't know how busy these dances usually are, but this? This is kind of crazy.

Whoever planned Homecoming picked an excellent location. It's an old library, reminding me of the one in *Beauty and the Beast.* With his hand on my lower back, Everett guides me toward the entrance. Ahead of us is a massive stone building with heavy oak doors propped open and a long, thick maroon rug laid out, leading to a large open corridor. It reminds me of a castle or something. Dark and rich oak accents. Marble floors. Crazy high ceilings. Chandeliers hung overhead. The warm, almost cozy light gives me hope I won't wind up with a headache by midnight in spite of the thumping music, and my shoulders relax as I take it all in.

"Yo, Reeves!" Maverick calls from the front of the group.

My heart jumps as I search the open space despite my best effort to appear unaffected by a guy who *isn't* my date. But I can't help it. The last time I had any one-on-one time with Reeves was in his room when he kissed me. I can't believe he kissed me. Even so, it didn't necessarily mean anything. He was proving a point, and boy, did he ever prove it. Chemistry is...chemistry, and with Reeves? I felt it in spades. The problem is, it's his literal job to make a girl feel special, and here I go, falling for it after one freaking kiss. At least with the masked guy from the party, I knew it wasn't his job to make girls feel seen and appreciated. Reeves? Well, it's messing with my head.

Peeking around Maverick's massive frame, I spot Reeves passing a marble pillar. As he strides toward us, people part like the Red Sea. It's fascinating to watch. Like maybe, just maybe, I'm not the only one affected by his presence. The lights are dim, but the mischief in his eyes and his wide grin are on full display, causing my stomach to tighten with anticipation. He's already lost his suit jacket, and his sleeves are rolled up to the crooks of his elbows, leaving his muscular forearms entirely visible. The top button of his dress shirt is undone, too, and his tie is loose, making the guy look so effortlessly sexy, it should be a sin.

I've avoided him since the kiss. Since the moment I realized the chemistry I thought I felt for the guy was nothing but a drop in the bucket, turning my attraction to Oliver Reeves into a full-blown nuclear bomb capable of exploding at any second.

When he reaches us, Reeves tugs Maverick into a hug and slaps his back. Grabbing Ophelia, he spins her around like she's a princess. Her laughter echoes through the massive room, mingling with the music and the clink of glasses filled with likely-spiked punch from the banquet tables on my left. She's let go a second later and replaced with an amused Finley. With a final spin, Reeves releases her, then lifts his chin at Drew in a silent hello while I stay glued to Everett's side.

"Hey, Brittany," Reeves greets Griffin's date.

"Hey, you." She gives him a friendly side hug and turns back to my brother. "I believe you promised me a dance."

"I did, didn't I." Griffin offers her his arm, and they head to the dance floor without a backward glance.

Then, Reeves' eyes are on me. His smile softens as his gaze rolls over my dress. Well, me *in* my dress. The spark in his eyes when he realizes I most definitely am not wearing black like he requested tugs at my insides when Everett steps in front of me, blocking most of my body from Reeves' view.

"Hey, man. Where's your date?" Everett asks. The question is tense. Forced.

"I decided to go stag." He dips to the left and finds my stare. "Hey, Dylan."

"Hi."

"I like your dress."

"Thanks." I look down and smooth out the front while seriously second-guessing my bold decision to wear it in the first place.

"It's colorful," he notes.

Peeking up at him, I lie, "It's all I could find."

His mouth quirks. "Guess it's my lucky day, then."

"Drinks?" Everett interrupts.

My attention snaps from Reeves to Ev as he turns around and faces me. "Uh, sure?"

"Awesome."

"I'll have one, too," Reeves calls from behind him.

Everett's eyes narrow as he, once again, puts himself between me and Reeves and faces him. "I'm not your waiter."

"Yet you delivered the perfect snack." Reeves winks at me. Turning back to the rest of the group, he announces, "I snagged a table. You guys wanna come claim it with me?"

"Lead the way," Mav returns.

Everett's fingers find mine as we follow our party, and it's...strange. We've never held hands before, and I can't help but wonder why? Why now? Is it because he's actually making a move, and Finley's right about Cinderfella's true identity? Or is it because he feels the need to stake a claim since Reeves is here? And why do I care? Why do I feel like I'm being torn in two? Do I like the feel of my hand in his? Do I *want* to hold hands with him? Do I feel the same spark I did with Cinderfella *and* Reeves? It's stupid. I should know, but I...don't.

We weave between people, following Reeves to the edge of a ginormous room, complete with a stage and live band playing a love ballad. It's romantic and beautiful and so over the top I can't help but take it all in with a smile. Once we find the table, Maverick and Drew disappear onto the dance floor with their dates, and I'm left witnessing a staredown for the record books.

Well, this isn't awkward at all.

After a moment, Everett clears his throat. "Dylan...I don't suppose..." He motions to the dance floor, and I grimace as memories of the last time I danced rise to the surface. It was bad. Like really bad. Like *America's Funniest Home Videos*, but you're the main character bad.

"Don't look so excited, Dylan," Reeves chimes in.

Ignoring him, I turn back to Everett and grimace. "I think I need the drink you mentioned first."

He smiles. "I got it."

"Awesome, thanks."

The same smile hardens as he gives Reeves a dark look. "Reeves..."

"Yeah, yeah. I'm aware of who she came with, Ev. No need to piss on her. You can lower your leg."

"Thanks," Everett grunts, though he doesn't exactly look convinced. Then again, neither am I. Not when it comes to Reeves. If I've learned anything about him over the past little while, it's he does whatever he wants. Period. And for some reason I can't understand, he wants me. The question is, is it because he likes me, or is it because he enjoys pissing off Everett? And honestly? I have no idea.

With a deep breath, I slide into the chair closest to the back wall and rest my elbows on the table, unsure what to do now that I'm actually here and my date is on a mission to find me something to drink. Part of me wonders how much the school bothers keeping the alcohol locked up at events like this. The other part? Well, one might say I'm well aware of how creative college students are when it comes to sneaking around and getting the things they want, especially when half the student body is already legal.

The legs from the closest chair scrape against the polished marble floor as Reeves spins it around and straddles it, resting his corded forearms on the backrest while pinning me with a stare I can feel from the top of my head to the tips of my toes.

"Can I help you?" I ask.

"I like the dress."

"So you mentioned."

"Do you dance?"

"Not when I'm sober."

His laugh is warm. "You look beautiful, you know."

I gulp. "Thank you?"

"Is that a question?" he teases.

"I'm, uh, I'm not sure. I'm not exactly great at taking compliments."

"Shocker. And don't get me wrong. You look gorgeous. But I think I miss the glasses."

I snort and lift my hand as if to touch the frames despite knowing they're absent tonight. "Of course you do."

"What? They're cute!"

"Mm-hmm," I hum, tearing my attention from those dangerous dark eyes and choosing to focus on the dance floor instead. Couples are paired together, their bodies pressed close, each of them swaying to a classic Broken Vows song. It's…kind of adorable.

"So, do you want to dance?" Reeves prods.

"Haven't had my drink yet," I remind him. "And even if I had, you're not my date, remember? You don't need to…" I wave my hand around. "You know. Babysit me or whatever."

"You hardly need babysitting, Dylan."

"Funny," I mutter.

"Why? Because it's Everett's favorite pastime with you?" he challenges.

My eyes snap to his. "Everett's protective of everyone."

"Yet his sister's on the dance floor, and you're sitting here waiting for him to come back."

"His sister is harder to push around," I mutter under my breath, well aware of how it paints me in the process. Honestly, I'm jealous of Finley. How she's confident. How she isn't afraid to speak her mind or put her brother—or anyone else for that matter—in their place. But I hate confrontation. I hate disappointing people. I hate causing friction or drama or...anything, really. Is it wrong to want to keep the peace, even if it means biting your tongue or going with the flow when it's moving in the opposite direction you want every once in a while?

Hearing my unspoken self-deprecation and how close it hits to home, Reeves leans closer. "Tell me something. Are you still thinking about our little experiment in my room the other day?"

Heat floods in my lower stomach, and my fingers itch to touch my lips, the memory of his kiss branded into me, but I keep my hands fisted instead. "Why would I?"

"Because you couldn't stop thinking about the one you shared with your masked wolf at the costume party," he replies. "I guess I'm trying to gauge if ours is on the same level." He brushes his finger against mine, and I peek up at him.

"No comment."

"Not an answer," he murmurs. "Let me ask you this. What made your kiss with Cinderfella so special? Is it because you like the mystery? The chase? Is it why you keep me at arm's length?"

"I don't—"

"Do you still think Everett's your Cinderfella?"

With a quiet huff, I face him fully. "You're full of questions tonight, aren't you?"

"Guess my mind's been busy lately. Normally, I'd distract myself with a solid fuck, but since the girl I want is hung up on a guy who isn't real—"

"You're saying I imagined the kiss at the costume party?" I counter.

"I'm saying you've built up unrealistic expectations for a guy you don't know. No wonder he hasn't come forward."

"The night's still young," I whisper.

He leans back in his chair, putting much-needed space between us. "So you *do* think Everett's your Cinderfella, and this is his bullshit attempt at wooing you."

"Wooing me?" I snort. "What are we? In the fifteenth century?"

"You're the one who wants the fairytale."

"I think Everett won the bet fair and square, thanks to you passing him the puck."

"Never gonna let me live it down, are you?" He leans even closer and rubs his hands together. Not in some weird, villainous, muah-ha-ha type of way, but more like he's intrigued. Really intrigued. By me.

"*And*," I continue, ignoring his interruption, attempting to focus on our actual conversation instead of the way my stomach fills with butterflies anytime he even looks at me. "Since Everett's my date for the evening, I should be polite and give him a real chance."

"The color of your dress says otherwise." His hot gaze slides down my body and snaps back to my face. "Told you aquamarine's my favorite."

"Happy coincidence," I volley back at him.

He chuckles. "Sure, it is. Let's say Ev isn't your Cinderfella. What then?"

"Then, I have a laid-back evening with a friend."

"A friend." His expression sours. "Your group has always been pretty tight-knit. Makes it hard for newcomers to find a place."

"Seems like you're doing an okay job so far," I point out.

"Depends on the circle. Getting close to you, however, feels like a bad visit to the dentist, thanks to your date for the evening."

"Really? This again?"

"Just trying to piece together a few things." He leans closer. "Like Everett's obsession with you."

I roll my eyes. "He likes looking out for me."

"Why?"

"Because we have history."

His gaze narrows as he pieces together a puzzle I didn't realize I laid out for him.

"History you don't want to share with me," he concludes. "What are you hiding?"

"Nothing."

"You're a terrible liar, Dylan."

"You know, I think you pointed it out a time or two," I tell him.

"Is it about the headaches?"

Oxygen stalls in my lungs, but I force it out in a careful, controlled breath. "What about my headaches?"

"Anytime Everett hears you bring them up, he turns defensive."

Lips bunching, I lean back in my seat and fold my arms, studying the man beside me through thin slits. "You're way too perceptive for your own good. You know that, right?"

He smirks. "I like to think it's one of my best traits."

"Depends on who you ask."

"So, what happened?" he pushes.

"It was an accident."

"Figured as much. Everett wouldn't hurt a fly. Not on purpose. Unless I was the fly and you were in the room. Then I think he'd be okay pulling out the swatter."

"Dylan." A glass is set in front of me, and I look up, finding a very restrained Everett staring down at me.

Shit.

"Oh. Hi," I murmur.

His chin dips as he lowers into the seat on my opposite side. "What were you guys talking about?"

"Nothing, really," I start. "Will you dance with me?"

"You don't dance," he reminds me.

"Normally, you're totally right, but at this moment, I'm pretty sure we could use the opportunity to cut a rug, don't you think?"

"Cut a rug?" Reeves snorts. "You're cute when you're awkward, Dylan."

I glare at him, then stand up, and Everett does the same. Linking my arm through his, I urge him to take me to the dance floor while ignoring a curious Reeves still sitting at the table. By some miracle, Everett gives in and humors me. We walk to the dance floor, and when we reach the center, I look up at him, waiting for him to pull me closer. To start dancing with me. Instead, he stands there, his hands flexing.

"You can touch my waist, you know," I murmur.

"Right." His arms are stiff, but he reaches for me, placing his palms against my upper waist, practically cupping my ribs. I'd laugh if it didn't feel so forced. It doesn't help that I have a clear view of a pulsing vein in his forehead.

"You're mad," I decide.

"Reeves is a dick."

"He was simply asking questions."

"What kind of questions?"

"Questions about you and me," I murmur. "He's convinced you have feelings for me since you're so protective."

"And?"

"Aaaand...nothing, I guess." I tear my attention from his hard gaze, choosing to focus on the top button of his white button-up shirt as the next song starts. It's slow and sexy and makes me feel like I'm crawling out of my own skin.

Why is this so...awkward? I've never felt awkward around Everett. Ever. I swear I can hear his molars grinding, but I'm too anxious to confirm my suspicion. When my foot lands on his, he curses under his breath, every muscle in his body turning to stone beneath my fingertips.

Shit.

"Sorry," I start.

He lets me go and stares up at the ceiling. "Fuck, Dylan."

"I didn't mean to step on you."

"Yeah, no shit," he grunts, taking a deep breath. "It's fine."

"Do you want me to—"

"I want you to not stir up shit. That's what I want you to do."

My brows dip. "Wow."

"Fuck," he seethes under his breath, taking another deep breath. "I'm being an ass."

"Yeah," I agree. "You kind of are."

"I'm sorry." The tightness around his eyes softens as he scrubs his hand over his face. "Seriously, Dylan." He takes another deep breath as if the third time's the charm or something. "I'm sorry."

Sensing his sincerity, I force myself to relax in his hold and move a little closer to him. "It's okay."

"I don't know what's wrong with me tonight," he adds.

"You're fine," I offer. "I think we're both a little on edge."

"Yeah." He nods and forces his muscles to relax beneath my palms. "Yeah, I guess you're right."

"So…I know I never told you, but…thank you."

He frowns. "For what?"

"For asking me to a dance. I didn't think they were your thing."

"They aren't," he grunts. "But Mav wanted to do something special for Ophelia after everything from the past few months, and he knew she'd want you guys to come."

"Well, yeah, but…"

"What?"

"I don't know? I mean, don't get me wrong. I get how

we've always been friends, and you wouldn't have ever crossed the line or whatever, but I guess I figured…" The rest of my sentence catches in my throat, and I bite my tongue because if I'm wrong—if Finley's wrong—this could seriously blow up in my face.

A crease forms between Everett's brows as he stares down at me. "What?"

"I don't know? I guess Finley assumed…and *I* assumed… you might be…"

"What?" he repeats.

Just say it, Dylan. Rip it off like a Band-Aid.

"Are you the guy who kissed me at the party?" I blurt out. His shoulders drop another inch as understanding paints his handsome features, causing his expression to fall. "Dylan…"

"Just answer the question," I beg.

"Why does it matter?"

"I dunno? Call me old-fashioned, but I'd like to know if we kissed or not."

"It was only a kiss."

"I know, and you're right. It doesn't really matter, but not knowing has driven me crazy, and ever since the party, you've acted strange around me. So it's left me trying to pinpoint whether or not I'm *actually* going crazy."

When he stays quiet, my anxiety eats at my stomach lining, leaving me more than a little uncomfortable as I hold his stare. Or at least try to. The guy looks like he'd rather study the beams along the ceiling than the girl he asked to Homecoming.

"So you're not interested," I mutter. "Or am I so dense I can't tell the difference?"

"Dylan…" He says my name again, dragging it out, leaving me hanging until I want to claw at my ears to erase the weight accompanying it.

"Did you, or did you not, kiss me at the party?" I demand.

"If I say it wasn't me, are you gonna run to Reeves?" he counters.

"Would you care if I did?"

"I don't know?" He shakes his head, frustrated. "Yes. Yes, I'd care."

"Why?"

"We've already had this conversation, and I don't want to have it again."

"Did. You. Kiss me?" I grit out.

"Yes," Everett snaps. "Yes, I kissed you, but it didn't mean anything, so will you let it go?"

We aren't dancing anymore. We're just…standing here. In the middle of the dance floor. The strobe lights shining down on us make me feel like I'm under interrogation. Or maybe he is. Honestly, I don't even know anymore. I feel…blindsided. And incredibly stupid.

"If it didn't mean anything, why did you ask me to Homecoming?"

Nostrils flaring, he grinds out, "I asked you to come as a friend."

"Yeah, and I would've assumed so if you hadn't interrupted Reeves mid-sentence when he was trying to ask me to be his date."

"Dylan…"

"Stop saying my name like that," I order. "Like I'm your little sister's awkward friend, and you're trying to let me down easy."

His eyes close for a brief second, his lips nothing but a slash of white on his sharp features.

"So you *are* trying to let me down easy," I realize. "Let me get this straight. You kissed me, then asked me to a dance. Not because you actually wanted to be my date, but because if you didn't, you were afraid your friend would. And it's a problem because…?"

"Don't do this," he murmurs, and I can't decide if it's a plea or an order. "Not here."

"Don't do what? Force you to have a conversation instead of letting you hide behind bullshit excuses like guilt?" I spit.

"This has nothing to do with guilt."

"This has everything to do with guilt," I realize, too numb to pull away when he reaches for me. "You don't want me caught up with Reeves because you think I'm too fragile to handle the potential fallout. Am I right?"

His expression twists with unease. "Dylan—"

"And you think I'm fragile because you saw me at my weakest, and you're convinced I never recovered." I nod, hating how easily the pieces finally fall into place since I'm facing them head-on instead of shoving them under the rug like everyone else. "Yeah, you hit me in the head when we were kids, Everett. And yeah, it fucked up my eyesight and any future I had of being a professional hockey player, but guess what? I accepted it. I moved past it. Whatever screwed-up obligation you have when it comes to...whatever the hell this is, because let's be honest, it sure as shit isn't a friendship to you. Well? You can let it go. You owe me nothing. And I'm tired of accommodating you and your bullshit, overprotective actions hoping to ease whatever guilt you still carry. It's not on me to let it go. I already have. This is on you. Goodnight, Everett." I slip out of his hold. My body feels like it's attached to a car battery, and I'll be electrocuted at any second. I need to get out of here. I need to clear my head and swallow the shame filling every inch of my body for honestly believing the connection I felt with Cinderfella was anything more than physical. And even then, it must've been one-sided because this? This is so embarrassing I legitimately might puke.

Everett's attention darts around the dance floor like he's

afraid I'm making a scene. When he steps closer, he keeps his voice low, gritting out, "Where are you going, Dylan?"

"I'm not sure it's any of your business." He grabs my arm again, attempting to keep me from bolting, but I jerk away. "Don't follow me."

I head to the empty table, grab my clutch, and rush out the door.

20

REEVES

ameron's chatter goes in one ear and out the other as I watch them on the dance floor. My pretty wallflower and the stubborn teammate. For them to know each other as well as they do, they look awkward as shit out there. Either Everett's game is trash, or I've misread him because *this*? This is downright pathetic. Her hesitant smiles. His forced ones. Fuck, she might as well be asking him to turn his head and cough with how uncomfortable the bastard looks.

What's going on in your head, Ev?

Her smile falls, and her eyes drop to the floor. Like she's embarrassed. Ashamed. My hands clench, and I nod my head, pretending to listen to whatever bullshit story my buddy's spewing as I turn back to the trainwreck on the dance floor.

Dylan pulls away from him, her movements tight and jerky. He grabs her wrist, and she pulls away from him, her upper lip curling with contempt. Suddenly, she darts away, clutching her aquamarine dress in her hands, grabs her purse from the table, and rushes outside like my very own broken Cinderella.

I'd laugh if the situation wasn't so messed up.

It's midnight somewhere. Right, Dyl?

"What do you think, Reeves?" Cameron asks.

I shake my head, stepping around him. "I'll be back in a few." I stride straight toward the motherfucker on the dance floor. It takes everything inside of me to keep my expression as if I don't care, as if I don't have skin in the game, as if I don't care how Everett, holier than thou Everett, pissed off the girl we've fought over for far too fuckin' long.

"What did you say to her?" I demand.

"It's none of your business, asshole."

"Answer the question."

Everett and I are pretty evenly matched in height, and our weights are the same. Hell, we're even two peas in a fucking pod when we're at the gym and go back and forth on who can do more reps, etcetera. But I have no problem beating the shit out of him if he made her cry.

The calloused asshole glares back at me, his own frustration consuming him as the people around us start to form a circle, sensing the brewing tension.

"Back up, man," he grits out. "I'm not in the mood."

"I don't give a shit. What did you say to her?"

"She isn't your date, so this has nothing to do with you."

"You forget she isn't my date because I passed you the puck for the good of the team instead of taking the shot myself."

He scoffs. "You never would've made it."

"And you'll never let me smooth things over with you after I fucked up the playoffs."

"You're right. I won't. You don't deserve her," he grits out.

"Says the guy who made her cry," I spit. "What the fuck is

your problem, man? All she wanted was a night out with her friends."

"My problem is you're a selfish prick who doesn't think of anyone but himself." He shoves me in the chest, and I stumble back, almost hitting the edge of the crowd surrounding us.

Game on, motherfucker.

21
DYLAN

Stupid.

I feel so freaking stupid. Angry tears well in my eyes, and I wipe them away, searching in my clutch for my phone so I can hire an Uber or something. It doesn't matter how we're only a couple miles from home. I'm not stupid enough to walk there by myself when it's dark outside. Okay, I'm stupid, but I'm not *get-yourself-killed* stupid.

I know this. But the idea of going back in? Of ruining everyone's night or facing Everett after admitting our kiss meant a hell of a lot more to me than it ever did to him is more than I can stomach.

Oh my gosh. The fact Finley told him I'm hung up on the guy at the costume party without actually knowing it was him in the first place is so freaking embarrassing. Did she say anything else? Relay the play-by-play I gave her? She promised she wouldn't but at this point? Who the hell knows? I'm not sure how I'll ever be able to look him in the eye after this. After seeing the pity in his gaze and the way he brushed the kiss aside like it meant nothing when I spent countless nights replaying it?

Dammit, Dylan! How naive can you be?

I double over, putting my hands on my knees as I force my breathing to slow. It's cooler outside, and if I wasn't so pissed about my conversation with Everett, I'd probably freeze, but I like it. The cold. The way it eases my nausea. The way it cools my heated skin and my frazzled nerves.

Breathe.

Folding my arms, I look up at the night sky. Why didn't I stand up for myself and tell Reeves I wanted to go with him instead of letting Everett and Griffin have any say in the matter? It would've made this entire night so much less painful. I shove the thought aside, noticing a new energy inside the building. People rush around, pulling out their cell phones and crowding into the dance area at the back of the hall.

My forehead wrinkles when someone mentions a fight between Reeves and Everett. I don't even think as my feet move on their own volition. Bodies are sandwiched together, packed tighter and tighter as the sound of flesh hitting flesh mingles with hushed voices and quiet gasps.

"What's going on?" I ask, pushing between two people. Then, I see it.

Reeves and Ev. Two of my favorite people. Fists up. Shirts rumpled. Hair a mess. Reeves' knuckles skate across Everett's jaw, and his head swings to the side, spittle flying from his mouth. He recovers with a blow to Reeves' stomach. The air's knocked from his lungs, and he bends forward, taking a shoulder to the gut as Everett tackles him.

"Stop!" I yell. "Fucking stop it, you two!"

They don't hear me, too lost in the fight, in the pent-up aggression and frustration they ignored for too long.

Somehow, Everett makes it on top, straddling Reeves'

waist. He cocks his arm back, nailing Reeves in the eye. Reeves raises his arms to protect his face while Everett pummels him over and over again.

"Get off him!" I yell, not realizing I'm too close. Much too close. The tussle turns into a full-blown brawl, and they roll into me, the pair of bodies knocking me to the ground. When an elbow slams into my head, I see stars. A sharp pain explodes in my skull, and I groan, curling into a ball beside the chaos. A pair of hands find my waist, dragging me to the edge of the open space while keeping us blocked by the wall of classmates still recording everything.

"Fuck." Griffin cradles my face. "Dylan? Dylan, are you okay?"

Blinking rapidly, I try to convince my brain to work.

The sounds of flesh hitting flesh escalate further, and the situation crashes into me all over again, so I yell out, "Help them!" I attempt to scramble out of my brother's embrace and do it myself, but the asshole's a hell of a lot faster than I am, and he tightens his grip.

"Dylan, stop," Griffin grits out. Somehow, Reeves is now on top, and his face is twisted with a rage I've never seen before. Not on him.

Cross. Jab. Cross. Jab.

Everett's head rolls back and forth with every hit, making my stomach pitch.

"You need to—"

"Then stop fighting me, and let me help them without worrying about you doing something stupid. We clear?" He grabs my chin and forces me to look at him instead of the blood pouring from Everett's nose. "Are. We. Clear?"

I blink in an attempt to erase the haze in my blurry vision. When the view finally comes into focus, my fight dissipates.

"Yeah," I breathe out. "Yeah, we're clear. Help them!"

By the time Griffin lets me go, blood and spittle paint Reeves' knuckles and his once-white dress shirt. His face is also cut up, proving Everett gave as good as he got. My stomach coils as Griffin grabs his friend's arms, dragging him off a raging Everett as some of his teammates get their heads out of their ass and hold him back.

Where the hell is Maverick?

The familiar sound of heavy footsteps on marble echoes through the stifling library, and the air shifts around us again like a hurricane. In an instant, the teammates who were holding Reeves back disappear into the crowd, leaving Ev, Reeves, Griffin, and me in the circle. The beam of a flashlight is like an icepick to my brain, and I lift my hand to block it as my mind tries to catch up with what's happening. But I feel like I'm two steps behind. Hell, I feel like I'm ten.

"Put your hands up!" a deep, menacing voice demands, but I'm too dazed to register it, let alone comply. "Hands up, Reeves!" the stranger growls.

Reeves?

The officer knows his name?

My attention snaps to Reeves in the center of the circle. His hands are at his sides, his body poised and ready for another battle. I'm terrified he might throw down all over again, which would be...really, really bad.

"Reeves," I murmur. His angry gaze snaps to mine, causing the fight to seep out of them. I step closer, moving slowly as a mask of indifference slides into place on Reeves' bruised face.

"Now!" the officer booms as his hand reaches for his holster.

I flinch at the sound, and my blood runs cold as Everett and Griffin lift their hands into the air. But the officer? He isn't looking at them. His eyes are pinned on Reeves and *only* Reeves.

And Reeves? His bloody hands aren't raised. They're loose at his sides as he stares numbly in front of him.

"Look, it was a stupid fight," I interrupt, desperate to cut the tension. To explain how they aren't needed here. "They're over it. It's fine."

The cop ignores me, reaching for the cuffs on his utility belt as he takes a step toward Reeves and continues to *not* acknowledge a very guilty and bloody Everett beside him.

What the hell is this guy's problem?

I move closer, putting myself between Reeves and the cop who clearly has it out for the guy, though I have no idea why. "Look, the fight's over, okay? We'll get out of here right now and—"

"Miss, if you could please step back." The first cop's partner moves closer, his hands half raised as if trying to look unthreatening. It would work if the first cop wasn't acting like an ass.

Fingers brush softly against the inside of my wrist as Reeves murmurs, "It's gonna be okay, Dylan." When he turns back to the first cop, he raises his hands fully into the air. "Hey, Dad."

What the actual fuck?

I blink, convinced I'm hallucinating.

"You're his father?" I whisper. The bastard doesn't even deem me worthy of a response. "Listen, I know fighting is stupid, and I have no doubt Reeves and Everett realize the depth of their stupidity at this moment. But if you could... back off, we'll go our separate ways, and..." my voice trails off as I shove my fingers through my hair and search the premises.

Feeling his pity, the partner takes another step toward me and touches my shoulder. "Miss, what happened to your face?"

I touch my cheek, then wince.

"He hit you, didn't he?" the first officer snaps.

"What? No! He didn't—" I turn to Everett. "Everett, tell them!"

The first officer doesn't even bother acknowledging my argument. Instead, he orders, "We're gonna need your statement, and we also need you to decide if you want to press charges."

"Are you kidding me?" I seethe.

The same pity shines in the second officer's eyes as he shakes his head back and forth. "Your boy here has priors, miss. We have no choice but to take him in."

"Then take him in, too," I seethe, pointing to Everett.

Everett's muscles are poised as he steps forward. "She's right. I'm the one who started it."

"Everett," Reeves growls. A warning. A threat.

"What's your name, son?" the unhinged officer demands.

"Everett. Everett Taylor."

"Never heard your name. You ever been arrested?"

He shakes his head. "No, sir."

"Then it seems we can let you off with a warning."

"What?" I screech. "That isn't fair!"

"She's right, it isn't," Everett argues. "If you take Reeves in, you might as well take me, too."

"You want to be arrested, boy?" the first officer demands. "Have a mark on your permanent record?"

"Let it go, man," Reeves warns as he stares at Everett. A look passes between them, and Everett backs off.

"Thought so," the first officer replies. The condescension in his voice is so thick I swear I could choke on it.

This is bullshit. I shake my head, convinced I've entered an alternate universe, when Griffin tugs me into him. "Let him go."

"But this is bullshit!" I repeat, voicing the words aloud instead of letting them fester inside.

The first officer finally looks at me and cocks his head, daring me to have another outburst.

Part of me wants to. Not because I'm an idiot. Or maybe I am, but I've never looked for trouble. Never skipped school. Never stole anything or even had the nerve to argue with my teachers. But this? This isn't fair. Clearly, this cop, his fucking *father*, has it out for Reeves, and seeing the injustice of it all? It makes me sick to my stomach.

Everett moves closer, blocking the first officer from my view as he towers over me. "We both know this is bogus. But the faster you cooperate with the police and let him cooperate with the police, the faster they'll know it's bullshit, meaning he'll be home sooner."

Everett's right. I know he is. But this feels wrong. So freaking wrong.

"Reeves," I whisper. My eyes well with tears as I watch the officer slap the cuffs into place around Reeves' wrists.

"It's gonna be okay, Dylan," he promises.

I wish I believed him.

22

DYLAN

Someone called the cops. It makes sense since, ya know, there was a full-on brawl in the middle of a university's Homecoming dance. The view of his father's hand on the back of Reeves' head as he was forced into the back seat of the police car is ingrained in my memory, and the unfairness of it all makes me see red.

Everett drives me back to our house in Reeves' car while Griffin takes his date home with Finley and Drew. Mav and Ophelia offered to come over after Griffin told them what happened—they were hooking up in an empty room and missed the entire thing—but I didn't see the point. There's nothing we can do.

It's a short but silent ride. Resting my throbbing head against the cold passenger window, I watch as trees blur together, blending in with the inky darkness. When we pull up to the garage, he cuts the ignition but doesn't reach for the door handle, and honestly, I'm too numb to do much of anything.

"I'm so fucking sorry," he mutters.

My eyes cut to his. "What the hell happened, Ev?"

"We fought."

"Duh." I scoff. "Did you know his dad's a cop?"

He hangs his head and squeezes the steering wheel as the lights from the dashboard highlight the regret in his stoic expression. "Yeah."

"Did you know how much he hates Reeves?"

Wiping at the corner of his eye, Everett nods. "Yeah, Dylan. I knew."

"Why didn't you say anything? Why didn't you defend him?"

"I tried."

"Yeah, and you were too worried about your precious record for any of it to actually mean anything." My nose wrinkles in disgust. "You're a coward."

His hands tighten around the steering wheel. "I'm trying to protect you."

"I can protect myself."

"How?" he demands. "By putting yourself in the crosshairs and hitting your head?"

My fingers move to the bruise along my cheekbone as if they have a mind of their own, and I flinch despite the light pressure. "I'm fine."

"Bullshit."

I shake my head, caught between disgust, resentment, and resignation, as I lick my bottom lip. "Don't start this again. Don't you *dare* start this again and treat me like a victim."

"You're right, okay?" He lifts his hands in defense. "You're right. Reeves did nothing wrong, and I deserved what I had coming to me. Happy now?"

"No, I'm not happy," I retort. "I don't want either of you hurt or carted away in handcuffs. It isn't you against him, and I'm not picking his side by acknowledging he was treated unfairly by the police tonight, so stop being such a selfish dick and only looking at this from your perspective."

A bit of fight seeps out of me, and I rest my head against the leather headrest.

"You're right," Ev admits. "I treated him unreasonably." He pinches the bridge of his nose and draws in a breath. "And I've done it for a long time."

It's true, he has. But even though Everett's always been stubborn, he's also always had a big heart, and I know this is killing him.

Reaching over, I squeeze his knee, hoping he knows he isn't alone and isn't a bad person for making a mistake, even if it was kind of a doozy.

"What's going to happen to him?" I whisper.

"He's been arrested before."

"I know. For a DUI."

"And assault charges."

My lungs cease. "W-what?"

"A few of them."

Panic blooms in my chest. "Everett—"

"He hit his dad, and his dad pressed charges," Everett explains. He sounds so cold. So detached. "He's also been in fights with his clients' exes, which didn't turn out so great, either."

Chewing on the edge of my thumb, I play out a million scenarios, but none of them fit. None of them make sense. And neither does tonight's fallout.

"So, what does this mean?" I whisper. "Even with his priors, we gave our statements, and you admitted you started it. There's no way...there's no way he'll be in serious trouble, right?"

"Honestly, I don't know." Ev rubs at the five o'clock shadow along his jaw and stares blankly out the windshield. "As you saw firsthand, Reeves' dad is a dick and has always had it out for him. Always."

"But it was only a fight. If you were on the ice, no one would've batted an eye."

Okay, it's a lie, and we both know it. Sure, hockey fights can be brutal, but whatever the hell that was tonight? It was more.

As if he heard my thoughts, Everett points out, "It was in the middle of a school dance, Dylan. Don't get me wrong. I get it. But when you add in his priors, it doesn't look good."

He's right. It doesn't. At all. None of this does. But it isn't his fault. It *isn't*.

Scrambling through my clutch, I say, "I need to call my parents. Maybe they can help."

He reaches for me, sets his hand on mine, and halts my search. "You sure you wanna do this?"

"Do what, exactly?"

"Get...mixed up in this?"

My expression twists with hurt, and I pull away from him. "The boy I grew up with wouldn't have had any issue standing up for Reeves tonight."

"I don't want to see you hurt."

"We already discussed how you owe me nothing, Everett. And guess what? I'm starting to think I don't owe you anything, either. Now, get out of the car so I can call my parents."

It doesn't take long for my mom to answer. I word-vomit everything that happened, and Dad promises to call his lawyer.

23

REEVES

My wrists are raw as I stare at the two-way mirror on my left. I should've known fate would deal me a shit hand tonight. Should've known my dad would wind up on campus. Any chance he has to fuck me over, he's always first in line. The fact he's made a point of spreading lies about me to all of his buddies doesn't help, either. Fuck, pretty sure any officer from the Lockwood Heights Police Department would pull out the cuffs as soon as they saw me, thanks to dear old Dad's after-work ramblings when he's downed three too many beers. Too bad none of his accusations hold any weight.

It doesn't matter, though. Not to them, anyway.

Rolling my shoulders, I look at the ceiling as the clock ticks on the wall.

Tick. Tick. Tick.

Get your ass out here, boy, or I'll get my belt!

Tick. Tick. Tick.

What the fuck you been doin', boy?

Tick. Tick. Tick.

I could kill you, boy. I could kill you, and no one would bat an eye. No one would miss you. Fuck. No one would even notice.

The door hinges squeak, snapping me back to the present as the heavy metal door opens, revealing my sperm donor.

Disgust oozes through me, leaving a black, oily trail along my skin, but I don't cower. Can't wait to get the fuck out of here and shower, even though I know I'll still feel dirty afterward. It's how it is with me and my dad. Every interaction takes weeks for me to recover from. To let his bullshit words go.

"Hello, boy."

"Where's your partner?" I ask.

"He'll be here in a minute. Figured I'd start without him."

Of course, he did.

I rip my gaze from his to stare at the dried blood on my knuckles.

"So, who's the girl?" he prods.

It shouldn't surprise me, but it does. His question. Where his mind is. It doesn't make me feel any better.

"She's pretty," he notes.

My lips gnash together.

"Seemed enamored with you," he adds. "You like her?"

My attention shifts from my knuckles to the red, angry skin beneath the metal cuffs.

Fuck, those are gonna leave a mark.

"Nothin' to say?" he asks.

We've played this game often. More times than I can count. I never struggled to remain indifferent. Unaffected. By whatever bullshit he spews at me. But this time? It's harder. Because this time? I have something to lose.

"Dylan Thorne," he says thoughtfully. "Pretty name for a pretty girl. Can't figure out what she sees in you."

I clench and unclench my fists, letting the pull of my bruised knuckles ground me.

"Not very talkative today, huh, boy?"

The pressure in my jaw strengthens, but I don't bother answering.

The sound of his work boots scuffing against the concrete ground grates on my nerves as he circles me slowly, but I don't follow the movement. I simply wait. For what? Who the hell knows. But communicating with the bastard is a waste of breath, so why give him the satisfaction? Nah. Especially not where Dylan's concerned.

He doesn't even deserve to think her name, let alone say it. And if he pieces together my feelings for her, I'll never forgive myself.

"Tell me something," he demands, trying a different tactic. "Do you actually think I'll let you walk out of here without assault charges?"

I ignore him, choosing to stare at the two-way mirror instead. Is someone in there? Is someone watching?

"You always were a stupid, stupid boy. Causin' trouble. Fuckin' up your life the same way you fucked up mine." My eyes snap to him, and he tilts his head. "You think you'll keep your scholarship after I finish with you?"

Annoyance licks through my veins, but I don't give in. Don't throw a fit or say a fucking word. Because I know what he wants. I know *exactly* what he wants. He wants me to be mad. To make a scene. To muddy the waters and incriminate myself when we both know he already has enough on me.

The slap of his palms against the cold surface of the table rings throughout the otherwise silent room as he glares down at me. "Might as well kiss your NHL career goodbye right here, right now, boy, which means you can kiss your girl goodbye, too, because it's clear a girl like her would only slum it with you for one reason."

My molars threaten to grind, but I keep my face blank,

staring straight ahead of me as if the asshole doesn't exist, which, to him, is worse than death.

The door opens again, and our heads snap in its direction. My dad pushes himself away from the table, smoothing out the front of his uniform. "McDonnell," he acknowledges.

"His lawyer's here," McDonnell tells him.

A grating laugh cuts through the tension as my dad slaps his hand against his knee like he's fuckin' Santa Claus. "Reeves? Reeves doesn't have a lawyer."

"The attorney at the front of the station says differently," McDonnell argues.

My brows raise as McDonnell's words wash over me. My dad's right. I don't have a lawyer. I'm saving every fucking penny for a rainy day, since I'm not stupid enough to believe I can play in the NHL forever.

So, who the hell is McDonnell talking about?

And why does my dad look scared shitless for the first time in his life?

Shifting in my chair, I can't help the shit-eating grin from nearly splitting my face in two as I take him in.

Well, would you look at that? Seems my dad does have something he's afraid of, and someone gifted me with a front-row seat to see his fear up close and personal.

24

DYLAN

I can't sleep. I stare up at the bedroom ceiling, counting Finley's breaths in the otherwise silent room. She's out cold beside me. Has been for at least an hour.

After showering, I slipped on Reeves' hoodie, headed back to my bedroom, and received a call from my parents. All they said was the lawyer was at the precinct, and they'd keep me updated.

That's it.

Now, here I am, attempting to sleep despite knowing it's pretty freaking impossible. Annoyed, I throw off the covers. Remembering the sleeping zombie beside me, I slip out of bed more carefully. After sliding on my glasses from the nightstand, I close the bedroom door with a quiet click, then pad down the stairs and into the kitchen. The lights are off, but I don't mind. Honestly, the dark is the only thing quieting my brain right now. I grab a glass from the cabinet and fill it with water. The cool moisture seeps into my parched tastebuds. When I lick my bottom lip, it stings, reminding me of everything that happened tonight.

My head still pounds, making it hard to see straight, let alone form a coherent thought, even though I took my contacts out as soon as I turned on the water for my shower.

I search the cupboards for some Advil, hoping I won't have to pull out the big boy pain meds. They knock me on my ass. Then again, I could probably use the sedative after my shitty night. When a soft creak echoes behind me, I almost jump out of my skin, and the glass crashes to the ground. It splinters into a thousand pieces around my bare feet as I turn around, searching the dark kitchen. My heart rate rivals a hummingbird's wings as my already-drained body floods with the last of my adrenaline. Honestly, I'm surprised I have any left. The patio light paints shadows through the window, highlighting the man in front of me, and my body sags against the counter in relief.

Reeves.

He's back.

The realization doesn't ease my galloping pulse, but I force my lungs to expel the oxygen they hold.

Sensing how on edge I am, Reeves' eyes fill with concern. "You okay?"

"Yeah, it's just...you're back," I whisper, careful not to wake anyone else in the house.

"I'm back." He steps closer, keeping his hands raised as if to placate me while his amused gaze skims across every inch of my body. Finally, his attention lands on the broken glass dusting the floor around me, and his brows tug.

"Don't move." Disappearing down the hall, he comes back wearing a pair of hard-soled grandpa slippers, wielding a broom and dustpan. With precision, he crouches down and collects the larger shards from around my bare feet. Once they're tossed in the trash, he sweeps up the smaller pieces. Methodically. Expertly. Effortlessly. Like cleaning up after me is the most natural thing in the world.

Embarrassment coils in my abdomen as I helplessly watch him pick up my mess, debating how I can minimize it or at least help without making things worse like I did earlier tonight.

As he drags the broom along the floor one more time, he sighs, sets it and the dustpan on the floor, glances up at me, and turns around. "All right, my little bull in a China shop, hop on."

"What?"

"I don't want you walking around in here with bare feet until I can vacuum without waking everyone up." He pats his shoulder and repeats, "Hop on."

"You're serious?"

"You gonna make me whinny like a pony to prove it?" He smirks. "*Whinny. Whinny.*"

A laugh bubbles out of me. "Horses don't say whinny."

"What do they say?"

"Uh, *neigh?*"

He rolls his eyes. "I'm sorry, but you sounded nothing like a horse. Now, hop on."

Gripping his shoulders, I jump on his back, and he carries me away from the mess, setting me on the couch in the family room.

"Thanks," I whisper.

"Nah, pretty sure you're the one I should be thanking." The cushion dips as he sits beside me. Tilting my head up with a nudge of his bruised knuckles beneath my chin, he locks his gaze with mine to examine my cheekbone. "Quite the shiner you got there."

My imagination runs wild as his calloused fingertips skate across my skin with visions of how differently tonight could've turned out if I had gone to the dance with him instead. We would've danced. Laughed. Probably even kissed. And no one would've wound up in handcuffs.

237

Closing my eyes, I shy away from his hold. "I'm fine."

"Was it my elbow or his?" he questions.

"Does it matter?"

"Yeah." He nods. "To me, it does."

I shrug. "Honestly, I have no idea. It happened so fast... Regardless, it was an accident."

His eyes fill with regret as he holds my stare for a few moments, then leans back against the cushions. "Doesn't make me feel any less like shit, though."

"How are you?" I ask. "How was..."

"Jail?" he offers with a smirk. "Surprisingly good once my *lawyer* arrived." He says the word like it's a smoking gun and shakes his head ruefully, watching me like he doesn't know what to do with me. "You didn't have to do it, you know."

"Do what?"

"Call in a favor."

"Pretty sure you didn't deserve to be arrested tonight."

"Pretty sure it didn't matter. Most people wouldn't call their family lawyer to swoop in and save the delinquent on the team from their asshole father."

I bite my tongue to keep from arguing with him. To keep from pointing out how he's hardly a delinquent and most definitely worth saving. A guy like Reeves? Call it a hunch, but I'm not sure words hold much weight for him. Actions, though? Actions are a different story, and I really hope he grasps mine.

Tucking my feet beneath my butt, I mention, "Your dad seems like a real piece of work."

He scratches along his jaw, avoiding my gaze. "You could say so. He's not so bad as long as I keep my distance, but thanks to my side gig, sometimes it's a little easier said than done."

"He seemed like he had it out for you."

"He's always had it out for me," he explains. "But at least now I'm able to defend myself."

My body ices at his insinuation. At the idea of anyone hurting *anyone* under the guise of discipline. "He hit you?"

"All the time." Reeves smiles, but it doesn't reach his eyes as he stretches his legs out in front of him, getting comfortable beside me on the couch with only the moonlight peeking through the windows. "A few of my teachers had a hunch about what was going down, but that kind of accusation, in general, is messy. That kind of accusation against a cop when you live in a small town?" He grimaces. "Yeah, not so much."

He's right. Who do you call when the police aren't an option? I mean, technically, they are, but I'm not an idiot. I've heard the stories. Officers band together, and it's usually a good thing, but there's a flip side to camaraderie, and in this instance? A teacher's word against a police officer's, especially if they're wrong, would make a huge mess for everyone involved. But to deal with something like that and to see so many people turn a blind eye to your pain would be...awful. And so unfair, I can barely stomach it.

"I'm sorry," I whisper.

"Don't be." He shrugs. "Sometimes we get the shit end of the deal. What matters is how you handle it."

"And how do you handle it?" I ask.

"By protecting those I can," he murmurs.

Noticing his bandaged knuckles resting in his lap, I grimace. "Speaking of protection, are your hands okay?"

"I'm a hockey player. My hands have been busted up more times than I can count."

"Yeah, but it doesn't exactly make me feel better." I grab his hands from his lap and bring them between us, examining the damage to his knuckles. Blood splotches the white bandages, and I can only imagine how busted up they must be beneath the gauze.

"Speaking of damage," Concern creases the outer corners of his eyes. "How's the head?"

"I already told you I'm fine."

"All right, I'll be more specific. Any headache? Is it the reason you were rummaging through the medicine cabinet?"

My brows dip, but instead of confirming or denying him, I keep my lips pressed tightly together.

"You gonna tell me about it?" he pushes.

"I believe we already had this conversation," I point out.

"And yet you still manage to dodge it anytime I ask for specifics."

"Fine." Blowing the air from my lungs, I give in. "Let me repeat for the billionth time how this isn't a big deal."

"Small deal. Got it." He winks. "Continue."

"When I was younger, I took a hit to the head with a puck." I touch my hairline and the scar hidden beneath it, then place my hand back in my lap. "I don't even remember it. We were playing roller hockey, and then I woke up in the hospital. I was out for two days. They were afraid I wouldn't wake up at all."

I wait for the inevitable pity to spark in his eyes, but it's absent.

"It was Everett, wasn't it." It isn't a question. It doesn't need to be. "He's the one who hit you."

With a nod, I curl the sleeves of his hoodie into my palms and fold my arms. "Like I said, it was an accident. No one holds it against him, but…well, it is what it is, and apparently, he's dead set on spending the rest of his life feeling like he owes me or something."

"What makes you say that?"

"Our fight tonight," I admit, hating how stupid it was.

Everything. My reaction. His response. The last few weeks altogether.

So. Freaking. Stupid.

"What'd you fight about?" Reeves prods.

Just say it. Say it and get it over with.

"Everett told me he was most definitely the culprit behind the kiss at the party."

His brows raise in surprise. "Everett told you he's your Cinderfella?"

"Yup." With a pathetic laugh, I pick up one of the hoodie strings and rub it along my bottom lip. "But you were right. It was only a kiss. A very stupid, very meaningless kiss."

He hesitates and inches closer. "Only a kiss, huh?"

I gulp past the sharp pain in my sternum, unable to look at him. To see his amusement or pity or secondhand embarrassment when we both know how hung up I was on the said kiss.

"Yeah," I mumble.

"No offense, but I don't think any kiss with you is meaningless, Dylan Thorne." The rasp in his voice skates over my skin, causing my pathetic heart to skip a beat as the memory of another kiss rises to the surface. A kiss meant to prove a point. To prove chemistry's chemistry, and I can't help but wonder how many girls he's felt it with. How many girls he's left swooning over him. How many girls he's swept off their feet like he could so easily do with me. I peek up at him, and my breath hitches.

He's so close.

So damn close.

I can feel it. The chemistry. The pull. It's like a magnet. A *strong* magnet. I want to lean into him. I want to let go of my silly reservations and kiss him. Without fear of rejection or fear of comparison.

What's real and what isn't with you, Oliver Reeves?

His gaze falls to my lips as we sit in the dark family room, and I swear I can feel him bending closer until the space between us grows, and a soft exhale hits my ears. "We should get some sleep."

My brows pull. "Sleep?"

"Yeah. *Sleep.*"

"Why?"

"Because if you don't stand up and walk out of this room right now, I'll kiss you, Dylan Thorne. I'll kiss you, and I'm sure as fuck not gonna be able to stop. *Go.* I'll vacuum in the morning."

The sting of rejection hits like a lash, and I start to stand when his hand darts out, and he grabs my wrist. "Not a fan of the miscommunication trope, remember?"

Staring at his long fingers, I whisper, "W-what?"

"I said, I'm not a fan of the miscommunication trope."

I rock back against the couch again, lost. "Okay?"

"Okay, so maybe stop looking at me like I kicked your puppy."

"We already discussed this," I remind him. "I don't have a puppy."

"And I don't have the willpower to not kiss you when we already discussed how, for me, a kiss with you isn't simply a kiss, so stop looking at me like I hurt your feelings by not kissing you two seconds ago."

My gaze falls to the ground. "Reeves..."

He drags his thumb against the back of my hand, and I swear I can feel it on every inch of me. "If you honestly think you aren't kissable or I haven't woken up every morning since our first kiss with a hard-on and jacked off in the shower at the memory of what you tasted like, then I have no problem proving it to you. But let me make one thing clear." My gaze snaps to his, and the heat in his eyes? The need? It makes me almost combust. "You deserve all of me, Dylan

Thorne, and I won't kiss you again until you have it." The absence of his touch kills me as he lets my wrist go and leans back on the couch. "Goodnight, Thorne."

As I brush my fingers against the tender patch of skin he caressed, I whisper, "Goodnight, Reeves."

25
REEVES

"So, are we gonna talk about it?" I ask as the sun peeks over the horizon. Everett's in the backyard. His eyes are still bloodshot from last night, his face mottled with bruises as he sips his coffee. He looks like shit. Then again, so do I. I've been in a lot of fights in my life and Ev? He can throw down better than the majority of them. My split knuckles flex at the memory as I wait for him to stop being such a tough nut to crack.

Without looking at me, he mutters, "Talk about what?"

I want to laugh as I watch him avoid me at all costs, but I bite it back. No use kicking the asshole when he's down.

"About the fight or the fact you've had it out for me since day one," I tell him. "Or we could always talk about how you lied to Dylan and told her you were the one who kissed her at the costume party when we both know it isn't the case. Take your pick."

His shoulders fall, the guilt he's carrying practically engulfing the bastard. That's the thing about Everett, though. I want to hate him sometimes, but I can't. Because he isn't a bad guy despite his reasoning being skewed sometimes. But

I'm tired of waiting for him to have the balls to tell me why, especially after my conversation with Dylan last night.

"I haven't had it out for you," he mutters.

I chuckle dryly. "Bullshit."

He opens his mouth to argue, then nods slowly, giving in. "Fine. I have. But you gotta understand, man. My family is everything to me."

"Not trying to take anyone's place, Ev."

"You broke my trust," he argues.

"I fucked up," I volley back at him, "but you can't tell me you haven't."

He nods again, knowing I'm right, as he drinks some more from his mug. "I didn't want her to get hurt."

"And you thought lying to her was the solution?"

"It's complicated—"

"Tell me this," I interrupt. "Do you love her or not?"

"Of course, I love her," he argues.

"But not enough to actually claim her."

The fight seeps out of him, and he takes a seat on the top patio stair leading to the grass. "It's not the romantic kind of love." He shakes his head and sips more coffee, letting the mug dangle from his fingertips as he leans forward, resting his elbows on his knees. "She's one of the best people I know. She's good. Kind. Innocent. She deserved more than falling for a guy like you and being let down."

I don't call him out for having such little faith in me. He's right to have reservations, but even I can't deny the sting accompanying it.

"Lying to her, though?" I add. "When she finds out, she'll never forgive you."

"Add it to the list."

"Are you talking about the head injury?" I challenge.

His eyes close, and his head falls forward. Like the memory alone is enough to make him drown in shame. In regret. Disgust. "She's different than she was before," he murmurs. "She might not be able to see the difference, but I do. Her parents do. Her brothers do. Her best friends do." He hesitates. "Before, she was..." He smiles. "She was fucking snarky, man. Wouldn't take anyone's shit. And then...then I got pissed, and I hit the puck as hard as I could during a game and...and she collapsed." He shakes his head again as if he's picturing it. As if he'd give anything to erase the image of her tiny body falling to the ground. "Just...collapsed. I thought she was dead. I'd never seen her dad run so fast as he raced toward her. Her body...it fucking flopped like a rubber toy or some shit." His expression tightens, and his Adam's apple bobs in his throat. "They took her to the hospital, you know? Found out it was a brain injury. She could've lost her speech. Her ability to wake up entirely. Her complete eyesight. Her personality. Everything. And it was all because I lost my temper. Because I was pissed she scored against my team." His eyes are glassy as he looks up from his mug. "I can still see her like that, Reeves. In her hospital bed. Tied to tubes and shit. And the migraines after? Fuck, man. You don't even know. She pukes. She cries. She begs for it to stop. And you have to watch her. Watch her go through it. Fight through it. With your hands tied behind your fucking back. Helpless."

Helpless.

I know what it's like to feel helpless. To feel like you're up against a wall. Like no matter what you do, who you fight, who you beg, it's out of your control, and for a guy like me or Ev, it's a hard fucking pill to swallow.

"It wasn't your fault," I murmur, knowing how little my words will sink in but needing to say them anyway.

"It was," he pushes. "Everyone knows it was. They don't say it, but they know." His head falls forward, and he shakes it back and forth. "I can't...I can't see her like that again.

Hurting. Crying. Miserable." Those bloodshot eyes shoot straight through me as he looks up at me again. "She gets a fucking splinter, and I crumble, Reeves. You have no idea."

"I'm not gonna hurt her, Ev."

He draws in a breath, turning back to his cup. "I know you won't. I lied about the costume party before I knew. Seeing her try to save you last night...the way she fought for you. The way you willingly went with your dad after all the shit he's put you through... I get it. I don't even know if *you* get it," he adds wryly, "but I see it now. You care about her."

"I do."

"I'll back off," he decides, "*if* you promise to be done with the escort shit."

"It's not really any of your business, but I decided to retire before Homecoming. I have one more job to clean up, then I'm done."

"Good."

"Yeah. You still owe me, though," I add.

"Oh, I do?"

"Yeah, man. You do," I tell him.

Setting the coffee between his feet, he rests back on his hands and turns to me. "What do you want, Reeves?"

Since last night, I considered this question long and hard. The possibilities. The options. The ways I can have my cake and eat it, too. The ways I can keep my superhero cape or, at the very least, pass it on to someone else. Someone capable. Someone with a hero complex and a guilt complex, no matter how much it fucks with our heads.

"I want you to take over helping the girls on campus," I announce.

Groaning, Ev rubs his hand from forehead to chin. "Tell me you're joking."

"I'm not," I say with a laugh. "You'll be surprised how many girls find themselves in shitty relationships and have no clue how to escape them unscathed. You'll also be surprised by how many are able to stand up to the assholes if they feel like they have someone in their corner. Someone who builds them up. Someone who has their back in case things go south." I sit next to him on the stairs and pat his shoulder. "And that guy is now you. Congratulations."

He snorts but stays quiet.

"Six months," I push. "Do it for six months, and we're even."

Giving me the side-eye, he asks, "You're serious?"

"Yeah, man. And since I'm not gonna do it anymore, not gonna do that to Dylan, I need you to take over."

"For Dylan," he repeats.

"Yeah, for Dylan."

The bastard glances at me one more time, then sighs. "Fine."

"Thanks." I slap my hand against his shoulder again and push to my feet. "And for what it's worth, I won't hurt her. You have my word."

"Yeah, I know."

26

DYLAN

T he scent of coffee wafts through the air as I walk down the stairs, finding Finley in the kitchen with a cute little strawberry apron wrapped around her. Covering my yawn with my hand, I croak, "What time is it?"

"It's seven-thirty," she answers, handing me a cup of coffee. "Here. Reeves said you like peanut butter in it lately? That's new."

My brows bunch. "You already spoke with Reeves?"

"Yup. He's at the gym with the guys. Glad to see your parents' lawyer had him home quickly."

"Well, aren't you a plethora of knowledge this morning," I reply. She was MIA when everything went down at the dance, so I assumed she was blissfully unaware of the fight, arrest, and...everything else.

A gleam hits her gray eyes. "Griffin filled me in on the rest on the way home last night," she explains.

"Got it." I look around the empty kitchen. "Did Drew go, too?"

"To the gym?" She snorts. "Yeah, no. He works out, but he

doesn't exactly feel close to the guys in general. Take away his awesome girlfriend as a buffer, and the guy would have a meltdown."

With a laugh, I point out, "To be fair, it's probably hard being the long-distance boyfriend who's expected to step into your girlfriend's friend group without any friction, especially when your girlfriend is so close with her family and friends."

"Yeah, well, I don't really care at this point because he's kind of on my shit list, so…"

"Trouble in paradise?" I ask.

"He's mad at me because I didn't put out last night. And don't get me wrong, I get it. He flew here for the dance and missed a big test or something, but forgive me for not wanting to get laid after Griffin filled me in on all the drama from the dance, you know?" Her eyes turn glassy, and she shakes her head again. "Blah. I think I'm gonna start soon or something because"—she waves her finger around her face—"this is not on my Bingo card today."

"Well, a Harry Potter marathon wasn't on my Bingo card, either, but it looks like we're both in for a treat."

"It's tonight?" she asks.

"Yup."

"Well, damn." Her nose scrunches. "But first, coffee."

I smile against the rim of my cup. "Coffee."

"And sleuthing," she adds.

My amusement falls. "What now?"

"You really like him, don't you?"

Him.

She doesn't even have to say his name. I know exactly who she's referring to. So, what does it prove about me? I'm smitten, is what it proves. And being smitten over a guy like Reeves?

Am I really this dense?

"Oh, Dylan," she sing-songs. "The sooner we have this discussion, and I can give you my words of wisdom, the sooner you can shower."

I shoot her the side-eye over the rim of my cup but give in. "Fine, but you won't like my answer. I'm not entirely sure how I feel about him."

She tilts her head, looking less than convinced. "Be careful. Any relationship is...really freaking hard. A relationship with a guy who takes other girls out as a side gig?" She hesitates, letting her words hang in the air. "I like Reeves, I really do," she adds. "The chiseled jaw. The charisma. The snark? He's a little tempting even for me, but...be careful, okay? I don't want to see you hurt."

"I think you're reaching," I point out.

"Reaching?" She shakes her head and sits down at the kitchen table. "No. Projecting?" An amused yet dejected scoff escapes her. "Maybe a little."

Joining her at the kitchen table, I take a seat and stare into my coffee. "I thought he was going to kiss me last night."

"Last night?"

"I couldn't sleep. I ran into him in the kitchen. We talked, and...I thought he was going to kiss me."

"*Thought* he was going to kiss you?"

"He didn't." I shrug. "Obviously, I was a little butthurt, and the guy saw right through me, which is when he said he won't kiss me again until I have all of him."

Her jaw drops. "He said that?"

I nod.

"Holy shit, Dylan. He *really* said that?"

My eyes thin, and my lips bunch on one side. "Gee, thanks for not sounding super shocked, Fin."

"It's not that, it's just...huh." She leans back in her chair, lost in thought. Then, a smile spreads across her face. "Who would've thought you'd be the one to tame the infamous Reeves?"

"I'm not taming anyone," I argue.

"No, but you *are* tempting him to settle down, and from what I heard? No one on campus thinks they'll ever see the day."

"Which is the terrifying part," I mutter.

With an understanding nod, she watches me from over the rim of her cup but doesn't say anything else. And a speechless Finley? Well, it's about as unnerving as a hurricane warning.

I guess we'll have to wait and see.

FUN FACT. MY MOM AND HER FRIENDS ARE A LITTLE CRAZY. They also killed it when it came to brainstorming and decorating. Give three sad women an opportunity to throw a party, and it's all hands on deck, people.

And boy, does it show.

Finley and I arrived early to help my mom, Aunt Mia, and Aunt Kate set everything up. Aunt Kate is Finley's mom. She's in town with my Uncle Mack for the foreseeable future. It's mainly to stay close and support Aunt Mia and Uncle Henry after Archer's passing. However, I doubt they haven't already recognized the benefits of being near their kids, too, despite raising such independent hellions. Thankfully, they have a cabin in the mountains about a half-hour from campus, so it hasn't been too much of a headache for them to relocate.

I'm not going to lie. It's nice hanging out with everyone, and it's exactly what I need. My muscles are sore from all the lifting and decorating and icing, but it's a good sore. A comforting sore. The kind of sore you feel from hard work.

Or at least, it's what I tell myself. I'm not stupid enough to think my bruised tailbone and sore cheek are from hanging battery-powered candles from my parents' ceiling, but still. The distraction is nice. Really nice.

Once the glowing candles hang along the ceiling of my mom and dad's house, I stretch my arms over my head and walk into the kitchen. Uncle Mack made a smorgasbord of Harry Potter-themed food, and Aunt Mia found a sorting hat, themed cloaks, and wands for every guest. Oh! And let's not forget their fake British accents, the giant spider stuffed animal, and the custom dog collar Aunt Mia purchased for her German Shepard to make him look like he has three heads instead of one.

It's corny and ridiculous, and I love it way more than I ever guessed I would.

"So, what do you think?" my mom waves her hand around, indicating the kitchen and family room turned banquet hall.

I bite back my grin. "I think you're crazy."

"Crazy awesome or just crazy?"

"Obviously, the answer's crazy awesome," Aunt Mia interjects. She wraps her arm around me and squeezes all the air from my lungs. "Thanks for giving your mom the idea to throw this party."

"Pretty sure you can thank Reeves for this little nugget, but you're welcome."

"Yeah, Reeves is a real peach." She gives me one more squeeze and lets me go. "Now, when is everyone else supposed to get here? I want some butterbeer."

"Speak of the devils," my dad says from the top of the second-floor stairs as the front door swings open, revealing Mav, Ophelia, Jax, Everett, Finley, and Griffin. Each of them takes turns hugging everyone and gushing about the decorations. Rory arrives a few minutes later with her dad, Henry, and their dog, Kovu. As soon as Aunt Mia sees them, she rushes toward her fluffy dog and slips on the three-headed dog collar, earning cackles from the rest of the group. Well, everyone but Rory, who's apparently too cool for her mom's whims.

Aunt Blakely and Uncle Theo turn up shortly after. They are in full-blown Dumbledore and Professor McGonagall attire—enough to make any fan gush—and I find myself grinning from ear to ear as I hug them.

A few minutes later, I give into my own curiosity and ask, "Where's Reeves?" I haven't seen him since we talked on the couch. I assumed he'd tag along with the rest of the group. But with him missing, I can't help feeling…anxious.

"He's coming," Maverick answers me. "Had to wrap up a few things."

"He's such a cutie," my mom adds.

"Mom." My eyes bug at her in a silent attempt to say, "*Zip it*," without actually voicing the words aloud and drawing more attention to our conversation. I may or may not have caught her up on a few things during decorating—while leaving out the jacking-off-in-the-shower portion—and she's yet to stop grinning.

She lifts her hands in defense. "What? I'm not allowed to say he's cute?"

"No pressure from us, babe," Aunt Mia interjects, giving my mom a look mirroring my own.

She nods back at her best friend, then turns to me. "Aunt Mia's right. Take your time, girlie. Seriously."

"There's no time to take," I remind her, "but thanks."

"So, who's ready for a tour of Hogwarts?" my mom announces.

"And who's ready for some beverages?" Aunt Kate chimes in from the kitchen. "The polyjuice potion is for adults only, but the pumpkin juice and butterbeer are kid-friendly."

"Gee, thanks," Rory mutters. Being the sole well-under twenty-one partygoer, she rolls her eyes, strolls through the family room, sidesteps the sorting hat and stool in the center, and heads straight out the back door, her dog trailing behind.

"Party pooper," her dad yells, but the girl doesn't stop her retreat.

As I watch her disappear, I ask, "Where's Tatum?" mentioning Ophelia's little sister.

Aunt Blakely, their mom, shakes her head. "She decided to stay home tonight. I'll tell her you asked about her, though."

With a weak smile, I nod. "Thanks."

Tatum's been absent since Archer's death. There's so much to unpack there. I wouldn't even know where to begin, so I stay quiet and am saved by a loud knock on the front door.

Griffin opens it seconds later, revealing an effortlessly sexy Reeves on the other side.

"Hey, man," Maverick greets him. "You get it done?"

He shakes his head but steals a quick glance my way. Turning back to his best friend, he tells him, "Not yet. Soon, though."

Mav nods but doesn't say anything else as Reeves runs his fingers through his shaggy brown hair. His massive bicep bulges beneath his white T-shirt, making my mouth water. I'm not sure why he decided to ditch a coat despite the cold weather, but with a view like this, I'm not complaining. He does the weird man-hug thing, patting Griffin's back, then Jaxon's and Everett's. He pulls the rest of the girls into friendly hugs while I wait at the back of the line. It feels weird. Like I'm sitting on pins and needles for a guy I shouldn't be sitting on pins and needles for. What was he finishing up, anyway? A date? A class? Something with the police? Something for his G-rated gigolo side gig? The thought makes my expression sour. I almost forgot about his extra-curricular activities until Finley mentioned them earlier today. Whether or not I want to admit it, the reminder doesn't exactly give me a lot of hope to hold on to despite his super sweet comment last night.

A kiss with you isn't meaningless.

Aaaand the butterflies are back.

A guy like Reeves has the power to own me—let alone every other girl on campus—and what happens if I'm not enough? And why am I even thinking about this? He dates other girls for a freaking living! Finley's right. Is Reeves tempting? Yes. But am I strong enough for the mess he brings with him? Hardly.

Boundaries, Dylan. Find some.

When Reeves reaches me, he smiles and pulls me into a side hug. Like he did with Finley. And Ophelia.

It's sweet.

Thoughtful.

Platonic.

It also makes me feel insecure and on edge, which is completely ridiculous.

What do I have to be insecure about?

Ha! Only everything.

Letting me go, he murmurs, "Hey, Dylan."

"Hi." I peek up at him and fold my arms. I don't know what else to say or how to act.

Sensing the tension around us, my mom steps in and pulls him into a hug. "Good to see you again, Reeves!"

"Good to see you, too, Mrs. Thorne." He steps back and lets out a low whistle as he takes in the themed decor. "The place looks great."

"Aw, thank you. I think it turned out pretty awesome, too." Arms folded, my mom rocks back on her heels, practically beaming. "We're so happy you could make it. And now that everyone's here, let's sort everyone into their houses, shall we?"

She guides us all into the family room, where a Harry Potter playlist is already on repeat, along with a tall leather stool from the kitchen sitting in the center of the carpeted area. Couches, LoveSacs, pillows, and blankets occupy the rest of the space, creating a cozy theater with room for everyone.

"All right, Griff, you first," my dad orders, motioning to the stool.

As he steps over a stuffed spider on the ground, Griff mutters, "You guys are insane," but plops down on the stool, playing along with our parents' antics.

Practically beaming, my dad slaps the sorting hat onto his youngest son's head, and Uncle Theo begins reading from a script one of the moms wrote. It's corny and silly and over the top and has my abs hurting from laughing so hard within minutes.

I kind of love it.

"Ravenclaw," Uncle Theo booms.

My dad takes off the hat and turns to me. "You're up, Dyl."

Slipping through the gap between Maverick and Reeves, a gentle brush of fingers tickles my wrist, and I turn back, catching a glimpse of a smirk from Reeves. Then I sit down on the stool.

The same spiel repeats as my dad places the worn sorting hat on my head.

"Hufflepuff," Uncle Theo announces.

Reeves is next. He's placed in Gryffindor, though I'm not surprised. I can feel the guy's main-character energy from a mile away. The red and gold colors make his warm under-tones even brighter as my mom slips on his house-themed cloak. However, when Reeves catches me checking him out, he gives me a cocky grin and moves to the side so Finley can take her place on the stool.

The hat barely touches her head before Uncle Theo yells, "Slytherin!"

"Called it," Griffin points out from the couch.

She scoffs. "Whatever, *Ravenclaw*. You're basically a glorified book nerd."

"Says the girl obsessed with books," he volleys back at her.

"Only murder mysteries, so watch your back, or I might find a place to bury your body."

"There are those Slytherin roots," he quips.

"All right, all right," Uncle Mack calls. "No fighting on school premises, or I'll have to take away your house points. Everett, you're up."

About half an hour later, everyone's spread out in the family room with custom cloaks and handmade wands while balancing plates of goodies on their laps as the first Harry Potter movie plays on the television screen in front of us.

A few minutes later, Reeves stands from his spot on the floor and disappears into the kitchen, returning with two fresh glasses of butterbeer. Instead of returning to his original seat, he takes the spot next to me on the couch. My breath catches in my lungs, and I sneak a peek at him in my periphery. It's stupid. I know it is. He's just a boy, and I'm just a girl, and we're only sitting on a couch. He isn't making a move. He isn't putting his arm around my shoulders. He isn't even touching me. Yet here I am, feeling like a livewire. Is he going to touch me again? Do I want him to touch me again? Yes. Yes, I want him to touch me again, but how do I show I want it without looking like an idiot?

Dipping closer, he offers me the cup, whispering, "Here."

I smile back at him and take it. When our fingers brush, a zing shoots up my arm, and I almost spill the stupid drink as he catches it at the last second.

"Shit, good catch," I blurt out.

My mom glances my way with a smile, then faces the television again.

"Don't worry, Thorne." Reeves offers me the drink again. "I have quick reflexes."

"Thanks." Carefully, I take it, turn back to the movie, and sneak a sip of the drink while over-dissecting how I can feel his attention on the side of my face.

"Are you having fun?" he adds, keeping his voice low enough for only me to hear.

I nod. "Yeah. You?"

"Yeah. Kind of surprised I was invited, but, hey, I'll take it."

"Why haven't you ever come before?" I whisper, sneaking a glance his way. "To family stuff? I mean, you're friends with the guys. I'm surprised I never saw you until this year."

He hesitates. "I'm not sure they consciously left me out of these things, but they're pretty protective of this." He looks around the room again. "This place. These people. These moments." His eyes find mine. "I'd be pretty protective, too."

My brows bunch, and I steal another taste of butterbeer while staring at the screen without registering anything happening in the movie. I can feel it, though. His envy. It's stupid, but it's true. *This?* A family hanging out together with friends and watching an old movie? It should feel juvenile or corny. And yeah, I guess it is. But knowing it isn't the norm— knowing some people wish they had the same thing and don't—I guess it puts things in a different perspective. One I should be grateful for. I can't help but feel sorry for him. For Reeves and the childhood he endured. The idea of a family like this, a loving, welcoming one, must be so foreign to him. As foreign as a wizarding world with a Dark Lord is to me.

The urge to move closer to him, to comfort him when he's one of the strongest people I know, while also knowing the house he grew up in, is overwhelming. But I keep my butt where it is and drink more of my butterbeer. I wonder what it was like to be raised with a dad like his. It took me about two whole seconds to see there wasn't exactly good blood between them. And if he doesn't have his mom or anyone else... How lonely it must be. A guy like Reeves doesn't deserve to be lonely. Someone who's kind and thoughtful and confident and sexy, and—

"What are you thinking?" he murmurs.

"I'm thinking..." I rub my lips together, watching how his attention drifts to the movement, "you're in the fold now, and there's no getting rid of us."

"I appreciate it." His chuckle warms my stomach, but I don't miss the way his smile falls flat.

Frowning, I point out, "You don't look very convinced."

"There's an old tale about a man who went through life," he explains. "Sometimes, he was lucky. Sometimes, he wasn't. And every time, people around him would say, 'You're so lucky,' or 'You're so unlucky,' and every time, he always replied, 'We'll see.'"

My lips pull at the corners. "Doesn't sound very optimistic."

"It's realistic," he clarifies. "There's a difference. It means life is always changing, you know? Archer's death. Maverick's transplant. This. *You.*" He takes a sip of his butterbeer and licks the foam from his top lip. "It isn't positive or negative. It's...appreciative of the now while recognizing the future can hold anything, and it's okay because it isn't our job to control shit. It's our job to roll with the punches and make the best of what we get. So, for now, I'm happy to be here. And as to whether or not I'll be invited again, all I can say is... We'll see."

I kind of hate it. How logical he looks at things. How matter-of-fact. But the worst part is I can't even argue with him. He's right. We can't control everything. Looking back over the last few months only confirms his outlook.

"We'll see, huh?" I repeat.

"Yeah." He smiles, and this time, it's more genuine. "We'll see. Now, I'm trying to let you take the lead on whatever's going on between us, but when I first walked in here and hugged you like I did the rest of the girls, you almost looked disappointed."

"I wasn't disappointed," I lie.

"Careful." He moves closer, and the heat in his gaze threatens to burn me from the outside in. "You're many things, Dylan Thorne, but hard to read isn't one of them."

Shame flares in my stomach as I set my butterbeer on the coffee table in front of me. "Ouch."

"Nah, it's a good thing," he argues. "It means you're real, and for a guy like me, I like *real* a lot. So, I think the real question is, why were you so disappointed?"

I open my mouth, then close it just as quickly, unsure what to say or how to explain the ridiculousness of the entire situation.

"Let me guess." He manages to bend even closer. "After our conversation last night and the lineup of hugs, it made you feel...dejected?"

I press my lips together.

"Unimportant?" he offers.

I must make a face or something because the guy nods his understanding. "Trust me, Pickles. The only girl I saw when I walked into the house was you." His knee bumps against mine as he drinks more of his butterbeer, oblivious to the movie on the screen. Hell, it's as if I'm the only person in the room. The only person who matters, and for a girl so used to blending in, it leaves me squirming.

"My pretty little wallflower." There's a slight rasp in his voice, and it scrapes over my skin, spreading goosebumps along every inch of me. I'm not sure if the words are meant for me or if he's saying them to himself, but the awe? The fascination? The knowing lift of his lips? I can't wrap my head around it, but for the first time ever, I want to. I want to wrap my head around it. I want to understand it. I want to see what he sees.

He sets his butterbeer beside mine on the coffee table and wraps his arm around the back of the couch, leaving his side wide open. "Come snuggle with me."

Staring at his welcoming side, I counter, "Are we on snuggling terms?"

"I mean, you left a puddle of drool on my pillow the night you slept in my bed, which is pretty intimate, especially when I don't let anyone sleep in my bed."

I gasp. "I did not."

"You most definitely did," he argues.

Tugging the collar of my cape up, I cover the bottom of my face, hoping to hide my embarrassment, but it feeds his amusement and attracts a few curious looks my way. Thankfully, my friends turn back to the television without any fuss.

Once we have a semblance of privacy, I beg, "Tell me you're joking."

"Definitely not joking, but don't worry." He leans closer until his breath tickles the shell of my ear. "I like my girls wet." He pulls away, winking as he tosses his arm around my shoulders and tugs me into him.

And for some reason I literally don't understand, I let him.

Besides, it's only snuggling.

Isn't it?

27

REEVES

I t's late. The lights are off on the main floor, so I flick
on the hallway light as I head to the kitchen, keeping
my footsteps quiet in the silent house. Finally home
from my last job, my head is killing me. After grabbing some
ice from the fridge and placing it on my fresh black eye, I
head upstairs, change into a pair of sweats, and collapse onto
my bed. All I want to do is watch a show and wind down,
maybe unplug my brain for a few. I reach for the remote on
my nightstand but hesitate when soft, feminine voices slip
through my closed bedroom door.

"Are you sure?" one of them asks.

"Seriously, not a big deal," the other girl replies. It's Dylan.
I'd recognize her quiet voice anywhere. "Have, uh, fun, I
guess?" she adds.

The other person snorts. "Don't worry. I will. And thanks
again. Seriously."

With a quiet click, the door across from mine closes, and I
press my ear to the solid piece of wood separating me from
Dylan. I wait for the soft pad of feet against the floor, but all I
hear is silence. Curious, I twist the handle, finding Dylan

cross-legged on the floor. Her back is pressed to the wall, her giant sleep shirt hangs off one shoulder, and her black glasses are propped on her button nose.

I haven't seen Dylan since her parents' house. Not gonna lie. I've kept my distance on purpose, afraid of overstepping my boundaries until I could fulfill my contract with Lilah. As of tonight, it's finished, and all bets are off.

"Hey," I murmur.

She jerks in surprise and looks up at me. "Oh. Hey." Her forehead scrunches as she squints. "Shit, what happened? Are you okay?"

It's still dark in the hallway, so I'm not sure how she noticed the fresh shiner, but I offer my hand and help her stand. "Never better. What are you doing out here?"

"Never better, my ass," she mutters. Reaching up, she brushes her thumb along my bruised cheekbone and sighs. "Seriously, Oliver. What happened?"

"Did you just call me Oliver?"

She frowns. "It's your name, isn't it?"

My mouth lifts. "Guess so."

"Am I not allowed to call you by your name?"

"You're allowed."

"And yet, you act like I said two plus two equals five."

"Nah, just not used to pretty girls slipping past my defenses so easily. I like it, though," I add. "Keep it up, yeah?"

"I'll see what I can do," she replies, peeking up at me again through those dark glasses. When her eyes land on my bruise again, her frown deepens. "So?" she pushes. "What happened?"

"You should see the other guy."

Her hand falls. "You got into another fight?"

"Appears so."

"How...stupid."

"Necessary."

"Pretty sure fights are never necessary."

"Depends on the crowd," I hedge.

Her lips purse. "You should put some ice on it or something." I lift the bag of ice in my palm, and she nods. "Good."

"What are you doing out here?" I ask.

"Drew wants to…" She sucks her lips between her teeth. "Ya know…"

I chuckle knowingly and glance at the closed bedroom door. "Phone sex, huh? I tell ya, video calls brought a whole new angle to the game."

"You act like you were around before video calls."

"I heard stories."

"Mm-hmm," she hums. "From who? Your current geriatric clients?"

I snort. "Past clients, but yeah. Guess you could say so."

Her lips part, and I swear I can feel the question on the tip of her tongue, but instead of asking me why I corrected her, she darts right back into her little tortoise shell like a baby turtle and changes the subject. "Apparently, Drew didn't get laid while he was in town and figured Finley could make it up to him tonight."

"And you're the one paying the price by having to hang out in the hallway."

"Yeah. And it's not like I can go downstairs since I might run into Everett, and if he asks why I'm not hanging out in the room—"

"You'll crumble like the Cave of Wonders and tell him his baby sister's doing the hanky-panky over the internet?"

"Cave of—" Her yawn cuts her off, and she covers her mouth. "From *Aladdin*, right?"

"The one and only." Tilting my head toward my bedroom door, I add, "Come on."

"Oh, I don't have to—" she yawns again.

"Come on, sleepyhead. You can hang out in my room until Finley's finished."

Grudgingly, she places her hand in mine. "Fine. But only because you insist."

"Glad I can be of service."

She pauses and tilts her head, taking in the fresh shiner on my cheekbone. "Okay, seriously, though. What happened?"

"It's a long story."

"Not exactly an answer," she murmurs.

"Come inside?"

"Fine." Her bare toes are painted blue. I don't know why I notice, but I do as she makes her way into my bedroom. Staring at the bed, she rocks back on her heels and folds her arms.

"There a problem?" I ask.

"I feel weird."

"About what?"

"Being in your space."

"You've been in my space before," I remind her.

"Yeah, but last time I was in your space, I was exhausted, and I wasn't thinking straight, and I, apparently, drooled on your pillow, and..."

"And what?"

"I don't know? You're the one who mentioned crusty sheets when we were cleaning out Griffin's room, and—"

"Are you asking if my sheets are crusty?" I muse.

Her nose wrinkles. "Ew. No. Um...forget I said anything."

"I don't have sex in my bed," I interrupt.

Damn, this girl's cute when she's flustered and talking about sex? It works like a charm.

Her brows bunch as if the s-word rendered her speechless. "Huh?"

"I said, I don't have sex in my bed, so you don't have to worry about crusty sheets."

"Technically, it's none of my business."

"And technically, I want to make it your business," I argue. "So let me."

The wrinkle between her brows softens, and she lets out a quiet exhale. "Reeves…"

"You won't find any crusty sheets in here. Promise." I lift my chin toward the bed. "Take a seat."

Carefully, she sits on the edge of the bed. Her mouth twitches as she takes in the room with fresh eyes.

"Something funny?"

Tearing her attention from the flatscreen TV hanging on the wall, she asks, "Have you always been a sucker for movies?"

"Have you always *not* been a sucker for movies?" I toss back at her.

"I like movies."

"Yet you never know what I'm talking about when I quote them," I point out.

Her fingers brush against the side of her head. "After the accident, it took a few years until I could watch anything on a screen without getting a migraine or feeling nauseated," she explains. "What's your excuse for your obsession?"

"You caught that, huh?"

"Mm-hmm," she hums. "I'm not the only one who's easy to read, Oliver."

Oliver.

Fuck, I like the way my name sounds when she says it.

Squeezing the back of my neck, I debate how much information I should throw at the girl. Giving in, I explain, "You could say some of my favorite movies were more like a parent than my dad ever was."

"What do you mean?"

"Movies were my escape growing up." I pause. "Actually, they're still my escape. Do you want to watch one?" I motion to my black eye, adding, "I kind of had a shit night."

Her curious gaze bounces around my face a few times, but she nods softly and scoots over, leaving me some room on the bed to sit beside her. After turning on a movie, I steal the offered space and lift my arm to wrap around her shoulders when she stops me, grabbing my hand and assessing the damage along my knuckles. Her bottom lip juts out as she softly drags her fingers against the split flesh from the bastard's tooth cutting into me.

"You're cute when you worry about me," I murmur, fascinated by the concern in her aqua depths.

"It isn't funny."

"Never said it was funny."

Her gaze flicks to mine. "I can hear the amusement in your voice. Your knuckles haven't even had time to heal from Homecoming."

Sobering, I cup her cheek with my other hand. "I'm fine, Dylan. Promise."

"What happened?"

With a sigh, I scratch my temple. "My client's ex didn't like seeing me with her."

"Then why hire you?"

"So he would see me with her."

She frowns. "I don't understand."

"You can blame your brother," I mutter.

"Griffin?"

"Jax," I clarify. "During my freshman year, I got a lot of attention from the, uh," I clear my throat, "the puck bunnies. A few of the guys asked how I did it. I joked about how dating is nothing more than a game, and they requested pointers. Since I was short on cash…"

"You made them pay you."

"Yeah."

"And Jax paid you?"

I laugh. "Nah, but I'm definitely telling your older brother you thought he needed my help getting laid."

"Hey!" she argues. "You're the one who said I can blame Jax."

"True," I concede. "But no. I'll get to the part Jax played in a second. Word got around how I was helping the guys, and a girl asked if the same went for them. I joked around, saying she didn't need any help 'cause she was already beautiful. Unfortunately, she didn't see it, so I had to explain it to her. Guys are simple. All we want is what we can't have. Make the girl untouchable, and the guys will fall at her feet."

"So?"

"So, I proved it by taking her out. As soon as the guys saw me acting like I was interested in her, they became interested, as well."

"And the woman at Rowdy's?"

"Like I said, she wanted to feel desirable and to be told which quirks might *not* be desirable."

"And you're a big enough asshole to oblige."

"Exactly," I agree dryly.

"What does all this have to do with Jax?"

"One day, a girl approached me and asked how to be *un*desirable. She'd found herself on her ex-boyfriend's bad side, and he wouldn't leave her alone. The problem was I didn't know how to fix it. I started brainstorming with the guys, and Jax had a suggestion."

"What was it?"

"Well, you might want to ask your dad for the details, but from what Jax told me, your dad wound up fake dating your Aunt Mia to protect her from an abusive ex when they were in college. Supposedly, it worked with your dad and aunt, so I tried it with the girl."

"I thought you said fake dating made girls more desirable?"

I blow the air from my lungs, trying to find a way to explain a possessive person's psyche. "Abusive assholes aren't like most guys."

"You say it you like you know from personal experience."

"My dad's an ass, remember?" I offer. "Sometimes all it takes for a guy to leave their victim alone is learning there's someone in their corner. Someone who isn't afraid to kick their ass if they keep bothering her. Usually, all it takes is one altercation, then they leave the girl alone."

"Usually," she repeats.

"If it turns into anything more, I make sure they press charges, and that's that."

"So, you're willing to get the crap kicked out of you for money?"

"I don't make them pay. Not when they already feel isolated and unworthy of someone's time or empathy. I don't usually take on clients who attend LAU anymore, either. It started messing with my reputation and shit, but after seeing Lilah's bruises on the quad, I had to say yes."

"Lilah," she repeats. "The girl from the party before Homecoming."

"Yeah."

"So, you're a saint," she surmises.

"Nah, I'm still an ass. But an ass who doesn't like to see girls being hurt."

Her eyes fall to my mouth. She blinks slowly and clears her throat. "Do you, um, have any more clients lined up?"

"Nah, Lilah was the last one."

Her eyes widen in surprise. "Why?"

"I'm retiring."

"Why would you retire?"

"Guess I realized something."

Fuck, I can see it. The spark of hope in her eyes. The slight hitch of her breath. The way she's anxious and on edge. Like I have the power to make or break her right now, and fuck, do I hope it's the first.

"And what did you realize?" she whispers.

"Maybe Ron and Hermoine aren't so bad together."

Her brows furrow. "What?"

"Don't get me wrong. I'm a sucker for enemies to lovers and all, but this whole will-they, won't-they friends tension we got going isn't too bad, either."

The sound of her quiet amusement causes my chest to tighten as she turns to me fully. "Are you serious right now?"

"Tell me you don't feel it."

"Reeves—"

I grab her chin and tug her closer. "Tell me you don't feel it."

Those aqua-blues bounce between my eyes, and her lips part.

"I like you, Dylan Thorne. I like you a lot. And even though it isn't my MO to care, with you, I do. I care a lot. Seeing the way you blush or how you look at your feet when you're uncomfortable... I like you, and I'm stubborn enough to fight for what I want. The real question is, do you like me, too?"

Her straight white teeth nibble on her bottom lip as she stares at me. Eyes wide. Innocence gleaming. I wasn't kidding when I told her I wouldn't kiss her again until she had all of me. Without my side gig to overshadow my feelings or make her second-guess them in the first place. And with my obligation to Lilah over? Fuck me, Dylan's never looked more tempting.

"Answer the question, Dylan," I push. "Do you like me, too?"

"Yes." It's nothing but a whisper. A breath. A secret.

I bask in it, nonetheless. The last of my restraint feels like loose strings of thread, and she's tugging at them one by one.

"Let me kiss you."

She hesitates, her breathing staggered and unsteady as her eyes fall to my lips. But she doesn't answer me. Doesn't put me out of my misery. Doesn't give me her consent when I desperately need it.

"Gonna need your permission, Pickles."

Her breath of laughter touches my cheeks, but she stays quiet, refusing to give me what I need.

"Do you not want me to kiss you?" I ask.

"I do," she whispers. "It's…"

"What is it?"

"I've only kissed a very small handful of guys, Reeves." She wets her bottom lip, her breathing growing more and more shallow with every passing second. "And even though we kind of explored our chemistry the last time we were in this room, I feel like right now might be different." Her teeth dig into the inside of her cheek. "Might be…more? Or maybe, I'm… I don't know. It isn't the point, though. My point is, with you, I…I don't know what your expectations are."

I pull back, surprised by her honesty. "I have no expectations."

"Every guy has expectations."

"Okay," I concede. "Let's lay them out for you, then. I expect you to tell me how you feel. What you like and what you don't like. What makes you uncomfortable—if anything," I clarify. "And if or when you want me to stop, I expect you to communicate with me."

"I don't, uh, I don't always do well with communication." She pauses, running her fingers through her hair as she pushes it away from her face. "Is that weird? What am I saying? Of course, it's weird. It's *me* we're talking about."

"Not weird, Dylan."

"Debatable."

With my knuckle, I lift her chin. "Does this feel weird? My hands on you?" Her lids flutter slightly, though I doubt she even realizes it, so I push, "Answer the question."

"If I say yes, will you stop?"

I nod.

"Then no, it's not weird."

My lips twitch. "You're lying."

"You said if I tell you the truth, you'll stop."

"Tell me the truth," I murmur.

She closes her eyes and lets out an exasperated sigh. "Yes, it's weird, but not for the reason you think."

"Care to expand?"

"Thanks to my lack of experience, any guy touching me would be weird," she admits. "But it doesn't feel *wrong*, so..."

I nod again, enjoying the torture she's putting me through way more than I should. "Do you trust me?"

"Should I trust you?" she counters.

"Probably not." My lips tilt up. "But we've come this far, right?" Shifting closer, I whisper, "Does this feel wrong?"

She shakes her head in my gentle grasp, causing her silky skin to skate along my knuckle as she stares up at me, those doe eyes wreaking havoc on my restraint. She's fucking silk, and I want to wrap myself up in her.

"What are you thinking?" she whispers.

"I'm thinking I want to kiss you."

"Anything else?"

My mouth twitches again. "I'm thinking you're awfully chatty right now."

"Is that a bad thing?"

"It's a *you* thing," I joke.

"Is *that* bad?" she repeats.

"Are you stalling, Pickles?"

"Yes." I lean even closer, my lips barely brushing against hers, when she adds, "And no."

Pulling back slightly, my brows furrow. "No?"

"Honestly, I'm not sure? When you're sitting close like this, it's hard to think straight."

"And that's a bad thing?" I ask, throwing her own words back at her.

Her breath quivers across my lips. "I'm not sure."

"Again with the back and forth."

"The push and pull," she adds.

"The will they, won't they," I murmur. "And fuck, do I want them to, Dylan."

"Me too."

My chest tightens at her acquiescence, and I swear, if I died right here, right now, I'd be okay with it. Keeping my movements slow and controlled, I lean in again, waiting for her to push me away. Instead, her lashes flutter, and she closes her eyes. I kiss her softly, holding on to the last of my restraint as I taste the girl in front of me. No tongue. Just lips. Hell, there's barely any pressure either. But the feel of her. Warm. Pliant. Fucking supple. The combination shoots straight to my groin, and I nearly crumble from the assault, desperate to fall to my knees and worship her the way she deserves. Sliding my hand along her cheek, I thread my fingers through her hair and tilt her head further up, keeping the same gentle pressure.

When a soft whimper hits the back of her throat, I pull away, my eyes bouncing around her face as I wait for regret or fear or whatever the fuck she might feel, but her eyes are still closed. Only the tiniest of divots between her brows gives me a clue as to what might be going on in her head.

"What's wrong?" I ask.

"Nothing," she whispers.

"Dylan…"

She blinks slowly as if forcing herself to come back to earth when she'd clearly been lost in the clouds. Her hands press against my chest, but instead of pulling away, she keeps her palm on my heart, feeling the steady rhythm as if it's the one thing keeping her from floating away.

"What are you thinking?" I ask.

"I'm thinking you're kind of a terrifying guy to fall for, Oliver, and yet, for some reason I genuinely don't understand, I can't help myself."

My mouth twitches. "Is that a bad thing?"

"It depends," she whispers. "Are you really done dating other girls? And I'm not trying to be controlling or whatever by asking you this. But I need to know how deep I should let myself go, and one boundary I realized before Homecoming is you fake-dating other girls, even when it's weirdly chivalrous, is a no-go zone for me, so—"

"I told you I wouldn't kiss you until I was all yours, Pickles. Tonight was the last time," I reassure her. "I promise."

"Promise?"

"Promise," I repeat. "Lilah's been my last client for a while now, but since her ex wouldn't rear his head anytime we tried to lure him out, it took a little longer than I anticipated to finish the job. But after tonight? He won't be a problem anymore, and neither will she."

The tension in her muscles melts away, and she scoots closer, giving me a fucking Eskimo kiss as a smile toys at the edge of her lips. "Where were we?"

My mouth is on hers in an instant, our bodies melding together as I snake my arms around her waist and memorize every curve. Every whimper. Every fucking inch of the girl plastered to me.

I should be softer. I should be more patient. More willing to let her take the lead when we both know I'm more experienced than she is. But I can't help it. I feel like we've played this game for so long. Dancing around what we could be. What I could give her. Tonight, I've finally snapped, and there's no going back. To be honest, there's been no going back for a while. I think of her. Dream of her. Worry for her. She's on my mind constantly, and I can't let her go.

Her body molds to mine as her fingers toy with the edge of my shirt. I doubt she knows how close she is to touching my cock. I doubt she knows how much I'm craving her fingertips to run along my stomach or the patch of skin she's dangerously close to skating across. My abs tighten at the thought, and my dick fucking weeps in my pants as I angle her head higher. Running my tongue along her bottom lip, I taste her slight gasp and dive in further, licking her playfully and smiling against her mouth when she moans softly.

"Is this like you remembered?" I murmur against her lips.

"Pretty sure you were taking it easy on me the last time we were in this room."

I chuckle, nipping at her bottom lip one more time. "And now, all bets are off."

Leaning forward, I kiss her again, savoring the slight inhale as soon as my lips touch hers. She melts against me. My hands ache to touch her. To push her onto her back and slip between her pretty little thighs, but I hold back, forcing myself to take things slow. To be patient, no matter how impossible it feels. She slides her tongue against my bottom lip, and I groan, shifting closer to her on the bed. Her hands find my shirt, and she twists the fabric in her fingers. My abs tighten when the soft brush of her fingertips hits my bare stomach, causing my dick to jump.

Forcing myself to pull away from her, I rest my forehead against hers and let out a slow breath. "Need you to slow down, Pickles."

Eyes closed, she laughs. "Still with the pickle bit, huh?"

"Come on, it's kind of cute."

"It's terrible."

"What do you have against pickles?"

"Nothing, I—"

"What about cucumbers?" I shift softly against her, letting her feel my erection against her hip, and she laughs even harder.

"Does this work for you? Talking about cucumbers while rubbing your..." she gulps, and her eyes fall to the outline of my dick in my sweats.

"You have no idea how well it works," I warn, but instead of going in for another kiss, I toss my arm around her shoulders and tug her closer. "But for the time being, we're gonna snuggle and watch a movie." I hesitate. "Actually." My eyes gleam. "One sec."

I feel her watching me as I head to the closet and rummage through the top shelf.

"What are you doing?" she questions.

My fingers hit the edge of a grocery sack, and I grin, pulling it down.

"What is it?"

Without answering, I toss the bag onto the mattress.

Curious, she searches the grocery bag, a soft laugh escaping her. "Peanut butter cups?"

"Is there a problem with peanut butter cups?"

"Not at all. I guess I assumed you were a sucker for variety."

"Until I find what I like," I murmur. "Then I can't get enough." Once my back is pressed to the headboard, I raise my arm and urge her closer. "Where were we?"

28

DYLAN

"Stop. Dad, stop. I'll be good. I swear, I'll be..."

The muffled plea trails off as I peel my eyelids open. It's dark, nothing but the small night-light in the corner of the room to give the space any kind of illumination, but it provides enough of a glow for me to see the tight expression painted on Reeves' face as he shakes his head back and forth on the pillow. He's asleep. He's dreaming.

"Dad." He groans and rolls onto his side, giving me his back and bringing his knees to his chest, his voice tainted with agony.

Sitting up, I touch his shoulder, and he flinches away.

"Reeves," I murmur. "Reeves, wake up."

Pained whimpers slip out of him, but he doesn't stir, so I touch him again, shaking softly. "Reeves, wake up," I order. "Reeves!"

He jerks upright, and his head hangs as his shoulders heave with uneven breaths. Eyelids fluttering, he turns to me and frowns, scrubbing his hand over his face. "Fuck."

"You okay?" I ask.

"Nightmare."

"Gathered that much." I reach for him again and touch his bent knee. "Is everything all right?"

With a slow exhale, his hand drops to his lap, his exhaustion palpable. "Just the usual, Pickles."

I smile at the sentiment. "Do you want to...talk about it?"

"Not much to tell. My dad's an abusive fucker who liked locking me in the closet. Sometimes, the memories haunt me at night."

A closet? He was locked in a closet? What kind of asshole locks their kid in a closet?

Rage flares inside me, but I force it back because he doesn't need me to add fuel to the fire, not when he's already heated. He needs me to stamp it out. To calm him down. To help him relax.

"I'm sorry, Reeves."

"No need to apologize. It isn't your fault."

"Still," I offer. "It doesn't make it okay."

"Nothing makes the shit my dad put me through okay. But waking up next to a beautiful girl helps take away the sting. Thanks for waking me up." The night-light's glow makes the warm brown of his eyes look like brownie batter as he settles back onto the mattress, and then it hits me.

"It's why you use a night-light, isn't it? Because of the closet."

"Yeah." He smiles, but it doesn't reach his eyes. "Childhood trauma's a bitch. Now, come here. Let's get some sleep."

Settling beside him, I rest my hand on his chest, but his breathing feels...forced almost. Like he's trying too hard to control it. Like he can't catch his breath.

"Are you going to be able to relax?" I whisper against his chest.

"I'll be fine."

"Not an answer." I try to sit back up again, but his grip tightens.

"I like this side of things."

"What side of things?"

"The girl looking out for me instead of the other way around," he muses. "Don't get me wrong. I love a good damsel in distress, but having someone look out for me, willing to fight my battles? It's nice." He drops a kiss on the crown of my head, then lays his head back on the pillow. "Like a fresh, crispy...pickle."

With a laugh, I smack his opposite pec, pulling a rumble of amusement from him. When we both quiet down, we fall back to sleep. And by some miracle, he doesn't move for the rest of the night, holding me tightly against him as his breathing slows and the fight dissipates from his body.

He was right about one thing. I have a feeling no matter how our relationship—or whatever this thing is—plays out, I'll always look out for him. After everything he's been through, everything he's endured all by himself, he deserves it.

29

DYLAN

After Reeves' nightmare, I slept like a baby but woke up alone. By some miracle, Finley didn't give me any crap at the breakfast table the next morning for sleeping in Reeves' room. I have a hunch it's because Everett sat across from us, and she didn't want me to spill the beans about why I wasn't in my room in the first place.

It's getting cooler, but I choose one of my own jackets instead of wrapping myself in one of Reeves' hoodies scattered across his messy room. Messy. Not dirty. No. On a deeper level, the place is practically pristine. But the clothes? The unmade bed? The stack of Blu-rays on the dresser and the handful of candy wrappers littered next to them? It's... fitting, somehow. Like the man himself. Underneath everything, he's kind of perfect.

My lips kick up at the memory as I walk to class with Everett and Griffin. They're up ahead, chatting about tomorrow's game while I trail behind, lost in thought, remembering last night while fighting the butterflies attacking my stomach at the prospect of today's photography class.

After saying goodbye to Griff and Everett, I head to my

seat. My muscles relax into the chair as Dr. Broderick stands from his desk and walks to the front of the room.

When he starts talking, Reeves appears in the doorway, and the girls in front of me start whispering like they did during our first class at the beginning of the semester.

"Nice of you to join us, Reeves," Dr. Broderick comments.

A second later, deja vu hits me as Reeves takes big steps, striding toward me and collapsing into the seat beside mine. He pushes something across the table in my direction, and my forehead wrinkles as I study the contents.

It's a box.

A plain cardboard box.

No label. No picture. No hints as to what's inside.

Curious, I peek up at Reeves, and he murmurs, "Maybe open it after class."

"What is it?"

"You'll see."

"Reeves…"

He grabs my hand from toying with the edge of the lid, slips it under the table, and rests it in his lap. His touch is gentle—casual—as he plays with my fingers, dragging the tip of his own along every crevice. Every surface. It feels amazing. And intimate.

"What are you doing?" I whisper.

"Distracting you."

"From what, exactly?"

"From what's in the box." He leans closer. "Don't want you going all Brad Pitt on me from *Seven*."

My brows bunch. "Huh?"

"*Seven*?" he repeats. "The movie?"

"I don't know what it is—"

"Aw, come on, Pickles. *Seven*? About the serial killer. *'What's in the box? What's in the box?'*" His face contorts like he's caught between begging and fear. I stare blankly back at him until his usual persona clicks back into place, and he tsks, "So disappointing."

Like an egg, my indifference cracks, and I shake my head. "You're insane."

He grins. "Yeah, I know."

"Hey, Reeves," the girl in front of us interrupts.

Annoyance flashes across his face, but he covers it in an instant. "Yeah?"

"You excited for the game tonight?"

"Uh, yeah. It'll be good."

He turns back to me, effectively dismissing her as she adds, "You should keep an eye on the crowd. I got you a present, but I can't give it to you until the—"

"You know who loves gifts?" he interrupts. "Griffin. Me? I hate gifts unless they're from my girl here." He rests his arm on top of my chair and leans back, making sure I'm fully included in the conversation. "But Griff? Griff's a big fan of presents. Whatever you have planned should definitely be for him."

"Oh." Her bottom lip juts out in a pout. "But my friend likes Griff and—"

"Miss Brown," Dr. Broderick snaps from the front of the room. Like a top, the girl spins around in her seat and crouches down, trying to make herself smaller. With another stern look, he continues, "As I was saying, today, you'll discuss the second emotion for your project. Talk with your partner about which emotion you'd like to focus on and schedule a time to make it happen. I need a list of props and a description of the desired setting on my desk by Friday. Any questions?" The guy barely waits a millisecond. "Good. Get started."

Reeves rolls his shoulders and scoots closer, bringing us knee to knee. "So. Emotions."

"Emotions."

"Should we go straight to horny? Or—"

"Reeves!" I smack his chest and bury my face in my hands.

"Hey, there's nothing wrong with horny, Pickles. Ha! Horny pickles. Get it?"

"Oh, yeah," I mutter into my hands, "I definitely get it, which is saying something, considering I've never—" I smash my lips together and rest my forehead against the desk, praying it'll open up and swallow me entirely as my words hang in the air. And thanks to the tension I can literally feel rolling off Reeves beside me, I know he heard me loud and clear.

Well, isn't this a great way to start my day after spending a pretty incredible night beside a guy I really like.

Why? Why do you have to blurt out random shit, Dylan? Can you please learn to keep your freaking mouth shut?

I'm lost in my head, so I barely notice when Reeves leans closer and keeps his voice low. "You're cute when you're embarrassed, but I already figured out you're a virgin. You don't need to be ashamed."

Oh, boy. The things I could say that would unhinge this man's jaw.

Instead, all I squeak is, "Yup."

"But it doesn't mean you've never masturbated and shit, right?"

I bury my face even more, cradling the back of my head with my hands. "You did not just ask me that question."

"Dylan," he says with a laugh. Yanking me up, he grabs both sides of my face, then looks around the room, making sure no one's eavesdropping. I do the same, grateful everyone seems as invested in their own conversations as Reeves is with ours. "Look, you have nothing to be ashamed of, Pickles. There's nothing wrong with a little bean flicking or meat jerking. Trust me, if there was, I'm pretty sure my dick would've fallen off by ninth grade."

We are not having this conversation. We are not having this conversation. We are not—

"Why do you look like you're about to puke?" he questions, though he has the decency to stay quiet as his eyes bounce around my face like a pinball. "Seriously. Did your parents catch you once or something? Honestly, I think it's kind of hot. Not your parents catching you— gross—but the idea of you getting all worked up and slipping your hand—"

"Stop. Talking." I try to cover his mouth, but he swats my hand away, undeterred, and goes back to framing my face with his very large hands. I have zero doubts he won't drop this topic until he gets the answers he's searching for. Avoiding his gaze, I mumble, "My parents didn't catch me doing anything because there was nothing to catch."

"Nothing to… What are you saying?" His eyes widen, and he lets my face go. "Have you never come before, Dylan?"

"I, uh," I gulp, "I think that's a question for a better time and place."

Stunned, he falls back in his seat.

"Fuck." His attention falls on my lips. "Yeah. Yeah, we'll definitely have a very long conversation about this later, and, uh." He smiles. "And I think you should be excited. But on that note." Clearing his throat, he leans his elbows against the hard surface of the table. "I gotta calm the hell down. What's another emotion, Pickles? One that doesn't make me want to toss you on the table and make you come with my mouth?"

My jaw drops, and I scan the room again, freaking flabbergasted by the lack of response from my classmates after the words that just came from this man's mouth.

Came. Mouth.

Dammit, he's rubbing off on me.

Focus, Dylan.

Realizing no one heard us, thankfully, I try to stay on the topic at hand, or at least attempt to search for a new one.

"Right. Emotions. Uh...sadness? Anger? Embarrassment? Surprise?"

"Surprise," he grunts. "If you had a camera to capture the last three minutes, you'd already be done." He shakes his head and clears his throat. "But yeah, I like it. Let's go with surprise."

"Perfect."

Grabbing my hand, he tucks it under the table and rests our entwined fingers on his thigh. "Perfect."

The rest of class crawls by at a snail's pace, but he doesn't let go of my hand. Not once. And by halfway through, I relax a little more, savoring the feel of his hand in mine. When the teacher excuses us a little while later, the other students push to their feet and head to wherever they're going while Reeves and I stay seated.

Brushing his thumb along the back of my hand one more time, he lets me go, grabs the box, places it on the table, and sits back in his chair, lifting his chin toward it.

"Can I open it now?" I ask.

He nods.

Unfolding the flaps, I find almost two dozen DVDs. They're the same ones from his room. My brows pinch as I look up at him again. "Your movie collection?"

"Yeah. Like I said last night, in a weird way, *these* raised me." He motions to the box. "I want to introduce you to them. Keep digging, though. There's something else in there."

Curious, I pick up a few of the DVDs to find a small, laminated card. When I recognize what it is, I laugh but don't bother lifting it from the box. "Are you serious?"

"Take a look, *Dani*."

Giving in, I reach for the fake ID and study it, surprised by how legitimate it actually looks. Dani Reeves. "Who's Dani?"

"From *Game of Thrones*? You know, Daenerys? Daenerys Targaryen?"

"Oh, yeah. The girl with the white hair, right?"

He clutches at his chest. "You're killing me, Smalls."

"And you're killing my good girl persona with a gift like this."

"A guy can hope," he quips.

Ignoring the heat in my cheeks, I study the card more carefully, my brows pinching as I drag my finger across the name printed on the driver's license. "You picked Reeves for the last name instead of the dragon lady's name."

"I'm subtle like that."

My gaze locks with his. "Mm-hmm."

"What, you're not convinced?" he challenges.

"Pretty sure subtle is the last word I would use to describe you."

His mouth lifts. "You're not wrong." He scoots a little closer to me. "Come with me to the Halloween party at SeaBird."

"SeaBird throws a Halloween party?"

"Yeah. Don't get me wrong. It's nothing like the costume parties we throw,"—he winks—"but it's still pretty fun. Come with me."

"I didn't hear a question," I snark.

Grasping my hand, he runs his thumb along the back, then brings it to his lips. "Will you, Dani Reeves, go to the Halloween party at SeaBird with me?"

"Are you asking me out?"

He nods. "It's exactly what I'm doing. Say yes."

It's official. I'm reeling. I mean, sure. After last night, I knew this was a possibility, but it's Oliver freakin' Reeves. And he's asking me out. Me. Dylan Becca Thorne. Like, what alternate universe am I in right now?

"You gonna leave me hanging, Pickles?" he challenges.

"Yes."

"Yes, you're gonna leave me hanging, or yes, you'll go out with me?"

"The second one," I rush out.

His smile widens. "It's a date."

"What's that?" Dr. Broderick demands, snapping me back to reality and the fact Reeves and I are most definitely the last two students still in the room.

With a clatter, the box slips from my fingers and falls onto the desk. Reeves closes the top and scoops the whole thing into his large hands, tucking it under his arm. "It's a dildo. I keep telling her to leave it at home, but—"

"Reeves!" I smack his chest, and a loud laugh rumbles up his throat.

"I'm kidding." He turns to Dr. Broderick and shakes his head with wide eyes like he most definitely is *not* kidding.

As I shove him in the chest, he laughs even harder.

Dr. Broderick loses interest, and he waves toward the door. "Get out of here, you two. And keep your sex toys at home."

"Did you hear him?" Reeves asks. "He said *our* sex toys."

"No, he didn't. He said your—"

"The *plural* your," Reeves corrects me. He tosses his arm over my shoulder, guiding me toward the exit.

As I peek up at him, I mutter, "You're insane."

"You know, I think you mentioned that already."

And it's strange. Being under Reeves' arm. Feeling the stares from those around us and the assumptions I have no doubt they're making. How I'm simply another flavor of the week, and he'll grow bored with me by Friday. But for some reason, a small part of me doesn't buy into those assumptions. Not when I slept in his bed last night. Not when I know his past with his dad or how he still has nightmares from his childhood. Not when he's been so open and vulnerable with me from the very beginning, making me wonder if I'm brave enough to do the same.

No. I think this is real for both of us. And even though it should terrify me, it doesn't. Because Oliver Reeves said it himself. He likes real. And you know what? So do I.

The air is cool as we walk outside, and the slight breeze ruffles my hair, causing a chill to run up my spine. I burrow a little closer to Reeves and steal some of his body heat. If he doesn't like our proximity, he's a good actor because he pulls me closer, not even bothering to stop and chat with one of his friends when they call his name.

"So, what do you say?" he asks. "Want to skip class and have a movie marathon with me?"

"I can't. I have a test," I admit. "But, uh, thank you. For the gifts. They mean a lot, Oliver."

His muscles freeze, and he turns to me. "Did you pull out the first name again?"

I lick my bottom lip and repeat, "Is it a problem, *Oliver*?"

He steps closer, and my pulse quickens. "Careful. There's a lot of power in a name."

"What kind of power?"

"The kind making me want to push you up against the nearest wall and bury my head between your thighs so I can hear you chant it over"—he dips forward, the heat from his breath skating across the shell of my ear—"and over again. Is that what you want, Dylan?"

"I, uh," I gulp again, my voice failing me as my eyes fall to his lips. I'm not stupid. I know where we are right now. I know we're surrounded by other students. I know they're staring because it isn't every day hockey god Oliver Reeves spends his time chatting with nerd-extraordinaire Dylan Thorne. But I can't stop picturing it. Reeves and me. My back pressed against the wall. His knees on the ground and his hands on my thighs, spreading me. "You already know I've never..." The words catch in my throat as I shake my head back and forth. The idea alone is enough to make me pass out, but I am curious. For the first time ever, I want to know what it's like. To be vulnerable with someone. To let someone in. To share something so...intimate with someone I care about, and I do care about Reeves. Way more than I'd like to admit.

His mouth twitches, and his hands find my waist as he snakes them around me. "You aren't helping your case, Pickles." He kisses my temple, releases me, and laces our fingers together. "Now, come on. If I don't start walking you to class, I'll cave, and I have a hunch you don't want me to pop your oral cherry on the quad. Let's go."

30

DYLAN

"**W**hat are you doing?" a low voice asks
behind me.

Everyone went to SeaBird, but I decided
to stay home and catch up on homework. Turning around in
my seat, I find Reeves leaning against the wall with his hands
tucked in his pockets and his ankles crossed, one over the
other.

"What are you doing home?" I ask.

"Well, since I'm retired and all, I have more free time on
my hands."

"You could always go to SeaBird like everyone else."

"And who would I dance with if you aren't there?" he
counters, grabbing the chair opposite mine, flipping it
around, straddling it, and taking a seat. "You finished for the
night?"

"I haven't decided yet," I lift a shoulder. "You sure you
don't want to catch up with everyone at SeaBird?"

"Depends."

"On what, exactly?"

"You."

"What about me?" I ask.

"Well…I don't get a ton of nights off. Between hockey and Game Nights, it can be kind of busy."

"And school work," I muse. "Right?"

He chuckles. "Sure."

"What? You don't have homework?"

"I'll have a degree when I graduate. Not much else matters."

"You have all your eggs in the hockey basket, I assume?"

"Nah, it's more like when I find what I want, I go for it. I'm all in, you know?"

I nod, surprised by his perception and how fitting it really is since I've gotten to know him. Honestly, I'm kind of jealous. The way he rolls with the punches no matter what life throws at him. How he adapts while still being passionate about what he wants. I think the balance is hard to accomplish, but Reeves pulls it off in spades.

"I think that's…really cool, actually," I admit.

"Thanks. Speaking of being all in, can I hang out with you tonight?"

"Me?"

"Yeah." He smiles. "You're kind of hard to pin down, Dylan Thorne. Between your family, your friends, Rowdy's, and all your school work, I'm trying to be patient."

"You've been very patient," I murmur.

"*Trying* was the key word," he argues. His voice is thick with amusement as his eyes fall to my lips. Clearing his throat, he pulls back and adds, "I can help you study if you aren't finished yet, or we can grab some food, we can go to SeaBird, we can hang out here and grab takeout. Whatever you want."

"You really want to hang out?"

"Have I not made my feelings clear to you yet?" he challenges.

"You have, it's... Well, you don't seem like the type of guy who's a fan of boring nights in."

"Nothing's boring when you're around."

I bite the inside of my cheek to keep from smiling as I take in his sincerity.

"Okay," I decide. "I'd love to hang out."

"Yeah?" His brows raise as if he's surprised by how easily I gave in.

With a laugh, I push my laptop to the center of the table. "Yeah, sure. Why not?"

His wide grin makes my stomach clench with anticipation. "Is this our first date, Pickles?"

"Maybe." I stand up, then look down at the hoodie hanging off my body and covering my pajama shorts beneath. Reaching up, I touch my crooked, messy bun. "I should probably shower."

"Nah. I think you look perfect."

Again, I take in my appearance and scoff. "I look like a crazy person."

"A cute crazy person," he argues.

"Dude."

"Dude," he mimics. "Don't get me wrong. I like when you're all dolled up and shit, but this?" He reaches for my hand and spins me around. "This is just as perfect." Lifting our entwined fingers, he brushes a kiss against the back of my hand. "You're perfect. Now, come on. Let's grab some food."

IT'S DARK. EVER SINCE I SAW THE NIGHT-LIGHT IN OLIVER'S room, I wondered if his aversion to the dark extends to being out at night or only when he's sleeping—when his nightmares can hold him hostage and fight to keep him trapped in his past. But right now, Reeves looks as right as rain. With one hand on the steering wheel and another on my thigh, he seems more content than I've ever seen him. It's nice. Really nice. The roads are mainly empty. It's like most of Lockwood Heights has already gone to sleep, giving us a sliver of solitude except for the occasional passing headlights as we drive over the rolling hills. My belly is full of street tacos, and there's a half-empty cup of Diet Coke in the cup holder. Music filters from the speakers, the heat is blasting, and the windows are rolled down. A mixture of Blink-182, Green Day, and a bunch of other punk bands I never heard of acts as our playlist for the night, and the contrast of frigid fall air combined with the car's heating system leaves me feeling at odds but weirdly comfortable.

The dashboard highlights Reeves' sharp features as he pulls back on to our street, making him look even more handsome than I've grown to expect from the guy.

When the song ends, he reaches for the volume knob and turns it down, giving me a panty-melting smile while he's at it. "You know, this is usually the part where I kiss the girl good night and make sure she gets inside safely."

"Oh?"

"Yeah, but since we live together, I can't decide if I kiss you now or when we reach your bedroom door."

"Is *both* an option?" I ask.

With a quiet laugh, he leans over the center console and reaches his arm toward me, cupping my cheek and pulling me into him. When our lips meet, I melt a little more, relaxing into his touch.

It's sweet. Innocent. Soft.

Breaking our kiss, he murmurs, "I had fun tonight."

"Me, too."

"Will you let me take you out again?"

The idea alone causes a kaleidoscope of butterflies to flutter inside me, so I nod. "Yes."

Running his thumb along my jaw one more time, he drops his hand, climbs out of the car, and rounds the front, opening my door.

The lights are off inside the house. I look around the dark main room, folding my arms across my chest as he locks the door behind us.

"I'm not ready to go to bed," I admit.

"Movie?" he offers.

"Sure."

We search the family room for the remote, but when we don't find it, he suggests his room, and I agree. Candy wrappers surround us a little while later as *Game of Thrones* plays on the television. When a spicy scene starts, I catch myself staring at the people on the screen. I shift slightly on the bed, both embarrassed and aroused.

"Fuck, Thorne," Reeves murmurs. "You turned on?"

"I—what? No!"

"You know, it's okay to be turned on, right?"

"I mean, obviously." I roll my eyes. "But I'm not."

"Why not?" he asks. His gaze flicks to the screen, then back to me. "It's hot."

"It's...fine, I guess, but—"

A moan from the screen cuts me off, and my breath hitches as the girl writhes.

"You've never watched porn, have you?"

I can feel his stare on the side of my face as I wring my hands in my lap, avoiding whatever's happening on the screen like my life depends on it. "Did you seriously just ask me if I've watched porn?"

"It's a simple question."

"Okay, then." I force myself to stop fidgeting and meet his stare. "No?"

"Is that a question?" he challenges.

"It's a...let's change the subject."

"Humor me," he begs. "I've been curious as fuck since photography class." He scoots closer. "Have you seriously never masturbated?"

I squeeze my eyes shut. "Way to get right to the point, Reeves."

"I think we both know I don't beat around the bush."

With a huff, I turn to him. "It's not like I haven't...felt down there or whatever, but..."

"But you've never actually masturbated."

"Stop saying that word," I beg.

Reaching for the remote, he turns off the show, then sits up as if I'm the most interesting person in the world. "Have you ever wanted to?"

"I don't..."

Is it getting hot in here?

I gulp. "I don't know?"

"You don't know?" He chuckles, but it isn't condescending. It's almost like he's intrigued. Fascinated. "Dylan, have you ever orgasmed?"

"Reeves," I groan.

"Fuck me." He looks up at the ceiling and shakes his head. "You've never come?"

"Reeves," I repeat.

"Do you want to?" he asks.

"I don't—" I shake my head. "Look, I'm an awkward person in general. Adding awkwardness to *sex* sounds like a major turn-off, don't you think?"

"You want the truth?"

I nod.

"Nothing about you is a turn-off, Dylan."

"You're being too nice."

"No, I'm being honest," he argues. "Do you have any

fucking clue how sexy you are?"

I scoff. "Sexy? No. Cute? Yes."

"Sexy," he pushes, "yes." Rolling onto his side, he studies me. "You don't believe me, do you?" I stay quiet, and he grabs my hand on the comforter, bringing it to his lips. "Do you trust me?"

"Reeves…"

"Just answer the question, Pickles."

My mouth twitches at the ridiculous nickname, and I nod. "Yes, I trust you."

Slowly, he moves our entwined hands to his crotch, where his very erect, very hard shaft stands at attention. "Do you feel this?"

I roll my eyes. "Obviously."

"You turn me on, Dylan."

"Yeah, for now, but what if I…" I clamp my eyes shut, shoving aside my first two experiences with kissing and exactly how shitty they were. "What if I mess up or I'm bad at it?"

I can hear his smile as he argues, "Not possible."

"You don't know that. Trust me, my kisses with you were very different than my experiences with the other guys and—"

"Thank fuck."

"Reeves, I'm serious," I push. "This is scary."

"Trust me, you have nothing to fear. When the time comes, and you want me to prove it, I'll happily oblige." He reaches for the remote again to turn on the show, but I grab his hand and stop him. I can't help it. Blame the show. Blame the very hard dick from two seconds ago. Blame my pent-up libido and the fact I've only touched the surface. But lying here? In bed with a very attractive guy willing to show me the ropes? Call me a crazy person, but I kind of want to see where it goes. To see if I'm cursed or not. Because I wasn't kidding when I said I've felt around down there, but actually orgasming? I've never been able to reach it, always getting too caught up in my own head to actually fall apart.

"Prove it," I whisper.

His brows lift. "What did you say?"

"I said, prove it," I repeat. "Prove I have nothing to fear."

His wary gaze slides over me, and I can see the indecision in his warm chocolate eyes. "I didn't bring this up to pressure you."

"I know you didn't," I rush out. "It's just...I'm always in my own head, and with you? I don't know, it's different." I nibble my bottom lip, lost in my thoughts.

He reaches up and plucks the flesh from between my teeth. "You're in your head again." He smiles, and it's patient and kind and so damn inviting I swear I could spill every secret and desire, and he'd welcome them with open arms.

"Teach me," I beg. "Help me. Guide me or...whatever."

His smile widens as he slowly shifts his hips into my hand, letting me feel him. "Do you remember my expectations, Dylan?"

"If I'm uncomfortable, I say something."

"Good girl." Moving his hand from mine, he scoots closer and kisses me. It's soft at first but turns bolder with a sweep of his tongue. My breathing is staggered, like I can't catch my breath. Like I'm distracted. Anxious. And I am. I wasn't kidding when I mentioned my fears over being awkward or bad at anything physical and intimate, especially with Reeves. Even alone, I couldn't come because I was too caught up in my own head. This? This puts those tiny moments to shame.

"Breathe," he orders against my lips, then kisses me again. He's so warm. So patient. With a gentle tug, he threads his fingers through my hair, and a jolt of pleasure shoots down my spine. I open to him, and he rubs himself against my hand, letting out a soft groan. It races straight to my core. My skin feels hot. Tight. And my eyelids flutter as I lose myself in him. His weight. His scent. And the feel of his bulge. I like it. Seeing what I do to him. How he responds to me. My lips. My tongue. I open my mouth a little wider, and he takes advantage, kissing me deeper. My legs fall apart on their own, making him smile against me.

"Awkward, my ass," he mutters, shifting onto his elbows and caging me in. I spread my thighs wider, and he settles into me, his weight a heady aphrodisiac I never expected. But I need more. I need him to touch me. I never understood what it was like to feel empty. Desperate. To want to chase the pleasure just out of reach. Until now. Until *him*.

My clit pulses as I shift beneath him, feeling the length of his cock against my center despite our clothing.

Tearing his lips from mine, he kisses the edge of my mouth, then right beneath my ear, slowly moving lower as his hands find my hips. When he pushes me into the mattress, my shirt slides up, and his calloused hands tickle my bare skin, making me want to arch into him. To press our bodies together until there isn't any space between us. It isn't enough. I want him all over me. My pulse gallops, and I raise my hips, the same desperation leaving me on edge and way more turned on than I've ever been in my entire life. Rolling his hips into me, he softly rocks against my core a few times.

When his fingers play with the waistband of my leggings, he rasps against my lips, "Stay with me."

I part my thighs a little more, fighting off the tiny voice inside my head. The one reminding me of how inexperienced I really am.

"You're fucking perfect," he murmurs. "Every inch of you. It's like you were made for me, Dylan."

He dips his hand beneath the fabric of my pants and tugs them down my thighs. My hips lift as if they have a mind of their own, and cool air hits my upper thighs, threatening to snap me out of the moment. As Reeves drags his hands up my bare stomach and palms my breast, he kisses me even harder. I could get lost in this kiss. Could die from this kiss. My nerves settle, and my need builds again, leaving me squirming on the mattress when his fingers trail down my stomach once more. But he doesn't touch my sex. He simply drags his fingers from one hip bone to the next until I honestly think I might die from the torture.

"Reeves," I beg. "Please."

He swallows my plea as I spread my legs further apart. His hand slides closer, cupping my bare sex and playing with the seam but not dipping into me. He deepens the kiss, dragging his tongue in and out of my mouth. When he *finally* pushes into my center slowly, I gasp at the intrusion, ripping my lips from his as I bask in the foreign feeling. It's only one finger—one. Freaking. Finger, but I sense myself stretching around him. The fullness. My heart races faster and faster. When his thumb finds my clit, my jaw drops, and he smiles.

"You like that, Dylan?"

"I think it's a stupid question," I pant.

With a low laugh, he pushes into me again, hitting the little bundle of nerves inside of me, and I grab his wrist, overwhelmed by the sensation. I can't decide if I want to push him away or keep him where he is. He thumbs my clit again, slowly pumping his finger in and out of me, holding my gaze until I'm convinced I might burn up on the spot.

"Do you have any idea how fucking sexy you are right now?"

I swallow and shake my head. The building pressure is too much. Like a rubber band ready to snap as it's pulled too tight, and I'm not the one in control of when it happens.

"Prettiest thing I've ever seen." He adds a second finger, and I gasp at another intrusion. His thumb draws small circles above my entrance, and my muscles slowly relax. The feeling is…incredible. Fucking incredible. And I don't want it to end. Don't want it to stop. Not now. Not ever. Is this it? What I've been missing?

"That's it, baby. Let me in," he orders.

As the muscles in my thighs soften, he scissors his fingers, adding a bit more pressure to my clit and leaning down to swallow my moans with another drugging kiss. I roll my hips into his hand, surprised at how good it feels to have them on me. *In* me. The same foreign pressure builds, starting low but slowly rising with each brush of his fingers until I'm pretty sure I'll explode, and I have no idea how to survive the aftermath.

"Oliver," I whimper. "Shit, Oli—"

"You're close, baby. I can feel it. Feel the way you squeeze my fingers so good. You're so fucking perfect. Can't wait to bury myself inside you. Fuck. Open your eyes and watch the way you take my fingers."

My eyelids feel heavy as I lift my head and look down.

"Do you see it, baby?" he murmurs.

With my legs spread, his wet fingers pumping in and out of me, and his thumb playing with my clit, it's the hottest thing I've ever seen.

"Look at me," he orders.

My gaze snaps to his.

"Let go, baby. I got you."

As if it were waiting for his command, the last of my restraint finally snaps, and an explosion hits, spreading from my core out to my fingers and toes like fireworks. Tiny shock waves of pleasure follow as he keeps playing with me, letting me ride his hand as wave after wave of euphoria pulses through me. It's a high I can't describe. Foreign. Addictive. Freaking mind-blowing as I blink away the stars in my eyes and slowly drift back down to earth.

Melting into the mattress, he pulls his hand from my center and licks his fingers. "You have no idea how good you taste." He slips them into my center again, then lifts them to my lips. "Unless you want to know."

My brows dip as I realize exactly what he's asking. I've never thought about it, but now, I'm curious. Opening my mouth, I suck his fingers, rolling my tongue around the tips and pulling a groan from him. It's...different. The taste. But I kind of like it. Not necessarily sweet or bitter. Just...different. What I really like, though? Is the way Reeves' eyes flare with heat. With want. With desire. At a simple caress of my tongue. I've never been desired. Not like this.

Resting his forehead against mine, he sighs and shakes his head. "And you think you're awkward. Fuck, Dylan." He chuckles. "You have no fucking clue. Come on." He reaches for the remote and tugs me against him. "Let's finish the show."

I try. Trust me, I really do. But knowing what I've been missing, it's not like I can close the door on it again. And he wants me to focus on the show? A silly show when I know for a fact only one of us orgasmed tonight, and I really want it to be two. But how do I tell him?

Lifting my leg, I hook it over his waist and scoot closer until every inch of my front is pressed to his side as the show plays on the screen. He settles even more against the stupid pillow, either oblivious or with a hell of a lot more restraint than the guys my parents warned me about. Curious, I shift my leg and brush up against his crotch, finding a very hard bulge.

Aaaand there it is.

"What are you doing?" Reeves growls.

"Finishing the show," I answer innocently.

"Pickles."

"Mmm...what I wouldn't give for a big, juicy cucumber

right about now."

His chest rumbles with amusement. "Are you going for subtlety? Because if you are, you're failing. Hard."

"Maybe I like *hard*."

"Dylan," he warns.

"And maybe I'm not done exploring things."

His body tenses beneath my cheek. "What kind of things?"

I drag my knee against his crotch one more time. "This kind of thing."

"Tonight's about you," he reminds me.

"And maybe I want this." I lift my head and look him in the eye. "Maybe I want...more."

His brow quirks. "More?"

I nod, slipping my hand beneath his jeans and boxers and grabbing his penis, slowly pumping him up and down. I'm not completely naive. I know what jerking off is. But I've never actually done it.

"Can you show me?" I ask.

He leans his head back on the pillow and stares at the ceiling as I continue my assault. "You sure?"

Nibbling at the edge of his jaw, I murmur, "Pretty positive, actually."

"Take me all the way out."

I sit up on my knees and unzip his pants. He lifts his hips and lets me slide everything off him. His hard cock springs in front of me, and I grab it, moving my hand up and down, gathering the moisture from his slit to use as lube. I've never seen a dick up close and personal. He's so hard, but his skin is so smooth. So warm.

"Fuck, Dylan." He grabs the outside of my hand and forces me to slow down. Without words, he shows me how to pay special attention to the head before moving from base to tip. "Just like that," he encourages me to continue.

I do as I'm told, mirroring the movement. Satisfied, he lets me go and leans back again, but his eyes never leave my hand, and honestly? I'm almost jealous. Moving lower, I continue pleasing him with my hand, then bring the tip to my lips. His eyes snap from my hand to my eyes, his chest heaving with pent-up frustration.

"Dylan—"

I kiss the tip. It's barely even a touch, but his dick jumps in my grasp, and my tongue darts out, licking the bead of moisture from my bottom lip. With a smile, I say, "It's kind of salty."

He laughs and shakes his head. "It's precum."

"I kind of like it." Holding his gaze, I dip down again, licking the slit with the tip of my tongue, wrapping my lips around him. His hand finds the side of my face, his eyes turning a molten chocolate. Bobbing my head, I suck on him, the motion surprisingly…natural, almost.

"Fuck, Dylan. You have no idea how good it feels. Slowly," he urges. I ease up on my pace, using my hand to give the base of his dick attention while I focus on the head with my mouth. His breathing quickens, and his hips shift off the mattress. "Yes. Perfect." He drags his thumb along the edge of my lips where his dick is. "Fucking perfect, Dylan."

My chest fills with pride as I continue licking at him, sucking him, and savoring the little grunts of pleasure. My jaw aches. He's so big; it fans my curiosity. What would it be like to let him inside me? To feel him stretch me the same way his fingers did a few minutes ago? I press my thighs together at the thought and take him deeper, letting him hit the back of my throat.

"Fuck," he grunts.

Peeking up at him, I find his molars grinding.

"I'm gonna come," he warns, "so if you don't wanna taste me, you need to get off now."

I keep him in my mouth, bobbing my head and watching his abs flex when a spurt of cum hits the back of my throat. I almost gag but keep my mouth on him, swallowing every drop. It's weird and messy, and I swear I might choke as my eyes gather with tears, but I don't stop. I suck him like a straw, drawing out his groans and the way his hands grip the sides of my head. Like he wants to push me away and pull me closer all at once. It's addictive and dizzying and turns me on way more than it should. When he stops jerking between my lips, I let him go with a soft pop and lick my bottom lip, my insecurity rearing its ugly head as he stares at me.

Was it good? Was it bad? I mean, I thought I did pretty well, but *I'm* the newbie here, not Reeves. And with the way he's looking at me? Is he only being nice? Because I'm an A+ kind of girlie. Give me a grade, dammit! How can I improve? Did I completely fail? I don't think so, but how am I supposed to know? I've never done this before! Do we talk? Do we go our separate ways? No, that feels wrong. I don't want to go anywhere. I want to stay with him. I want to snuggle and fall asleep in his arms. I want—

"You're cute when you're overthinking things," he murmurs.

"Then do us both a favor and put me out of my misery," I push. "How was it?"

"Fucking hell, Dylan." He grabs me and pulls me into him. "Do you have any idea what you do to me? It was incredible. *Perfect.*" Pushing my hair away from my face, he cups my cheek, his eyes full of wonder and awe and appreciation. "Never thought I'd consider myself a lucky guy, but every time I'm with you, I wonder if I might be."

His smile softens, and my nerves settle, letting me ride the high from my first sexual encounter. And damn, it was a doozy. One I can't wait to recreate.

But only with Oliver Reeves.

31
REEVES

I wasn't kidding when I told Dylan the Halloween parties at SeaBird aren't as good as our costume parties but still pretty fun, and for some reason, I'm even more anxious to have her on my arm tonight. To show the rest of the world she's mine, even if it's only for one night. I decided to go all out for our costumes and gave Dylan a choice between Little Red Riding Hood—she's yet to see the irony— or Princess Charming. She vetoed both almost instantly.

However, when Finley showed up at my bedroom door with a costume bag over her arm and promised she'd take care of everything, I didn't fight her.

And here I am, waiting at the base of the stairs for Dylan to appear. I told everyone else to meet us at the bar, and they left without protest. As I check the time on my phone, a creak sounds at the top of the staircase, grabbing my attention. The view is even better than I anticipated. My mouth goes dry as I take her in. Every curve. Every freckle. Every inch of pale, creamy skin. Her light blonde hair is half up, the rest cascading around her shoulders. The twists and braids are an exact replica of the dragon queen herself, and so is the royal blue dress robe *thing*. Honestly, I'm not sure what to call it, but she looks incredible.

"No glasses?" I ask.

"Does Daenerys Targaryen wear glasses?" she challenges.

"So, you're going all out, I take it?"

"Uh, heck, yes." Stopping at the last step, she takes in my dark leather straps, inked shoulders, and Dothraki armor. "And apparently, so are you, Khal Drogo."

I drew the line at the dark wig and couldn't braid my scruff even though Finley insisted on trying after she knocked on my door with a makeup kit in her hands earlier tonight. I caved, letting her add dark shadows around my eyes as Dylan finished getting ready in the room opposite mine.

When their kitchen burned down, I was a little worried the close proximity might be too much for me, but it's proven the opposite. I like having Dylan around. Seeing her in my space. The kitchen. The family room. The classroom. The bathroom. It's one benefit after another, and knowing I get to bring her home tonight and kiss her goodnight in my hallway instead of on her doorstep makes me feel lighter than ever. Hell, part of me hopes the contractors never finish the damn thing, and she moves in permanently.

A guy can dream, can't I?

Reaching for her hand, I guide Dylan down the last step until I tower over her tiny frame. With a gentle nudge, I lift her chin, nearly getting lost in those aqua pools. "You look perfect, Dylan."

"You don't look too bad yourself, my sun and stars."

Laughter booms out of me as I throw my head back. "Did you just quote *Game of Thrones?*"

"Finley and I watched another episode while we were getting ready."

Well aware I'm the luckiest bastard in the world, I tug her

against me, wrap my arms around her waist, and breathe in her scent. I don't know if it's her shampoo or perfume or her natural pheromones, but I swear I could wrap myself up in it. In her.

"Your friend's something else," I tell her.

Dylan rolls her eyes. "Just wait 'til you see her fairy godmother costume. Come on. Let's get going."

Threading our fingers together, I lead her out the front door and lock it behind us. Then, we make our way to SeaBird.

The drive is short, but the place is already packed. Coconut and lime hang in the air as I push the door open. The bouncer dips his chin as we enter, barely scanning Dylan's fake ID. I guide her to the bartop at the back. A live band is playing on the stage to our left, and the dance floor is packed with people grinding on each other.

With wide eyes, Dylan scans the area, a soft smile playing at the edge of her lips.

I bend closer to her and ask, "What are you thinking?"

"Will you think I'm weird if I say my parents?"

Cocking my head, I bend closer, convinced I misheard her. "Did you say you're thinking about your parents right now?"

"This is where my mom and dad became an official couple, or at least it's what they told me," she adds. "It's kind of surreal being here."

"Good surreal?"

She nods. "Definitely."

"What would you like to drink?" I prod.

Her shoulder lifts in a shrug. "Whatever."

"Sweet?" I ask.

Her smile grows. "Always."

"A girl after my own heart." I kiss her cheek. "Come with me." After ordering two fruity concoctions in tall glasses, I pass one to Dylan, and we make our way toward one of the booths near the back of the building. The guys are already here, and so are Ophelia and Mav.

"Dylan!" Ophelia practically squeals as she shoves her boyfriend out of the booth so she can pull her best friend into a hug. "You look gorgeous!"

"Ditto," Dylan replies.

"Oh, good, you have drinks," Lia adds. "We're playing Truth or Dare, but it's Finley's turn, so we're waiting until she gets back."

Scanning the bar, Dylan frowns. "Where'd she go?"

"Drew called," Griffin announces from deeper inside the booth.

"I hate the fucker," Everett grumbles.

Mav chuckles across from him. "Yeah, but you hate anyone who touches your sister."

"Pretty sure a saint could say hello to her, and you'd still be pissed," Griffin adds.

"Because no one's good enough for her," Everett argues.

"No one's good enough for anyone from your perspective," Ophelia chimes in.

"You're right, they aren't," he tosses right back at her, but I don't miss the way Griffin stares at his best friend for a beat too long, picking up his cup and swallowing the rest of what's inside.

"I'm gonna grab another drink. You guys want anything?" he asks.

Everyone shakes their heads as Griff slips out, heading back to the bar. Dylan and I take his place and scoot along the vinyl cushion until we're tucked in the corner.

"So, you guys are cute," Ophelia notes. Her caramel-colored eyes bounce between Dylan and me like we're the two most interesting people in the world. It makes Dylan shrink a little further into my side.

Tossing my arm around her shoulders, I stretch my legs out in front of me and motion to her and Mav. "I could say the same about you two. Tinkerbell and Peter Pan? What'd it take to get this man in tights?"

Mav doesn't bother hiding his grin as he scratches the side of his jaw. "No comment."

"You dog, you," I joke as Griff and Finley appear, drinks in hand.

"Okay, so when you guys win the award for the cutest couple, you better thank me in your acceptance speech," Finley says as she slips in beside Lia.

"There's a costume contest?" Dylan asks while Griffin follows behind Finley and rests his elbows on the table, cradling what looks like a Jack and Coke between his hands.

"Yup, but it doesn't start for another hour or so," Finley replies. "Now, where were we? Oh. Right. Dylan, truth or dare?"

Dylan pauses, then finally answers, "Dare."

"I dare you to give Reeves a kiss on the lips."

The wallflower shrinks beside me, glaring at her friend across from us as Finley grins back at her.

"Dylan." I keep my voice low enough for only her to hear. "You don't have to."

Peeking up at me, she scoots up a little more in her seat, desire and unease fighting for first place in her big, round eyes. We've kissed. A lot. But only when it's me and her. Only when there aren't any witnesses. And yeah. I asked her here as my date, but when we both know a kiss means more to her than it does to a lot of people, does this bother her? Kissing me in public? With the way she's acting, I'm not sure.

"Dylan, I'm serious," I mutter. "You don't have to."

She swallows thickly, and her body trembles as she lifts her chin to kiss me. It's soft and careful and very PG, all lips and no tongue, but it makes me crave her more. Pulling away, she touches her fingers to her soft lips.

A squeal echoes from across the booth. Finley claps her hands in triumph as Dylan's haze of interest vanishes, and she gives her friend another death glare. "You're a brat."

"No, I'm your fairy godmother," Finley reminds her, then turns to me. "You passed, by the way. Congratulations."

My brows bunch. "Did I miss something?"

"We have a rule," Ophelia explains. "Each of us has an...I dunno, a no-fly zone, if you will. We've had it since we were little, and everyone's red tape is different. Mine is no heights because, duh, Finley's is no frogs—"

"Because, duh," Finley repeats with a look like I'm a lunatic if I dare to disagree with her.

"And Dylan's red card is no kisses during Truth or Dare. And yet, she kissed you." Finley smirks. "You know what it means, right?"

"It means it isn't your turn anymore," Dylan interjects. "Griffin, truth or dare?"

"Truth," he answers.

"What's it like sharing a room with Everett?"

Laughter erupts as his face scrunches. "Smelly."

We all laugh even harder, and Griff turns to Everett. "Truth or dare?"

"Dare."

"I dare you to..." Griff scans the table, grins, and reaches for the Tabasco sauce. With a few rough shakes, he adds a couple of tablespoons to Everett's beer. "Chug the entire thing."

"Aw, come on." Everett groans but lifts the glass to his lips as the red sauce swirls with the pale yellow alcohol. Pinching his nose, he chugs the rest of his drink, then sits it on the table, his mouth twisting with distaste. "Disgusting."

We take turns, going back and forth until we're all at least four drinks in—except Finley—and the room starts spinning.

"So, Finley," Dylan prods, "Truth or dare?"

"Dare," Finley decides.

"I dare you to ask the band if you can take a moment to make a speech lasting at least one minute while you propose to Griffin on stage."

Ophelia busts up laughing and shoves her friend's shoulder. "Shut up! That's the best dare of the night!"

"Why'd you have to drag me into this?" Griffin groans.

Glowering at Dylan, Finley mutters, "This is payback for the kiss thing, isn't it?"

"Hey, I could always find a frog."

"I'm going!" she snaps, scooting out and heading to the edge of the stage. With a crook of her finger, she convinces the lead singer to bend down. We all watch as they have a short conversation, and he nods, offering his hand to help her onto the stage.

I can't decide if I'm too bombed to think straight or if the image of Finley in a princess dress being yanked onto the stage by a hot rockstar is as funny as it seems, but this? This is fucking priceless.

"Don't forget to time her speech," I remind Dylan.

"Oh. Right." She pulls out her phone, then lifts it into the air, showcasing the timer app as her thumb hovers over the start button.

Tapping the end of the microphone, Finley confirms it's on and clears her throat. "Hello, ladies and gentlemen. First of all, everyone looks amazing. If I were a judge of the costume contest, I'd definitely have a hard time picking a favorite, but, uh, I wanted to come up here today to talk about love, you know? Love is..." She stares at Dylan and smirks. "Love is an incredible thing, and I could not be happier for my best friend and her new fiance. Who knew a surprise pregnancy could end with such…"—she sniffs and dabs the corner of her eye—"such a beautiful proposal. Dani? Get up here, girl! You, too, Reeves!"

Jaw on the floor, Dylan grits out, "That's it. We're buying a frog."

"Aw, come on, babe." I grab her stomach and rub my hand against it. "It's for the baby."

"Oh, shut up."

She smacks my shoulder as the crowd begins chanting, "Da-ni! Re-eves! Da-ni! Re-eves!"

"They won't stop," Griffin muses. "Might as well get it over with, *Dani*."

After one final glare at her brother, we scoot out of the booth and wave at the crowd gathered.

"How 'bout a dance for the lovely couple?" Finley suggests. Her voice echoes through the speakers, and our audience cheers.

Yeah, Dylan's gonna kill her.

I raise my hand, silently asking Finley for the microphone. Eyes narrowed, she gives in and hands it to me. I turn toward the audience while Dylan uses me as a human shield, hiding behind me.

"I want to thank our dear fairy godmother for setting this whole thing up," I start. "Unfortunately, our Dani here, well, her pregnancy is high risk, so we're sitting this dance out. But we'd love it if our best man and maid of honor would take our place on the dance floor. Griff?" I call as I wrap my arm around Dylan and bring her to my side so she can have front-row seats to tonight's main event. "Come on, Griff. Get out here."

The rest of the band watches from the side of the stage before the rhythm of a slow song begins playing.

"Gonna kill you," Griff mutters as he passes me.

I bring the microphone to my mouth again, adding, "How

'bout you dance on the stage, you know? Let the whole world see."

"Woo-hoo!" the audience cheers.

Shaking his head, Griffin grumbles under his breath, climbs onto the stage, and grabs Finley's hips. The fluff of her dress prevents them from getting too close, but it only adds to the ridiculousness of the situation as they sway back and forth to the slow love song.

"She's gonna kill you for beating her at her own game," Dylan says as her fingers trail against my chest.

"She'll get over it," I decide. "Besides, she looks pretty comfortable up there with your brother."

"Yeah, but the real question is, how comfortable is Ev?" Dylan challenges.

I glance at the table where Everett is watching, his expression unreadable. "Poor bastard."

"Who? Griff or Ev?"

I laugh a little harder. "Both, I guess. Come on." I reach for her hips and pull her into me. "Dance with me."

"But what about the baby?" she quips.

With a grin, I bend down and kiss her nose. "Worth it."

32

DYLAN

With a yawn, I roll onto my side and peel one lid open. I'm still in Reeves' room. I must've fallen asleep during the movie he insisted we watch last night. Searching the bed, I find the sheets cold on the opposite side, which means I'm most definitely alone. He's probably at the gym. It makes sense. He spends most mornings at the gym with his team. Like a cat, I stretch on the mattress. Slipping from the sheets and out of bed, I smooth the covers until you'd never know anyone even slept here.

After a quick shower, I head to the kitchen to find Finley with a plate of eggs Benedict in front of her.

"Hey, stranger," she quips. "There's more on the stove."

I dish up a plate for myself, then sit across from her at the table as she chews slowly, watching me.

"Is there a problem?" I ask.

"Just trying to figure out if I can see the I've-been-thoroughly-fucked glow or not." She tilts her head. "Don't get me wrong. I'm definitely seeing a glimmer, but..."

"We didn't sleep together," I answer, stopping the fork an

315

inch from my face. "Okay, we did, but I mean *actual* sleep, not what you're referring to."

"Mm-hmm." She watches as I chew my bite, adding, "But you definitely did something. Am I right?"

"Finley," I whine. "Can you give it a rest? Please?"

"I heard he's done with his side gig."

"He *is* done with his side gig," I confirm.

"So? It's good, right?"

"Yeah." A smile stretches across my face as I push the eggs around my plate. "Yeah, it's good."

"Good."

We stay silent, both of us enjoying her kickass eggs. When my nerves get the best of me, I look up at her again. "You like him, right? Like, you think we're a good fit?"

"Yeah, of course, I like him."

"So you don't think I'm crazy for wanting to see where this goes?"

"I mean, I most definitely think you're crazy," she returns dryly. "But no, I don't blame you at all. You guys were really cute together on Halloween."

"You think?"

"Yeah, I do. Have you guys had the talk yet?"

My smile falls, and I set my fork down. "Talk?"

"You know, about the relationship."

"Are we supposed to have a talk about the relationship?"

"I mean," she laughs, "at some point, yeah. Probably. Why? Are you nervous?"

"I don't know?" I frown. "Maybe a little."

"Why?"

"Because Reeves is…Reeves, I guess."

"What do you mean?"

"All any girl on campus has ever wanted from him is a fake commitment so they can show him off like a prized pony." I shake off my annoyance along with the knowledge that the list of girls he's connected with, both professionally and physically, is probably a mile long. "I don't want him to think I'm doing the same thing."

"Trust me, after seeing you two together, I guarantee he won't. He really likes you, Dylan. Everyone at SeaBird could see it. Hell, we could *feel* it, and honestly? I'm kind of jealous." She smiles.

"I just...I want to make sure I keep my head on straight through all of this."

"Which is super romantic, by the way," she teases. "I take it you guys haven't gone all the way yet?"

I shake my head. "We've done...a lot, actually, but not the whole shebang."

"Shebang?" she laughs. "As in she-bang?"

"Finley," I whine.

"I'm kidding. Kind of," she clarifies. "It is pretty funny. But for real, what's holding you back?"

"I don't know?" My face scrunches. "I want to, but..."

"But you're scared?"

I nod. "Yeah. I guess I am."

"Honey, you have nothing to be scared of, especially with a guy like Reeves who clearly cares about you. Besides, he's hot as fuck, and I have no doubt he'll be so good in bed it's not even funny."

Pushing my eggs around my plate some more, I snort. "Yeah, so not the part I'm worried about."

"Falling for someone is a leap of faith, Dyl. Sometimes it's worth it, and sometimes it isn't, but refusing to fall in general won't get you anywhere. You need to have a little more faith in yourself," she counters. "Are you coming to Game Night with him tonight?"

"I haven't decided yet. My mom wants to take me out to dinner, so it depends on when we finish."

"I hope you do. I have a feeling he'll love showing you off

to the rest of his friends, and afterward, you can chat about what you both want out of the relationship." She stands up and sets her dishes in the sink. "Now, if you'll excuse me, I have a paper to work on. Oh, and PS—you're on dish duty as payment for breakfast. Thank you!"

I roll my eyes, watching her go as I call out, "You're welcome!"

∾

AFTER SPENDING THE ENTIRE DAY CLEANING THE HOUSE FROM top to bottom, my mom picked me up for dinner. It was fun. Catching up on everything going on in the families. I needed it more than she knew.

Now, we're on our way home, and when we reach my street, I lean closer to the windshield, taking in the cars parked along the curb. Like always, it's packed.

"What's going on?" my mom asks.

"Game Night."

"Oh?"

"Yeah." I glance at her and turn back to the scene unfolding in front of us. "They're chaos."

With a rueful smile, she pulls up to the crowded driveway. "Aw, I miss college chaos."

"You're crazy."

"And you're adorable if you honestly think I believe you don't kind of love being here."

She isn't wrong. I do kind of love it. I kind of love a lot of things about college, especially when I'm around a certain someone.

"It's…a lot," I reply.

"Life is…a lot," she repeats, mimicking me. "The trick is to soak it up while you have it and not lose track of your goals while trying new things and figuring out what works for you and what doesn't."

"Look who's a sage old woman," I quip.

With a gasp, she shoves my shoulder. "Excuse me? Did you just call me old?"

"And sage."

Her eyes thin. "Mm-hmm. And to think I let you talk me into stopping at the grocery store to get more Ben & Jerry's. I feel played."

I laugh. "Learned from the best."

"Yeah, yeah, whatever. Get out of my car, missy." As I climb out, she calls out, "Love you!"

"Love you, too." I give her a small wave, letting the ice cream we stopped for hang off my arm in its grocery sack. "Thanks again for dinner."

"Anytime, babe. Tell everyone hi for me."

"I will."

"Including Reeves," she adds, and I swear I can hear the amusement in her voice as my body freezes.

Turning back to her, I bend forward through the passenger door and give her a look. "Excuse me?"

"You really think I didn't notice how you two snuggled on my couch during the Harry Potter party?"

"Mom," I warn.

"He likes you, babe, and I have a feeling you like him, too."

She's right. I do. I like him a lot. Especially after our little...teaching session the other night. But said session is between Reeves and me, and *only* Reeves and me. Add in the Halloween party, and I'm pretty much walking on cloud nine. However, admitting it to myself is one thing, but admitting it to my mother? Well, it's different.

"You're making an assumption," I point out. "Two of them, actually."

"Am I?" She quirks her brow. "Because from where I was sitting, it was pretty clear—"

"We haven't...defined the relationship or whatever, so..."

"Take it from your sage old mom. Sometimes, you don't need a label to know you care about someone."

"Mo-om."

"I'm just saying, if there's any reason you think you need our approval, you have it. I've heard a few things about Reeves that might make some mothers nervous, but I know you, and I know you wouldn't put your heart on the line for just anyone, okay? We love you, and we trust your judgment. *Yours*," she emphasizes. "Understand?"

A burn hits behind my eyes as her words wash over me.

We trust your judgment.

Since the accident, I've second-guessed myself more times than I can count. Whether I'm strong enough or coordinated enough or confident enough or smart enough to trust my gut and to trust the not-so-tiny voice in my head telling me Oliver's a good guy. Telling me he cares about me. Telling me he might even love me one day. I spent so much time pushing the voice away, knowing my mom has faith in it means more than she'll ever know.

Digging my teeth into the inside of my cheek, I let out a slow breath and nod. "Thanks, Mom."

"You're welcome." She smiles, and I swear the woman can read my mind. "Now, get in there and have fun."

"Mm-hmm." I give her a small wave. "Bye."

"See ya!"

Closing the door, I weave around the busy entryway but stop short when I realize exactly how crowded the family room is. Seriously. Bodies upon bodies are pressed together like sardines in a can. In the center of the family room lies a giant, custom-made Twister mat with rows and rows of colored dots reaching from one end of the room to the other.

The rules of the game are simple. I remember playing it when I was a kid. Someone names a body part and a color, and you have to put the body part called out on the specific color. When a person falls or loses their balance, they're out. The last one standing wins.

Clearly, the game is already underway.

Everett's standing on the coffee table at the edge of the room with his feet spread wide, spinning an oversized arrow on a giant cardboard wheel. The arrow points to a color and a body part, like in the smaller version of the game. It seems there's a twist, though. People are wearing T-shirts with solid colors matching the mat on the floor, and I swear it isn't a coincidence.

Curious, I slip between a pair of bodies.

"Right hand, green," Everett announces.

One of the girls puts her right hand on a guy beside her. He's wearing a green shirt. She squeezes his pec, and they both laugh as a few of the people around them shift into different positions, making sure they're each touching green, whether it's the green on the mat or green from one of their fellow players.

"Hey, you in?" a guy asks from behind me.

I turn around, confused to see him staring at me expectantly. "I'm sorry?"

"Here."

He presses a yellow T-shirt to my chest, and I take it on reflex. "What am I supposed to do with this?"

"Put it on."

"Oh, I'm not—"

Without another word, he leaves, disappearing through the crowd, not allowing me to finish my sentence.

Ooookay, then?

"Hey, Dyl!" Griffin calls from the edge of the mat. "You're late."

"Sorry, I was with Mom."

"No excuse," he argues, but he sports a playful grin to take away the sting. Lifting his chin at the bunched fabric in my hands, my brother adds, "Put it on. Come play."

I know what he's doing. He's trying to make me feel included. Trying to help me make friends and memories, and I kind of love him for it despite the many pairs of eyes staring at me as they wait for the game to continue.

I lift the grocery bag into the air. "Can't. I have ice cream."

Griff snaps his fingers and gives a freshman in my math class a pointed look. "Put it in the freezer."

Like a dog, the guy jumps into action and snatches the thing from my hands, weaving toward the kitchen.

What the—

"Dylan!" Finley squeals from the opposite side of the room. Her butt is in the air, and she's in a downward dog yoga pose, but she lifts her head with a grin, keeping her hands in place. "Come play! It's fun!"

"You've already started—"

"Pretty sure I make the rules, Dylan," Everett announces from the coffee table. "Jump in. Left foot, red. Right foot, yellow. Left hand, yellow. Right hand, green. Ready?"

Ah, so you're all in on it, huh?

Buttheads.

Heat hits my back, causing anticipation to pulse through me as I peek over my shoulder without turning around. It's Reeves. I should've known. He's wearing a blue shirt. I like it. It's bright. Bold. Fitting for the man wearing it. Slowly, he reaches around me and, with a single tug, snatches the shirt from my grasp, bunches the fabric, and slips it over my body. As my head pops out the neckline, he orders, "Arms." On autopilot, my body responds, following his instructions. He turns me around, and tingles spread over every inch of my body as he glides his hands along my neck and pulls my hair from the shirt, letting it cascade down my back. And with a gentleness that leaves me melting, he adjusts my glasses, straightening them with a smirk.

"You're cute when you look at me like this."

"Like what?"

"Like you don't know what to do with me." He bends even closer. "Even though I want to kiss the shit out of you right now, I also know how much you hate the spotlight. Since Everett refuses to call out the next directions until you're a participant, everyone is looking at us. I'm gonna let you off the hook and turn you back around so you can play. But know it's killing me to keep my hands to myself after the way we...left things."

The way we left things. As in, me in his bed and his fingers inside of me. Yup. My body heats at the memory alone, and I stare at the ground, hoping no one notices when his hands find my hips. He turns me around, giving me a gentle nudge toward the mat and stepping beside me.

Everett repeats the placement, helping us catch up to everyone else. Once we're in position, I crouch, feeling like a frog. Reeves is behind me, stealing different circles on the ground.

Satisfied, Everett calls out another order. "Right hand, yellow."

Heat slips around my waist, and I look down, finding Reeves' hand spread across my abdomen. It seems so big there, his thumb reaching to my ribs and his pinky barely above my pubic bone. It's intimate. Possessive. And makes my knees weak.

I glance over my shoulder. "Is this how we're supposed to play?"

"Why do you think we each have on a colored shirt?" he counters.

"Clever," I note.

He smirks. "You have no idea."

"Right foot, blue," Everett calls.

I take note of Reeves' shirt. "Does this mean I should put my foot on your chest?"

"I mean, if you're into it."

A laugh escapes me, but I ignore him and shift my right foot catty-corner from where it was.

"Nice move," he comments. "Now, I can do this." He slides his right foot between my thighs, placing it on one of the blue circles in front of me, leaving my back and butt practically plastered to his front while straddling his upper thigh.

Well, this is...interesting.

"Sneaky," I say, peering back at him from our new position.

"Never been one to turn down an opportunity, Pickles."

I snort.

Of course, he isn't.

"Left hand, blue," Everett yells.

I reach behind me and blindly grab onto Reeves' blue shirt while he moves his to one of the blue circles behind him, turning him into a sand crab.

"Left foot, green," Everett announces.

Considering how close Reeves is to me, finding a spot is hard. Can't say I'm complaining, though. It's nice. Being close to him under the guise of a game. Like it's innocent when this feels far from it, especially as something very hard presses against my butt. And after the other night? It makes me want to take things a step further.

"You gonna move, Dyl?" Reeves asks. "You still need to put your left foot on green."

Oh. Right.

Clearing my throat, I lift my leg and rotate my entire body until I face him, sitting on his right thigh instead of straddling it. His right hand stays splayed against my shirt, rubbing my waist and turning me on way more than it probably should as I move into my new position. I like it, though. Feeling his hand on me. It helps to have so many people squished on the mat. Everyone's in their own world, oblivious to whatever innocent or not-so-innocent brush of my body against Reeves and how it makes me feel.

As Reeves' heated gaze slides over me practically laid out before him, Everett calls out, "Right hand, blue."

Pushing myself up, I latch onto Reeves' shoulder, hooking my hands around his neck to keep from falling and making us both lose. Once he's sure I won't make us topple over, he moves his hand from my waist and reaches behind him, finding a blue circle on the mat. His body is basically a tabletop, and I'm straddling his waist while his very hard erection strains against my center.

Fucking hell.

"You like this position, Dylan?" His breath is hot against my ear, and my tongue darts out between my lips. It's new. All of this is. Part of me wants to run. To call it a night and hide in my room. The other part? Well, I'm kind of tired of running and hiding and pushing away a man who's only ever treated me like I'm his queen.

I shift a little more in his lap, getting comfortable. "I'm, uh, not complaining."

"Right foot, Red," Everett announces.

I slip my foot a little more forward, and Reeves scoots his back, bringing our chests closer.

"You been in a position like this before, Dylan?" he murmurs.

"I think we both know the answer."

"Yeah, but hearing you say it means more than me assuming."

"Never been this close with anyone."

"And you're okay being this close with me?"

I hesitate but nod, my gaze falling to his lips, realizing how close they are.

"You're cute when you're turned on," he breathes out. "Scratch that. You're sexy as shit."

There's a slight rasp in his voice, and it does me in. "Who says I'm turned on?"

He smiles. "Let's see. It could be the way your cheeks are flushed."

"They aren't—"

"Or maybe it's the way your hips shift ever so slightly against me."

My face floods with embarrassment, and I start to pull off him, but he lifts his hips, hitting me in the exact right place.

I freeze.

"Tell me something, Pickles. How competitive are you?"

I shake my head, my attraction and libido and embarrassment all fighting to make my thoughts about as clear as mud while I consider his question.

"Well,"—I lick my lips—"considering how clumsy I usually am and the fact I usually wind up losing anyway, I'm gonna go with not very."

"Perfect." His ass hits the ground, and I tumble onto him with a gasp. I didn't realize how much weight I was putting on him. I barely have time to register the thought when he jumps to his feet, pulls me up, and flips me over his shoulder.

"Yo, what are you doing?" Griffin yells as Reeves heads toward the stairs.

"She has a throbbing headache," Reeves tells him. "It's terrible. A pity, really. Don't worry, I'll take care of her!"

I'd bet a thousand dollars my brother doesn't buy his lie, but he doesn't call him out on it, either. I sway back and forth on Reeves' shoulder, feeling like a sack of potatoes as he takes the stairs two at a time.

Once we're sheltered behind his closed bedroom door, I ask, "What are you doing?"

He sets me down carefully, well aware I'm probably light-headed after his little stunt on the main floor. He isn't wrong. The ground tilts beneath my feet as his hands find my hips while he waits for the blood to drain from my brain and back to where it should be.

"You good?"

"Uh, yeah. I'm good. But seriously, what are you doing?"

Satisfied, he lets me go. "Taking care of you."

"But I don't have a headache," I point out. "Especially not a throbbing one."

"Something's throbbing, though. Am I right?"

I press my thighs together and shake my head. "You're ridiculous."

"No, I'm charming and dying to touch you. The question is, will you let me?"

Will I let him? I want to laugh and throttle him all at once. I think we're both aware I've been holding back, even if it's only a little bit. But after my conversation with Finley, then my mom? I don't know. I guess I'm tired of it. Tired of letting fear keep me from the things I want. The person I want. Maybe I should trust my gut. And my gut is screaming at me to give myself to him. Oliver Reeves. He's charming. Thoughtful. Protective. Snarky. And so freaking sweet, it hurts.

"I think you should touch me now," I whisper.

His grin widens, and he grabs the back of my legs, lifting me up. Wrapping myself around him, I tangle my fingers in his hair and kiss him. My back hits the wall with a thud as his hands slip beneath my shirt. I love it. The desperation. The desire. The need. Tilting my head to the side, I make room for his lips. He obliges, kissing the side of my neck as he slips his hands higher, shoving my bra up and palming my breasts.

I arch into him, loving every single second of it as he dips down and sucks my nipple into his mouth. With the tip of his tongue, he flicks it, causing liquid heat to pool between my thighs. Shamelessly, I grind against him, holding his head to me and shaking my head back and forth.

"Ollie, Ollie, I need…"

"What do you need, Dylan?" he asks.

"I need you inside me."

He freezes as if the words are a bucket of ice water, and he's drenched. He lifts his head and stares at me. "You sure?"

"Positive."

The sincerity in his eyes does me in, and when a beaming smile spreads across his face, I have no doubt I made the right decision.

"Come here." He grabs my face, kissing me with a fervor I feel from the top of my head to the tips of my toes. Hooking his hands right beneath my ass, he carries me to the bed. Then he's on me. His hands. His mouth. His scent. His need. Within minutes, I don't even know where my pants went, but his mouth? Yeah, I know exactly where it is as he slowly trails down my body, kissing my ribs, then beneath my belly button.

"What are you doing?" I ask.

His eyes lift to mine. "Kissing you."

"Ollie—"

"You don't want me to lick your pussy, baby?"

Fuck.

My thighs press together with need. He coaxes them open with his hands.

My heart pounds against my sternum as he moves lower, kisses the edge of my underwear, and tugs them down my legs. Without a word, he grabs his pillow and shoves it under my hips. With his hand on my lower belly, he presses me down.

"What are you—"

My hips bow off the bed as the heat from his mouth covers my core, branding me with a wet, hot kiss.

Holy shit.

With a groan of appreciation, he laps at my folds, slipping his finger along my seam but not pushing into me. It pulls me tighter, making me feel like a taut string on a guitar, ready to snap at any second.

We've fooled around, but this? This is new. And I like it. I like it a lot. Maybe too much. Who needs a dick when you have a tongue like this? The heat from his mouth sears me, leaving me hot and wet and already on the edge of falling apart when I catch myself holding my breath. But this feels too good. *He* feels too good. Clit aching, I twist my hands in his shaggy hair, holding him to my core as I moan his name. I'm close. So close. How does he do this to me? How does he rip away my barriers like they're nothing? How does he know exactly where to apply pressure and when to pull back, leaving me desperate and needy?

"Please," I beg. "Please, Ollie."

Swirling the tip of his tongue around my clit, I tremble beneath him. It's too much, yet not enough, as he pushes his finger inside me, finds the little bundle of nerves he's all too familiar with, and massages it. Heart pounding, my back arches off the mattress, and stars explode behind my eyes as I come. Hard. It's incredible and addictive, leaving me satiated yet greedy for more. Of this. Of him.

Slowly, I float back down to earth, and my legs fall open. Muscles softening, I'm surprised he hasn't passed out from lack of oxygen. When he climbs back up my body, his chin glistens with my juices. I wrap my arms around his neck, pulling him into a kiss. When he ends it seconds later, he rests his forehead against mine, and I slip my hand between our bodies.

"What are you doing?"

"I said I want you inside me," I remind him.

"Dylan," he warns.

I love it. The affection in his warm gaze. The restraint. The desire to respect my boundaries and the way he's so willing to put me first. My wants. My needs. And at my speed. Always.

"I want you to be my first, Oliver," I whisper. "I want it more than you know."

A divot forms between his brows as he stares down at me, brushing my hair away from my face. "I don't want to pressure you."

"Pretty sure I'm the one pressuring you," I point out.

With a dry laugh, he shakes his head. "You're fucking perfect."

"I think the same can be said for you, Oliver Reeves. Now, help a girl out because I'm not entirely sure how this works."

The same dry laugh kisses my cheeks as he undoes his belt, shoves his pants down his muscular thighs, kicks them off, and makes himself at home between my thighs.

"Condom," I remind him.

"Fuck, I almost forgot." Grabbing one from his nightstand, he slips it on and comes back to me, nestling himself between my parted legs.

"You trust me?"

"You ask that a lot."

"Guess I'm still getting used to it."

My heart cracks, and I bob my head. "Yes, I trust you."

He nods, lining himself up with my entrance and slowly rubbing against me. But he doesn't push in. Doesn't give in.

"Do you like torturing me?" I tease.

"Savoring this," he clarifies.

"Well, if you keep it up, I might come again."

"That can be arranged."

"Oliver…"

He pushes into me slowly—gently—but nothing prepares me for the blinding sensation. I gasp, the intrusion almost more than I can bear as a hot, searing pain makes my jaw drop in a silent scream.

Holy shit.

He freezes on top of me, letting me adjust to his size while keeping his weight on his elbows as he stares down at me. Resting his forehead against mine, he murmurs, "You're perfect, Dyl. Fucking perfect."

"And you're too big," I joke.

He chuckles quietly, shifting his weight onto one elbow and brushing my hair away from my face with his opposite hand.

"You'll get used to me."

"Debatable."

"Nah. This is only the beginning, Dylan." His smile softens, and I swear I can see his soul as he adds, "You were made for me."

I don't know why his words hit me so hard, but they do. Maybe it's because I'm already close to crying, thanks to his massive dick splitting me in two. Maybe it's because a quiet voice inside my head mentioned this *might* only be sex for him, in spite of everything we've been through. Maybe it's the way he climbed the walls around my heart as if they were barely an inch tall, despite how many years I spent building them. Maybe it's because a small piece of me didn't want to believe this could be love. This could be everything.

Regardless, there's something in this. This moment. Even if I'd slept with a hundred men before him, I have no doubt it would still feel like this. Like I really was made for him, and maybe, just maybe, he was made for me.

A tear slips from the corner of my eye, and he leans forward, kissing the trail of moisture, slowly moving his hips in and out of me. He's careful. Gentle. Thoughtful. Like even now, my pleasure and my pain are more important than his, proving the kind of man he really is. And it means more than he can ever imagine.

Curling my arms around his neck, I keep him close as I lift my ankles and hook them around his waist until I cling to him like a monkey. I feel his smile against my neck as he burrows deep, thrusting into me over and over again, slowly picking up speed as my need builds. All too soon, we both tumble over the edge in more ways than one. The seams of my heart unravel more and more with every tremor of pleasure.

It's perfect. He's perfect. And even though I know without a doubt Oliver Reeves has the power to break me, I trust him not to.

33

DYLAN

"**I** got you something," Reeves announces as he strides toward me in the kitchen. It's been a couple weeks since we officially hooked up, and to say things have been pretty close to perfect would be a massive understatement.

Looking up from my Captain Crunch cereal, I ask, "You got me something?"

"Yeah, I got you something."

"You mean *another* something?" I prod.

He shrugs. "Sure."

"Okay, no more buying me things."

"Why not?"

"I don't know? Because you're too sweet, and it makes me feel guilty?"

"Not gonna stop buying you things." He slaps a cardboard box onto the kitchen table, his face beaming with pride. "Open it."

Curious, I push my bowl aside, drag the package closer, and lift the lid. Inside is an...honestly, I have no idea. It's a Taser, I think? Only this one is more like a gun than a small, handheld rectangle with teeth on top. I pick it up to examine it further. It's black and yellow and bulky and absolutely insane. With a laugh, I look up at Reeves again and shake my head. "Are you serious right now?"

"I thought about getting you and the rest of the girls one for a while now."

"Why?"

"One too many horror stories," he offers. "Supposedly, it hurts like a bitch, but I want you to try it on me to be certain."

I shake my head, convinced I heard him wrong. "I'm sorry, what?"

"You should test it on me. Make sure it works."

My eyes bulge at the ridiculousness of his suggestion, and I argue, "I'm not going to tase you."

Rolling up his sleeve, he grips the edge of the table until his knuckles are white and grits his teeth. "Come on. I'm ready."

"Oliver—"

"What are you guys doing?" Griffin asks as he strolls into the kitchen.

"Trying to convince your sister to tase me," Reeves replies, barely casting him a glance as he fills him in.

Surprised, Griffin's attention shifts from me to Reeves and back again. "No shit?"

"Dude, I heard some are nothing but a nasty beesting," Reeves interjects. "I want to know if this one will actually drop a guy if she's using it for protection."

"Protection from what?" I demand.

"Look, do it for me, all right?" Reeves interrupts. "I got one for each of you girls. Figured it would help all of us sleep at night."

"Uh, I sleep fine, thank you very much."

"Humor me, Pickles," he begs.

"Yeah, humor him, Pickles," Griffin adds. He folds his arms across his chest like this is the funniest thing in the entire world. "Besides, Reeves is right. We'll sleep better if we don't have to stress about you guys, and there's only one way to see if it works."

"Come on, Dyl. Do it," Reeves pushes.

"I won't tase you," I all but yell.

"Yeah, you will," Griffin interjects.

Glowering at my brother, I point out, "This has nothing to do with you."

"You're my little sister. Honestly, I'm disappointed I didn't think to buy you one myself. Come on. Let's see what kind of power it has." He lifts his chin at the massive Taser in my hand. It's heavy and masculine and at least twice the size of any other Taser I've ever seen in my entire life. It's probably twice as powerful.

"I refuse to shoot Reeves!"

Griff rolls his eyes. "Dylan, he's a big boy."

"Fuck yeah, I am," Reeves adds. His eyebrows bounce up and down.

My brother's nose wrinkles. "Gross."

"Hey, you brought up size and shit."

"What the fuck did I just walk in on?" Everett demands from the front door. He's dressed in his gym clothes and holding a protein shake.

"They're about to pull out their dicks and compare sizes," Finley comments from the couch in the family room as she files her nails. I should've known she was eavesdropping instead of listening to whatever murder podcast is supposed to be blaring through her headphones.

No wonder she's a sleuth.

"You'd like that, wouldn't you?" Reeves returns with a grin.

Finley's eyes snap to his, and she winks, blowing on her nails.

"Aaaand, no one's showing anyone their dicks, thank you very much," I interrupt.

"Aw, come on, Pickles."

"Did he call you Pickles?" Everett asks.

"You know, as in Dyl?" Reeves grins like he's the most clever human on the planet.

Griffin snorts. "Yeah, you should definitely shoot him."

"Oo, what about Rock, Paper, Scissors?" Finley offers. "Loser gets tased."

The guys exchange looks, but I slap my hand against the table to cut through the staredown.

"You guys, this is *my* taser, and I'm not going to—"

My forefinger slips on the trigger, and a pair of wires shoot from the end pointed directly at Reeves. Like a rock, he drops to the ground, his entire body strung tighter than a bow as he jerks repeatedly.

"Shit!" Releasing the gun onto the table, I rush around the corner and collapse on my knees. "I'm so sorry, I'm so sorry, I'm so sorry," I repeat over and over while the rest of my friends surround us in a small circle, their jaws practically unhinged. Then again, so is mine.

I cannot believe I did that.

"Reeves?" I lift his head, place it in my lap, and pat his chin softly. "Reeves, I am so sorry. Tell me you're okay. Please tell me you're okay."

Reeves' skin is paler than normal as he slowly stops twitching from aftershocks and lifts his hand to hold the one I have pressed against his cheek. "Always knew you'd be the one to knock me on my ass, Pickles."

Bouts of laughter surround us, and by some miracle, it eases the tension in the room. I let out a slow breath of relief. "Are you okay?"

"I'm all right."

"You sure?"

He nods. "Wanna know what would make me feel even better?"

"Don't say it," Everett grumbles.

Ignoring him, Reeves finishes, "If you could kiss it better."

I roll my eyes and smack his chest. He grabs the back of my neck and tugs me toward him, kissing me in front of my friends. It's sloppy and silly, and I catch myself smiling against his lips until he lets me go. Stunned, I stay on my knees as he rolls off my lap and pushes to his feet.

"Well, damn," Finley murmurs from the couch.

"Yeah, I did not need to see that," Griffin states. "But at least we know the Taser works."

"Yeah. We also know my bladder's more resilient than I thought," Reeves quips with a grin as he offers me his hand.

When I take it, he yanks me to my feet and wraps his arms around me like it's the most natural thing in the world. I lean into him, surprised by my lack of embarrassment despite the public display of affection. Peeking up at Reeves, I smile. "Thank you for the gift."

"You're welcome."

"I should probably go shower. I have work in a few hours."

"No worries." He drops another kiss on my forehead. "I'll be ready to take you whenever."

"You sure?"

"You're cute when you're unsure."

"She's cute all the time," Finley points out.

Tapping his finger against his chin, Reeves says, "You know, I think you're right, Fin. She *is* cute all the time."

"And you guys are weird. All the time," I counter. "Good-bye, people."

"Don't use all the hot water!" Everett calls.

"No deal," I say over my shoulder. When I turn the heat to full blast in the bathroom and step under the spray, I'm blown away by how I gave Oliver Reeves a very *real* kiss in front of everyone, and no one even batted an eye.

What a strange world.

34

DYLAN

The place is hopping. Seriously. It's packed. I shouldn't be surprised. The arena is always packed when the guys play. Especially after last week's win. The energy missing since Archer's death has returned. The memory hurts, but instead of shoving it away, I let it sink in as I look up toward the rafters. It's silly. I don't necessarily believe in Heaven and Hell, but I say a silent prayer anyway, hoping Archer can hear me.

Miss you.

The announcer's deafening voice shakes me out of my thoughts as the players take the ice. My dad sits next to me, and I cup my hands over my mouth, cheering the guys on.

"Woo-hoo! Go, Reeves!" a group of girls shouts from a few rows behind me.

I turn around, my nose wrinkling as I take them in. There are at least a dozen of them. Girls in short skirts and LAU jerseys knotted right underneath their massive boobs, showcasing their tan, toned abdomens. Each of the guys has their own fan group. Some of the players have no problem claiming their little groupies. Pointing to them. Blowing kisses. Putting on a show. Others are more subtle. More strategic. Like they're in it for the long game and have no problem being lusted after from afar. It's annoying. I've been coming to these games long enough to know which category Reeves fits into, and the knowledge makes my stomach tighten.

I shouldn't be jealous. I have no reason to be. Sure, most of them probably slept with Reeves at one point or another. But I knew what I was getting into with him before we started dating. Doesn't mean I enjoy the reminder, though. Of his past. His experience. And my lack thereof.

Ignoring them, I try to focus on the game, and before I know it, the first period passes by in a blur, but neither team scores.

As they head into the locker room for their short break, my dad bumps his shoulder with mine. "Been meaning to talk to you."

Finley leans forward and gives him a look. "That doesn't sound ominous at all."

The fine lines around his dark eyes deepen as he chuckles. "Just checking in."

"On what, exactly?" I ask.

"You. You're my baby girl, Dyl. How are you?"

I lift a shoulder. "Fine, I guess."

"Yeah, I'm pretty sure you need to be more specific, Uncle Colt," Finley chimes in. "Are you asking about school or her dating life?"

"Both, I guess," my dad answers. "Although, I'm not sure this conversation involves you, Finley Taylor."

"Every conversation involves me," she volleys back with a cheeky grin and turns to me. "The question is, would our dear Dylan like me to answer for her, or are you going to catch him up on your life willingly?"

"I, uh—"

"Well, for starters," Finley interrupts, diving right into my life like it's her one true calling, "she probably isn't a fan of the homemade jerseys sporting her new boyfriend's last name plastered all over the puck bunny section."

"Boyfriend?" My dad quirks his brow at me.

"I'm not sure we're official—"

"They're totally official," Finley interrupts. "Don't worry, though. They're super cute together and definitely being safe, so—"

"Finley!" I screech.

"What?" she argues, utterly oblivious to my dad's unhinged jaw. "It's true!"

"That's it. I'm putting a frog in your bed," I grind out.

With a gasp, she clutches at her chest. "You wouldn't dare!"

"I think we both know I most definitely would."

"Hey, we share a bed, or at least we would if you weren't always so busy sleeping in your boyfriend's—" Her mouth snaps shut when she realizes exactly what she's aired out in front of my dad. "Aaaand…." She starts scooting past us, heading toward the aisle. "I'm gonna go grab a pretzel."

My dad digs a twenty out of his pocket as she slips past him, handing it to her. "Pretzel's on me."

"Gee." She rolls her eyes. "Thanks. But if your daughter actually does slip a frog in my sheets, you'll be paying for my therapy, too."

Chuckling, he replies, "I'll keep it in mind."

Once she's gone, my dad turns back to me and folds his arms. "We can skip over the gory details. Does he make you happy?"

My heart squeezes in my chest as I look up at him. He's tall and handsome and kind, and he basically set the bar really high when it comes to my expectations of the opposite sex. To be fair, he kind of set the bar high for all of his kids.

Jaxon has spent his entire life trying to live up to him, and Griff? The same goes. I'm not going to lie. It hasn't always been easy for them, and I didn't ever think it was possible to find a guy who could even compete with those notions, but Reeves?

My mouth tilts up as I think about the last few weeks with him. I nod. "Yeah, Dad. He makes me really happy."

"Then I'm happy for you." He gives me a quick squeeze. "Although, I do think we need to invite him to our next family brunch or something."

"I'll see what I can do," I murmur.

He bends closer and narrows his gaze. "I'm serious. How's next week sound?"

"Fine," I concede because I know he won't quit pushing me until I do.

"Good." Backing away, he stands to his full height again while still managing to tower over me. "How's school?"

"Fine."

"And how are the headaches?"

"The usual."

His head bobs in understanding. "And Reeves? He treats you right?"

"Yeah." I smile and bite my bottom lip. "He treats me really well. He even bought a Taser for me and each of the girls, and—"

"He bought you a Taser?"

"Yes."

"You sure it's a good idea?" he teases.

"Probably not, since I accidentally shot him with it."

His guttural laugh makes me flounder as he holds his stomach and bends forward. It's so loud and boisterous people start looking our way, so I elbow him in the ribs. "Will you shush?"

"I'm sorry, but that's the best thing you've ever told me."

He wipes at the corner of his eyes, not even bothering to hide his amusement, as he stands to his full height again and shakes his head in utter disbelief. "Tell me someone recorded it."

"It was an *accident*," I emphasize. "Don't get me wrong. I know I can be clumsy, but it's not like Finley's pointing a camera at me twenty-four-seven, hoping to catch me doing something stupid."

"You mean like shooting your boyfriend with a Taser?"

"Da-ad!"

"All right, all right, I'll stop." His shoulders bounce as he fights back another round of laughter. "Aw, man. Wish I could've been there. Your mom's gonna crack up when I tell her about it tonight."

Smacking him one more time for good measure, I mutter, "Well, I'm glad you find entertainment in my embarrassing stories. But back to our conversation. I'm doing good and... yeah." My attention darts to the empty rink a few rows down.

He nods again. "Well, then I'm even happier for you." Tugging me into his side, my dad kisses the top of my head. "Now, about the homemade jerseys with your boyfriend's name on them..." He lets me go and motions to my generic LAU fan shirt. "Why aren't you wearing one?"

"I don't know?" I tug at the hem of my red and white T-shirt, then fold my arms. The girls have been wearing them for a few weeks now. Ironically, the homemade jersey was the gift the girl in my photography class mentioned to Reeves not long ago. And despite him saying not to bother, she's worn the stupid thing to every game.

Ignoring the reminder, I turn back to the game in time to catch Westbrook, one of LAU's new defensemen, steal the puck from the opposing team. He chips it off the boards and straight to Reeves. The screaming heightens, and I squeeze my eyes shut, knowing how fruitless it is for me to try to block them out. He dribbles it down the ice, heading straight for the net before sending the puck flying across the ice over to a waiting Griffin. With a crash, someone checks him, and he's slammed into the glass. Everett steals the open puck, passing it behind the goal line where Reeves is heading. Ice sprays as Reeves stops short, pivoting around the back of the goal and dropping it into the top left of the net.

The crowd goes crazy, and squeals ensue from the puck bunnies as Finley returns with a soda and pretzel. "Hey, was that your boy?" she asks.

"Apparently, it's our boy," I mutter, glancing over my shoulder at the fan club behind us.

With a frown, Finley follows my gaze, then turns back to me. "Don't worry about them. They're jealous he's finally tied down."

Is he, though? The question crashes through my mind before I can stop it. It's stupid. I know he is. But I'm not the one wearing his jersey. They are.

"Did you ever get sick of them?" I ask my dad. Considering he played in the NHL for years, he has plenty of experience when it comes to this, and I can't help but put him on the spot. "The puck bunnies?"

He frowns. "Unfortunately, they come with the job, Dyl. Some fans are awesome, and others are kind of a pain in the ass, but it is what it is."

"How comforting," Finley chimes in.

He cuts her a look but explains, "Dating a hockey player means you gotta have thick skin, especially when it comes to the fans. Thankfully, your mom and aunts have quite a bit of experience on that front. If you ever need someone to commiserate with, you have a couple pretty great experts. But if you're afraid of blending in with the bunnies while supporting your guy on the ice, I have good news."

A spark of hope ignites inside me. "What is it?"

"When you're out there?" He lifts his chin at the rink beneath us. "The fans are nothing but a blur of people. But your girl?" His smile softens as the team takes the ice. "They're like a homing beacon. I promise."

"Thanks," I murmur. "And you're right. Reeves has been nothing but a gentleman, and I trust him. It's the girls wearing his number I have to get used to."

"Yeah. Besides. They aren't worth it."

"Exactly." I sigh and turn back to the game. "Go, Hawks!"

35
DYLAN

My head is killing me. I've been at Rowdy's for six hours now, but my shift ends in about one more, and I'm counting down the minutes. The sooner it ends, the sooner I can go home, remove my contacts, and take some painkillers. The idea sounds even better than ice cream, which is saying something.

"Hey, Dylan," Finley prods, "Someone's at table seven." She pauses. "You okay?"

"Headache," I mutter.

"Yeah, you look pale. Do you need me to cover the rest of your shift?"

"I'll be fine."

"You sure?"

"It's one more hour. I can do one more hour," I answer, grabbing a tray of drinks for table five. Once they're delivered, I pull a pad of paper and pen from my apron and head to table seven.

"Hey, my name is Dylan, and I'll be your..." my voice trails off as my eyes connect with a familiar shade of brown. Convinced I'm hallucinating, I blink slowly, but the image doesn't dissipate. Nope. Reeves' dad is still here, and he's still staring at me. I never thought I'd have to see him again. But being face-to-face with a guy who tortured his son for years? It pisses me off and makes me want to run in the opposite direction as quickly as possible. Adrenaline shoots down my spine, and I swallow thickly, throttling the pen in my hand.

Snap out of it, Dylan!

"I'll, uh, I'll be your waitress for the evening," I finish.

"I'll take a Corona," one of the officers announces. There are three of them, and they all look at me like I'm a crazy person. Then again, I probably look like I just shit a brick, so...

"Corona," I repeat. "Of course." I scribble the order on the paper and turn to the second officer. "And you?"

"Dr. Pepper."

"Got it." Sucking my bottom lip into my mouth, I turn to Reeves' dad as the pounding in my head grows stronger and stronger. "You?"

His attention shifts from one of my eyes to the next, and he tilts his head. "Do I know you?"

"I, uh—"

"Yeah, I do. You're..." He snaps like he can't quite put a finger on my name when a grin spreads across his face. "You're the Thorne girl. My, uh, my boy's girlfriend, right?"

Oh, so now he claims him.

Forcing a smile, I mutter, "The one and only."

With a booming laugh, he counters, "Not from what I heard."

"Aw, come on, Reeves," his partner interrupts. He introduced himself to me the night of the fight, but I'm too distracted by my throbbing headache and his current company to remember his name. "Give the girl a break so we can get our drinks, man."

Grateful for the reprieve, I smile at the partner. "I'll be

right back." As I start to step away, Reeves' dad grabs my wrist, holding me in place.

"Nah, nah, nah," he tsks. "I haven't ordered yet."

His warm, clammy hand leaves me nauseated, and I carefully pull out of his hold, hoping he can't see how disgusted I feel in his presence. "What can I get you?"

"I'm not sure." His weathered face tightens as he scans the menu. "What's my son's favorite drink?"

"You'd have to ask him."

"What, you don't know?"

"It depends on the day," I answer vaguely.

"Like his taste in women." He laughs.

"Reeves," the partner interjects. *Again.* "Give the girl a break, yeah? You already had your fun with your kid at the station."

"Hey, I'm only tryin' to help her out. Right, McDonnell?"

So that's his partner's name.

McDonnell. Got it.

"Yeah, man, I know," McDonnell says. "But I'm also parched after tonight's shift, so…"

"You're right, you're right," Reeves' dad returns. "I'll have a…Bud Light."

"Coming right up." I step away from the table and can finally breathe once I'm at the back of the restaurant. I don't know what it is. How someone can look so similar to someone else, yet their presence elicits the exact opposite response from my body. One leaves me feeling like a warm drink of hot chocolate. The other? Like I'm being pricked with needles over every inch of my skin. Then again, maybe it's the headache.

Attempting to shake it off, I place their beverage order at the bar and return to the table. "Your drinks will be right out." I glance at the clock on the wall beneath Bruce, the mechanical bull. Forty-seven more minutes. "Any food for you guys?"

"What do you suggest?" McDonnell asks.

I ramble off the specials as well as some of my favorite menu items while ignoring the persistent stare from Officer Reeves. If I can pretend like he doesn't exist, I might be able to hold back the bile coating my throat. *Might,* being the key word. Tonight is not the night to have to deal with him. Not when I already feel like shit.

The drumming in my ears makes it hard to focus, but I manage to write down everyone's order until Officer Reeves is last.

"Country fried steak for me," he announces, closing his menu. Instead of handing it to me, he tucks it under his hands and stares up at me expectantly.

With my hand outstretched, I say, "Got it. Now, if I can have the menu?"

"You'll have to forgive me for dragging my son off to the station the other night."

Lowering my hand, I slip my pen into my apron and fold my arms. "Why did you?"

"Well, you see, there was a fight, and with his history..." His words trail off, leaving me to fill in the blanks.

Honestly, it's a little pathetic.

I know what he's doing. He's baiting me. Toying with me. Daring me to ask for details. For whatever twisted perspective he has on his son, hoping to scare me away. To make me want to leave him.

"I know everything about his past," I lie. "And it's no excuse. Yeah, he made a mistake, but you treated him like a criminal."

"He is a criminal."

Frustration bubbles beneath my skin, but I ignore it. "I'll be right back with your dinner."

I turn on my heel, ready to get the hell out of here and call it a night, when he calls, "Are you sayin' you don't agree with me? Caught him jaywalking the other day and—"

"That's nice," I call over my shoulder.

"What about him killin' his own mother?" he yells. "Does *that* make him a criminal?"

A stone drops in my gut, and I face him again, keeping my head held high as the last of my patience evaporates into thin air. "Is that what you tell people? He killed his mom?"

His face is blotchy and red, his upper lip curling. "It's the truth."

"Bullshit." Giving him one more glare, I turn to McDonnell. "She died in childbirth, but I'm not surprised your partner is so fucking delusional he believes an accident involving an infant constitutes murder since he spent the following eighteen years torturing his son physically, emotionally, verbally, and who knows what else? The fact he still holds a badge and has any right to carry a weapon in this town is not only absolutely disgusting, but so is the fact people like you clearly see how unhinged he is, yet you cover for him. Brushing off his shitty behavior under the guise of... what, exactly? Protecting your own? Well, call me crazy, but I think innocent children should probably be a priority, don't you? Now, if you'll excuse me." My legs feel like Jell-O, but I force them to carry me away from the table while Reeves' dad curses at me. Or at least, I think it's what he's doing. My throbbing headache drowns out his insults, and for once in my life, I'm grateful for it. Heading to the kitchen, I give the cook their order, then find Finley in her section.

When she sees me, her eyes widen. "Hey, are you okay?"

"I need to go home."

"What's wrong?"

"Nothing, I just..." I force my breaths to lengthen, terrified I might actually pass out. Tonight is not the night for a confrontation with Reeves' asshole of a father. But even then, I can't get his stupid comment out of my head.

What about him killin' his own mother? Does that *make him a* criminal?

Fucking asshole.

"Dylan?"

"Take over for me?" I dig my fingers into my forehead where the sharpest point of pain radiates, adding, "I don't know who you have to tell or whatever, but I have a migraine and—"

"I get it." She rubs her hand along my back and pulls out her phone, requesting an Uber for me while guiding me to the front of the restaurant. When we reach the hostess table, she gives the girl at the front the license plate number to look for, then passes me off to her. "Go. I'll take care of everything here."

"Thanks, Fin."

"I got your back, Jack."

36

REEVES

FINLEY

Hey. Dylan ended her shift early and took an Uber home. She has a nasty migraine. I'm not sure if you've ever had to help anyone with them, but you might want to have the lights turned down low.

ME

Thanks for the heads-up.

The garage door sounds a minute later, and Dylan stumbles through the door, her forehead scrunched and her face tight like she's in pain.

Pushing to my feet, I switch into hero mode and stride toward her. "Hey, how can I—"

"My head is killing me." She presses her fingers above her left brow and squeezes her eyes even tighter as she lets out a slow breath.

"What can I do? How do I help?"

"Will you get me a glass of water while I grab my meds?"

Before I can say yes, she pushes her sluggish body away from the wall and heads to the stairs. With a death grip on the railing, she forces herself up the steps, one slow, uncoordinated movement at a time. I've never seen her like this. Like she's in so much excruciating pain she can't even function. Can't think straight. Can't walk straight. Moving as fast as I can, I fill a glass with water and follow her up. The lights are off in her room, but the glow from the hallway highlights the lump on the mattress. She's curled in a ball, her knees to her chest and her eyes still squeezed tight as tears roll down her cheeks.

Fuck.

"Come on, Pickles." I help her sit up and hand her the glass.

"Nightstand," she breathes out. "Orange bottle."

I find the medicine in the drawer, and she peeks one eye open, nodding. With a quick twist of my wrist, I undo the cap and hand her a large, white pill. She pops it into her mouth without hesitation and swallows the water greedily, wiping the corner of her mouth with the back of her hand. She looks so miserable. So...tortured.

"Did you already take out your contacts?" I ask.

Her shoulders hunch even more, like the thought alone is enough to drain her. "It hurts too much."

"Come on, Dylan. Leaving them in isn't an option."

Her head rolls forward like it weighs a thousand pounds. "I think I'm going to be sick."

Reaching for the lined garbage can beside the nightstand, I offer it to her, and she grabs it, cradling the container to her chest. Her hair is in her face, so I shift on the mattress to pull it back as her body heaves, and she pukes into the bin. The sound. I know it well. Heard it more times than I can count when I was in the trailer with my dad. He usually left me to clean it up. At some point, I stopped doing it out of spite. The smell hits like a train, and I open my mouth, breathing through it instead as I fight back the memories.

"Shit," she mutters once she's finished.

I check the vomit for her pill, and sure enough, it's floating front and center. Handing her another one from the bottle, I grab the half-empty glass on the nightstand and give it to her again. "Slower, this time," I murmur.

She takes the pill, along with a slow sip of water. Swallowing, she rests her head on my shoulder, her body spent.

"Your contacts." I shift in front of her and lift her chin. As she slowly opens her eyes, I pluck the contacts from her and place them in the container next to the alarm clock while my concern and sympathy battle for first place inside me.

With a sigh, she murmurs, "I'm sorry."

"*I'm* sorry," I counter.

"No." She shakes her head, her eyes nothing but slits as her forehead scrunches. "No, you don't understand. Ooooh," she groans. "This is a bad one." Folding forward, she cradles her head in her hands, her body rocking back and forth as we wait for the medicine to kick in.

"Sh, sh, sh." I rub my hand up and down her back, anxious to take away her pain while shoving aside the helplessness eating me alive. I hate it. Hate seeing her like this. Hurting. Uncomfortable. Fucking wrecked. This is what Everett was talking about. What he warned me about. How much it affects her even though she hides the repercussions of her injury well most of the time. But this? This you can't unsee. Something that hits her out of nowhere. Something she has to live with for the rest of her life. But if I've learned anything, it's Dylan will persevere through something like this. She's the strongest person I know.

"It's gonna be okay, Dylan. Just relax. You'll get through this." Slipping my hand beneath her bent knees and my other around her upper back, I cradle her to my chest and carry her to my bedroom so Finley won't wake her up when she gets home. Assuming Dylan's able to find sleep in the first place. With a soft whimper, my girl curls closer to me, her hot breath brushing my neck as I close my bedroom door behind us. I kick one of my T-shirts over the night-light, then set Dylan on my mattress.

Her fingertips are white as she squeezes her head, her lips parted in a grimace. Taking over, I place one hand on her forehead and the other at the base of her skull, hoping the pressure will relieve her pain. A low breath of relief escapes her, and she leans into my hands a little more, the tension in her body easing a bit. We stay like this. Dylan rocking back and forth in the fetal position, my hands on either side of her head, the lights off, blanketing the room in darkness. Soon, her tiny whimpers soften, and her muscles relax even more. The pill is finally doing its job. Shifting on the mattress, I keep my movements slow, realizing she's fallen asleep, and I bring her against me, holding her close. Soon, my eyes grow heavy, and I pass out beside her.

I WAKE SLOWLY. THE MORNING LIGHT FILTERS IN THROUGH THE blinds. Dylan's snuggled beside me. Her head is on my chest, and a little pool of drool is on my shirt. I smile when I notice it. The reminder of the last time we were in this position. I never slept with a girl until Dylan. Never trusted one enough to be vulnerable around them. To turn off the Reeves' charm and simply…be. Yet, with her, it's different. It's always been different.

As if she can feel me watching her, her brow wrinkles, and she squints her eyes open. They're clearer than last night. Not clouded with excruciating pain. If anything, there's barely a hint of discomfort in her pinched expression. The sharp pain in my chest softens as I take her in.

"What time is it?" she croaks.

"No idea."

She nods and smacks her mouth. "My breath tastes like shit."

With quiet amusement, I sit up and reach for the almost empty glass of water, offering it to her. "Here."

She takes it. "Thanks." After a small sip, she licks the moisture from her pouty lips. "And thank you for taking care of me. It was...a bad one, obviously."

"You mentioned that." I push her hair away from her face and over her shoulder. "Are you feeling better?"

"It's still there, only not as bad. It's more like...a crappy headache instead of the my-brain-being-is-stabbed-with-a-million-ice-picks feeling."

"Progress, I guess," I say with a laugh.

She joins in. "I guess." Sitting up a little more, her blonde, wavy hair cascades over her shoulder, and she sobers, looking like she's seen a ghost or some shit.

And just like that, whatever peace I felt this morning is replaced with a heavy unease.

"What is it?" I ask.

Chewing on the inside of her cheek, she looks at war with herself. Finally, she lets out a quick breath and faces me. "Look, it isn't a big deal."

"Because that's the first thing a guy wants to hear in the morning."

She rolls her eyes, taking another breath, but it's deeper this time. "I, uh, I ran into your dad."

My stomach plummets. "What?"

"He, uh," she pinches the bridge of her nose but lets her hand fall to her lap with a soft thud. Dejected. Embarrassed. Annoyed. "He came into Rowdy's with his partner and another guy. Go figure, he was seated in my section, and then he recognized me and—"

"What did he do?" I growl.

"Nothing."

It's a lie. I can see it. Feel it. Fucking taste it.

"Tell me, Dylan."

"He said you're a criminal, and when I didn't take the bait, he told me you, uh... He said something despicable. I can't even repeat it."

"Let me guess. He told you I killed my mom."

Her teeth dig into her bottom lip, but she nods softly. "I couldn't believe he would say something like that."

"I can." I hesitate, shoving aside my frustration. "My dad...he lives in the gray area. He thrives on people not communicating. On him holding all the cards."

"Yeah, I noticed." She reaches for her glasses on the night-stand, slides them on her face, and squeezes my hand. "But I couldn't let him get away with it, you know? Painting you like that."

Dread spreads in the pit of my gut, and I push myself up, pressing my back to the headboard. "What did you do?"

"Well...uh, the night's kind of a blur, but I'm pretty sure I kind of yelled at him and then told his partner your dad is an abusive asshole."

My spine turns into a steel rod, and I tilt my head, convinced I heard her wrong. "What?"

Pity and regret shine in her eyes as she holds my gaze. "I told his partner you were abused as a kid. That he abused you."

"Dylan—"

"I know it was stupid," she rushes out. "I know I should've kept my mouth shut, but after he accused you of killing your mom, I couldn't..."—she shoves her hair away from her face —"I couldn't sit there and let him manipulate everyone at the table."

"Dylan—"

"I know you'd never—"

"Dylan," I repeat.

Her lips press together, and she lets out all the oxygen from her lungs. "I'm sorry. If I overstepped my bounds or...if I did anything wrong."

My eyes close from the weight of our conversation as I try to quiet the voice inside my head. The one warning me to lay low. To figure out how to get Dylan off his radar. How to protect her from him. But she fucked up. She did it for me, which I appreciate more than she'll ever know, but my dad knows how to make life a living hell for people. He knows how to dig up dirt and to plant shit and to manipulate and torture and—

"Oliver," Dylan's quiet voice cuts through the chaos as she places her hand on top of mine. "It's going to be okay."

I lean my head against the solid piece of oak behind me and look at the ceiling. "You don't know him like I do."

"Tell me about her," she begs. "Your mom."

Lifting our entwined fingers, I kiss the back of her hand. "There's not much to tell." A bitter laugh rumbles from my chest. "They were high school sweethearts. I was her miracle baby. And then...I took her from him, and he never let me forget it. I grew up across town, but after I found out my mom went to LAU, I dunno. I guess I wanted to be close to her, so I applied and got in. First thing I did was look her up in one of the old yearbooks." I smile at the memory.

"What did she look like?" she whispers.

"Brown hair. Brown eyes. Beautiful." I smirk down at her. "Like you."

A blush hits her cheeks, giving me a glimpse of the wallflower I fell for when we first met. She asks, "So you chose to put up with your dad being within a twenty-minute drive all because you wanted to be close to your mom?"

"It didn't hurt how coming here pissed him off."

She laughs. "Wow."

"Never said I wasn't an ass."

"Yeah, you were pretty clear about it from the beginning. But since we're being honest, what else is on your criminal record?"

Scratching my jaw, I give her the side-eye. "You sure you wanna know this?"

She nods.

"Assault charges for beating the shit out of a few abusive motherfuckers over the years and a DUI after a run-in with my dad."

"The night before the playoff," she realizes.

I nod. "Yeah. He recognized my car and pulled me over. Lied about the breathalyzer reading, said it wasn't working, but since I couldn't walk a straight line, he had to take me in." I scoff. "It was bullshit, but it didn't matter. He's also gotten me on jaywalking a few times, and, uh," I pause. "I *think* that's it?"

"You think?"

With a shrug, I admit, "Never claimed I didn't have a shady past, Pickles."

"I'd say shitty over shady."

I laugh. "Thanks for the benefit of the doubt. And now, all my dirty laundry's been aired, but I have one more thing to add."

"What is it?" she asks.

"I'm the one who kissed you at the party."

Her brows pinch, and she tilts her head. "What?"

"It was me. I'm Cinderfella."

"But Everett—"

"Lied, hoping you'd let go of your mission to track him down. He knew it was me, and he wanted you to keep your distance."

Her expression falls as she registers the truth, the one I kept from her for far too fucking long. "I'm gonna kill him."

"Don't," I argue. "I get why he feels the need to protect you. Especially after seeing you last night with your migraine. That shit—knowing he's the one who caused it—would fuck with anyone's head."

The anger seeps from her, and she leans her back against the headboard beside me. "Doesn't mean it's okay to lie to me, though."

"You're right, it isn't, and I shouldn't have covered for him, either, but don't worry. I'm making him do his time."

"How so?"

"Well, since I'm off the market now and can't protect innocent women from assholes, I figured I'd send them Everett's way. It'll be good for him to have his ass handed to him once or twice."

Her jaw drops. "You're joking."

"Definitely not," I say.

With a laugh, she smacks my chest and snuggles closer to me. "You're terrible."

"Meh. He'll make some money while he's at it, so I think it's a win-win."

"Mm-hmm," she hums.

"Thanks for talking to me about last night, though. You could've easily run in the opposite direction after interacting with my dad, but you didn't."

"Of course, I didn't." Her voice is soft. Hushed. As she drags her fingers along my chest. "You're not the only one willing to put in the work, Ollie."

I shut my eyes, surprised by how much I needed to hear it. How I'm worth the work. Worth the effort. Worth... anything at all.

"Love it when you call me Ollie," I rasp.

"And I love saying it. *Ollie.*" She says the name as if she's tasting it. As she sits up again, a giant grin nearly splits her face in two. "I kind of love the name."

Chuckling, I reply, "You know, I think you mentioned it once or twice."

"No, seriously. Can I please call you Oliver all the time instead of mainly when we're alone? After my interaction with your dad yesterday, I..." She shivers. "I have a feeling it's going to be a problem."

"My last name?"

"Mm-hmm. A big problem, actually."

With a low laugh, I sit up and kiss the side of her neck. "Who knew you were a snarky little thing?"

"Uh, jokes on you. I've always been snarky. You had to wiggle past my defenses to see it."

"I like wiggling past your defenses."

"And I like wiggling past yours," she replies. And fuck me, but the sincerity shining back at me? It hits me right between the ribs, and I'm blown away. By the way she's stuck around so far. The way she's given me a chance, a real chance. The way she likes me. Despite my past. Despite my dad. Despite my reputation. I'm the luckiest bastard alive.

"All right, here's the deal," I decide, pushing her hair away from her face and cupping her cheek. "You can call me whatever you want as long as you ride my dick every once in a while."

Tossing her leg over my lap, she murmurs, "I think that can be arranged...on one condition."

"Oh?"

"You let me brush my teeth first."

With a laugh, I slap the side of her ass, and we both head to the bathroom to brush our teeth, returning to lounge in my bed once again. Like it's the most natural thing in the world. To spend a day being lazy in bed with the person you care about. No expectations. No rules. No time restraints. Nothing but each other's company, and I like it. A lot.

Resting her chin on my chest, she draws circles along my bare chest. "So."

"So?"

"My, uh, my family's having brunch, and…"

I push her hair away from her face and tilt her head toward me.

"And?"

"My dad's wondering if you'd like to come."

"And what about you?" I ask.

With a shy smile, she murmurs, "I was wondering if you'd like to come, too."

"As a friend like at the Harry Potter party?"

"As…whatever this is."

My mouth lifts. "We still haven't had the DTR talk yet, have we?"

She frowns. "DTR?"

"Define the relationship," I clarify.

"So this is a relationship."

"You've trusted me enough to let me inside you." I drag my fingers along her bare thigh. "I think it qualifies, don't you?"

"What are you saying, Ollie?"

"I'm saying I want you to be my girlfriend."

Her straight white teeth dig into her bottom lip as if she's trying to stifle her smile. Her hope. Her fucking joy. And dammit, my chest swells as soon as I see it. Her joy. I never wanted to make a girl as happy as I want to make her. Because this feeling? It's indescribable. Addictive.

"You want me to be your girlfriend?" she asks.

"Yeah, Pickles. I really do."

Giving in, a grin spreads across her face, and she bends down, kissing me. "Okay."

"Now about the dick riding you mentioned earlier…"

Her hand slips down my torso, and she raises her hips, letting her hand graze my stiff cock, lifting it.

My lips part on a groan, pulling a laugh from her as she lines me up with her entrance. "You were saying?"

"Uh, what about a condom?"

"Uh, I'm on birth control, boyfriend, so you're welcome."

And just like that, I know I'm a goner. Dylan Thorne. Wallflower. Daenerys doppelganger. And stealer of hearts... including mine.

I wouldn't have it any other way.

37

DYLAN

I love my childhood home. Seriously. It has a smell no candle can replicate. It's a combination of whatever's cooking in the kitchen, fresh linen, and my mom's perfume. I love the cozy furniture and the way I know ice cream is stashed in the freezer. I love the gray stone fireplace in the family room and how a fire is almost always blazing from November to February. I love the fuzzy blanket hanging along the back of the cozy, cream-colored couch I spilled juice on when I was a little girl and the way my parents soaked it up with dish towels as I cried in the corner, feeling guilty as hell for ruining the fabric until they gave me a hug, then flipped the cushion over, proving everything was still perfect, and I had no reason to be bawling my eyes out over spilled juice.

I love the love emanating from every corner. Every surface. Every picture hung on the walls.

But it's a little strange being here now. Knowing you came from a loving home without thinking much of it until you're standing next to someone who hasn't. Who wasn't lucky like me. Who didn't have amazing parents. Opportunities galore. A full belly and a happy childhood.

Slipping off my jacket, I hang it on the coat rack near the front door as laughter echoes from the back of the house. Oliver's behind me, and he follows suit, making himself comfortable.

"You okay?" he murmurs when I stay frozen in my family's entryway.

I nod but remain quiet as a burn hits the back of my eyes.

"Hey, what's wrong?" He cups the side of my face and lifts my chin. "Another headache?"

I shake my head, my heart aching at his thoughtfulness. "It's not that."

"What is it?"

"Nothing, it's just…I was thinking about how different our childhoods were."

His chuckle is low and dry and sardonic at best. "And it made you want to cry?"

"I'm sorry, is all."

His eyes soften. "Don't apologize, Pickles."

"I'm serious," I push. "After seeing how horrible your dad is and how intimidated I was after a single interaction with him as an *adult*," I emphasize, "I can't imagine how rough it was growing up with him as a father. And walking in here, I took a second to imagine what it must look like through your eyes, comparing it to what I assume your childhood looked like, and…" I swallow thickly, blinking away the sheen in my eyes. "I'm so sorry."

His soft smile greets me as he bends down to kiss my forehead. "You're cute when you're thoughtful, Dylan."

Glaring up at him, I smack his chest and start to pull away, but he drags me closer.

"Ollie, I'm serious."

"So am I." With a rough tug, he pulls me back into him like I'm his own personal yo-yo and kisses my forehead one more time. "No one's ever cared about me, Pickles. No one's ever looked out for me or stood up for me. Not like you do. So, thank you." He leans even closer, whispering, "And you are cute as shit. Now, come on. Let's see if your family hates me."

"My family already knows you," I remind him.

"Yeah, well, we're official now." He grimaces. "I have a feeling my work's cut out for me." Threading his fingers through mine, he adds, "Lead the way, Pickles."

So, I do.

My family is gathered around the granite island covered with waffles, sausage, hash browns, and fruit. As we enter the kitchen, my dad steals a piece of watermelon from the bowl, and my mom snatches it from his hand before he has a chance to eat it. Then, she tosses it into her own mouth.

With a playful glare, he points out, "I thought you said we had to wait for—"

"We're here!" I announce.

"Dylan!" my family greets me.

My mom rounds the island and pulls me into a hug. My dad takes her place, then Jax, then Griff. Each of them takes their turns until a pair of hands lands on my hips, and a familiar heat hits my spine. Peeking up, I find Oliver.

I can't decide whether I'm grateful it's only my immediate family here or if a bit more chaos in the form of Finley and the rest of the gang would make today's brunch a little easier. Not that it matters. We're here, and there's no going back. Not anymore.

"Hey, Reeves. What's up?" Griffin greets him, doing the manly hand grasp, pull-in, back slap thing guys do.

Ollie returns the gesture, lets him go, and lifts his chin to greet Jaxon. "Hey, man."

"Hey."

"Hi, Reeves." My mom hugs him, and Oliver's eyes widen in surprise as they connect with mine over her shoulder. His body stays frozen in place until she steps back, giving him space.

My dad, however, only offers his hand for Reeves to shake. "Reeves."

"Mr. Thorne." Reeves takes it, his jaw tight as he holds my dad's stare. And with a single shake, they each step back.

Okay, this is weird. Nothing over the top, but the last time my dad saw Reeves, he was friendly. Now, he's...I don't know, more tense? Defensive, maybe? And it's strange because I've literally never seen this side of him. Then again, I've also never introduced him to a boyfriend, so maybe this is normal?

Ignoring it, I smile up at Reeves one more time and announce, "Should we eat?"

"Finally." Without waiting for any further prodding, Griffin grabs a plate and dishes his food. The rest of us follow suit and move to sit around the dining room table. It's quiet and weirdly tense, and I kind of want to crawl into a hole and never come out.

"Juice?" Reeves asks from beside me.

I nod. "Yes, please."

He pours us some orange juice, and my dad leans forward, watching with interest as I reach for my glass and take the first sip.

"So," my dad clears his throat, "tell me about yourself."

Reeves shrugs. "Not much to tell."

"I'm sure there's something," my dad counters, as chilly as he was earlier.

"Let's see..." Reeves scratches his jaw. "I grew up right outside of Lockwood Heights with my dad. I've played hockey my entire life. I like movies, TV shows, games, sports, your daughter, uh...yeah."

"Way to slip it in there," Jaxon notes behind the rim of his coffee mug.

Griffin's chuckle cuts off when my mom elbows him in the ribs.

"That's interesting, Reeves," she tells him as she dishes up a few cubes of fruit. "Do you have any other family? Siblings or anything?"

"None I'm aware of. My mom married my dad pretty young, and her parents weren't fans of the guy, so they never came around, especially after she died." He pauses, looking thoughtful. "I think they passed away three or four years ago, but honestly, I'm not sure. It was hard to keep track of any of it. As for my dad's side of the family, he wasn't from around here. From what I understand, he also had a shi—uh, not good—relationship with his parents, and...yeah. As far as I know, I'm an only child, but that's taking my father's word for it, and from my personal experience..."—he forces a smile and stabs a piece of pineapple—"it's not always the brightest decision."

My mom's fork makes it halfway to her mouth before she frowns and sets it down on her plate. "Oh? Was your dad... *active*?"

"Mom, don't ask about his dad's sex life," Griffin interrupts. "It's gross."

With wide eyes, my mom argues, "I wasn't, I was—"

"Don't worry about it, Mrs. Thorne," Reeves interjects after he swallows the piece of fruit he'd eaten. "I know what you're asking. There were rumors when I was little about another brother from a previous relationship or something, but when I asked my dad about it, he said it was bullsh—uh, not real, and it hasn't come up since."

My mom's mouth twitches, and she glances at me as she picks her fork up again.

"So, I take it you're not close with your father?" my dad demands.

Holding his chilly gaze, Reeves answers, "Not in the slightest."

"Dad," Griffin mutters through a mouthful of waffle, giving him a look telling him to back the hell off, and my chest warms.

At least someone's on Reeves' side.

"Nah, it's all right," Reeves tells Griff. He shifts in his seat and stretches his legs out. "My dad's an abusive asshole in the Lockwood Heights police department. I've had run-ins with him here and there, which is what most of my records revolve around, but I was also arrested for assault when I found a girl in one of my freshman classes was being stalked by an ex-boyfriend. She asked me to walk her to and from classes because she was scared. Sure enough, the guy was following her. I got fed up, we got into a fight, and he wound up in the hospital with an eye socket fracture and a broken wrist, so he decided to press charges. Let's see, what else? Uh, I had a DUI a couple years ago right before the Hawk's championship, which led to the team losing, and, uh…a few citations for jaywalking, and yeah. I think that's about everything." He exhales, and his attention snaps to my dad. "It's what you really want to know, right? I mean, if I had a daughter, the first thing I'd do is pull a background check on her boyfriend when she's officially bringing him home to meet the family, even though we technically already met."

I blanch, realizing exactly what he means.

I glare at my dad. "Tell me you didn't."

My dad blinks. Twice. He throws my mom an indecipherable look, sighs, and turns back to me, setting his napkin on the table. "Dylan—"

"Dad," I snap. "You did not—"

A warm hand touches my thigh, and I look down to find Oliver's massive hand squeezing my leg to get my attention.

"Like I said, it's the first thing I would do," he murmurs.

"We do like you," my mom interjects. "And, even though I'm sure Colt would've probably looked into you a little more since you two are official now, it was a moot point. Yesterday, Officer Reeves called to tell us all about you. He wanted to give us a heads-up about the boy our daughter's dating and living with."

"Yeah, he's a real saint, " Reeves mutters under his breath as he stares down at his hand resting on my knee.

"I figured," my dad returns. "But it's clear the apple fell quite far from the tree."

Reeves looks up from the table. Surprised. Stunned. Humbled. Forcing a smile, he reaches for his juice but hesitates before taking a sip. "I hope so." Then he swallows it back and sets the glass down.

"Trust us," my mom adds. "The older you get and the more run-ins you have with shitty people, the easier it is to tell them apart from the good ones. And you, Reeves, are a good egg, despite your dad's shitty sperm."

Oliver snorts, and the tension in the room dissipates as my brothers groan in unison, "Mo-om…"

"Oh, boo-hoo," she replies. "You two are fine. Now, let's finish breakfast."

38

REEVES

It's been a few weeks since brunch. Somehow, between classes, Game Nights, hockey games, and spending every waking moment together, Dylan and I managed to finish the second part of our photography assignment. When we got our grades from Dr. Broderick, both of us were pleased to find we received an A on the project. I forgot how pretty she looked in the photos I took. After seeing them again, I decided to frame them. They should be here soon. But the photos? Those were a gift for me. The jersey burning a hole in the white box on the kitchen counter is for Dylan, and I'm praying she likes it.

When the front door opens with a quiet squeak, Dylan appears in the doorway, and I scoop up the gift from the counter and announce, "I got you something."

I should've waited. Should've been more smooth and shit, but I can't help myself. Ever since Finley told me Dylan was jealous of all the puck bunnies in the arena wearing my name on their jerseys, I did something I never thought I would.

Slipping off her backpack and setting it on the ground,

Dylan tears her attention from the large box and looks at me. "Dude."

"What?"

"You have to stop spoiling me! This is like the third gift since school started, and—"

Snatching her arm, I pull her into me, silencing her with a kiss. Once she's practically panting, I smile against her mouth and lean back, soaking in the light pink tint on her cheeks. "I'm always going to spoil you, Pickles. Now, open it."

Letting her go, I hand her the box and wait for her to lift the lid. I've been dying to give her the present since Dylan's dad suggested it while she went to the bathroom at brunch. She'll either love it or hate it, but I really hope it's the first.

With a hesitant smile, she lifts the lid, tearing at the tissue paper inside and laughing. "Where did you get this?"

"Do you like it?"

"It's your jersey."

"Yeah?"

"But instead of Reeves, it says Oliver."

I nod. "You said you don't like my last name, remember?"

Her cheeks pinch as she shakes her head, examining the red and black jersey with my name stitched along the back. "Well, yeah, but…"

"But what?" I prod, sitting on pins and needles.

"You remembered."

"Of course, I remembered." Lifting her chin, I step closer and kiss her. "I never had a girl wear my jersey."

"You have a dozen puck bunnies who not only wear your jersey number but went through the effort to bedazzle them with your last name and happily wear them to every game," she argues dryly. "Trust me. I've seen them."

"There's the jealousy Finley mentioned," I note.

She frowns. "Finley told you I was jealous?"

"Finley told me she'd neuter me if I didn't grow a pair and

claim you in front of everyone while simultaneously putting all the puck bunnies in their place," I counter.

Her jaw drops. "I'm gonna kill her."

"Don't you dare," I order. "Besides, even if she hadn't said anything, your dad pulled me aside during brunch and suggested I give you something to help you stand out in the crowd."

"Bunch of snitches," she mutters.

I chuckle under my breath, pushing her hair away from her face. "I want to make something very clear to you."

"What is it?"

"Yes, plenty of girls have worn my jersey number."

"Mm-hmm." Her nostrils flare, and she presses her lips together, looking annoyed and fiery and pissy, and, fuck, it's hot as hell.

"*But*," I clarify, "I've never had anyone I actually want to see wearing my jersey. My name. My *real* name."

Her eyes soften, and the heat from her jealousy evaporates almost instantly as she looks back at the jersey with the name Oliver stitched in the bright red fabric. "I love it."

"You do?"

"Well, yeah." Amusement shines in her pretty blue-green eyes as they snap back up to me. "How'd you get it, though? Obviously, it's custom-made."

"I figured I could do the research, but Finley got in another fight with Drew, so I called her and let her work her magic."

"That was sweet of you," she admits.

"I can be sweet."

"Yes, yes, you can." She rises onto her tiptoes and kisses me softly. "Do you want to see me in it?"

"In my jersey?"

"Mm-hmm," she hums.

"Fuck yeah."

"Perfect. Meet me upstairs in five." She nibbles my bottom lip for good measure, lets me go, and skips up the stairs when a loud thud echoes from the staircase.

"Dylan?" I call.

Did she seriously just fall up the stairs?

"I'm okay!" she yells.

I hang my head in amusement until the familiar click of a bedroom door closing makes my blood flow south.

I wait, counting down the seconds. Once the last minute is up, I take the stairs two at a time, not bothering to knock as I push my bedroom door open. And there, in the middle of the bed, is the prettiest girl I've ever seen in nothing but a jersey. My jersey. With my name scrawled across the back.

"So?" she asks. "What do you think?"

"I think I've never seen anything sexier."

She grins. "And I think I like you, Oliver Reeves. I think I like you a lot."

"I like you, too, Pickles."

She bites back her grin and shakes her head. "Pretty sure I'll never be able to eat a pickle again without thinking of you."

"But only the big pickles, right?" I lift my hands, leaving a foot of space between the two. "Like a really *big* pickle."

With a laugh, she says, "Shut up."

"I'm just saying—"

"You're the only pickle I've had, so, technically, I can't compare the size, thank you very much."

The reminder that I'm her first, her only, makes my chest swell with pride. I don't care about the number, but rather how she trusted me enough to give me a chance she's never given anyone else.

Striding toward the edge of the bed, I climb on top of her, and she leans back, staring up at me. "I think we should keep it that way, don't you?"

"I think, as of right now, you have nothing to worry about, Ollie."

"And I think you're the only taco I ever want to eat again." I nip at her pouty lips, tasting her smile. "*Ever.*"

With a very unladylike snort, she pulls back and repeats, "Taco? Really?"

"What would you prefer I call it?" My hand slips between her thighs, and I start playing with her entrance, drawing small circles in her heat as she shifts on the bed, making more room for my hand between her pretty little thighs. She isn't wearing underwear, which might be my favorite surprise of the day.

"Call it whatever you want," she whimpers. "Just don't stop what you're doing."

A low laugh escapes me as I continue fingering her on my bed, the jersey riding up and showcasing the prettiest goosebumps racing along her pale, silky skin. Realizing she might be cold, I tug my comforter around us to keep her warm while continuing my assault. When her eyelids flutter, she grabs my wrist and rides me.

"Fuck, this feels so good," she whimpers.

Slowly, I kiss down her body, the sheets rustling as I slip beneath them. Her nipples are stiff little peaks, and I pop the left one into my mouth, sucking on the hard bud as she fumbles with my belt and shoves my pants down my thighs. Blindly, she reaches for my dick, rubbing her thumb along the head and pinning me between her hand and her thigh, spreading my precum along her silky skin.

"I like feeling you on me," she whispers. "On my skin. Like you're marking me."

"All you gotta do is ask, baby. I'll cover you with my cum any time you want."

She lets out a breathless laugh, letting me go. "Figured

you'd be happy to oblige. But first, I think you should eat my taco, don't you?"

"Someone's needy."

"Hey, you made me this way. I didn't know what I was missing with this thing, remember?" She drags her thumb along my bottom lip, then pushes me further down her body. I like it, though. I like it a lot. The way she trusts me enough to tell me what she wants and how she wants it. The girl who moved in next door wouldn't have. She wouldn't have wanted to inconvenience me. Little does she know, I fucking live for this, and if I died right here, buried between her thighs, it'd be worth it, and you could mark my tombstone with, "Happiest Man to Ever Live."

Her little gasps of pleasure mingle with the sound of her wet pussy as I pump my fingers in and out over and over while trailing open-mouthed kisses along her stomach and lower to the apex of her thighs. Spreading her folds, I replace my hand with my mouth, anxious to please her. To make her come. To make her mine again and again for as long as she'll have me. She's hot and wet and needy, and exactly how I like her as she lets her thighs fall open even more. Playing with the little divots between her thighs and pussy, I flick my tongue inside her, and she moans. Fuck, I love her moan. How it's breathy and needy and so damn quiet. Like she's holding back. Like she's afraid of letting go, and every time she does, it makes me feel like the luckiest bastard in the world. When her fingers find my hair, I know she's already close, her hips lifting and writhing and rolling as I French kiss her core.

"So sweet," I groan.

"And so close." She brings my mouth back to her. "Keep going."

I smile against her pussy, then suck her clit into my mouth. Her muscles tighten with pleasure as she comes against my tongue, her body arching off the bed and her thighs squeezing the sides of my head. She's nothing but goo as I drag her to the edge of the bed. Flipping her over, I take her from behind, lining up the head of my dick with her dripping entrance and pushing into her. It's as if she was made for me. Her tight, wet heat. Her creamy skin. Her muffled groans getting lost in my sheets. She grabs the fabric with her hands while meeting me thrust for thrust, and my blood flows further south.

"You take me so good, baby." I watch her pussy swallow my dick, the image tattooing itself into my brain. "So fucking good." Thrusting into her over and over again, my balls tighten, and I come inside her, throwing my head back as warmth spreads through me. Her core tightens around me. Her arms give out, and she collapses onto the bed, spent from her second orgasm.

"Let me get a towel," I offer as I slide out of her.

"Ah, come on," she peeks over her shoulder at me. "You don't want crusty sheets?"

I chuckle. "Do you want me to have crusty sheets?"

The girl pauses thoughtfully. "I mean, I kind of like the idea of being the only girl to ruin your bed—"

"You mean of letting *me* ruin my bed."

"Yeah. *That*." Her grin widens.

Tilting my head, I challenge, "You're seriously gonna make me wash my sheets all so you can prove you're the only girl I've fucked in my bed?"

She crumbles into a fit of laughter. "Okay, your face made this even more priceless, but no, I'm teasing. Get me a towel so we can snuggle without worrying about rolling around in your mess. Mmmkay, pumpkin?"

I smack her ass, and she squeals, laughing even harder. I step back, grab my shirt since it's close by, and clean her up, tossing the dirty fabric into the laundry basket. When I find her staring at me with a soft smile, I ask, "There a problem, Pickles?"

"I like it when you take care of me."

"Always gonna take care of you," I tell her, slipping back into bed and tugging her toward me. Once she's comfortable, I grab the remote from the nightstand and turn on the television. "Now, what movie should we watch?"

39

DYLAN

I'm not gonna lie. I feel a little ridiculous wearing Oliver's jersey, but it's a good kind of ridiculous. Like I scratched the winning number on the lottery ticket, and I don't know what to do with myself. Squeal? Do a happy dance? Pretend like my life hasn't been turned upside down, and everything is like it was, only I'm in on the secret, and damn, it's a good one. I'm no secret, though. Nope. Oliver has always made his intentions with me very clear. He's never hidden this. Me and him. He refuses to. And there's something about being claimed so openly. So confidently. I like it. A lot, actually. So, yeah. Sitting here in the stands while wearing his jersey with his number painted on my cheeks as I watch him score two goals in the first period makes me feel like the luckiest girl in the world, and I'm so here for it.

As the red light flashes behind the opposing team's goal, Reeves points to me in the stands and starts twerking in his gear. I shake my head, my cheeks aching as I grin from ear to ear. Seriously, he's the biggest goofball on the planet.

"Yeah, you totally love him," Finley points out beside me.

The word catches me off guard, and I tear my attention from Reeves heading back to the bench and pin Finley with a look instead. "What did you say?"

"She said you totally love him," Ophelia repeats from my opposite side. She's sandwiched between Mav and me. He's currently oblivious to our conversation, cheering for his team the same way I should be if I wasn't so distracted by my friends' accusations. When my head snaps in Ophelia's direction, she adds, "What? You're surprised you love Reeves?"

Tugging at the hem of my shirt, I consider her question while nibbling on the edge of my thumb. Love? Who said anything about love? I mean, I get it. I care about him more than almost anyone. When I'm not with him, I feel like a not-so-little piece of me is missing. And when he's around, I can't stop smiling. But *love*?

Holy shit. Do I love Oliver Reeves?

"Told ya," Finley teases.

I lower my hand and scowl at my best friends. "We've only been dating for a little while."

"So?" Finley prods.

Ophelia laughs, clearly finding way too much enjoyment from my bludgeoned epiphany. "Yeah. *So?*"

"So…" My voice trails off, and I stand, determined to avoid my best friends and their perceptive gazes even if it's the last thing I do. "I'm going to the bathroom."

"Aw, come on!" Finley argues. "You can't run from your feelings, Dylan!"

"Who said I'm running?" I call over my shoulder. I reach for the hem of the jersey I'm wearing and tug it down as if to shine a light on Reeves' first name sprawled across my shoulders while solidifying my point. I'm not running from anything. And even though it should be terrifying, it isn't. Because it's Oliver Reeves.

Ha. Who would've thunk it?

Weaving through the throngs of students and LAU fans, I head to the bathroom. It's almost empty since most people wait until the end of the period instead of sneaking out of the seating area a few minutes beforehand. I, however, don't feel like hanging out in line for the next twenty minutes, thank you very much. After finishing up in one of the stalls, I wash my hands in the sink. As I reach for the paper towels, an eerie feeling settles over me, and my body flicks into full alert mode when I turn to the exit and find Officer Reeves glaring back at me.

I haven't seen him since the restaurant. Since I tattled to his partner about his shitty parenting. Since I offended him and embarrassed him in front of his friends. Since I called him out for his lies and threw him under the bus without giving a shit about the repercussions.

And clearly, he isn't over it.

Hiding my shaking hands in the paper towel as I wipe them dry, I tell him, "You shouldn't be in here."

"I'm a police officer, little girl." He smiles and spreads his legs wide as if he's untouchable. "I can go wherever I want."

"Good for you." With a flick of my wrist, I toss the paper towel into the garbage and start to slip past him, but he blocks the exit. My nerves kick into overdrive, and I glare up at him. "What do you want?"

"Just wanted to check up on my son's girl."

Nausea burns up my throat, but I swallow it back.

"Nothing to say, Thorne?" he demands.

I can feel his annoyance. It sticks to my skin and makes me feel like I'm walking on eggshells. Like if I don't play this carefully, the consequences could be dire. Wetting my lips, I reply, "Not sure what you want me to say."

"You're right. You said enough at the restaurant."

"You mean when I called you out for being a liar and a shitty father? Or for exposing the truth to your friends?"

"You should be careful who you piss off," he warns.

"I'll keep it in mind." My head held high, I meet his gaze. "If that's all, I suggest you move so I don't miss the second period."

"Nah, I think I'll stay," he decides. He looks so cocky right now. Like he has me exactly where he wants me. Like he's already won whatever sick, twisted game he decided to play as soon as he followed me into the bathroom.

"You're trying to piss off your son. To get under his skin by coming after me. Cornering me in a girls' bathroom and intimidating me."

"Just trying to keep you safe, Dylan. Being alone, even in public, can be dangerous for a girl like you."

"A girl like me?"

"Vulnerable," he clarifies.

"Are you threatening me?"

"No, I'm looking out for you. My son is… He's a bad person, Dylan. He's manipulating you, but—"

"You perceive me as his weakness." I force a laugh, and his eyes thin, but it doesn't stop me. Instead, I lift my chin a little more. "You left him alone for the past couple of years because you realized you couldn't hurt him anymore. You couldn't isolate or control him anymore because you lost all your leverage."

His eyes darken. "All the leverage I need is standing in front of me."

"Is it?" I laugh again. I can see why Reeves ended up providing his G-rated gigolo services. Because he's dealt with shit like this man his whole life. Might as well deal with it from strangers, too. And if he was willing to protect random women from this kind of bullshit, then I have no problem protecting him from it, too. "I have news for you, officer. I'm not your son's weakness. I'm his greatest strength. And if you honestly think you can get to him by manipulating me or trying to mess with my head like you did at Rowdy's, you're wrong. I'm not stupid, Mr. Reeves. You want to use me against him. You want to control him. To keep him under your thumb. But it won't work. I won't let it work. You already took his childhood. Ruined it. And here he is, refusing to let you ruin his college experience or his future."

He's pissed. I can see it in the tight jaw. The flared nostrils. The veined, clenched fists resting on his hips. The bated breath.

When his silence stretches, I tilt my head, surprised. If I didn't know any better, I'd say he's surprised, too. Like I caught him off guard. Like he expected this to go differently. Like he assumed I'd cower like the rest of the women he's used to picking on, and now? Now, he doesn't know what to do with me.

"Careful, Ms. Thorne. You're walking a fine line," he finally warns.

"Good, maybe it'll knock you down a peg or two." He takes a step toward me, but I stand my ground, tilting my head up so I can continue our little staring contest. "I won't let you win, and neither will he. And if we're talking about walking a fine line, I believe it's you who should watch your step."

A vein throbs in his forehead as he cocks his head. "Are you threatening me, little girl?"

"No, I'm explaining things to you. You might think you're untouchable, Mr. Reeves, but I have something you don't. I have a family who's loyal to me. They're wealthy, well-connected, and not afraid to protect the ones they love. I hate to break it to you, but I'm just like them. Your son didn't have me before, but he has me now. Every. Single. Piece. So you're going to stay away from both of us. Because if you don't, I'm not afraid to call in any favors with my family, and my family sure as shit isn't afraid of calling in favors with people so far above your pay grade you probably can't even pronounce their names, let alone fully comprehend exactly what they're capable of."

He grabs my arm and squeezes roughly, cutting off the blood to my hand, proving I pushed him too far. It's scary and possessive and hurts like a bitch, but I don't crumble or cower. I don't even flinch.

Flexing my fingers, I look down at his massive sausage fingers strangling my arm and smile. "You should squeeze tighter."

Frustrated, he shoves me against the cinderblock wall behind me, stealing the breath from my lungs. "Don't tempt me."

My gaze flicks to his. "Keep on squeezing, Mr. Reeves. I want to make sure you leave a mark, so I have evidence of what a dipshit you really are."

His nostrils flare, but he lets me go. "This isn't over."

"I think we both know it is, but if you're still on the fence, I suggest Googling my dad, Colt Thorne. You know, the guy you called out of the blue and lied to, warning him about his daughter's boyfriend without taking into account how he might actually respect his kid enough to actually talk to her instead of believing a random man's accusation. Or better yet? Maybe skip my dad and go straight to my Uncle Henry. Henry *Buchanan*," I punctuate. "Billionaire businessman with political connections all across the world and a penchant for putting pathetic men like you in their place." With a syrupy, sweet smile, I step around him and grab the door handle. "Have a good evening, Mr. Reeves."

"You don't know who you're dealing with," he calls.

Ignoring him, I slip out of the exit without a backward glance and head back to my seat.

Come at me again, Officer Reeves.

I dare you.

4 0

DYLAN

The rest of the game passes by in a blur. I don't even watch the plays. I'm too busy scanning the rink for a familiar officer with stalking tendencies. I want to simultaneously throat punch him and avoid him like a bad flu. By the time the final buzzer sounds, ending the third period and the game, Finley loops her arm through mine. We follow Mav and Ophelia to the door leading to the locker room, where the team exits once they shower.

I'm not sure how long Finley's been talking, but I'm too lost in my head to really listen, let alone respond. Staring blankly into the distance, I chew on the edge of my thumb, debating whether or not I should tell Oliver about what happened in the bathroom. I mean, I know I should, but the idea of him flying off the handle after the fact seems…not great, especially when his father's entire motive when he approached me was to get under his son's skin. Playing into it feels wrong. But keeping my interaction with his dad feels even *more* wrong.

"Hey, are you okay?" Finley snaps her fingers an inch from my nose, and I jerk back.

385

"Sorry, what?"

"Are. You. Okay?"

"Uh, yeah," I lie. "I'm fine."

Her eyes thin, and she opens her mouth to continue pushing, but the heavy metal doors open at the same moment, the groan from the hinges cutting her off.

With his hair still damp from his shower and a duffle bag full of hockey gear hanging from his shoulder, Ollie appears. Sporting the same smirk I've most definitely fallen for—okay, Fin and Lia might've been onto something when they mentioned the L-word earlier—my knees go weak in an instant when his eyes land on me.

"You were fast," Finley notes as she pushes herself away from the cinderblock wall she was leaning on.

"Excited," Reeves clarifies. He gives her a wink as the rest of the guys file out behind him.

"Hey, good game," Mav congratulates him.

"Thanks, man." Reeves returns. " Hey, Lia."

"Hey, Reeves," she replies. "Mav's right. You killed it on the ice today. If I didn't know any better, I'd say you were trying to impress someone."

"You know, you're not wrong," he notes, turning to me with a shameless grin. "Hey, Pickles."

"Hi."

As he takes in my fake smile, it causes his lips to turn down. "What's wrong?"

"I asked her the same thing," Finley interjects. She folds her arms and gives me a stern look mirroring my mom's anytime I'm in the doghouse as we all start walking toward the exit.

"Seriously, nothing's wrong," I tell her—tell everyone, thanks to the curious stares of my brother, Ev, Mav, Ophelia, and Finley. Desperate to change the subject, I add, "Well, except for Griffin's lack of scoring."

"Hey!" My brother shoves me playfully, pretending to be offended, until Everett jumps in and gives him shit while the chatter grows around us. When Mav pushes open the door to the parking lot, a gust of cold wind hits my cheeks, so I tug my jacket a little tighter around me, preparing for the short trek to the cars while avoiding a certain someone's knowing stare.

Seriously, though. There are some major pros to having a very perceptive boyfriend, but right now? I kind of wish he wasn't quite so attuned to my emotions and my current inner meltdown.

"Okay, what's going on, Dylan?" he demands once everyone's a few paces ahead of us.

Oh, boy. What a loaded question.

I twist my hands in front of me, unable to look him in the eye. "Maybe we should wait until we get home."

With a gentle but firm grasp on my wrist, he pulls me to a halt as our friends continue walking through the crowded parking lot. Oliver caught a ride with Everett and Griffin to the game, I drove his car with Finley, and Ophelia went separately with Maverick, but since we all parked relatively close to each other, we're all headed in the same direction. "Dylan, you've got me worried here."

"Okay, here's the deal," I blurt out. "I need you to promise me you won't freak out."

"Not exactly a good way to start a conversation, Pickles."

"Promise me," I push.

"Fine, I promise."

"Good." I fist my hands, forcing myself to stop fidgeting as I look up at him. The concern in his eyes makes me want to bite my tongue and pretend like my run-in with his dad never happened. But if I do, and he finds out I lied to him... Well, neither of us is a fan of miscommunication, so where does it lead me? It leads me here. To an awkward conversation that may or may not push him over the edge and ruin the high from tonight's win, no matter how much he deserves it. The high, that is. Not the being pushed over the edge part. For shit's sake, I'm not a monster.

"Start talking, Dylan." He crowds me against a parked car until I'm drowning in all things Oliver. I'd give anything to ignore my tussle with his dad and pretend it never happened, but I can't do it. I can't lie to him. Can't sweep it under the rug.

"Fine." My tongue darts out between my lips as I reach for the edge of his shirt beneath his jacket, dragging my fingers along the thin material. "Your dad cornered me in the girls' restroom during the first period."

His jaw tics, but I can tell he's fighting it. His growing anger. "He what?"

"Your dad—"

Like a beast, Reeves shoves himself away from me, but I pull him in again, fisting his t-shirt in my hand as the cold from the metal bumper seeps through my jeans and hits the back of my legs.

"Listen to me," I snap.

"Did he touch you?" His eyes are dark and wild. Fear. Rage. Determination. They all swirl together like a hurricane of hurt and regret. Like, somehow, this is his fault, and it couldn't be further from the truth. "I knew he would come after you. I knew he'd be pissed you embarrassed him. I fucking *knew* it."

My eyelids flutter as the memory of my confrontation with his father sparks, causing his upper lip to curl.

"I'm gonna kill him."

"Ollie—"

Wrenching himself away from me, he storms further into the parking lot as if knowing exactly who's waiting in the distance. I rush to keep up, but his long legs close the space faster than mine ever could.

"Ollie!" I repeat.

"Dude, what's wrong?" Maverick asks as Reeves rushes past him. Mav had been walking slowly with the rest of the group, giving us space for our conversation while knowing we'd all leave together once we finished talking despite each of us driving in separate vehicles. When I catch up to him, I give him a panicked look and continue my pursuit of his very pissed-off best friend.

The parking lot is still full. Well, mostly full. Some fans have already left, but most still mill around, figuring out what to do with the rest of their night with the game now over. I slip between a red Corolla and a black F-150 when Reeves' car comes into view. Sure enough, leaning against the driver's side door is his father. And beside him? It's his partner, Officer McDonnell.

"What the fuck is your problem?" Oliver demands. He storms toward his own flesh and blood, completely ignoring the armed officer beside him and the plethora of witnesses scattered in the lot.

Why is McDonnell here? Oliver's dad, sure. But McDonnell? It doesn't make any sense. And why does this feel like a setup? People gawk from all sides. Most of them are wearing LAU's black and red, and even though they know it isn't polite to stare, watching one of the star players from tonight's game storm through the parking lot toward police officers is pretty hard to look away from.

The question is, is this what his dad wants? To cause a scene? To shine a light on Oliver's frustration while only giving them half the story? He's painted Oliver as a loose canon for so long it makes sense. And it also pisses me off. The way he manipulates the situation even now. With so many witnesses. So many cell phones poised and ready to document the moment and to record Oliver's potential explosion. It makes me wish I'd recorded my conversation with his dad in the restroom, too, but now isn't the time to reflect on wasted opportunities.

"Oliver, stop!" I call out. My tone is thick with desperation, but he's too furious to acknowledge it.

His dad glares at me, but it only lasts a second until his calm, collected persona slides back into place. With folded arms, he demands, "Sir, I need to look in your vehicle."

"Don't fucking *sir* me," Oliver snaps.

"Is this your vehicle?" His dad pushes off from the door and looks into the back seat window. His brows lift as if something caught his attention, and my insides fill with absolute dread.

He did something. I don't know what it is, but I know it's the truth. I borrowed Oliver's car before the game. I know for a fact nothing is in the back seat. Or at least nothing to garner such a look.

What did he do?

"Reeves—" I reach for his arm, but he dodges my hold, and, with a gentle but forceful touch, he pushes me behind him. Protecting me. When the only person his dad wants to hurt is him.

"Why won't you leave Dylan and me alone?" Reeves demands. "Is it because she embarrassed you? Because she told your friends the truth?"

His father's eyes darken. "I need you to open your car—"

"It's mine!" I yell. "Whatever it is, it's mine."

Everyone's heads snap in my direction, and I notice the cell phones pointed at us. At me. They surround me. Recording everything. Oliver's rage. My confession. Everything.

"Dylan," Reeves murmurs, but I shake my head, silently begging him to listen.

"If you're arresting someone for possession of whatever's in the back of the car, it's mine." I swallow thickly and fold my arms. "I drove here on my own."

"It isn't your car," Officer Reeves argues.

"Technically, it's mine," someone announces from behind me.

I glance over my shoulder to find Maverick. He isn't looking at me, though. He's glaring at Officer Reeves. His frustration rolls off him and hits my back with an air of... pride, almost. Griffin steps up beside him, and Everett joins, each of them folding their arms with their heads held high and their chests puffed out like they're ready to throw down at any second to protect their friend, even if it means going head-to-head with law enforcement.

Confusion consumes Officer Reeves' face. He shakes his head. "This is—"

"When I bought my motorcycle, I let Reeves borrow my car. His name isn't on the title, but mine is, so if there's a problem with the vehicle, you can take it up with me personally."

"Or maybe I'm the one who planted it," Everett offers. "You already know about my prior altercation with Reeves at Homecoming. Hell, you arrested him but didn't even take me in for questioning after I refused to press charges. Maybe I planted it to get him in trouble."

"And now you're confessing your scheme?" Oliver's dad scoffs. "Not likely."

Griffin steps even closer. "Yeah, well, it looks like you have three people worth arresting for whatever bullshit thing you planted in the back of the car, and your son isn't one of them. So, you're welcome to pull out the cuffs now and arrest any of my friends who confessed, but since Reeves is clearly innocent, I suggest you let him be on his way. What do you say?"

"You sure you wanna play this game?" Officer Reeves asks. But he isn't looking at me. He isn't looking at Mav or Everett or Griffin. He's looking at Oliver. And I swear I've never seen so much hatred in my entire life.

Reeves breaks the staring contest and reaches for me, but I shake my head again and turn to Officer Dickhead. "You going to arrest me, or what? I confessed to being the sole owner of whatever's in the back of the car, so—"

"Dylan," Reeves snaps. He's confused. Frustrated. Then again, so am I.

I step forward and squeeze his hand, begging him to trust me. To not let his father win.

"Do you even know what it is?" McDonnell questions. It's the first time he's spoken, and by the surprise in Reeves' expression, it's the first time he sees him, too. Sees the setup. The carefully orchestrated plan I'm shitting on at this very moment.

"Does it matter?" I counter.

McDonnell's expression falls. "Miss—"

"It's mine," I repeat.

"And mine," Maverick interjects.

"And mine," Everett chimes in.

My heart grows like the Grinch's as I look around at my friends, each of us stepping around a stunned Reeves, forming a literal barrier between him and his asshole of a father.

"As you can see by my boyfriend's very confused expression," I add, "he has no idea what any of you are even talking about. Now, if we can please get this over with…"

"Keys," Reeves' father snaps. "Now. Or I can always break the glass."

"Pretty sure it's not necessary," Maverick counters.

The familiar jingle echoes throughout the otherwise silent parking lot as I fish the keys from my pocket and toss them to Officer Asshole.

I don't have to step closer to know what's inside. Something illegal. It could be drugs. A weapon. Who the fuck knows? I'm not the mastermind here. Oliver's dad is. But if he honestly thinks he can pin something on his son because he's pissy and feels like throwing a fit, well, at least I threw a wrench in something.

I don't know how long we stand here before a bag of white powder is confiscated from the car's back seat.

With a wicked grin, Reeves' father turns to me. "The question is, who do we arrest?"

"I think we all know the answer, don't you?" I challenge. "Maverick hasn't been in his car in weeks, and I'm the one with the keys."

"And Mr. Taylor?" Officer Douchebag demands.

Everett steps forward and raises his hands in the air. "Do your worst."

Reeves' father's eyes narrow, but he shifts his attention back to me, his arrogance wafting off him like stinky cologne. It makes my nose wrinkle.

"Dylan Thorne, you're under arrest." He takes a step closer to me until Reeves matches his stance, putting himself between us again. It's like he can't help it. Like this is killing him.

I turn to Officer McDonnell, the only potentially sane man with any kind of authority at the moment. "Give me one minute."

"Not a chance," his dad snaps.

"Please," I beg.

"Give her a sec," McDonnell orders his partner.

The same familiar glare twists Reeves' father's expression, but he stops moving closer, and I take full advantage.

Carefully, I touch Oliver's back, moving around him until I face my boyfriend fully. "Ollie," I whisper. His jaw tightens as he glances down at me. "Let me—"

"Us," Maverick interjects. He steps closer, using his broad back to shield us from the cell phones pointed directly our way.

I peek up at him and smile. Then my eyes land on Oliver again. "Let *us* protect you for once."

The gravity of the situation finally hits him, and he closes his eyes. "Dylan…"

"Don't let him win."

"I can't let you walk away—"

"You can," I breathe out. "Go with the guys. Call my dad. Have him meet me at the station."

"Dylan—"

"Go with the guys," I repeat. "I'll be fine."

With a defeated nod, Oliver unclenches his fists.

I turn back around, facing McDonnell and Officer Reeves. "Okay, I'm ready."

His dad takes another step toward me, but McDonnell intervenes.

"I'll make the arrest," he grunts to his partner, pinning my boyfriend with a stare. "You need to step back."

Gravel crunches beneath Oliver's Nikes as he obeys the command.

Satisfied, Officer McDonnell steps closer, his dark brows pulled low and his face tainted with unease. "Miss, place your hands behind your head."

The metal is cold against my skin, the locks clicking into place one at a time, as the mumbo jumbo speech I've heard a hundred times on police shows distracts me. The Miranda warning. That's what it is. Funny. I never thought I'd listen to those words in real life, but here we are.

From the corner of my eye, I notice Officer Dickwad's

smug face, and I can't help but smile back as McDonnell puts his hand on the back of my head and helps me into the police car.

Smile while you can, asshole. You have no idea what's coming to you.

41

REEVES

Cocaine. Fucking cocaine in the back of my car. I've never touched drugs. Never had the desire to, but it's what the asshole planted. A tow truck came while I was on the phone with Dylan's dad. Mav's car was impounded so they could perform a more thorough search. They won't find anything. Not unless my dad stashed more drugs or other illegal items somewhere else in the vehicle.

My. Fucking. Luck.

I've been at the police station with my friends for a few hours. They gave up comforting me a while ago. There isn't anything left to say. I feel like shit, and I can't stop replaying what happened. What I could've done. What I should've done. Without losing Dylan. Without losing my NHL career. Without letting my dad win. My knee bounces, and I stare at my hands.

"Breathe," Mrs. Thorne orders.

I look up at Dylan's mom and shake my head. "I can't."

"If everything you said is true—"

"It is."

She smiles. "I know. We already talked to the lawyer. She's going to be fine."

A girl like Dylan shouldn't need a lawyer. None of my friends should. And I hate how this is what Everett was trying to protect them from. From me tainting their lives. Infecting them with the bullshit they have never and would never have dealt with if I'd kept my distance. And even though we're good, and Everett isn't acting like a dick anymore, which he proved firsthand by being willing to take the fall for planting the drugs in the car, it doesn't make me feel any better.

Fan-fucking-tastic, Reeves.

You let your shitty childhood touch them anyway.

"Listen," I mutter. "I really am sorry—"

"Stop apologizing," she orders. "This isn't on you, Reeves. This is on your father."

"If she hadn't met me..." My voice trails off, and I hang my head in my hands.

"If she hadn't met you, her soul would still be searching for the man who could make her whole again."

My chest tightens, and I look up at her again. Dylan's mom. Ashlyn Thorne. The resemblance is staggering. Same blonde hair. Same kind eyes. Same reassuring smile. It's like I'm looking at my future, and, dammit, I want it. A future with Dylan. A life with Dylan. I want everything with Dylan.

"My daughter loves you, Reeves," Mrs. Thorne murmurs, and the words hit me in the ribcage. "I see it. Her father sees it. Her brothers see it. I haven't seen Dylan smile the way she does these days since before the accident." Her lips lift, but she quickly sobers. "Honestly, I didn't think I'd ever see her smile the same way again. Without you, she'd still hate school. She'd still be a shy, anxious mess. She'd still do every-thing in her power to blend in and be invisible. What she did for you tonight? Do you know how much growth it demonstrated for a girl like her? How brave she had to be? Reeves, I've never been more proud of my daughter for standing up for someone—especially someone she loves—in my entire life."

"Yeah, but the videos from the parking lot—"

"If anything, they'll prove your dad's an asshole, and my daughter—and you—are completely innocent." She squeezes my knee gently. "If you were arrested tonight, your NHL career would be ruined—even when we both know the charges wouldn't have stuck—and your father would've won. What happened worked out for the best, and my daughter will be fine. We'll make sure of it."

We'll make sure of it.

I rub at the ache beneath my ribs. "I'm glad she has people she can rely on."

"You both do, Oliver."

Oliver.

Like taking a baseball bat to the chest, my lungs deflate, and my eyes burn.

"Hey," she murmurs. "I didn't mean to—"

"You're fine." My Adam's apple bobs, and I wipe beneath my nose. "Sorry, it's…um, I'm not used to anyone but Dylan calling me by my first name."

"Your mom picked it, right?"

I nod. "So the story goes."

"It's a good name," she notes. "A strong name."

I smile, but it feels forced. "Thanks."

"You know you have a family now, right? Me and Colt. Jax and Griff. Everett, Finley, Ophelia, Mia, Henry, Tatum, Kate, Mack, the list goes on and on." She leans closer and drops her voice low. "Seriously, if I keep going, we'll be here all day."

I chuckle dryly. "I appreciate it."

"I'm being serious," she pushes. "I have shitty parents, too.

I mean…not your level of shitty,"—she grimaces—"but they were never there for me, and I know what it feels like to wonder if anyone cares. To wonder if you'll be alone and if you'll always be the only one to fight your battles. But then I found my friends and Colt, and I think you'll be surprised at how strong of a bond you can have with someone who isn't blood."

"Thanks, Mrs. Thorne," I mutter. "I appreciate it."

"Now, if I could get you to believe me, that'd be great."

Another laugh slips out of me. "I do believe you."

"Liar."

With a shake of my head, I start to argue but stop myself. Do I believe her? Do I want to believe her? Am I too calloused to believe her? Too scared?

Fuck.

The people she named have shown up for me more times than I can count. Over and over, they've proven I'm not alone, even when I'm a dick. Even when I keep them at a distance. And yeah, they aren't perfect, and neither am I, but still. Maybe it's time I start believing in them.

"I'm not used to depending on others," I admit.

"Yeah, well…" she bumps her shoulder with mine. "You better get used to it, *Oliver,* because we kind of like you."

With another quiet laugh, I scrub my hand over my face and settle into the plastic chair. "I kind of like you guys, too."

"Also, if you don't want me calling you Oliver, I totally get it, but I have no problem adopting another son."

"Another?" I question.

She smiles. "You didn't know Jax isn't my son by blood?"

I shake my head. "Jax?"

"He's from one of Colt's previous relationships."

My eyes bulge, but I can't help it. I had no idea. Not a fuckin' clue.

"Shit," I mutter, unsure what else to say.

"Yeah. Finding out about him was a doozy, but honestly? He was one of the best surprises I could ever hope for, and so are you." She gives me the same sweet smile, looking so much like her daughter's it makes my chest ache. "Now, aren't you supposed to be in class?"

"Yeah, but Dyl—"

"We have no idea how long this will take," Mrs. Thorne interrupts. "Go." She raises her voice and looks around the crowded precinct littered with my friends. "All of you. We'll update you all as soon as we know more."

42

REEVES

I didn't want to go to class, but Mrs. Thorne insisted I attend, and since I didn't want to be on her shit list after she welcomed me into her family with open arms, I obliged.

The minutes tick by in slow motion when I receive a text a little while later.

PICKLES

Hey! I made bail. :) My parents are taking me home right now. I'm hitting the shower ASAP. I'll see you in a bit. Have fun in class!

I reread the text for the thousandth time as I sit on my bed. After receiving it, I rushed home, only to hear the shower running, so here I am, feeling like an addict looking for my next fix. My knee bouncing. My phone shaking.

The water shuts off, and my head snaps toward the bedroom wall separating me from her.

I wait, forcing myself not to rush in and bury my head in her neck when the hinges squeak a minute later, and she appears in the hallway. Her wet hair hangs down her back, and her body is covered by one of my hoodies. It's the same one I gave her when she was cold all those weeks ago. The sight eases the ache in my chest, but the relief only lasts a second. The guilt returns with a vengeance. She was arrested last night. Because of me. My family. My connections. My asshole father.

"Hi," she greets me, leaning against the doorjamb, looking sexy as sin.

Resisting the urge to rush toward her, I wipe my palms against my thighs. "Hey."

Her brows pull. "You okay?"

With a laugh, I shake my head. "Are *you* okay? Come here." I reach for her, and she sways toward me, wrapping her arms around my waist and burrowing into my chest.

"Mmm...I missed you," she murmurs.

"I'm so sorry."

Lifting her head, she gives me a look like I'm a crazy person. "Don't apologize for your dad being a dick."

"Dyl—"

"I'm glad he couldn't get his way this time. The lawyer says it might take some time, but there's no way the charges will stick, especially considering it isn't even your car. Also, since when did that happen?"

"I drove a beater for years. It broke down around the time Mav bought his motorcycle, so he let me use his car, and I never bothered to replace mine."

"Definitely a happy coincidence," she notes. "I can't wait for the lawyer to present that little nugget when the case goes to court."

"What do you mean?"

"You really think we're going to let your sperm donor get away with all this bullshit any longer?" She scoffs. "I wish I recorded my conversation with him in the restroom, but once my lawyer saw the bruises your dad left on my arm, he says they should be more than enough."

"What bruises?" I demand.

"It isn't a big—"

"What. Bruises," I seethe.

She slips off my hoodie until only a black tank top covers her body and lifts her arm. Purple and blue bruises marr her bicep, giving a perfect representation of the way he manhandled her. I skate my fingers along her bare skin, nearly drowning in guilt.

"Hey." She reaches up and cups my jaw. Forcing me to look her in the eye, she murmurs, "I promise I'm okay."

"This isn't okay."

"I didn't say this was okay. I said I'm okay," she clarifies. "Now, will you let me finish my story, mister?"

I bend down and kiss each of her bruises before helping her back into my hoodie. Once she's covered, she gives me a quick peck on the cheek, then continues. "Like I was saying, I didn't record the conversation in the bathroom, but my lawyer's looking for any footage of your dad sneaking into the girls' bathroom behind me so we can corroborate my story. His team is also checking the parking lot cameras to see if they find your dad messing with your car at all. And having Maverick's name on the title is the icing on the cake. My lawyer was practically frothing at the mouth over how easy this case will be to win. Like seriously, despite the fact your dad is a cop, he definitely didn't think things through last night. Then again, after I kind of, sort of threatened him that if he didn't leave you alone, I'd tell Uncle Henry about him, I'm pretty sure he wanted to retaliate as quickly as possible. Even without the footage inside the rink or the bruises, I think McDonnell knows your dad tried to set you up."

Unconvinced and still reeling from the information she's thrown at me, I shake my head. "You sound so sure."

"Honestly? I am. You should've seen how tense he was in the police car with me. McDonnell kept looking over at your dad and then at me in the back seat. I think he knows your dad's dirty and with a little pushing from the lawyer my dad hired?" She lifts a shoulder. "I dunno. Like I said, I think your dad screwed himself over and doesn't even know it yet."

She might be onto something, especially if McDonnell's catching onto things. I never minded the guy. He was always by the book and struggled to follow my dad's lead despite being the younger and less experienced of the two on the force. But even then, the idea of Dylan going after my dad? Of putting herself on his radar more than she already has? It's terrifying.

Bunching the thick hoodie material around her waist, I mutter, "I don't want you involved."

Rolling her eyes, she reminds me, "I've *been* involved. Your dad made sure I was. He's the one who wouldn't leave you alone, not the other way around. Besides, the asshole has had it coming to him ever since you were little. Now, you have someone on your side, so I think it's time karma catches up to him, don't you?"

Karma. I'd laugh if the circumstances weren't so shitty. I never believed in karma. Never believed anyone was looking out for me or cared about what happened to me. But after meeting Dylan, I can't help but wonder if maybe there's more to it. More to life. More to random occurrences I always thought were meaningless until my little wallflower stumbled into my life. But even so, the idea of Dylan being within a hundred-mile radius of the man who made my life a fucking hell feels wrong.

"I don't want you hurt by him," I admit.

Shimmying away from me, she spreads her arms wide and does a slow spin. "Do I look hurt, Ollie?"

When I hesitate, she faces me again, propping her hand on her hip. "This is the part where you say, 'No, but you're cute when you're protective of me.'"

My laugh eases the knot in my chest, and I breathe in deeply. "Is that what I'm supposed to say?"

She nods. "It's exactly what you're supposed to say."

Reaching for her, I drag Dylan into me again and slowly sway us back and forth, savoring the feel of her small curves pressed against me. I've been terrified since her arrest. Of the consequences. The repercussions. Whether she hated me after putting her neck out for me the way she did. Whether she'd ever forgive me for dragging her into this mess. Seeing her like this? Happy? Healthy? It's…fuck, I don't even know.

"You're cute when you're protective of me, Dylan," I finally murmur.

A grin nearly splits her face in two as she loops her arms around my neck. "Why, thank you."

"You're welcome."

"I'm also a badass prison girl," she adds.

"You spent one night in jail."

"And *survived*," she points out. "I hate to break it to you, but you're dating a badass."

"I'm in love with a badass." The words should scare me, but they don't. Fuck, they're almost cathartic. Cleansing. Soothing. I've never loved a girl before. Never loved anyone, really. Not like this. I didn't even know I was capable. Of loving. Of being loved.Until I met her. And even though I'm far from experienced when it comes to the true meaning of it, it doesn't make my feelings less true. And loving Dylan? It's like breathing. Natural. Easy. Inescapable.

Her smile falls, and she stops us from swaying as she peers up at me. "What did you say?"

"I said, I'm in love with a badass."

"And when you say badass…"

"I mean you," I clarify. "I'm in love with you."

Her breath hitches like she's not sure she believes me. "You're in love with me?"

"I'm one hundred percent in love with you."

"And it's not because I was arrested yesterday?"

"Nah." I kiss her nose. "Those glasses, though?" Letting out a whistle, I drag my hands up her bare thighs to cup her round ass. "Those were definitely the game changer."

Closing her eyes, she lets out a quiet laugh. It's laced with disbelief and fucking awe as she lays her head back on my chest.

"I love you too, you know," she whispers.

"You do?"

"Yup. But for me, the hoodies sealed the deal."

"My hoodies, huh?"

I swear I can feel her smile against me as she gifts me with another quiet laugh. "It's cute how you think they still belong to you."

"Oh, so they don't belong to me anymore?"

"I mean, I'm a seasoned felon now, remember? Stealing a hoodie or two is practically a cakewalk."

"Someone's cocky…joking about their rap sheet already, and all."

"Speaking of cocky and prison." She grabs my junk through my jeans and squeezes. "You should fuck me now."

Amusement spreads through me as I pick her up and toss her onto my bed. "If I knew handcuffs got you so hot and bothered, I would've introduced you to them earlier."

"Are you kink-shaming me?"

Jumping on top of her, I grab her wrists and pin them above her head. "Never."

And dammit, I mean it.

43
REEVES

It's been two weeks since Dylan's arrest. Neither of us has heard anything from my dad, but we did receive a letter from Officer McDonnell. He promised he was taking care of things from his end. He also promised we won't have any trouble with the precinct or his partner ever again. I couldn't help but smile when he didn't refer to the asshole as my dad, proving McDonnell's an even better man than I assumed. Part of me doesn't want to believe him. The other part? Well, I suppose Dylan's optimism is rubbing off on me. I guess we'll have to wait and see.

Regardless, it's been the best two weeks of my life. Dylan sleeps in my room every night. I even survived another brunch with the entire family. And my first name has started gaining traction with Dylan and her parents. I like it. A lot.

We just finished a game against the Grizzlies. We won, and fuck me, seeing Dylan on her feet, her hands cupped around her mouth as she cheered us on was the hottest thing I've ever seen.

"Hey." Griffin's shoulder falls into the locker beside my own.

I slap the metal door closed and turn to her brother. "Hey. What's up?"

"A girl's here asking about you."

"A girl?"

"Yeah." He sighs. "Look, I know you're retired, but—"

Adrenaline pulses through my veins as I shake my head. "I swear I'm done."

"Don't worry, man," he grumbles. "I trust you, but the girl's still asking for you. You gotta get rid of her."

My head bobs on autopilot, and I slip past him, heading to the exit.

The heavy metal door slams against the cinder blocks as I shove it open. People are still hanging around after tonight's win, but only one is staring at me. Expectantly. Anxiously. But with an edge of doubt I've seen a hundred times.

Fuck.

Pushing herself off the wall, she strides toward me, her arms folded and her head tilted toward the floor as she glances over her shoulder, scanning the corridor for the boogeyman.

She's pretty. Dark brown hair. Highlights. Petite. Sunglasses cover her eyes, and the asshole in me wants to point out that if she's trying for subtlety, she's failing. Badly. If I had a nickel for every damn time a girl showed up in glasses after an abusive dick got his hands on her, I'd be rich.

The dark frames hide her eye color, and my chest deflates as she keeps her gaze glued to the floor, approaching me cautiously. Carefully. Like I might *be* the said boogeyman. Despite seeing it more times than I can count, it still leaves me feeling like shit, especially since I can't be the one to help her.

"You were looking for me?" I ask.

The tip of her tongue darts between her lips, and she sucks the plump flesh into her mouth but stays quiet.

"Can I help you?" I try again.

"You're, uh, you're Reeves, right?"

I nod.

"I'm—"

"You can take the glasses off," I interrupt. "I'm not buying the bullshit."

With shaky hands, she lifts the glasses to the top of her head and forces herself to meet my gaze. Muddled purple and brown spreads across the bridge of her nose and along her left cheekbone. As I stare at the damage, my muscles tighten.

"I, uh, I heard you might be able to help me," she whispers.

"I'm retired."

A divot forms between her brows, and she shakes her head. "But I heard—"

"I know what you heard, but I'm retired."

"Oh." Somehow, the girl manages to curl in on herself even more, and my heart fucking cracks.

"Stay here. I'll be right back."

With a frown, she looks up at me, and I give her an encouraging nod then disappear back into the locker room.

"Ev!" I yell.

Cameron's attention snaps to me. "What?"

"Where's Everett?" I demand.

Glancing around the corner, Everett comes into view, rubbing a towel over his dark, straight hair, dressed in a pair of jeans but no shirt. "What's up?"

"Come out here."

"Why?"

If the asshole keeps asking questions, I have a feeling the girl will bolt. She looked spooked enough already.

"Come on," I push.

He strides toward me, the towel hanging by his side. "What is it?"

"Remember our deal? There's a girl outside. She needs your help."

His expression falls. "Fuck, man. I don't have time—"

"And I don't give a shit." Grabbing his arm, I shove him out the door and follow. Adrenaline pulses through me as I search the corridor, thankfully spotting the small-framed girl in a black jacket at the end of the hall.

"Come on," I repeat. Jogging toward her, I call out, "Hey, wait up!"

Her body freezes, and she slowly turns to face me. "Look, I'm sorry I bothered you."

"You didn't bother me," I argue, glancing over my shoulder as a shirtless Everett catches up. His muscles are tense as he scans the girl up and down. "This is Everett," I add, introducing him to her. "And you are...?"

"I'm Raine."

"Everett, Raine. Raine, Everett," I repeat as my attention catches on my girl at the end of the hall. When she sees me talking with Raine and Ev, her walking slows to a snail's pace, and she quirks her brow.

"Hello, Raine," Everett says, oblivious to Dylan's presence. His greeting is tight and forced, making him sound like he's about as comfortable as a guy who's been told to sit in on a pap smear. Slowly, he reaches out his hand for her to shake, but she only stares at it. Like it's a snake. One ready to lash out at any second.

"Raine," I interrupt, "Everett can help you with your... issue."

"Issue." A quiet scoff echoes past her lips. "So that's what we're calling him."

"Look, I gotta go, but, uh, you two chat. Figure shit out. And, Ev? If you need anything, let me know."

After officially passing the torch to him, I turn on my heel and jog toward a waiting Dylan.

"Everything okay?" she asks, eyeing Raine and Ev behind me.

"Not yet, but it will be." I wrap my arm around her waist and guide her around the corner so the two can have some privacy. "She's Ev's first client."

"Client?"

"Yeah."

"Oh." Her eyes spark with understanding. "As in…"

"Yeah," I confirm.

"She's pretty."

I nod. "Yeah, she is."

"You sure Everett's ready for this?"

"He's always had a God complex. Might as well let him lean into the role, right?"

She rolls her eyes. "You're insane."

"Nah, I'm a genius." I grip the back of her jersey and tug her closer to me. "I do like you in my jersey, though."

"Mm-hmm. Of course, you do."

"Might have to buy you a few more."

"You're gonna plaster me with your name every chance you get, aren't you?"

"Actually." I lean forward and drag my nose against hers in an Eskimo kiss. "I think it's a great idea."

"You're insane," she repeats.

"I think you mentioned that already." I kiss her nose one more time, then stand to my full height. "Now, let's get out of here."

She rises onto her tiptoes and drags me back down, planting a kiss against my lips. "Deal."

EPILOGUE

DYLAN

Warm lips hit my cheek, and my mouth spreads into a smile as I tilt my head, giving Oliver better access to the side of my face. "Merry Christmas, Pickles."

With a yawn, I cover my mouth and roll onto my back. I'm greeted with...my glasses?

"Here." Reeves slides them onto me, and I grin even wider as I look up at the most handsome man in the world. It's so surreal. To think he's mine and I'm his. The boy I found a little too tempting in my photography class. The boy who hates miscommunications and loves old movies and television shows. The boy who's a sucker for peanut butter and cosplay. The boy who loves me. *Me.* Seriously. I still can't believe I call him mine. It's been a few months since we started seeing each other, and every single day is better than the last. My family loves him. I love him. Things are just... great. Well, they would be if he'd actually let me sleep in this morning.

His hair is still mussed from sleep, but his eyes are bright with enthusiasm as he stares down at me.

"Why, thank you." I adjust my glasses and shift onto my elbows. "Merry Christmas to you, too, by the way."

"How'd you sleep?"

"Good. You?"

"Never better."

He dives in for one more quick peck, but I block it with my hands and fall back onto the pillow. "Morning breath."

"So?"

"So, I haven't brushed my teeth yet! No kissing until my teeth are brushed. PS—What time is it?"

"It's seven in the morning."

My brows pinch. "Why'd you wake me up so early?"

"We have to be at your parents' house at nine," he reminds me. "Besides, I got you something."

"I thought we agreed you weren't allowed to buy me any more presents."

"*You* agreed." He scoots to the edge of the bed but hesitates before revealing my present. "Close your eyes."

"Are you serious?"

"Dead serious. Close. Your. Eyes."

Covering my face with my hands, I listen for any clues but am only met with the softest of clinks. Then, his deep, husky voice orders, "Open."

My eyelids flutter for an instant, and I sit up fully, reaching for the glass aquarium resting on the nightstand that most definitely wasn't there thirty seconds ago. "What is it?"

"Look," he prods.

I lean closer, grateful for the morning light spilling in through the window and giving me a glimpse of what's inside the large glass terrarium. There's water. Dirt. Green plants with big leaves. A light. The thing is legit. And then I see it. A bright green frog in the corner of the aquarium. My jaw drops.

"You didn't."

"I did."

I shake my head, caught between laughing and full-blown peeing my pants. "No, you didn't."

"I most definitely did," he counters.

"You bought me a frog."

"I bought you a frog."

"Finley's going to kill you."

"Not when we can threaten her with this little guy." He shifts the glass terrarium, aquarium, *thing* a little closer to the edge of the nightstand without unplugging the light or the pump for the water. With my nose a few inches from the glass, I marvel at the little devil as he takes a little *hop-hop* and jumps in the water.

Clutching at my chest, I whisper, "My heart."

"Do you like him?"

"Like him?" I tilt my head, turn to my boyfriend, and move onto my knees. "Dude, I love him. What's his name?"

"He's yours. You get to name him."

"He's mine," I whisper. It's more to myself than anyone else as I steal another peek. He's so cute and tiny, and I just wanna kiss him. Well, *air* kiss him, then sneak him into Finley's bed the next time she pisses me off. A devious grin toys at the edge of my lips. "I cannot believe you got me a frog."

"Better believe it, Pickles. So what's his name?"

"Hmm." I click my tongue against the roof of my mouth, watching as he swims to the edge of the small pool. "Frankie. His name's Frankie."

"Frankie," Reeves repeats.

"Yup, Frankie. Frankie the Frog. The Frank-meister. My little Franken-froggie."

Amusement glows in his eyes as he nudges my chin with his fingers. "And you say I'm the one who's insane."

"Uh, you *are* insane," I reiterate. "But you're also perfect. And he's perfect." I wrap my arms around Oliver's neck and squeeze him tight. "And everything's perfect."

When I land a lip-smacking kiss against his lips, he pulls away, surprised. "I thought you said no kissing until you brushed your teeth."

"You just got me the perfect gift on the planet. I think I can make an exception."

"Well, in that case…" He kisses me deeply, shoving his tongue into my mouth because he knows how much it gets under my skin, then rolls me onto my back and pins me against the mattress.

When he finally lets me up for air again, I whisper, "I love you so much, Ollie."

"I love you, too, my tempting little pickled wallflower."

"A pickled wallflower?" My nose scrunches. "Really?"

He grins down at me. "The one and only."

HIJACKED EPILOGUE

EVERETT

L et's back up a bit.

Adrenaline lingers in my veins as I slide on my jeans after my shower. We just finished playing a game against the Grizzlies and won. LAU 3. Grizzlies 1. It was a rough game. I roll my shoulders as the ache from a particularly brutal hit spreads up my neck and down my spine. Yeah. I'm gonna feel it tomorrow.

Worth it, though.

"Good game, man," one of my teammates says as I rub my white towel against my head.

"Thanks."

The heavy metal door bangs against the cinder block walls in the locker room, followed by someone yelling, "Ev!"

"What?" Cameron, another teammate, answers for me.

"Where's Everett?" the person demands.

It's Reeves.

My roommate. Teammate. And just recently, *friend*. Still holding my white towel, I button my jeans the rest of the way and glance around the corner as Reeves comes into view.

"What's up?" I ask.

"Come out here."

"Why?"

"Come on," he pushes.

Forgetting about my shirt still hanging in my locker, I stride closer. "What is it?"

"Remember our deal?" he asks. "There's a girl outside. She needs your help."

Aaaand, there goes the high I was riding from today's win.

Yeah, I know exactly what my buddy's talking about, and it doesn't give me any warm fuzzies. Reeves and I have always been at odds with each other, and that's putting shit lightly. But, after sticking my nose in his relationship with our best friend's little sister, I decided I owed him one, and he cashed in on it. How? By making me agree to take over his side gig for the next six months. Normally I wouldn't complain about taking on a little something else, but when it involves fake dating girls under the guise of protecting them from their shitty boyfriends? Well, I'm less than enthusiastic about the whole thing.

Reeling in my annoyance, I throttle the towel in my hand. "Fuck, man. I don't have time—"

"And I don't give a shit." Reeves grabs my arm and shoves me out the door to the main hallway in the arena, scanning the premises with an urgency I'm not used to. Reeves doesn't give a shit about anything or any*one* but his girlfriend, Dylan. Or at least, it's the persona he shows everyone. After the last few months, I've caught glimpses of the real guy and learned his heart's bigger than any of us gave him credit for. But right now, something has him on edge.

When his attention lands on the back of a small-framed girl in a black jacket, he repeats, "Come on," to me and jogs toward the girl at the end of the hall. I hear him call out to her, "Hey, wait up!"

Her body freezes, and she slowly turns to face him. "Look, I'm sorry I bothered you."

"You didn't bother me," he argues, looking over his shoulder and giving me a look telling me to *hurry the hell up.*

Grumbling under my breath, I kick up the pace. When I reach them, my muscles tighten as I take in the strange girl. Long dark brown hair. Highlights. She's pretty. And *small.* Hell, she barely reaches my shoulder. Sunglasses cover her eyes, and I want to push them away to see what color they are. Her eyes. I shouldn't care. But having them covered when we're indoors causes warning bells to sound in my head. Like she has something to hide, and if Reeves' response is anything to go by, I'd say she does.

"This is Everett," Reeves adds, introducing me to her. "And you are…?"

He doesn't know her. Interesting.

A beat of silence follows, but she finally answers, "I'm Raine."

"Everett, Raine. Raine, Everett," Reeves repeats.

Raine.

If she weren't such a dark cloud on my day, I'd say it's pretty. Guess it's fitting, though, considering the circumstances.

"Hello, Raine," I mutter. It's tight and forced and makes me sound like a dick, but I can't help myself.

What the fuck does he expect me to do? Shake her hand and ask where her boyfriend is so I can beat the shit out of him? This is ridiculous. I don't fake date girls. I don't fake anything. Shit like this has always been Reeves' department, and he expects me to what? Jump in with both feet?

This is a bad idea.

Remembering the manners my mother spent years teaching me, I reach out my hand for her to shake, but she only stares at it. Like it's a snake. One ready to lash out at any second. It makes me feel like even more of a dick.

"Raine," Reeves interrupts my musing. "Everett can help you with your…issue."

"Issue." A quiet scoff echoes past her lips, surprising me. "So that's what we're calling him."

Him.

The asshole.

Great.

"Look, I gotta go." Reeves takes a step backward, adding, "But, uh, you two chat. Figure shit out. And, Ev? If you need anything, let me know." He turns on his heel and jogs toward the opposite end of the hall, where his girlfriend waits. I have no idea how long Dylan's been standing there. She gives him a quick hug, and they disappear from view.

Leaving me alone with a girl I should have nothing to do with.

Fucking promises.

What the hell are we supposed to do now?

Scratching the scruff along my jaw, I tilt my head. "So, uh, I don't exactly know how this works."

Her gaze darts from left to right as she curls in on herself. "Neither do I."

"Do you…wanna talk about it, or…"

The girl scoffs. "You know what?" She starts to turn away. "You're off the hook. I changed my mind."

"Wait." I reach for her arm, and she flinches away from me. And fuck, it hurts. The way her body tenses up. The way she thinks I'd harm her. I don't even know her. Lifting my hands in surrender, I rush out, "I won't touch you, all right? Just…wait for two seconds."

She scowls but stays in place, studying me. "Why?"

"I don't know? Because"––I wave my hand toward her––"I promised my friend I'd step in if someone wanted to hire him since he's in a relationship, and you obviously need... *help*."

Another scoff escapes her as her eyes fall to her feet. She shifts from one foot to the other. "Obviously."

"What, it's not obvious?" I push. "You're wearing sunglasses inside."

Her dainty fingers brush against the dark frames, but she doesn't take them off. "Maybe I don't want the world to see what a fist can do when provoked."

"Yeah, well, you're not fooling anyone, so maybe you should give the facade a break."

She nods, though I don't know if it's for me or if she's trying to convince herself it's a good idea. To give the facade a break. To not cover up the damage some asshole left her with. Regardless, her hands tremble as she slips the glasses off and folds them, lifting her chin and hitting me with a stunning pair of eyes. They're forest green and almost knock me on my ass as soon as our gazes lock. But the fire in them does me in. The anger. The determination. It's almost enough to distract me from the purple and black bruising along her cheekbone and the blood-red veins tainting the white surrounding her left iris.

"Fuck," I breathe out.

As if my words are a lash, she forces a smile and starts to unfold her glasses again, avoiding my gaze. "And this is why I keep the glasses on."

I reach for her, hesitating at the last second to keep from touching her and scaring her all over again, feeling like I'm going in circles. Like *we're* going in circles. I don't know this girl, but whoever she is, she's like a scared little mouse, and if I don't tread lightly, I have a feeling she'll bolt.

She stares at my half-outstretched hand the same way she did when I offered it for her to shake during our introduction. Then, slowly, her gaze trails along my bare torso. Fuck,

I forgot to put on a shirt when Reeves dragged me out here. When she reaches my eyes, she mutters, "I don't want your pity."

"What *do* you want?"

"From you?" She slides her glasses back into place. "Nothing."

"Then why come in the first place?" I ask. I shouldn't be offended, but, dammit, I am. When she stays quiet, I push, "What? I'm not good enough to help you, but Reeves is?"

"This wouldn't have been Reeves' first rodeo. Not if the rumors are true."

I move closer to her. "And you think it's mine?"

"By the look on your face? I'm gonna go with yes. This will be your first time helping someone in my situation, and I'm not stupid enough to risk pissing off my boyfriend even more than I already have by being here."

"Yet you're stupid enough to date him in the first place. Am I right?" Regret clogs my throat as soon as the words roll off my tongue, but it's too late.

Her sharp inhale of breath lingers in the otherwise silent corridor as she stares at me—glares at me. And I'm surprised. By this girl's tenacity.

"Fuck you, Everett."

The words slam into my chest, leaving a heavy dose of shame in their wake. Moving in front of her, I block her escape. "Look, I'm sorry—"

Heavy footsteps break the building tension and echo off the walls, distracting us both. Raine glances over her shoulder, searching for the culprit. The way her body tenses and how she looks like a ghost is chasing her is what gets me. What pisses me the fuck off.

"I have to go," she rushes out.

"Wait—"

"I *can't*." She scurries down the hall like the little mouse I pegged her for, disappearing around the corner and cutting off the heavy footsteps from moments ago.

I should be grateful. For the get-out-of-jail-free card. For the chance to wash my hands of this entire thing and go back to the locker room to celebrate today's win with the rest of the team. Instead, I fucking stand here. In the middle of the empty hallway. Waiting. For what, I'm not sure, but I can't walk away. I can't make my feet move.

"Where the fuck have you been?" a low voice growls.

"I was looking for you," Raine answers. There's a tremor in her voice, and, dammit, it urges me forward.

I have a feeling I'm gonna regret this.

Read Everett's and Raine's story in *A Little Jaded.*

ALSO BY KELSIE RAE

Kelsie Rae tries to keep her books formatted with an updated list of her releases, but every once in a while she falls behind.

If you'd like to check out a complete list of her up-to-date published books, visit her website at www.authorkelsierae.com/books

Or you can join her newsletter to hear about her latest releases, get exclusive content, and participate in fun giveaways.

Interested in reading more by Kelsie Rae?

The Little Things Series

(Steamy Don't Let Me Next Generation Series)

(Steamy Contemporary Romance Standalone Series)

A Little Complicated

A Little Tempting

A Little Jaded

A Little Crush

Don't Let Me Series

(Steamy Contemporary Romance Standalone Series)

Don't Let Me Fall - Colt and Ashlyn's Story

Don't Let Me Go - Blakely and Theo's Story

Don't Let Me Break - Kate and Macklin's Story

Let Me Love You - A Don't Let Me Sequel

Don't Let Me Down - Mia and Henry's Story

Wrecked Roommates Series

(Steamy Contemporary Romance Standalone Series)

<u>Model Behavior</u> - River and Reese's Story

<u>Forbidden Lyrics</u> - Gibson and Dove's Story

<u>Messy Strokes</u> - Milo and Maddie's Story

<u>Risky Business</u> - Jake and Evie's Story

<u>Broken Instrument</u> - Fender and Hadley's Story

Signature Sweethearts Series

(Sweet Contemporary Romance Standalone Series)

<u>Taking the Chance</u>

<u>Taking the Backseat</u> - Download now for FREE

<u>Taking the Job</u>

<u>Taking the Leap</u>

Get Baked Sweethearts Series

(Sweet Contemporary Romance Standalone Series)

<u>Off Limits</u>

<u>Stand Off</u>

<u>Hands Off</u>

<u>Hired Hottie</u> (A *Steamy* Get Baked Sweethearts Spin-Off)

Swenson Sweethearts Series

(Sweet Contemporary Romance Standalone Series)

<u>Finding You</u>

<u>Fooling You</u>

<u>Hating You</u>

<u>Cruising with You</u> (A *Steamy* Swenson Sweethearts Novella)

<u>Crush</u> (A *Steamy* Swenson Sweethearts Spin-Off)

Advantage Play Series

(Steamy Romantic Suspense/Mafia Series)

Sign up for Kelsie's newsletter to receive exclusive content, including the first two chapters of every new book two weeks before its release date!

Dear Reader,

I want to thank you from the bottom of my heart for taking a chance on *A Little Tempting*, and for giving me the opportunity to share their story with you. I hope you love Reeves and Dylan as much as I do!

As always, I would be very grateful if you could take the time to leave a review. It's amazing how such a little thing like a review can be such a huge help to an author! (Seriously, it can make or break a book. I'm not even kidding.)

Thank you so much!!! I couldn't do this "author gig" without you.

-Kelsie

ABOUT THE AUTHOR

Kelsie is a sucker for a love story with all the feels. When she's not chasing words for her next book, you will probably find her reading or, more likely, hanging out with her husband and playing with her three kiddos who love to drive her crazy.

She adores photography, baking, her two pups, and her cat who thinks she's a dog. Now that she's actively pursuing her writing dreams, she's set her sights on someday finding the self-discipline to not binge-watch an entire series on Netflix in one sitting.

If you'd like to connect with Kelsie, subscribe to her Patreon. Patrons receive a wide range of goodies including:

- Exclusive sneak peeks of works-in-progress
- ebook releases one week early
- Signed paperbacks on all new releases
- So much more

You can also sign up for her newsletter, or join Kelsie Rae's Reader Group to stay up to date on new releases and her crazy publishing journey.

Made in United States
Troutdale, OR
08/15/2024